ACCLAIM FOR VICTORIA DENAULT'S HOMETOWN PLAYERS SERIES

ON THE LINE

"Once again Victoria Denault has written a sexy, sweet story with characters who draw you in and get you invested in their lives as though you're living in this fantastic world of hockey with them."

—Fiction Fangirls

"*On the Line* was a complicated friends-to-lovers romance that was fun and sexy, yet intense and poignant."

—Guilty Pleasures

WINNING IT ALL

"Victoria Denault delivered a fantastic story that kept me glued to the pages. Between the sizzling chemistry and creative dialogue, I loved Shayne and Sebastian's relationship."

—Smut Book Junkie

THE FINAL MOVE

"Victoria Denault's writing is awesome, her character development is some of the best I've encountered and her dialogue is on point. This whole series is a must read!"

—Fiction Fangirls

"The perfect amount of heat, angst, romance, and humor."

—Shameless Book Club

ONE MORE SHOT

"This book is sexy, funny and has a lot of heart…I can't wait until the next book comes out!"

—Hashtag Avenue

MAKING A PLAY

"Victoria Denault's Hometown Players is sports romance perfection."

—Biblio Junkies Blog

"[*Making a Play*] was a breath of fresh air in a genre saturated with games and contrived misunderstandings…I loved the way the author was able to pull everything together in a plausible way."

—Badass Book Reviews

"I think this series might be turning me into a puck bunny because I cannot get enough of these hockey studs!"

—Fiction Fangirls

SCORE

VICTORIA DENAULT

FOREVER

NEW YORK   BOSTON

Forever
Hachette Book Group
1290 Avenue of the Americas, New York, NY 10104
forever-romance.com
twitter.com/foreverromance

First Edition: May 2017

Forever is an imprint of Grand Central Publishing. The Forever name and logo are trademarks of Hachette Book Group, Inc.

The publisher is not responsible for websites (or their content) that are not owned by the publisher.

The Hachette Speakers Bureau provides a wide range of authors for speaking events. To find out more, go to www.hachettespeakersbureau.com or call (866) 376-6591.

Library of Congress Cataloging-in-Publication Data

Names: Denault, Victoria, author.
Title: Score / Victoria Denault.
Description: First edition. | New York : Forever, 2017. | Series: San Francisco Thunder ; 1
Identifiers: LCCN 2016057328| ISBN 9781455597666 (softcover) | ISBN 9781478915614 (audio download) | ISBN 9781455597673 (ebook)
Subjects: LCSH: Hockey teams—Fiction. | Hockey players—Fiction. | Man-woman relationships—Fiction. | BISAC: FICTION / Romance / Contemporary. | FICTION / Contemporary Women. | GSAFD: Romantic suspense fiction. | Love stories.
Classification: LCC PS3604.E525 S36 2017 | DDC 813/.6—dc23 LC record available at https://lccn.loc.gov/2016057328

ISBNs: 978-1-4555-9766-6 (trade pbk.), 978-1-4555-9767-3 (ebook)

Printed in the United States of America

LSC-C

10 9 8 7 6 5 4 3 2 1

For the Ocean Park, Maine, crew

ACKNOWLEDGMENTS

The first and biggest thanks for this book go to my family. I edited this book beside my dad's hospital bed. He's fine now, but it was a big, unexpected scare that, as big, unexpected things do, brought our family closer together. Thanks to my mom, Ken, Sonia, Max and Zoe for allowing me to lug a hard copy of my manuscript around everywhere, even the hospital, so I could still meet my deadline. You guys are a great group of humans, and I'm lucky to call you my family. And thanks, Dad, for being superhuman and proving the doctors wrong. Again.

To my husband, Jack, thanks for providing me with humor, encouragement and support. You're the best, and I love this adventure we're on together. To my dogs—yes, my dogs—Belle and Gus. Thanks for snuggling me while I write and for letting me finish a chapter before I take you on walks. Now if you could stop stepping on the power bar and turning it off, that would be nifty.

Thanks to my agent, Kimberly Brower. You've been nothing short of perfection from day one. With this series in particular, you guided me through unexpected twists and turns, and thanks to your advice and encouragement, I know I produced the best book possible.

To my editor, Leah, thank you for coming up with a crazy, big change. This series is better off thanks to your efforts, and I'm more grateful than I can express. I'm so lucky to have you in my corner. Thank you to everyone at Forever for all you do to edit, publish and promote my books.

Thanks to all the other authors who have been an amazing support system. To my friends like Ari D, his sidekick Peter M, Ray and Mel M, Bev T, Jenn D, Katherine H, Des G, Mike "Shoelaces" H, Joe D, Carlos "One More Shot" M, Sarah J, DeAnna Z and so many more, thank you for showing me such overwhelming love and support. Thank you, Ruthe Douglas, my Fiesta sister, for bringing "Oh Mylanta!" into my vocabulary so I could put it in Zoey's. Sorry, Devon, but my goal is to make that catchphrase world famous. And to my friend and Realtor extraordinaire, Chris W, thank you so much for answering all my realty questions for this book.

Last but never least, a million thank-yous to the bloggers who work so diligently and passionately to promote books and authors and share the reads they love. You all rock!

SCORE

1

JUDE

I lock my car and make my way across the hospital parking lot. It's a gorgeous day—the sun is shining in the cloudless sky, and the temperature is a perfect seventy-eight degrees. I'd be bitching about having to spend it indoors if it weren't for such a good cause. Today I'm doing a meet-and-greet at the children's hospital with a few of my teammates and the Stanley Cup, the second in a row for the San Francisco Thunder. The only thing that beats lifting that Cup above my head on the ice after our win is sharing it with kids.

Not everyone is back from summer break yet, so it's a small but excited group. I normally wouldn't be back in San Francisco yet either, but this hasn't been a normal summer for me. Nothing has been "normal" for me in a long while. It's not that things are bad; they're just…different. And I have been realizing I am not the best with dealing with changes on my own.

The last big change I'd faced in my life was being traded to San Francisco from the Milwaukee Comets, but I didn't do that alone. They traded my teammate, my best friend since I was seventeen, Levi

Casco, as well. And then there was my dad getting sick, but I had my family to go through that with me.

As I reach the sidewalk where the team is gathered, I see my youngest sister and Thunder publicity dynamo, Dixie, pacing a hole in the concrete a few feet from a bunch of guys from the team. I make my way toward her, stopping to hug and high-five a couple of the guys on my way by. Dixie's got her face buried in her phone, which is typical when she's working. She doesn't look up, but somehow she knows I'm coming. As soon as I'm standing beside her, she says, "Are you sober? Are you hung over? Oh, and no hitting on the moms or nurses."

"Nice to see you too, sis," I reply and roll my eyes.

The word "sis" finally gets her blue eyes off her phone screen. They land on me with an expression that could wilt flowers. "Do not use that word in public, Jude."

"Sorry." I roll my eyes again, and she frowns. "And FYI, I'm sober, and I will keep my dick out of the staff and mothers. Thanks for thinking you have to tell me that, though."

"Of course I have to tell you that," Dixie replies matter-of-factly. "Unfortunately, I know your dick and your brain are mortal enemies. Anything your brain says, like 'don't bang people at team events,' your dick purposely defies."

"You are a total weirdo," I tell her for what's probably the millionth time since she was born into the family. "And you need to stop saying 'dick' in front of me."

She stops pacing, just out of earshot of the team. She shoves her phone in the pocket of her off-white summer blazer and tilts her head up to hold my eye. "If it makes you feel any better, this is Dixie Wynn, publicist for the San Francisco Thunder, talking, because it's my job to keep the dick of our best player in its pants at public events. It's not your sister Dixie Braddock talking. That said, both of us—Dixie Wynn and Dixie Braddock—are still disgusted your Little Jude ended up on the internet."

"There's no proof it's my not-so-little Jude. And you don't think it's weird that your job is to keep my dick in my pants?" I can't help but ask because, damn, she could have gotten a job anywhere else. My two other sisters, Winnie and Sadie, are living and working in our hometown of Toronto.

"Oh, it's weird," she agrees and gives me a humorless smile. "But you know what's really weird? You're the only player on the entire team who needs to be reminded to keep his dick in his pants at team events. Not even creepy Eddie Rollins needs the reminder."

Ouch. I must look as wounded by that as I feel, because her expression softens for a second before her eyes dart around to make sure no one is watching. She's ridiculously anal about keeping the fact that we're related a secret from the rest of the team. A lot of the management is aware, but no one from the team except Levi knows. It's kind of weird that no one has guessed. Especially since we have almost identical blue eyes and high cheekbones. We're both blond too, but my hair is more of a sandy color than hers is.

"We're scheduled to be inside in five minutes," Dixie tells me, and I simply nod as her eyes scan the players gathered on the sidewalk. "Where's Levi? He's never late. In fact, he's usually the first one here. Can you call him for me?"

"No." She frowns at my quick and assertive response.

"He called you a lot this summer," she counters.

"Yeah, because he thought my dick was on the internet, and management made him," I reply. Her frown deepens, as does that little crease between her eyebrows she gets when she's annoyed. The truth is Levi had called me a few times this summer, and some of the calls came before the dick pic scandal. I just ignored them because I was still pissed at him for dating my ex-girlfriend behind my back.

In an effort to avoid Dixie's judgmental stare, I look away, and my eyes land on Levi. I knew he'd never be late. He's the same old calm, reliable, emotionless Levi. Only I can't help but notice as he gets closer, he doesn't look like that Levi anymore. His posture is loose, his hair longer than I've ever seen it, careless stubble covers his jaw, and his smile is light, jovial. Everything about him seems to be the opposite of the cool, emotionally detached, almost moody guy who was my best friend until two months ago. Now he looks like someone I don't know, and that stings, like a sunburn inside my chest.

He glances up, our eyes connect and he gives me a Levi smile I recognize—tight, small and quick. I smile back, but it isn't completely authentic. This is what we are now. This is what we've become. Best friends with a deep crack running through the foundation of our friendship. One I don't think can or will ever go away. And it's eating at my soul to admit that. But I don't know how to get around the fact that he started sleeping with my ex-girlfriend without telling me.

"Hey!" Levi reaches out and grabs me in a hug. I hug him back, but it's awkward and brief. "How was your vacation time?"

I shrug and keep my smile light. "Fine. Not long enough."

We are due back for training camp in two weeks, after only ten short weeks off. Levi nods. "Yeah. It's gonna be a long season, but it was worth it."

He rolls his shoulder, probably without even thinking about it. He was injured last year in the playoffs, and I'm sure the shoulder is still not one hundred percent. "When did you get back to San Fran?"

I shrug again. "Two weeks ago. I went back to Toronto for a while, but after the picture thing happened, I came back here. Needed some alone time."

His brown eyes grow dark, and he nods tersely at that. I'd sworn to him it was a misunderstanding, the picture wasn't me, and in true Levi fashion he didn't believe me but backed me up anyway. Between his support and the fact that the dick pic taken by the puck bunny didn't have my face in it, the team management decided not to cut me loose. Thankfully.

"How's your dad doing?" Levi asks, his face filled with sympathy. It's the only unfiltered expression he gives me now. I know he truly is gutted about what I'm going through with my father, who was recently diagnosed with ALS, and I do appreciate his concern. My family is also like a family to Levi. He became an honorary Braddock the summer after high school, when he lived with us.

But the fact he's been like a brother to me is why the shit he pulled with my ex hurt me so much.

"He fell this summer. Had to spend a couple days in the hospital with a fractured wrist and some broken ribs, but you know him, he's bouncing back," I explain quietly. I'm still having a hard time dealing with the fact my big bear of a dad may only have a year or so left.

I pull myself together as Duncan Darby walks over, his phone to his ear. "Okay, babe. Yeah. I'll call you when I'm done. Love you."

He drops his phone from his ear and pulls me into a bear hug. I hug him back easily. Duncan is a giant, hilarious man-child. He's a defensive beast on the ice and as sweet and loyal as a puppy off. "Braddock! You *Playgirl* centerfold, you!"

I roll my eyes. "Wasn't my dick."

He nods emphatically. "Right. I forgot."

I ignore the completely un-ignorable exaggerated wink he gives me. Levi clears his throat. "Was that Carla on the phone?"

I watch Duncan nod. He started dating Carla Soto almost a year ago. She's best friends with Tessa Haynes, my ex and Levi's girlfriend. Yeah, we're one big happy family. Not.

"Yeah. She wants me to swing by work when I'm done."

"I was going to swing by and see Tessa too," Levi tells him. "I was going to surprise her with lunch. Carpool?"

They're like suburban husbands now. The realization makes me feel very lonely. Luckily, I don't have to stand here awkwardly and listen to them talk any longer, because Dixie is walking toward us. She stops in front of us and claps her hands to get the group's attention. "Okay, everyone! We're going to go into the lounge on the main floor, and the kids will filter in a few at a time to get pictures with you guys and the Cup."

Everyone nods. "The PR staff will be giving out Stanley Cup cookies and little stuffed mascots. Any questions?" Dixie asks.

No one has any questions, so she leads everyone inside. A couple minutes later we're in the long, antiseptic-smelling room, and the kids are starting to come in. It's brutal to see so many kids pale, frail and in some cases attached to tubes and IVs, but there's no place I'd rather be. I always take the time to shake their parents' hands and chat with them a little bit. Not because I'm trying to flirt with the hot moms, but because I can only imagine how hard this is on them. I'm feeling helpless and furious about my dad's health; I assume those feelings are even deeper when it's your child.

As the event winds down and the last of the kids finish with the photos and make their way to the cookies and toys, I see Dixie huddled in the corner with one of the nurses. She glances at me but doesn't really acknowledge me. That crease between her eyebrows seems deeper than normal, so I walk over to find out what's going on.

"He's just devastated," the nurse says to Dixie as I approach.

"Who?" I ask. Dixie hasn't realized I've joined them, and she jumps a little when I speak.

"A little boy," the nurse tells me as she smiles a big, flirtatious smile and smooths her bright pink scrubs. "Christopher. He's a huge Thunder fan, but his white blood cells got low last night. He's in isolation until we can pump them up again, so he couldn't come today. I'm Kina, by the way."

I smile at her and shake her hand. She bats her eyelashes at me with a smile that tells me I could violate Dixie's little rule with her.

"He's one of the reasons we organized the event," Dixie explains, and her brow pinches so tight I'm tempted to press my thumb between her eyes and flatten out the crease. I decide against it, because she'd probably slap me. "His mom wrote us with a few of the other moms and asked us to visit."

I feel for this kid. I hate the idea that he's going to miss us. Dixie's expression perks up a little. "Could we have Levi hold the Cup up outside the window to his room?"

"Why Levi?" The question flies from my mouth with a hard edge that has both Dixie and Kina startled. "I mean, I could do it."

"Well, you are his favorite player," the nurse explains with that flirtatious smile, adding, "And mine."

I ignore her last comment, because Dixie told me to, and nod.

"Well, I'd love to see him. Can't I go in the room if I'm sanitized or whatever?"

"You'd have to wear full scrubs and a mask and everything," she explains. "It's a bit of a pain."

"You know what's a bigger pain?" I ask and smile. "Being a sick kid and missing your chance to see the Cup and meet your favorite player."

The nurse smiles; this time it's more excited than flirty, thankfully, because I've never been great at ignoring a flirty woman. Dixie, on the other hand, is staring at me with a stunned and confused look rather than a happy one. I shrug at her. "What? It's not a big deal."

She doesn't respond, so I ignore her and ask Kina to take me to his room. Twenty minutes later, wrapped in a bunch of scrubs and booties and with a giant mask on my face, I'm in Christopher's room. He's pale and skinny, but his smile is hearty and full of life. I give him a jersey with the whole team's signatures and I have Levi hold up the Cup outside his window and all the other guys wave at him. He's only nine, which guts me, but I don't let him see it. I joke with him and take pictures. We talk hockey and how when he's better his mom is going to let him play on a team. I tell him I'll get him tickets to a Thunder game when he's well and take him around our arena. He's thrilled. Then I let his mom almost strangle me with a grateful hug before I leave.

I strip out of all the special clothes and find Dixie waiting for me by the elevators with the rest of the team. "That was amazing of you."

"It was nothing."

"Jude!" I turn as Kina jogs down the hall toward me. "Thank you so much. You're amazing."

She shakes my hand and then hands me a folded piece of paper.

"My number. Call me if you're wondering how Christopher is doing or, you know, you want to hang out."

She flashes that flirtatious grin again before heading back to the nurses' station. Dixie glares at me and shrugs. Duncan, Levi and the guys are chuckling as we all crowd into the elevator. "Only Jude turns a good deed into a lay," Duncan quips, and it instantly pisses me off.

"I didn't do it because of that," I say, my tone flat and even.

"You do everything for that," Eddie Rollins, our backup goalie, chimes in, and the elevator erupts in laughter.

"Fuck you guys," I mutter and storm off the elevator as soon as the doors open.

I'm already opening my car door when I hear Dixie call my name. I want to ignore her and just drive away, but knowing her, she'll hunt me down, so I stop and wait for whatever it is she wants to say.

She is almost breathless when she reaches me, and I realize she must have been chasing me. She stops half a foot away and smooths her blond bob. "Thank you for doing that. You went above and beyond."

"It was nothing," I reply casually, but I'm happy she was impressed enough to say something. "He's a kid. He deserves a little above and beyond."

"Yeah, he does. So thank you for being an awesome human." She lowers her voice before adding, "And I'm proud of you, as a sister."

"Yeah, well, you could have defended me in front of those assholes," I reply and sigh.

She glances over her shoulder toward the guys who are jumping into their own cars. "They were just teasing you. And besides, it's not like it's a wild accusation."

"I wasn't nice to the kid because I wanted to bang the nurse." I can't believe I have to defend myself on this. "I don't bang every girl I meet, even when I can. And trust me, I could have gotten in those scrubs with or without being nice to the kid."

Dixie rolls her eyes, but she's smiling. "If you don't bang every girl you meet, then why are you currently staying at a hotel and not your apartment?"

"What?" Fuck. How did she find that out?

"I was coming out of the coach's office after a meeting last week, and I heard Duncan tell Eddie you'd moved into a hotel because too many of your prior hookups were showing up at your place unannounced trying to get another ride on the…how did he word it? Braddock-mobile."

She shivers—actually it's more like a convulsion—as she says that. I clench my jaw in anger. Fucking Duncan Darby and his big mouth. She's staring up at me with a smug smile on her face, and I know the only answer is to lie. "Darby is talking out of his ass. I checked into a hotel because I wanted a staycation."

"A staycation? Did you just honestly feed me that bullshit excuse with a straight face?" Dixie questions. She is the most annoying sister on the planet. She really is.

"Yeah."

"So why is it that for the first time since you moved here you aren't letting Sadie, Winnie and me stay with you for our annual girls' weekend?"

I wish my dad had indulged me when she was born and I requested we trade her for a puppy. "I thought I'd treat you all to a five-star hotel. It's not like I'm making all of you cram into that shoebox you call an apartment. But if you all want to stay with me instead, by all means, go ahead."

"Thanks. We will. See you tomorrow night." She turns and marches off toward her car.

Goddamn it, I think as I watch her walk away.

I pull the nurse's number out of my pocket and tear it into pieces.

The unexpected guests that were showing up at my apartment weren't just annoying; to be honest, it was embarrassing and a wake-up call. I was way too liberal with where I put my dick. I wanted to say it was because of everything that happened with Levi and Tessa, but even I couldn't sell myself on that lie.

Dixie's red Fiat buzzes by me, and as my sister catches my eye through the windshield, I stick my hand out my window and let the torn-up phone number trickle out of my hand and to the pavement. I don't even think twice about it.

2

ZOEY

It's not going to be a crappy day. It's not going to be a crappy day. It's not going to be…

"Morning, Zoey. Adam Penner's office called."

It's going to be a crappy day.

"Thank you, Anastasia." I give the receptionist at my office a smile and wave off the slip of paper she's trying to hand me. I know his number. I don't need the paper, and I don't want to see his name in front of me, even if it's in Anastasia's perfect penmanship.

I continue to the back of the office, where my desk is tucked away in the corner. Next to my co-worker Marti's desk, it sticks out like a sore thumb. Marti's desk is the exact same dark wood as mine, but it's covered with stacks of house listings and file folders full of pending deals. Mine is bare. Well, except for the tiny antique clock my grandma gave me and the phone, which is blinking, probably because Adam has left me a bunch of messages there too. Ugh.

I remind myself to pick up some flowers for my desk at lunch. They might not be pending deals, but they will still bring some life to the barren surface. Marti is hunched over her laptop, a coffee in one hand while the other darts around on the mouse. "Morning, Zo."

I hate being called Zo. Always have. But I'm new to Golden Gate Realty, and residential realty in general, and she's been my mentor, helping me with everything at the office and in this new phase of my career, so she can call me whatever she wants.

"Hey, Marti." I smile, and as I round my desk I pull my own laptop from my bag. "How'd the showing in the Presidio go last night?"

"They made an offer by the time I showed them the master bath." Marti smiles triumphantly. "I told them the client wanted to wait until the weekend to take offers, which made them panic about a potential bidding war, so they upped the offer to five grand over asking. My client took it instantly."

"Good job, rock star!" I praise her and try not to let that little ripple of jealousy poison my bloodstream. Marti's been at Golden Gate for a year. She's been in residential real estate for three years. She's established. I just moved from commercial to residential last month and have only been at Golden Gate for ten days. I'll be closing deals on million-dollar homes one day too. Hopefully soon.

"How about you? How'd that lead in the Haight work out?" she asks, absently twisting her light brown hair around her finger.

"They were a nice couple. I think they liked me, and I was fairly confident they'd hire me to sell their place," I explain and pause before the bad news. "But then I saw another agent buzz their apartment as I was leaving."

Marti's eyes cloud over briefly, but it's long enough that it makes me think the confidence in her words is fake. "Well, you've still got that one-bedroom condo listing. I know it's been a few weeks, but someone will make an offer soon. I know it."

I stare at the red light blinking on my desk phone and turn to Marti again. "I'm going to run next door for a coffee. Want another? My treat."

She glances at the phone and back at me. "I'm good."

I haven't told Marti the dirty details of my life. She knows I'm separated and that I worked in commercial real estate at Penner Realty prior to this. She doesn't know that my soon-to-be ex-husband is Adam Penner, owner of the company. Or that my husband isn't signing the divorce papers, even though it was his idea to end it.

Marti shakes her head. "One is enough for me this morning, but thanks."

I nod and make my way out of the office again, smiling serenely at Anastasia, who inadvertently obliterated my chance at a good day, and step back out into the warm early-September San Francisco air. I take a few steps and quickly enter Peet's Coffee. I look around at the other patrons, mostly businessmen in suits grabbing java before hopping on a trolley to their jobs in the Financial District. I used to love a handsome man in an expensive suit. That's what first attracted me to Adam, but now the sight almost makes my stomach churn. San Francisco is full of guys like that or men in skinny jeans, dark-rimmed glasses and ironic T-shirts who are equally rich but made their money in the tech industry. But right now neither look does anything for me, because another relationship is the last thing on my mind. I kind of feel like I am treading water, and a new relationship would be the equivalent of tying a brick to my ankle.

I reach the counter and order a chai latte, and as I step aside to wait, I pull my phone out of the pocket of my suit jacket. Taking a deep breath and letting it out as slowly as possible, I dial Adam's personal cell.

He must have forwarded it to his office line because his long-time secretary, Minerva, answers in her typical Waspy voice: "Penner Realty, how can I assist you?"

"Hi, Minerva. How are you? It's Zoey." Minerva has been with the company since I met Adam. She is an exotic-looking woman with wide brown eyes and sleek, rich hair that is never out of place. She has been warm and friendly toward me since the beginning. So I feel the chill when her tone goes from polite to taciturn. "Oh, hello, Ms. Quinlin. Thank you for calling me back."

I don't know why she isn't calling me Quinlin-Penner anymore. After all, I am still married, and she doesn't know I've dropped Penner. "I was calling Adam back."

"Yes, Mr. Penner has asked me to handle this for him. He's busy at the moment," Minerva explains, her voice still so chilly I feel my flesh prickle. "I need to know the name of your lawyer, so Mr. Penner's lawyer can be in touch."

"Lawyer?" I repeat the word in shock. "I don't have a lawyer."

"Oh. Well…" Minerva seems unimpressed. "When you pick one, have them contact J. C. McGuire at McGuire, Milbury and Cherry."

"Adam and I decided to do this without lawyers. The paperwork is just waiting to be signed." I tell her what was decided that fateful Sunday afternoon of the worst weekend of my life.

"Mr. Penner has come to the realization that legal dealings should be done with lawyers," she tells me. "So please let your lawyer know—"

"I'd like to speak to Adam, please," I interrupt, making sure my voice is still calm and even. "I think it's best if we have a quick chat."

"As I mentioned earlier, he's very busy right now." Minerva's clipped voice falters just a little, her tone warming, and she sounds almost guilty for it as she lowers her voice to add, "Zoey, I think you should hire a lawyer and discuss this with them."

Okay, now I'm not just annoyed, I'm scared. "It's amicable, and the pre-nup is pretty detailed, and I'm not going to challenge it."

I hate that I am telling this to her. An administrative assistant. This isn't her business, it's between Adam and me. Why is he doing this? Is this his family putting pressure on him? I can hire a lawyer, I guess, but why? The pre-nup was fair, and I don't want anything more.

"J. C. McGuire," Minerva repeats. "Would you like me to give you the number?"

The barista slides my latte toward me. I reach for it and give her a quick smile. "No. I know the firm. Adam's brother, Phillip, used them for his second and third divorces."

Phillip had been in the process of divorcing Catherine when I was dating Adam; he married Megan before the ink was dry on the divorce papers. Then, about twenty months later, Megan didn't come on the annual family summer vacation to Tahoe. I was told later they were done. That's all I was told, because Adam's family doesn't discuss their dirty laundry even among themselves. It was a shame. I had liked Megan, but Adam and I were just acknowledging our own marital issues at the time, so I didn't even try to find out what had happened.

Minerva's voice gets soft and low again. "Prust and Bissonette are a reputable firm."

"Oh. Yeah, I think I've heard of them," I mutter back, but I'm not even sure.

"Please let me know when you have it worked out." Her tone is back to being polite with a touch of chilly. "Have a good day, Ms. Quinlin."

The line goes dead, and I stare at the now blank screen. Oh my

God, what is happening? Why is Adam doing this? I seriously need to talk to him, and since he clearly isn't going to let me get past Minerva, I'm going to have to stop by the house. My house. Well, at least it will be when this is over. But I'm the one who moved out of it for now, because one of us had to go, and he was using the third floor of the house as his home office. It would have taken a long time to move his office, so I moved into my brother's place for a month; then Adam and I agreed I could move into the Four Seasons. I thought it would just be for another month or so because we have a pre-nup and we're both agreeing to end this, but I've been there for four months and he's no closer to signing the papers.

At first, Adam was on business trips, because before he announced that it was best we end our marriage, he'd already started working on expanding his commercial real estate business into Los Angeles. I wasn't in a rush at the beginning. I was still devastated and confused and holding out hope that this could somehow be mended. That he'd change his mind and at least try. Try for the life we'd thought we'd have. After all, the doctor hadn't said I couldn't have children. She said it wasn't going to be easy. Apparently Adam only wanted easy children.

Still staring at my blank phone screen, I stumble toward the door and of course I walk straight into someone. Of course. Because today is going to be crappy in every possible way. Luckily, I manage to avoid getting chai latte on either of us; it barely spills over the lid and only dribbles onto my hand.

"I'm so sorry!" I say at the exact same time she does, and I look up to see a familiar face staring back, but I can't place it.

She blinks azure eyes and then her whole face lights up. "Zoey? Zoey Quinlin? Oh my God!"

She's hugging me before I realize what's happening. I wrap the hand not covered in latte around her back and return the embrace. She pulls back, still holding my shoulders, and smiles. "Holy crap! It's been over ten years! Oh my God." She pauses and glances around before adding in a softer voice, "It's Dixie. Dixie Braddock. You used to babysit me at my family's summer cottage in Maine. You were friends with my brother, Jude."

"Holy crap! Dixie Braddock?" I can't believe it. The last time I saw her she was thirteen. Wheat hair; pink, suntanned skin; freckles across her nose and chronically scabbed-up knees from trying to keep up with her older sisters and brother, who were all daredevils on their bikes and skateboards and surfboards. Babysitting them—well, the girls, anyway—for the two years I lived in Maine was a highlight of my summers. And so was seeing their brother. Crap, I hadn't thought of Jude Braddock in a while. I find myself smiling now that I am.

"You live in San Fran?" she questions as she takes my elbow and leads me over to the counter and hands me a napkin for my latte-soaked hand.

"Yeah. Stayed local after college," I explain as I put down the latte and wipe my hand. "And you live here?"

She nods, her sleek blond bob moving like a curtain around her face. She looks close to the tiny thing I babysat but much more refined and beautiful now. I do the math: she's only twenty-four, but she looks more put together than any twenty-four-year-old I've known.

"Yeah. I went to school for sports media, then interned with the San Francisco Thunder hockey team, and they hired me full-time this year." Her eyes dart around, and her voice drops again.

"Jude plays for them, so I use my mom's last name, Wynn, so no one thinks he got me the job. He didn't."

"Jude is in San Francisco?" I don't know why I felt the need to say that with such breathless shock. I knew he made the NHL, but I had thought he was playing in Milwaukee. That's where he was last time I Googled him, which was three years ago, before I married Adam.

"Yeah. Got traded a couple years ago," Dixie explains. "So how's your family? Where's your dad preaching now?"

"He's retired. Mom and Dad are in Sacramento," I explain. "My brother, Morgan, is a teacher here in San Francisco."

"Morgan!" She laughs and her cheeks turn a little pink. "Sadie, Winnie and I had such a crush on your brother when we were little. Remember we used to keep begging you to invite him over when you were watching us?"

I nod and can't help but smile back. Yeah, that memory hasn't faded. The Braddock girls wanted my brother to come over, but I never invited him. Not because he was gay, which I already knew at that point, but because if Morgan was around, he would tease me about gawking at Jude, which I always did if he happened to come home before Mr. and Mrs. Braddock's date night ended.

Dixie glances at her phone in her hand, and I realize we both must have been looking at our screens when we collided. She frowns. "I have to go. I have a meeting at the arena in twenty." She puts a hand on my arm again. "But I would love to catch up with you, and I know Winnie and Sadie would too. They're going to be in town this weekend. Would you be able to do brunch?"

"Yeah, I can do brunch," I reply and am shocked at how excited

I am at her suggestion. I haven't really done much of anything social since the separation. I kind of lost touch with a lot of my friends after marrying Adam and adopted his circle of friends. And they all promptly orphaned me after the separation. I didn't care much because I didn't feel up to social interaction, but suddenly this seems like a pleasant distraction from my reality. The Braddock family was one of my favorite parts of my childhood.

"Amazing!" Dixie almost squeals. "How about tomorrow. Eleven?"

I nod. "Where?"

"You pick."

"MKT?" I blurt out because it's in my hotel and I'm too flustered to think of anything else. To be honest, I don't even know what they serve for brunch.

"Great! Sadie loves that place, and she's normally impossible to please." She hugs me again. "See you tomorrow! Winnie and Sadie are going to be so excited!"

And then, before I can even lift my hand to wave, she's back out the door. She never even got a coffee, but she doesn't seem to notice. I'm more dumbfounded and confused than I was from the phone call with Minerva. The Braddocks are here. Well, at least Jude and Dixie are here. In San Francisco. Where I live. When the hell did that happen?

I look around the coffee shop to make sure there's no one else from my past lurking around. A teacher, a neighbor, another sister of an old unconsummated love. Although Jude was my only unconsummated love, but he did have three sisters. Whom I will be having brunch with tomorrow. Crazy!

I slip out of Peet's and concentrate on the clicking of my heels as I make my way back over to my office. I finally take a sip of my jostled latte. It's barely warm but the caffeine still manages to clear my head a little. Not enough that eagle-eye Marti doesn't notice something is up.

"Everything okay?" she wants to know as she stands at her desk, gathering things she needs for her day and placing them in her bag. "You look more out of it than you did before the coffee."

"I ran into someone I haven't seen in a long time," I murmur, and for some reason Jude's seventeen-year-old face floats through my head, not Dixie's from this morning. "The last time I saw her was in Maine eleven years ago, so it was surprising."

"Wow." Marti takes a break from filling her Michael Kors satchel with listing flyers. "Small world, huh? I love when that happens. Unless it's someone I hate. Was it someone you hate?"

"No. Not at all," I reply and drop down gently into my seat. "She and her sisters were sweethearts. Seems like they still are. I'll definitely find out, because I'm having brunch with them tomorrow."

"Cool." Marti isn't paying attention anymore. Her eyes are focused across the room on Parker McDavid, who is the owner of our company. He's midforties, tall with a dad bod that is oddly attractive, probably because he covers it in perfectly tailored designer clothes. His dark hair is graying in all the right places, like George Clooney's, and his eyes are warm and his smile is kind. But he's an astute businessman who expects a lot from his Realtors, and Marti is constantly trying to impress him. I am too, if I'm being honest, but I'm new. She's not new, but she's still hungry.

"I'm going to tell Parker about the deal I just closed, and then I'm off for a condo showing," Marti explains and barely even waves good-bye as she hustles toward the kitchen Parker just disappeared into for his morning croissant and English Breakfast tea.

I open my laptop and pull up my email, determined to keep my mind focused on work. I need to send a follow-up email regarding the potential Haight listing, but my brain is bouncing from Adam to Dixie.

One future encounter I'm dreading—confronting Adam—and one I'm looking forward to—seeing the Braddock sisters. But the one that isn't destined to happen is the one that fills me with excitement I haven't felt in a long time—the potential that since I'm meeting three Braddock siblings I might also run into the fourth: Jude.

3

JUDE

My head is pounding. Fucking *pounding*. I groan and slide deeper into my king-size bed, pulling the sheets up higher so I'm buried under them. The pounding isn't painful but it's annoying. It won't go away. God, why the fuck do I drink? Seriously, why?

"Jude Fucking Joseph Asshole Randall Dirtball Braddock, would you answer your goddamn door!"

"Who the fuck are you?" I shout back to the voice outside my bedroom door.

"I will call Mom and Dad, and they'll make you do it!" the voice warns, and I know it's Winnie. "Or better yet, I'll answer the door myself, and take pictures of whatever horny skank is on the other side and send them to Mom and Dad."

"Sweet bloody hell," I mutter loud enough for her to hear and for the pounding in my head to match the pounding she's doing on my bedroom door. But I do what she's asking and roll out of bed. I grab my jeans from last night off the floor and tug them on, falling over and thankfully landing back on the bed and not the hardwood floor.

I zip them up, careful not to catch any important parts with the zipper, and leave the button undone as I stumble toward my bedroom door.

I swing it open and all three of them are standing, in perfect V formation, in a variety of pajama sets with their arms crossed over their chests and angry scowls on their faces. As soon as I've opened my bedroom door, I can hear the incessant ringing of the doorbell. Oh. That's why they're bothering me. I roll my eyes at them and stumble down the long hall to the front door. They do exactly what I knew they'd do: follow along behind, cackling insults like a bunch of pissed-off chickens.

"What self-respecting woman bangs on this jackass's door in the middle of the night?" Sadie wonders.

"I can't decide if it's more horrifying or pathetic," Winnie laments.

"We'll know when he opens that door and we see her face," Dixie explains. "If she's gorgeous and articulate, and mostly sober, then it's pathetic, because she can definitely do better."

I turn as I reach for the door and glare at all of them. "I'm right here. Maybe save the insults for later."

I make a shooing motion with my hand, and the sorority, as I like to call my sisters, begrudgingly takes a few steps back. I turn back to the front door, which someone is still banging on, unlock it and swing it open. I barely have time to make out a face before a warm, lithe female body is pressing itself against me. I feel lips brush my cheek and a voice I'm embarrassed to say I don't really recognize says, "Hey, gorgeous. I'm so glad you answered."

My hands wrap around tiny hips and I gently push her back so I can see her face. I remember her now. Kate. Never did get a last name. I met her a couple weeks ago at a nightclub. I was on a mission that night, looking for a quick, fun fuck, and this girl was good to go. She lives in Oakland. A fuck isn't quick or fun when it involves a long, expensive cab ride to and from, so I suggested my place. This was my chronic mistake, as it turns out. She's the third girl to show up here uninvited in the last two weeks.

"I kind of didn't have a choice," I say and try not to sound as annoyed as I am. "I was worried you'd wake the neighbors."

I glance past her, and thankfully the hall is quiet and empty. I live in a very high-end condo complex, and my neighbors have made it clear in the past that they're less than impressed with my frequent visitors. Yet they haven't hired a doorman who could actually keep these unexpected guests from making it upstairs. I've been suggesting it since I moved in.

"Sorry. I just really wanted to see you. Didn't you get my texts?" she says and smiles at me while her hands make their way up my bare chest.

"My phone is off," I reply, which is a total lie. I ignored her five texts asking me where I was and if I wanted to hook up tonight. I didn't.

"Oh," she murmurs and rocks up on her tiptoes so her lips graze my cheek again. "No harm done. I'm here now, and I'm dying to wrap my lips around your—"

"What the actual fuck?!" Dixie's voice rumbles down the hallway, bouncing sharply off the walls.

As Kate tenses under my hands, which are still on her hips, I know exactly what Dixie is doing. I'm embarrassed to say she's done it before. She's pretending to be my girlfriend so that Kate will freak out and leave—and never come back. Kate's eyes slide over my shoulder, and as soon as they land on Dixie, she recoils from me.

I glance over my shoulder, and my eyes nearly bug out of my head. My youngest sister is standing there, by the door to my bedroom, in one of my Thunder T-shirts and shorts, caressing a very round belly. Her eyes meet mine and I can tell, because I know her so well, she's biting back a smile. But her words are angry and her eyes hard. "Jude! My water is going to break any day now and you're still sleeping around? Are you kidding me right now?"

Kate steps back out into the hallway. "I'm going to go."

I nod. "Yeah. Of course."

She glances past me again. "I'm so sorry. I had no idea."

"They never do, honey," Dixie says, and she's suddenly got a southern drawl. Dear God.

Kate rushes toward the elevator but not before telling me, "You're a dick."

I close the door as soon as she steps onto the elevator, and the giggles from the living room erupt. I watch Dixie pull the pillow out from under her shirt and follow her as we turn the corner into the large living room. Sadie and Winnie are both sprawled on the L-shaped couch holding their stomachs and wailing with laughter.

Dixie throws the pillow at me and collapses onto my custom-made armchair with a gleeful smile. "I don't think she'll be bothering you again."

"Ya don't think?" I ask and cock an eyebrow while glaring at her. It just makes the three of them laugh more.

"Jude, you have texted me in the middle of the night and forced me to come over and play a jealous girlfriend in order to kick out clingers before," Dixie reminds me. "The role is getting old so I thought I would challenge myself."

"Yeah, I guess pregnant wife is a stretch since you haven't even had a boyfriend since high school," I reply and grin at my own catty retort. As expected, I get an "ooh" from Sadie and Winnie, but Dixie isn't bothered in the least.

"I'm not trying to rush into anything I'm not ready for." Dixie shrugs and then levels her blue eyes at me like lasers. "Unlike you."

The unison "ooh" from the peanut gallery gets louder. Great. As if being woken up at four in the morning, in front of my sisters, by a clingy and horny one-night stand didn't suck enough, now we're going to talk about Tessa. *Fucking great.*

"I'm going back to bed," I snap, and as I turn to walk back to the master, the sorority goes back to doing what they do best—talking about me like I'm not in the room, even though I actually am. Sisters. Worst invention ever.

I close the door to my room with a bang. I make my way over to my bed and stand at the foot of it staring at my rumpled sheets as I unzip my jeans. Tessa is a great girl. She's beautiful, kind, funny and smart. I think that's what upsets me the most—that she literally has everything I've always said I wanted in a girl and yet I couldn't take the relationship seriously. Holy fuck, I wanted to, but I just couldn't.

That's what I still get angry about. That's what stings every time I see her. Not that she picked someone else, but that she did it because I couldn't be a fucking man and stay monogamous. And yeah, okay, maybe the fact that she fell in love with my best friend stung a little bit. At first when I was really bitter and really drunk, I thought about revenge. But I honestly wasn't angry at her, only angry at myself. I saw the way she looked at Levi. She loved him in a way she never came close to loving me. I was angry because I would never have a girl look at me like that. I'm just not a one-woman kind of guy.

I drop onto my bed and tuck both arms under the pillow beneath my head. I stare up at my ceiling. I just want to stop thinking about it. About her. About the personal failure she represents. I wish I could.

I finally fall asleep a couple hours after the early-morning intrusion only to be woken up a little after nine by the sorority. They're yakking in the living room or kitchen or somewhere and cackling with laughter. They always fucking cackle when they're together. I've heard them laugh when they're not in a pack, when it's just one of them with me somewhere, and each has a pleasant, subdued laugh. But put the three of them in the same space, and it's this loud, shrill cackle.

It's Saturday, so why the hell are they up at this hour? The one thing I actually enjoy about my siblings is that they've always been late sleepers, like me. When we were teenagers, if my parents didn't have to wake us for our part-time jobs or hockey, we'd all sleep until well after noon. A few months ago, when Sadie and Winnie visited for the weekend and they all stayed here, they slept until almost two in the afternoon both days.

The yammering and cackling aren't subsiding and I can't block them out, even with my pillow over my head, which only serves to make me feel like I'm suffocating. So I groan and swear and drag myself out of bed. This time, instead of jeans, I make my way to the open walk-in closet and grab a pair of sweats and a tank top, and I open my bedroom door and pad barefoot toward the incessant noise.

Dixie is sitting on the counter next to the coffee machine. Sadie and Winnie are at the kitchen table, both holding coffee mugs, and they have their feet up on my table. I shove their feet off as I walk by, heading to the coffee machine. Dixie smiles at me and hands me her full, untouched latte. "Here you go, grumpy. I'll make a new one."

I grunt my gratitude and take a sip. Sadie puts her feet back on the table, shooting me a defiant glare. I ignore her, because it's the easiest solution. She turns to Dixie. "So eleven?"

"Yep." Dixie nods and puts a new mug under the spout and hits the button for another latte. The machine rumbles loudly. "I can't believe she lives here or that I randomly ran into her. I'm hardly ever in that area of town."

Good. They're going out, so I can go back to napping. I should hit the gym, but I'll do that later. Probably.

Winnie sits up and flips her dirty-blond hair. "Does she look the same?"

Dixie nods. "Yep. Still has that gorgeous dark red hair and that incredible freckleless skin."

I stop staring at the foam on my latte and move my eyes to Dixie. She's pouring milk into the little metal frothing cup and sticking it under the steamer arm, all while still planted on the counter. If she's not careful she'll fall on her face, but that's not my concern. My concern is who they might be talking about.

"Remember I used to say she looked like a doll? Her skin was like porcelain." Sadie sighs.

Porcelain skin. Dark red hair. That brings back memories. I take another sip of latte. "You guys are reminding me of Maine."

"That's because we're talking about who you think we're talking about," Winnie replies. I stop mid-latte-sip, the liquid scalding my lip. I pull the cup back and wipe foam from my top lip.

"Zoey Quinlin?" God. I haven't said her name in forever.

Dixie just nods casually as she sips her new latte. Casually. Like this isn't a big deal. And of course if I act like it's a big deal—which it is—they'll tease me mercilessly about it until the end of time. Because that's what the sorority does best.

"Crazy that she's out here in San Francisco," I say in a low-key tone, to stick with this "no big deal" façade my sisters have going on. "She's living here? Or is she visiting?"

Dixie ignores me. "Winnie, are you going to wear that cute blue sundress? Because, if not, can I borrow it? Blue looks better on me anyway."

"Fuck you. I look fabulous in blue."

"You look better in red," Dixie counters with a grin. "I'll lend you that cute red tank I have that would look amazing with your black print capris."

"Hello!" I bellow, and Dixie kind of jumps and then turns and stares at me.

"Yeah? What?"

"I asked you a question. Is Zoey visiting, or does she live here?"

Winnie laughs as she stands up, leaving her half-empty coffee mug on my kitchen table. She gives me a cocky smirk. "Wouldn't you like to know."

And then she saunters out of the room. Dixie gulps down the rest of her coffee and puts the empty mug on the counter, nowhere near my dishwasher, and chases Winnie out of the room. "Do not get in the shower first! I called dibs already, remember?"

I hear them both running through the living room and around

the corner to my guest bedroom and bath. I sigh heavily. Holy crap, they're annoying. I run a hand over my face as if trying to scrub the annoyed look off of it and then take the final sip of my latte. Sadie watches me like I'm a caged monkey at the zoo. "What?"

"She's living here," Sadie tells me as she stands and grabs Winnie's cup off the table. There's a wet coffee ring left in its wake. "She told Dixie that her parents retired and live in Sacramento and she and her brother, Morgan, are both in San Fran."

"Oh. That's amazing," I can't help but confess, because of all my sisters, Sadie is usually the one who doesn't attack me like a gleeful hyena when I let my guard down. "I wonder how long she's been here and how I haven't run into her before."

"I'll find out at brunch and let you know," Sadie replies and places her cup and Winnie's on the counter next to Dixie's. Still not the dishwasher but A for effort.

"Where's brunch?"

Sadie pauses, and a smile slowly spreads across her lips. Of all my sisters, Sadie looks the most like me, her hair the exact same shade of blond, her mouth the same width, her eyes the same color. That means her smiles always look devious. She used to always get blamed for shit when the three of them got into trouble because she, like me, can never pull off an innocent face. "You still have a thing for her? After a decade?"

"I didn't say that," I reply promptly. "I'm just asking a question. Making small talk."

She laughs a little as there's a loud thud from the guest room and one of them swears loudly.

"We're meeting her at MKT in the Four Seasons," Sadie tells me. She starts out of the kitchen but pauses and turns back. "Because it would be kind of cool if you did still have a thing for her. If she's single and everything. And you could hook me up with her brother."

Sadie leaves but doesn't head to the extra bedroom like the other two. I catch a glimpse of her heading into my bedroom at the end of the hall. Of course. She's going to use my bathroom instead of wrestling the other two for time in the guest bath. Sadie was always the brightest. I shove their cups and mine into the dishwasher and pad down the hall, calling, "Oh, don't worry about me. I don't need to shower." I leave the kitchen for the living room and drop down on the couch. I grab the remote and turn on the sound system, filling the room with some Tragically Hip so I don't have to listen to the sorority thumping around as they get ready.

Zoey Quinlin lives in San Francisco. Well, things just got interesting.

4

ZOEY

I laugh so hard my coffee almost comes out my nose. I lift my napkin from my lap and hold it in front of my face just in case, but I manage to swallow the coffee down. Winnie's snorting laugh almost ruined it for me, but I managed. God, I thought she would have outgrown that goofy laugh by now. She's been doing it since she was a kid, and somehow it's just as adorable even now that she's an adult.

I was kind of worried when I woke up this morning and dressed for brunch that we'd have little to talk about after we filled each other in on the last eleven years, but we've picked up like no time has gone by. Babysitting these girls was always a treat. They're fun and a little bit wild. I think that's why their parents paid me to do it even when Winnie was technically old enough to be in charge. The three of them together were unpredictable and a wee bit crazy.

We had spent the first hour of brunch catching up on each other's lives. Winnie is a teacher, just like her mom. In fact they work at the same school in Toronto. Sadie is a nurse at a hospital there too, but both Dixie and Winnie say she should have been a doctor. Sadie laughed it off but there was something in her blue eyes that said she agrees. Dixie works in PR for the San Francisco Thunder. I didn't have to ask about Jude. I knew he was a professional hockey player, but they freely threw more details at me. He won two Cups, he is alternate captain, he has won almost every award in the league at least once. He lives in the Pacific Heights area of San Francisco. I had to suppress a smile at that. Adam had wanted to live there, but I thought it was too ostentatious.

Winnie stops snort-laughing, and the cackling from Sadie and Dixie dies down too. I take a deep breath. My sides hurt and my cheeks are sore from smiling, which hasn't happened in…well, I can't remember the last time it did.

"So I feel like you know everything we've done in the last eleven years. What about you?" Sadie asks as she pours more green tea from the tiny ceramic pot the waiter brought her.

I shrug. "I told you all there is to know. Morgan was already going to Berkeley, and when I got in, my dad decided to take a job at a church in Sacramento to be closer to us. He retired, but he and my mom are both still there, and Morgan and I both settled in here. I'm working in real estate. I was in commercial, but I transferred into residential a month ago."

"That does seem like a good fit for you," Dixie tells me, absently brushing her ash-blond bob from her eyes. "You always loved houses. I remember when you babysat you used to take us for ice cream just so we could walk around the streets at night, and you could look into all the windows of the cottages."

"That makes me sound like a peeping Tom!" I protest, but she's right. I used to love to walk the streets of that tiny town and glance in any open windows. The cottages were all so old and there was amazing woodwork and elaborate staircases to glimpse. "I do still love old homes."

"So do you live in one of the Victorian charmers around here?" Sadie asks, her expression inquisitive. "With your husband?"

I lift an eyebrow; she smiles sheepishly. "Actually, I do own a Victorian. But no husband. Well, not anymore."

"What kind of moron can't make it work with you?" Winnie asks bluntly, and I smile.

"It was basically mutual. Just not a good fit, long term," I say, and I'm surprised by how accurate that is but how much it still hurts. Not so much the losing Adam but the failure in general. I never would have married him if I didn't think I could be with him until the end. But I realized too late that I can't. Even if this kid thing hadn't come up, we were not a good fit.

The three of them fall silent for a moment. Then Winnie sits straighter in her chair and grins at me. "So you're single then. We should go out and pick up boys!"

"Oh my God." Sadie rolls her eyes and chucks a napkin at her sister. "You aren't single, remember?"

"No. I'm not, but I like to pretend." She laughs sheepishly. "I mean, not the way Jude pretends."

"Jude doesn't pretend he's single, he forgets he isn't. Big difference," Dixie replies with a frown. "Big, cheating difference."

"Jude's married?"

Different noises erupt in unison from each of them. Winnie snorts again. Dixie lets out a high-pitched laugh and Sadie chuffs. The waiter gives our table a confused stare as he collects our empty plates and hesitantly asks if there's anything else we'd like. We all shake our heads no. He disappears, and Sadie turns to me. She still looks like she could be Jude's twin. I mean, if he still looks like I remember. Tall, blond, smoky blue bedroom eyes and that smile that makes you think he wants to do dirty things to you. Correction: makes you hope that he's thinking about doing dirty things to you.

"Jude is impossibly single," Sadie explains and tosses her napkin on the table. "He tried the serious relationship thing once."

"And it was a serious nightmare," Dixie interjects, rolling her eyes. "He can't keep his dick in his pants. It's like genetically impossible. I swear it just opens the zipper on his pants itself if a hot, willing woman is within five feet."

Winnie swears. "Jesus, Dixie, you have to stop being so graphic when it comes to Jude's body parts."

Dixie shrugs. Sadie turns to me again. "She wasn't the right fit for him, and deep down he knew it. Or his dick did, which is why he cheated. But when the right person gives him a chance, he'll be exactly like our dad. Loyal, faithful and completely trustworthy."

"Well, hopefully not exactly like Dad." Dixie's words are barely a whisper, but she's sitting right beside me so I catch them. I glance at her, but her face is hidden by a curtain of hair. Still, the melancholy in her voice is unmistakable. I'm about to ask if everything is all right with her dad when a shadow falls across the table. I look up, expecting it to be our waiter with the bill, but it's not. It's Jude Braddock.

Our eyes lock. They're just as impossibly, breathtakingly blue as I remember. There's no surprise or shock in them. He knew his sisters were meeting me. He's here on purpose. But judging by the groans and shocked murmurs around the table, he wasn't invited.

"Hey, Sunset."

Oh my God, he remembers that nickname? He called me that the first night we kissed. He told me I was more beautiful than a sunset, and then it started raining and he kissed me under a lifeguard stand on the beach. I smile at the memory. "Hey, Jude."

I half expect the girls to start singing a loud, off-key version of the Beatles song like they used to do when someone said "hey, Jude," just to annoy him. But I guess they outgrew that.

"What the hell are you doing here?" Winnie asks, but he ignores her, his eyes still glued to mine.

"You look like life's been good," he says. Oh God, if only he were right.

"You look like life's been great," I counter.

He grins. Oh my word, that bloody grin. Full lips part to reveal perfect teeth with just the slightest slice of pink tongue visible as his high cheekbones seem to get higher and his chiseled jaw more defined. Those perfectly arched eyebrows bend just a little bit more to give him that totally cheeky, undeniably attractive bad-boy quality. Holy shit, it was hot when he was seventeen but now it's downright inferno inducing.

"Dear God, go away!" Dixie mutters, rolling her eyes again. I get the feeling it's how she gets her cardio. "You're bringing down the property value of this place with that sleazy smirk."

He ignores her completely, again, and moves around the table. His body is big, wider and maybe even taller than I remember, but he still moves with this mesmerizing grace. He steps in between my chair and Dixie's, angling his ass toward her as he turns to me. He holds out a hand. "How about a hug?"

I lift my hand off the table and place it in his. I feel his strength and his warmth surround it as he wraps his fingers around it and helps me to my feet. A second later I'm pressed into his torso, his arms circling my waist, and that strength and warmth is like a blanket covering all of me. Yeah, he's taller now. And thicker. God, it's sexy—the large, wide, hard size of his frame. Muscles are everywhere. They aren't bulky, but you can *feel* them.

The hug ends, but we don't really break apart. My arms are still around his shoulders and his still circle my waist. Our heads are only far enough apart to lock eyes once again. And then, in a low rumble of a whisper he says, "Christ, you're still as beautiful as I remember."

Oh sweet snickerdoodles.

And then I remember we're in the middle of a restaurant surrounded by his siblings. I remember, because they don't give me any other choice. They all stand up and start talking.

"Jude, let go of our friend," Sadie requests calmly.

"Jude, I've told you before, no eye-fucking in public. It's rude," Winnie remarks, not so calmly.

"Hands off, dirtball, before your dick escapes your pants again," Dixie finishes off the trio of insults.

And *poof*! That incredible moment is gone. We step apart, and he turns to scowl at all of them. I remember that face too. He gave it to them a lot growing up. It's oddly comforting that that hasn't changed. "Can the sorority take it down a notch? Please. Zoey doesn't need to know you're all still a bunch of brats."

He gets three perfectly synchronized eye rolls with that. Winnie excuses herself to use the restroom, Sadie joins her and Dixie sits down and pulls out her phone, presumably to check her email or something. He turns back to me, and I find myself holding my breath. He gives me that insanely attractive smile again. "I was hoping to catch you guys mid-brunch so I could join, but I guess you're all done."

I nod.

"Do you have plans this afternoon?"

I do. I promised myself I would go to Adam's house—my house—and have that talk we need to have about the lawyers, the divorce and everything else. But the idea of spending the afternoon with Jude is way more appealing. "I do, but they're not set in stone."

He likes that answer. "Spend the afternoon with me."

"Doing what?"

He grins wider.

That's all he does, and it's the most obscenely suggestive thing that has ever happened to me in my life. And I love it.

"Mrs. Penner?"

I smile back at Jude, because it seems like the perfect response to what feels like an unasked invitation to spend the afternoon naked under him. Is that really what he's offering? The Jude I knew at eighteen offered it but not nearly as confidently. And it went horribly awry, to say the least. But I find myself very open, for the first time in my life, to second chances.

There's a deep rumble of a man clearing his throat and then, "Mrs. Penner?"

Oh, right. That's me. I blink and step, almost more like stumble, back from Jude. The concierge from the hotel is standing just behind Dixie. His expression is serene, calm, but I know something is off if he's sought me out. "Yes?"

Once I acknowledge the name Jude doesn't know, and more importantly the Mrs. part, Jude takes a step back, out of shock, I'm guessing. Great. Now he thinks I'm married. Wait, I am married. Technically.

"I was hoping you'd have a minute to chat with me, over at the desk. It's about your room," the concierge says casually. I try not to frown as I nod. Wow, this is bad timing. I reach for my purse on the back of the chair I vacated and take out my wallet to settle my part of our brunch bill.

"I'll grab your brunch, ladies," Jude offers, and before I can argue, because after all he didn't even eat with us, Dixie is shoving the little leather folder with our bill at his wide, chiseled chest as Sadie and Winnie return to the table. I guess his sisters don't mind a free meal.

I turn and start hugging each sister. "I'll say good-bye now, since I don't know how long I'll be. But it was so great seeing you all, and we should do this again next time you're all in town."

"Yes!" Winnie replies as she squeezes me. Sadie nods emphatically as she hugs me.

Dixie squeezes me hardest of all and suggests, "Let's do drinks sometime soon, since I'm always in town."

"Sure." I nod. Jude leans in next and wraps me in his arms again. This time, though, the hug feels less intimate, cooler. Against the shell of my ear he says, "Congratulations on your marriage. He's a lucky guy."

"You should be congratulating me on my pending divorce," I blurt back softly, and I'm a little stunned I said that. But I don't even feel the least bit reserved in front of him. It's odd, because it took about a half hour before I felt completely at ease and able to be myself with his sisters, but with Jude, from the minute he walked up to our table I've been one hundred percent me. He doesn't seem shocked by my announcement. In fact there's a hint of a smile playing on his lips that says he might actually be relieved by the news.

I give them all a good-bye wave and follow the concierge out of the restaurant. The hotel lobby is down one level, so we ride the elevator together in awkward silence. I wonder if they need to have me move rooms. I keep extending my stay, so they've moved me a few times to make space for existing reservations.

"Is my room already booked?" I ask him as the elevator doors slide open and we cross the pristine marble lobby. "Because I don't mind moving rooms again. I know I haven't officially extended my stay, but I will probably be here another two weeks."

"We'll gladly extend your stay, Mrs. Penner," he says easily, and I try not to frown at that damn name. I don't want to correct the staff here, because all my credit cards are still in my married name, and I don't want to confuse anyone. "We'll just need a valid credit card, for the current charges and the future ones."

"You have my credit card on file."

He's moved around the massive oak check-in counter now and bows his head to look at his screen. When he looks up, his voice is still calm and casual, but his eyes are sympathetic. "You left us your MasterCard on file; however, when we ran the charges for the week through, it was declined."

He lets his voice drop low, to a whisper, when he says that last word. Because it's a very dirty word at a five-star hotel. I feel like I'm in some alternate universe. Was my card number stolen? Did the company freeze it for my safety and forget to tell me? Adam and I agreed that I would charge my hotel costs until the divorce was finalized. I should be in the damn house and I'm only not because he uses the address for business, so it was easier like this, for now.

"There must be some mistake," I stammer, and the look on his face says that he's heard that before.

"Let me just call the credit card company," I say, and he nods. I dig my phone out of my bag and wander to the corner of the lobby.

The credit card company explains that Mr. Penner canceled the card and closed the account. I'm shaking by the time I get off the phone with them. It's a mixture of rage and humiliation that causes the tremors. I know, without even checking, that he's shut down all our joint accounts. Why is he doing this to me?

I have one credit card in just my name, but the limit isn't all that high. Luckily, it's got nothing on it, so I can probably pay the entire bill I've accumulated so far, but I'll have to check out today. I head back to the desk and smile at the concierge, whose name tag says Ryan. But I know the smile is wobbly and my eyes are starting to water. "What's the total?"

Ryan slides a discreetly folded bill across the polished wood of the counter. I unfold it with shaky fingers. Okay. I will be able to pay it off and still have $107 of available credit. That's it. It makes my stomach roll with panic, but there's nothing I can do right now, so I hand him my Visa, and in the strongest voice I can muster I say, "Please use this for my charges, and I'll be checking out now."

"Thank you and…we hope to see you again." He looks so sympathetic it makes me feel worse. When he's done and hands me back my credit card, I swear it feels like it's hot, like there should be smoke coming off of it. I just annihilated my entire available credit in one blow. How is this my life? Ugh.

"I'll just head up and pack my things."

"Take as long as you need. We're not in a rush to turn over the room," Ryan says. I nod and beeline toward the elevator. I start to scroll through my contacts to find Adam's number, but I'm still shaking, and I end up dropping my phone.

It falls screen down on the marble floor, and I know the screen cracked. I don't even have to pick it up. I just know it. One big fat tear starts to hover on the edge of my lower eyelid, and I raise my hand and catch it before it can fall. If I let it fall, it will bring its friends and then I'll be crying in public. I'm not ready to cry in public. I'm not ready to admit my life is that far off track.

Before I can bend to pick up my phone, someone else is doing it for me. That damn tear hovering in my vision makes the person just a blur of blond hair and dark shirt, but then there's a hand pressed to my back, and it feels so warm and comforting that I instantly start to take deeper breaths. He's gently moving me forward with that warm, strong hand on my lower back. We reach the bank of elevators. "Punch the up button."

I do what Jude tells me. The doors swing open, and we step inside. He punches the close button before anyone can join us, and his blurry face is turned to mine as he commands, "Hit your floor."

I hit seventeen.

His hand is still on my lower back, pressed flat and firm, as we ascend.

The elevator rises quickly, and before I can get the liquid in my eyes to stop multiplying we're at my floor. I have to pack everything. I have a lot of stuff, and it's everywhere. I hadn't planned on leaving. And I have nowhere to go. And Jude is going to see this—see me in this disastrous state—and suddenly that is the most horrifying aspect of this entire thing. Jude knew wild, fearless, confident and powerful Zoey Quinlin. That girl doesn't exist right now. I hope to resuscitate her, but that hasn't happened yet, and I don't want him to know this woman. Dependent, weak, confused and abandoned Zoey Penner.

Oh crap. My urge to cry is getting stronger, not subsiding. As we walk down the hall I concentrate on the warm, reassuring feel of his palm against me. I try to absorb that feeling, let it seep into me and spread through me. It helps, a little. So do his words.

"I don't know what's going on with you, but I know you'll be okay," he says as I slow in front of my door. I take the key card and will my hand to stop shaking, which it doesn't, as I swipe it and the lock flashes green. Jude puts his hand on top of mine and twists the doorknob with me. We walk into the room almost as one, our feet beside each other.

The door closes behind us with a quiet *whoosh*. The curtains are still closed, since I didn't open them before I left this morning, and the room is oddly dark. It gives this whole moment a dreamlike quality. His hand on my back slides around to my hip, and he turns me so I'm facing him again.

He lifts his other hand, the one holding my phone. The screen is facing him, and he winces and then tosses it on the bed. "You're going to need a new phone."

"I need a lot of new things," I whisper back and fight to keep the tears from falling.

"Anything I can help with?"

"No." My answer is firm and swift. "I can handle it."

"I know you can." His response is just as firm and filled with a lot more confidence than mine. I look up, and our eyes lock, and I feel the power of his stare. Jude's always held this inexplicable intensity behind eyes that are so light and faultless. Even when his lips are pulled into a teasing smirk and his eyebrows are quirked in a playful arch, his eyes crush you with a deep, penetrating stare. It creates that deliciously off-balance feeling I haven't felt since I was eighteen. "You don't look like you believe that, though, so I just wanted to be sure you didn't need a reminder."

"A reminder?"

He nods and moves closer, just an inch or two, but it feels like he's right on top of me now. It creates a feeling of excitement that eats away at my melancholy. "I don't care what your last name is now, you're Zoey Quinlin. You're the most beautiful girl I've ever known with the best smile and the biggest attitude. You could do anything, get anything, be anything and make any man into your personal lap dog."

I almost laugh at that. Air escapes my lungs in a puff, and I feel the corners of my mouth lift. He grins back, big, bold and confident. "So whatever is happening in your life right now, it might have knocked you down, but it didn't knock you out. Zoey Quinlin doesn't get knocked out; she does the knocking out."

"Okay."

"You bet your sweet ass okay." He smiles. "And it's still a very sweet ass."

I laugh, full and complete this time.

"I'm going to go, unless you need me for anything," Jude says, his hand dropping from my waist. I instantly feel its absence. "And I mean anything. I will help you with anything, whether it requires clothes or not, so I should go because, Mrs. Penner, I might get myself into trouble."

He turns toward the door, and I take a deep breath that is, surprisingly, not shaky. "Jude," I say, and he stops, door pulled open, one foot already in the hall. "Thank you."

"I'll see you soon, Zoey," he promises, and then he leaves.

I have a fleeting but overwhelming urge to follow him into the hall and drag him back in here and rip his clothes off and finish what we started eleven years ago. I know he'll let me, Mrs. Penner or no

Mrs. Penner. But my life already feels like a meteor barreling out of control through the atmosphere. Sleeping with Jude right now would only create an even more obliterating impact when my life finally lands somewhere. No matter how fantastic it would feel to finally get naked with him.

5

ZOEY

I don't knock on the door, I bang on it with the side of my closed fist. One of my suitcases slips off the stoop and down a step. I reach for it and stumble and almost fall headfirst down the stairs. A big chunk of my hair escapes my topknot. I slip down another step and grab the railing for balance, and of course that's the moment Adam chooses to open the front door. He's wearing black running shorts and a gray-and-yellow dry-weave tank top. He looks bad in yellow; I've told him that. It gives his skin a jaundiced tone and makes the salt in his salt-and-pepper hair dull.

"Zoey." My name comes out in a flat, annoyed tone. He steps out onto the porch, crossing his arms over his sweat-stained chest. His earbuds still hang around his neck. "What are you doing here? Minerva said she explained to you that you need to hire a lawyer."

"Yeah, she told me. I'm not here about the divorce, I'm here about my credit cards," I explain as I abandon the bag on the step to climb up and be at least on the same level as him. Adam isn't overly tall. He's only about five nine, so with my high wedge sandals I'm close to his height. I straighten my spine to extend my height and I cross my arms too.

"Zoey, cutting off the cards is part of the divorce," Adam explains, sighing loudly. "If you'd hired a lawyer, my lawyer would have explained that to him."

"We agreed I could live in a hotel," I remind him.

He nods tersely. "But you should be paying for it."

"When the settlement is sorted, I'll pay half the bill," I offer.

He looks offended by that. "Half?"

"Remember, I'm only in a hotel because I was trying not to disrupt your business and let you use the home office," I say, and I hate that there's a little shake in my voice again. I hope he doesn't hear it.

"It's time to find a permanent place to live," Adam tells me, completely ignoring my last statement.

"I have a permanent place to live. This house." I point to the pretty blue-and-white front door I repainted myself less than a year ago. "The pre-nup clearly states I get the house."

He frowns, the deep crease between his eyes getting deeper. "It states that you and our future children will retain the house. There were no future children, so the rest is up for debate as far as my lawyer is concerned."

"You can't be serious."

"Zoey, please do yourself a favor and hire a damn lawyer." He turns to walk back into the house.

He's just going to leave me out here like I'm the trash. Jude's words echo through my head. *You're the most beautiful girl I've ever known with the best smile and the biggest attitude. You could do anything, get anything, be anything...*

I step onto the stoop and grab his arm. He bristles and turns slowly in disbelief that I would be so aggressive. "Zoey, there's no need to be uncouth."

"Yeah, well, there's no need to be a giant raging asshole, but you're doing it anyway," I retort cuttingly. His eyes grow wide. I don't swear. I was brought up not to, and it's one of the only rules my parents gave me that I adhered to—then and now. But fuck rules. "This house is mine. You were the one who wrote the pre-nup, and you gave it to me. I'm not backing down on that. You wanted to end this marriage because of the possibility I can't carry your future pretentious offspring, fine. But you don't get to take everything."

"Hire a lawyer," he repeats and slams the door in my face.

I could do a million things right now. Pound on the door again, repeatedly ring the bell or walk away. Give up. Do what he says and let some high-priced lawyer figure it out for me. But I don't. That might have been how Zoey Penner would react, but not Zoey Quinlin. And I want to be Zoey Quinlin again.

So I walk right up to the front door, open it and start hauling my luggage into our immaculate hallway. He's halfway up the ornate staircase. He's pulled off that hideous yellow-and-gray shirt, and his earbuds are on the hall stand by his phone. His brown eyes flare with shock, but I ignore him and pull my last suitcase over the threshold.

"Zoey, what the hell do you think you're doing?"

"I'm living in my house, Adam," I reply with a fierce intensity I haven't heard from myself in a long time. "I'm still on the mortgage, so I have every right to be here. If you don't want to leave, fine, but I'm not going either."

"How the fuck is that going to work?" He never swears. He's furious. Good.

I add to his anger by giving him a patronizing scowl, which I know he hates. "It's a four-bedroom, three-bathroom house, Adam. And if you don't like it, you can borrow my suitcases as soon as I unpack."

I start to lug the first one up the stairs. He lets me pass him without a word, but his face is red, and it's not from his little run. I ignore him and make it to the second-floor landing, exhausted and out of breath. Only two more suitcases to go. I could demand the master. It would be fun to piss him off even more, but the truth is, I don't want it. It's got too many sad memories, so I turn and wheel my suitcase down the hall to the largest of the three guest rooms. It doesn't have an ensuite, but I'll live.

As I place the suitcase in the corner near the closet, I hear a door slam, and it makes me smile. I go back downstairs and spend the next five minutes lugging my other two bags up to the guest room. I gently close the door, walk back to the bed and drop down across it. I'm not sure, in the long run, whether this is the right move, but right now it feels right. It feels good to stand up for myself. And I love this house. I was the one who begged Adam to buy it. He hates old things, especially in architecture. The only reason I convinced him to buy it was because it was a status symbol to own one of these iconic homes known as the Painted Ladies. They rarely come on the market, and Adam loves rare things that elevate his status, so he agreed despite the age of it.

I dig my phone out of my purse and text my brother, telling him I've moved back home. It's only cracked on one side, so I can still use most of the screen; it's just annoying. He texts back right away and asks if the divorce is final. I tell him no, and he asks where Adam moved to. I text back *nowhere* and then whisper a countdown. "Three…two…one."

My ringtone for Morgan, which is Hanson's "Mmmbop," fills the room.

"No, we are not back together."

"Thank you, sweet baby Jesus." My brother sighs dramatically. "Then why the hell are you living under the same roof as that loser?"

"He canceled our joint credit cards," I explain. "And I couldn't afford the hotel."

"You can crash here again," Morgan offers. "Ned is away for work until Sunday and besides, he loves cooking for more than just me."

"I know, but this is my house." I sigh and pull the elastic from my hair, letting the red tangled mess fall down the side of the bed. "He's trying to take it back."

"It's yours. It's in the pre-nup."

"Something about how the pre-nup mentions that it goes to me and our children, but we didn't have kids, so he doesn't seem to think it applies anymore." I hear a door slam again, this time upstairs, and I know he's in his office. "I spoke to Minerva and she told me to hire a lawyer. It's going to get ugly."

Morgan swears under his breath. "I hate to say this, Z, but I thought it might. He's too much of a greedy, self-serving bastard to be civil about this."

"You know I worked my ass off to grow his business. And I put way more blood, sweat and tears into restoring this house than he did. He's the one who asked me for the pre-nup. I didn't de-bate one word of it either, I let him craft the whole thing, and now he's going to change that too as punishment for an aggressive uterus I can't control."

I finish my rant and feel my eyes watering again. Ugh.

"I don't think your uterus is aggressive," Morgan tells me in his best soothing big-brother voice. "I think it's just protecting you from his snotty, uptight, bitchy sperm."

I laugh. "I said something similar to his face. Called his future children pretentious."

"There's the Zoey Quinlin I know and missed. Glad to have you back."

"Thank Jude Braddock."

There's a pause. "That Canadian kid who played hockey?"

"Yeah. He plays professionally here, and I ran into him," I explain. "I was having a moment, and he gave me a pep talk."

Morgan's deep laugh rolls through my phone. "He had it bad for you back in the day."

"Yeah, and his sisters had it bad for you," I remind him.

"If only they had penises," Morgan laments. "But I would have banged Jude, though, if I were you. He was hot."

"Still is hot. Even more so, I think." I smile as Jude's image fills my brain. "And we tried to hook up once. It didn't work out."

"Oh, right! How did that go again?" Morgan laughs again. "He tried to woo you with booze and pizza rolls and you barfed all over him."

I laugh. "Not exactly. It was Boone's Farm apple wine and Fireball and pizza rolls. It was actually pretty romantic at the time. And I threw up all over the floor, not him. In fairness, he threw up too, after he saw me do it."

"And then he left for school the next day, and you left for Berkeley, and then Mom and Dad moved away from Maine, and the rest is unconsummated history," Morgan announces dramatically.

There's another pause in our conversation. My house is silent, which isn't comforting, because I know Adam is around somewhere. God, I can't wait until it's all mine.

"I'll ask around and see if someone knows a good divorce lawyer."

"Thanks."

"Zoey-Poey, hang in there, okay?" Morgan says. "You'll get through this."

"I know."

"Call me day or night if you need anything. Even if it's just to come over there and remove the frozen rod from your ex's ass."

I laugh. "I will. Thanks, Morgy."

He groans at the nickname he's hated since birth and hangs up.

If Adam doesn't bend and move out, living with each other is going to be awkward and annoying. But I still feel better—about myself—for having taken this stand, so I know I'm not leaving first. Not unless the lawyer makes me.

6

JUDE

"Hey, Ry," I say with a light smile as I lean on the counter.

He gives me an easy but professional smile. "Mr. Braddock! Will you be staying with us again? Renovations still ongoing at your condo?"

I shake my head. "No. Well…maybe."

He looks confused, and I feel it. What the hell am I doing? I know that he can't tell me if Zoey is still staying here. It's against hotel policy. Still, I'm only here so I can ask that very question. And if she is still here, you bet your ass I'm checking in, even though there hasn't been a wayward hookup knocking on my door since my sister pretended to be my pregnant wife. Of course, that was only thirty-six hours ago.

"We have some availability," Ryan tells me, glancing at the screen in front of him. "But it's going to fill up, so if you want me to hold something…"

"You know, I was in my friend Zoey's room, and I really liked her view." I pray that Zoey's room had a good view. I didn't look out the window at all. I only looked at her. Ryan repeats the name with a furrowed brow, so I elaborate, in a casual tone. "You probably know her as Zoey Penner. I knew her before that, as Zoey Quinlin. Anyway, I don't know if she checked out or not, but if she did, I would love that room. It had fantastic light."

Ryan still looks confused. Good. Confusion will lead to being less guarded with his response…I hope. "Oh, wait. You mean Mrs. Penner. Zoey Penner. You know her?"

"Since I was a kid. She was here having brunch with my sisters, and I asked to see her room because, you know, I stay here all the time, and I haven't found the perfect suite yet. I'm particular about the layout and the light. Feng shui and all that." I am rambling like an idiot. I'm pretty sure Ryan thinks I've got some weird interior design fetish now. Oh, well, who gives a fuck, if it gets me the information I want.

"Well, actually, her room is available, since she checked out. Do you want that exact suite?" he inquires, his overly bushy eyebrows still pinched together. "I didn't know you liked views of the alley, though. We rarely have requests for that."

I smile as my phone starts buzzing in my pocket. It's my alarm. I have to get to the rink for a photo shoot. I pull it out of my pocket. "Shit. Sorry, Ry, I have to go. I forgot that I have an appointment. Thanks for checking availability for me. I'll call if I need the room."

I head out of the hotel lobby and hand the valet my ticket. I text Dixie to tell her I'm on my way. She texts back, Hurry up, dirtball. I jump in my Tesla and pull out into downtown San Francisco traffic. It was a little bit dumb swinging by here before the photo shoot. There was no way it wasn't going to make me at least a little late. But I had to know how she was. I couldn't get her out of my mind.

Something was wrong with my Zoey. I could tell, even before

I saw her at the concierge's desk. She was exactly the same on the outside—beautiful in a classic, pure way and yet sexy as hell in a wild, untamed way. But on the inside, I could tell despite her smile that something was not the same. I could see a glimmer of the girl who had been my teenage obsession, but it was weak, like a flickering ember on a dying fire. Then I touched her, we hugged and more of the inner flame seemed to glow. She smiled again, but it was the one I remember. Wild, carefree, unabashedly joyful. And then Ryan had interrupted.

I was going to leave with the sorority, but as we filtered down to the main lobby, toward the valet station, I glanced over and saw her standing at the desk. Her shoulders drooped, her head hung in defeat and she was biting a quivering lip. So as Dixie, Winnie and Sadie, oblivious to what I saw, disappeared out the front door to go shopping for the day, I found myself being pulled toward her.

In the hotel room, I wanted to take her. I wanted to strip her naked and worship her body, because it's what I've wanted to do since I was sixteen. And it wasn't the name Mrs. Penner that stopped me. I looked at her ring finger as soon as I walked into that restaurant, before I even approached the table. She wasn't wearing a wedding band. And she wasn't staying with anyone in that hotel room either. She wasn't married, no matter what paperwork still had to be filed.

But I knew she didn't need a reminder of how physically desirable she was. She needed to hear how incredible she was in other ways. So I gave her the words I could find, but honestly, even they don't express what I feel about this girl. She was this bold, confident and happy teenager when I first met her, and I know that girl is in there still. I know she just needs to be reminded of how strong and radiant she really is. And I want to be the one to remind her.

My phone rings and Levi's name flashes across the screen. I shouldn't ignore a call from the captain of my hockey team. But since he's also my best friend who'd been lying to me for months, I let the call go to voicemail as I get on the freeway in the direction of the arena. Levi and I have always been a great pair—on and off the ice. We balance each other out. I'm the upbeat, brash extrovert, and he's the rational, intense introvert. We never talked about it or purposely picked roles, it's just who we were, and it worked.

One thing we had talked about was the bro code. You didn't touch another guy's girl. This wasn't just a friend rule, it was a team agreement. The San Francisco Thunder is one of the youngest teams in the NHL, with most players under the age of twenty-five and only two players over the age of thirty. We're an untamed bunch of athletic, horny, rowdy guys. There have to be rules about women, or else off-ice drama would affect our on-ice chemistry. And that's exactly what happened when Levi started seeing my ex-girlfriend.

Yeah, Tessa was an ex, but she wasn't just a random hookup. We dated for a couple of months. It wasn't a smooth or easy relationship, but it was still a relationship, my first and only one. Even though we'd been broken up for ten months, they started hooking up behind my back, and even after it got serious, he didn't tell me. I caught them. I was a lot of things—impulsive, wild, willful—and I may not have been honest with Tessa, but I was always honest with Levi. And he wasn't with me.

And now I was on what felt like an emotional seesaw. I had to work with him and see him almost daily, and sometimes I could push past the betrayal. Sometimes it felt almost like old times. And then something happened—Levi said something, or, worse, he avoided saying something—to remind me that he betrayed me, and I would have never done that to him.

My phone rings again. This time it's my mom, so I answer it. "Hey, Ma."

"Hi, honey. Just wanted to make sure you're surviving your sisters," she says.

I smile. "I'm making it through. How are you doing without them?"

I know that having Winnie and Sadie close by is a blessing she's eternally grateful for, although she won't admit it. She's worried that they feel obligated to stay in Toronto, since Dad is so unwell and Dixie and I are so far away.

"Oh, it's fine," my mom tells me quickly. "It's only a few days, and your dad is doing well right now."

That news lifts my spirits instantly. "So the new meds are working?"

"It seems that way, yes." My mom has been, sometimes aggravatingly, realistic about my dad's diagnosis with ALS. She knows there is no miracle cure, and she works really hard to keep the hopes of her four children in check. I know that it's for the best not to get too excited, but I fucking hate it.

"So maybe he'll make it to the beach this year," I say, because my heart seems to actively rally against my mother's realism at all costs.

"Honey, I thought I told you, we're not going to Maine."

"What? Why?"

"It's too much, and I can't rely on your sisters."

I frown as I ease off the freeway. "You can count on them."

"Oh, I know. I know they'll come with me and they'll help me with him and won't leave our side." She sighs and it's heavy. It's always heavy. Growing up, my mom never sighed. "I meant I can't rely on them because I won't let myself. Your dad doesn't want to either. It would ruin their vacation. I told them to go ahead and use the cottage without us this year."

I get that feeling I always get when we talk about my dad's declining health. I feel like I did that time I had a concussion and I had to have a CT scan and they put me in that damn tube. I hadn't realized I was claustrophobic until that second. Being in that tube made me feel panic like I've never felt before. This irrational, uncontrollable clawing fear tore at my insides—my heart, my brain, my lungs—everywhere. And I was fully and completely aware that I could not do a damn thing to stop it, and that made it worse.

I swallow hard and pull as much air as I can into my lungs, working to let it out slowly so my mom doesn't hear it. I don't want her to think I'm about to freak out, even though I am. "Mom, I told you I can hire a nurse. She can go with you and help Dad out so the sorority doesn't feel like they're responsible. And I'll swing by for a weekend. It'll give you some time off."

"I don't need time off from my husband, Jude." Her tone is pointed, but only for a second. She knows I didn't mean it that way. "It's very sweet of you to offer, but hiring a private nurse to travel with us would be obscenely expensive."

The players' entrance to the arena is just up ahead, so I start to slow down. "Ma, I don't know if you got the memo, but I'm a millionaire."

She laughs like she always does when I bring up my financial situation. I still can't tell if she's doing it out of disbelief that her only son is absurdly wealthy, or because it makes her uncomfortable to think about all that money, but either way it's cute. My mom and dad lived a barely middle-class life supporting four of us and all our extracurricular activities on the salary of a high school teacher and a bus driver. We grew up in a small three-bedroom house in a so-so suburb of Toronto, meaning all three of my sisters shared a room until the fighting got to be too much and Dad renovated the attic.

The cottage in Maine was honestly where we lived like kings. It was owned by my dad's family. His grandparents had bought it and left it to his dad when they passed. Dad spent his childhood summers there and made sure we did the same. It wasn't fancy—in fact it was rustic. Four small bedrooms up a rickety staircase. One downstairs, sandwiched between an archaic bathroom and an ancient kitchen. But we loved it. All of us. We never fought at the cottage. We never complained about chores like washing dishes or cleaning our rooms. We spent all day at the beach and all night running around the safe, small seaside town so my parents also got a break from us.

"Dad loves that place," I remind her, even though I know she hasn't forgotten. "And by next year he really might not be able to go, even with a nurse, so he should go. You should all go. I'll be upset if you don't."

She sighs again. God, I hate that sound. "I'll consider it."

I swipe my pass at the gate, and the barrier moves upward. I see Levi leaning against the back of his G-Wagen as I pull into a spot. "Okay. Thanks. Just keep considering it until the only answer is yes."

She laughs at that. "You're incorrigible."

"I am. Love you."

"Love you too."

I hang up and turn off the engine. I glance at Levi in the rearview mirror, since I parked directly across from his car. He's tucking his phone into his pocket and is slowly walking toward my car. I jump out, hit the lock button and meet him near the trunk. "Hey. Did you just get here?"

"I got here about ten minutes ago but thought I would wait out here for you," Levi explains, shrugging. "Dixie won't go off on you for being late if we both are."

I glance at my phone for the time and then shove it in my back pocket. "It's only like ten after one. It's only late if it's thirty minutes or more."

"Jude logic." Levi chuckles.

"It's the only kind worth having," I say.

He smiles as I open the door to the arena, and we make our way down the hall. Okay, so far this is going well. I hope it stays that way. Sometimes he just tries too hard ever since I gave him and Tessa my blessing. He thinks I did him some kind of favor. I really didn't.

Dixie is standing at the end of the hall, near the dressing room. Her arms are crossed, creasing her fancy blazer and silk blouse. "Well, better late than never."

She's looking right at me, not Levi. But he pats her shoulder as we walk by and gives her his best soothing smile. He's got a lot of them. "We'll make up the time by changing quickly, I promise, Dixie."

She just nods. Man, how I wish she would just nod at me. The girl always has something to say to me.

We change into the clothes Dixie has laid out at our lockers. It's a photo shoot for a new line of Under Armour. We have the same sports agent, and he inked a deal for both of us.

As promised, we change with lightning-quick speed and make it down the hall to the training room Dixie has set up as a hair and makeup room. I give my sister a pointed stare and pretend to look at my watch, pointing out that *hello, the makeup artist is still setting up so you can suck it on tantrumming over me being late*. Dixie just rolls her eyes at my gestures and then promptly ignores me. I laugh to myself.

"Jude, you going to Darby's tomorrow?" Levi asks as the hairstylist motions him over.

"I don't know," I mutter. Duncan Darby usually spends the off-season in his hometown with his parents, but he's been bouncing back and forth all summer because his girlfriend, Carla, lives here full-time. I vaguely remember an email about a dinner party or something.

"You should come," Levi encourages as the stylist runs her fingers covered in some kind of paste through his dark brown hair. "It's not a couples thing or anything."

"But you're bringing a date?" I ask, trying to sound casual as the makeup artist motions me over, finally ready.

He swallows and shifts a little in his seat. "Well, yeah, Tessa is going. I mean, she's best friends with Carla, so even if we weren't—"

"Yeah, I know." I cut him off because I can't handle one more awkward explanation from him. There's a lot of that lately when we see each other. "I'm just saying, do you think I could bring a date?"

"Oh." Levi blinks. "Yeah. I guess. I mean, are you involved with someone? Because it's not like a couples thing, but it's also not like a huge party or anything."

"Don't bring your Bunny of the Week is what he's trying to say," Dixie interjects oh-so-helpfully.

"A PR assistant isn't supposed to talk to me like that, Ms. Wynn," I remind her as Levi bites back a chuckle. He finds it hysterical when my sisters take the piss out of me.

"No other Thunder employees here, so I'm your sister right now," Dixie rationalizes.

"Then speaking as your brother, mind your own business, you brat," I reply, but my tone is subdued, not angry. I've given up expecting my sisters to mind their own business, so saying it is a habit, not a warning. I turn back to Levi as the makeup artist stops putting powder on my face. "I'm not talking about some girl whose last name I don't know. I'm talking about an old friend I'm reconnecting with."

Levi looks stunned. Dixie looks terrified.

"You are not talking about who I think you're talking about," Dixie says, her blue eyes wide and her mouth quickly turning into a frown before I even confirm her thoughts.

"So you're allowed to catch up with her but I'm not?" I question and wave off the makeup lady, who is coming at me with a mascara wand. "She was just your babysitter. She was my friend."

"Please. You barely said two words to her when we were kids." Dixie lets out a *pft* and tucks her hair behind her ears. "You mostly just stared at her and drooled."

Levi laughs. It's loud and annoying. I glare at him momentarily before turning back to the makeup artist, who I pray signed a nondisclosure. Dixie is usually excellent about going above and beyond when it comes to protecting the team, so I'm not worried. "I just need the powder for shine. Nothing else. Trust me, I'm flawless on camera."

"But we'll need extra lighting to overcome the giant cloud that is his ego. Follows him around everywhere," Dixie mutters. The makeup artist just gives me a small smile and steps away as the hair person finishes up with Levi and they switch positions.

I go back to the original and important topic. "You were thirteen, Dix; you don't know everything that went on between us."

"Please. You were a bumbling virgin. Nothing went on between you," Dixie retorts with a snarky grin.

She hit the nail on the head, not that I'll ever admit it. Levi catches my eye, and I can see the wheels turning in his head. He's honestly the most intelligent person I know. He had a killer GPA in high school, and he could have gotten into any Ivy League school he wanted, without a hockey scholarship, but he chose to jump right into the league and use his intelligence to break down hockey plays, his extensive vocabulary to give motivational speeches in the locker room and his keen intuition to figure out my love life.

"Are you talking about Zoey?"

Dixie looks stunned. "You know about Zoey?"

Levi nods at her but keeps his gaze on me, which annoys the makeup artist because his head is turned. "Zoey is back in the picture?"

I nod, and I can't help but smile. He smiles back. Dixie keeps being Dixie. "How the hell do you know about my babysitter?"

"Jude talked about her all the time our senior year," Levi explains, and I give him a hard glance. He'd better not mention anything more. Dixie will use the information to tease me for the rest of my life. "She's the one that got away."

Dixie rolls her eyes. "If you mean she's the only female currently residing in San Francisco that he hasn't boned, then yes. But that doesn't mean he should. I like Zoey. I want her to keep liking us."

"I don't want to bone her, Dixie, relax," I bark, annoyed that she's still participating in this conversation. Of course now both my sister and Levi are looking at me with total disbelief. I sigh. "I mean, that's not all I want to do. Jesus, can everyone just keep their opinions to themselves?"

I stand up abruptly. The hairstylist steps back, almost tripping, so I reach out to steady her. She flushes and smiles that typical flirty smile at me as she whispers a thank-you. I give her a smile and a wink back. It's not even on purpose, it's just habit. I glance in the mirror and adjust what she was doing to my hair a little, finishing her job, because I've never been one for all this primping they make us do for shoots. It's weird to have people fussing over your face and hair.

Dixie says something about going to check on the setup on the ice, since that's where we're doing the shoot, and disappears out the door. The hairstylist leaves too, heading out to wait at the rink, where she'll do touch-ups during the shoot. The makeup artist leaves next, as I'm lacing up my skates. Levi walks over and sits down beside me, shoving his feet in his skates too. Without looking over at me, he says, "So how did the girl from Maine end up in San Francisco?"

I shrug. "Not completely sure, but it's fucking awesome."

"Yeah, it is." Levi nods and glances up quickly before concentrating on his skates again. "She's special. I mean, you've never stopped thinking about her this whole time."

Wait a minute…does he think this makes us buddies again? Screw that. "It's not a big deal."

Our eyes meet; his get darker and he's fighting a frown. He's right, though; I've always thought about Zoey. But in recent years it's become more of a mythical thing, like she was something that didn't actually exist, something I dreamed. Only she's one hundred percent real again, and I'm as excited as Levi thinks I am. I just don't want him to know it for some reason.

"Well, you should invite her to Darby's," Levi says, ignoring the elephant that lives in the room with us constantly now.

We both stand and walk—although it's always more of a waddle on skates—out to the rink. He's right. I should invite her and I will. I just have to find her again.

7

ZOEY

"Yeah, I completely understand," I say into my phone in the calmest, sweetest voice possible, even though inwardly I want to shriek like a tantrumming child. "Well, if it doesn't work out, or you have any other real estate needs, please keep me in mind."

He says he will, but I don't believe him, and then I hang up. Marti is watching me from her desk. And before I can even tell her that the Haight couple I had been wooing to sign decided to sell with another agent, she says, "Fuck them. You'll snag an even bigger client. Just watch."

"I hope so," I reply and try not to look as devastated as I am. Since starting with Golden Gate Realty I've only had three clients. One small condo—which I sold, yay!—one that's still on the market, and one buyer who, no matter what I showed her, couldn't find what she wanted. The divorce settlement, according to the pre-nup, meant I would get the house and five hundred thousand dollars. I was planning to pay off the mortgage on the house and use the remaining seventy-five grand as a buffer while I built up my business here, but now that Adam is delaying everything I don't know if that plan will happen. I need more clients now. "In the meantime, I need to find some more clients who want me now."

Marti gives me a sympathetic smile. "Something will work out."

I nod. I love real estate, but I hate this stage of it—scrounging for listings—but I know this is temporary. I'm going to have to use my last bit of available credit to make more flyers and pay for postage. Ugh. Still, I love residential real estate way more than I loved commercial. Homes, especially in San Francisco, have such character and history, and I love getting to know my clients, analyzing them and finding them places that make their eyes light up. It's addicting and makes me feel great.

I flip open my laptop and watch as a petal from the already wilting flowers I bought the other day tumbles to my desk. I take a deep breath and repeat my morning chant.

Today is going to be a good day. Today is going to be a good day. Today is going to be a good day.

My email icon is blinking as I wait for Photoshop to open, so I click on it. I have an email from Morgan. He says Ned's cousin's wife is a divorce lawyer, and she'll take my case and she's good. There's a number and a name—Cordelia Van Pratt. Okay, then. I have a divorce lawyer. I guess that's a win.

The receptionist buzzes my phone. I pick it up. "Hey, Anastasia."

"There's a Mr. Braddock here to see you."

"What? No, there isn't."

"Umm…yes. Yes, there is," Anastasia argues quietly. "He's a hockey player for the San Francisco Thunder!"

She whispers that last part excitedly. I scoot my desk chair over so I can stare down the long hall toward the reception area. And yes, there is Jude Braddock, looking all Jude Braddock-y in a pair of jeans and a khaki-colored shirt that's hugging him the way I think Anastasia probably wants to. Oh Mylanta.

"Yeah. Okay. You can send him over. Please. Thank you. Okay." I hang up and scoot my chair back over to my desk, where I frantically dig through my purse for a compact to check my makeup and hair. I look okay, I guess. I mean, my hair is good. I could stand to reapply my lipstick, which has faded a little thanks to my morning chai, but I don't have time. Ugh.

I shove my compact back into my purse and look up as Anastasia leads him through the open space. She didn't need to do that, and she's never done it before. It's a loft-like area for all the agents, so she usually just walks the guest to the main entrance and points at the right desk. But there she is, walking him all the way to me. His eyes find mine immediately, and he grins a slow, sexy smirk of a grin that I can feel touching every part of me. Hot dang.

Every single agent in the room looks up from whatever they're doing. Not because he's talking or because Anastasia's heels are clicking on the wood floor, just because he has this presence—he creates this incredible shift in the atmosphere when he enters a room—and you can't help but look at him. It's been that way since he was a kid, before he even realized it, but now I know he realizes it. I can't help but wonder if he uses his powers for good or evil now that he knows he has them.

"Mr. Braddock," Anastasia tells me as they land in front of my desk. I just nod. She puts a hand on his forearm gently. "If you change your mind about that coffee or that water or anything, please just let me know. I'd be happy to make you more comfortable."

Did she really just say that? I bite my lip to keep from laughing, but a smile tugs the corners of my lips up awkwardly, so I dip my head toward my desk. I can't look up for fear of laughing. I'm honestly not laughing at Anastasia. It's cute that she's flirting with him and also very reasonable. I mean, *look at him*. "Thank you, Anastasia, that's very sweet. I'll let you know, but it's doubtful I'll need anything more than Zoey."

Did he just say that?

My head flies up now. Our eyes meet. He knows exactly what he said, and its double meaning, and he's darn proud of himself. God, it's sexy, even though it makes me blush in embarrassment.

Anastasia gives him one last flirty smile and then saunters back to her post. She's swaying her hips like a supermodel, hoping he'll look back, but he doesn't. He's still locked on me. I grin at him and laugh. He walks around the desk and pulls me into a hug. It's brief, but it feels incredible. "Hey, Sunset."

"Jude." I step back, but only because I'm at work. Otherwise I would keep my hands on his shoulders and probably try to put a lot more body parts on him. "What are you doing here?"

"I wanted to see how you're doing," he explains, his blue eyes shifting to my desk. "I hope you're better than your flowers."

I laugh again. "Yeah. I'm better than my flowers."

I want to add "barely" but I don't want him to feel bad for me. Or think that I'm a mess. Because I kind of am, but his opinion of me—the way he seems to see me as this badass woman he's imagined me being since we were kids—is somehow really important to me. Even if it's a lie.

"Good," he says quietly and then adds, "Are you free tomorrow night?"

"What?" I heard him very clearly but I say it anyway—out of shock.

"Are you free tomorrow night?" he repeats. "I have a barbeque thing at a friend's and I'd love some company. Your company."

"How did you find me here?" I blurt out because, seriously, I never told him where I work.

"Dixie said you worked in real estate, and there's this crazy thing called Google," Jude explains and winks at me, and I laugh again. He steps closer, so now we're inches apart, and looks down at me, his expression turning serious, which thickens the sexual tension already choking me. "I know that might seem like stalking and I'm sorry, but I wasn't going to wait until you made plans with the sorority again to run into you. I wanted to see you again."

"I'm glad," I whisper.

He heaves a deep breath and clears his throat. "I should take a step back, because I am pretty sure everyone in the office is still staring at us."

I shift a little to glance around his wide frame. Marti is staring at us from the photocopier. Anastasia is almost falling out of her chair to sneak a look from reception, and my other four co-workers currently in the office are also focused on us from their desks. I look up at him. "Yeah, they are."

"Damn. I like being close to you." He sighs and steps back, putting my desk between us and shoving his hands in his pockets. "So tomorrow night? Come with me."

"I shouldn't," I say more to myself than him, because I really shouldn't. I'm still married and it's messy and I need to focus on my career and we don't even know each other anymore. I mean, we're not kids anymore and…"But I will."

His smile lights up his whole face. "That's my Zoey."

God, the look in his eyes is like a meal placed in front of me. I devour every inch of it, like I'm starving. He's literally feeding my ego—or maybe even my soul—with the happiness and desire in his eyes.

"Okay. Can I get your phone number?" he asks as he pulls his own phone from his back pocket. I tell it to him and watch as he punches it in. He's typing for longer than necessary and then suddenly my phone buzzes on my desk. He grins as I reach for it. It's a text from him with an attachment.

I open it up. It's a shirtless selfie. Wait…he's more than shirtless. He's naked. At least I think he is. The picture cuts off precariously low, where his hip muscles cut into a V and there's the slightest tip of well-groomed pubic hair. The background is a bathroom, a beautiful gray and white marble room, and the mirror behind him is steamed, but I can see the blurry silhouette of his body, including his bare ass. Water drops glisten all over his torso. Sweet mother of Mylanta!

I feel a blush hit my cheeks as I tear my eyes away from my screen and catch him grinning wider than before. Then he reaches into his back pocket and pulls out a brand-new iPhone and places it on my desk. "This is for you."

"Jude, I don't need a free phone," I say quickly.

"But you haven't fixed or replaced your broken one."

I shake my head. "But I mean, I can. I'm not poor or anything."

He smiles. "But you seem to be busy. And I need you to have a functioning screen." He puts a hand on my desk and leans across it so he can whisper. "I like to send dirty texts, and I need to know you'll be able to read them."

He steps back, away from me and the desk with that effortless yet sexy way he moves. Damn. He is blowing my mind in the best possible way. And for the first time in over a year I feel that delicious, hot tingle in the long-dead place between my legs.

He points to the phone on my desk. "Call your provider and hook it up. Use it. Text me. Make sure not to lose that picture or my number when you import your contacts."

I nod, and he turns and walks out of the building, with every set of eyes watching him go, including mine. My gaze, very blatantly, slips from his broad, strong shoulders to his tight, round butt. Boy, oh boy...and then down to his legs, which carry him in that powerful easy glide. Yeah, he grew up to be even more incredible than I thought he was as a kid. This is yet another time in the past decade that I really wish that our one attempt at sex had worked out. I think it might have changed my entire life.

"What did Jude Braddock want?" Marti asks. I hadn't noticed her walk up to my desk because I was too busy ogling Jude's backside. "You know he's the second-highest-paid hockey player in San Francisco, right? Is he looking for a house? Are you signing him as a client?"

"No. I mean, he's just here for..." I don't want to say the word "date." For some crazy reason I can't explain, I don't want to tell anyone—even Marti, whom I trust—what's going on here. I'm not even sure I know what's going on. I just know what I want this to be, which is something more than a rekindled flirty friendship. "I mean, I think he's looking into real estate."

"Buying or selling? Investment or personal?" Marti asks eagerly, her eyes excited. "He's going to be a big get with lots of high-end needs; if you want help on this one..."

"I'll keep you posted," I tell her absently.

"Okay, well, seriously, Zoey. I can help you with this one. It'll be great," Marti assures me.

"Yeah, I'll let you know if he decides to hire me," I mutter and sit in my seat as I examine the new phone. It's the latest model, and it should be simple to switch it to my plan. I put it down on my desk, pick up my original phone and pull up the picture he texted me. Holy sweet mother of Mary. I am going to do obscene things to myself while I stare at this picture. In fact, I want to lock myself in the bathroom and do it right now. But I quell the urge, which is a momentous feat, and stand up, grabbing my purse.

"I have to run some errands," I announce. "I'll be back soon."

Marti nods, but she's looking at me with this new, weird appreciation on her face. She's in awe of the fact that I might have Jude as a client. She sees him as a bunch of dollar signs, which I guess I would too, if I didn't have my past with him and I was looking at him professionally. But I will never be able to look at him that way, because I've sort of, almost seen him naked. "Let me know if you need anything."

I nod and head for the door. Outside, the warm air engulfs me and does nothing to quash the hot and bothered feelings Jude woke in me. He makes me feel young and happy and crazy and all the things I was at eighteen. The problem is not all of it was good. I was a wild child in both the good and bad senses of the term.

I was creative and inquisitive and other good things that parents are happy about, but I was also rebellious and brash and a bunch of other things that parents dread. Especially mine. My father was a Baptist minister. He wasn't overly strict, and he didn't shove the religion down our throats, and I believed in it—and God—but I hated the way we constantly had to move for his job. He never stayed at a church more than four or five years, and he always picked communities that were small and felt claustrophobic to me. When you're the pastor's daughter in a small town, everyone makes a point of watching you. I hated it, and as I got older, I made a point of rebelling the most typical way a teenage girl can: I drank, I smoked and I had sex.

I know the nosy parishioners were telling my parents what they heard and saw about poor, wayward Zoey Quinlin, but to their credit, my parents never yelled at me about it. They had a few serious, heartfelt talks about my self-esteem, and there was a little talk of how this wasn't God's will for me, but they always told me they loved me no matter what. I tested that statement more than I should have, but they never wavered.

I don't regret my past. I had a lot of fun, but I do regret any pain it caused my parents. And that regret was one of my motivating factors in marrying Adam. Not the only factor, for sure, but I knew they would approve of him. I knew they would feel like I was finally making a smart choice.

And even when I told them about the divorce, they were unwaveringly supportive. My parents are truly the best. But I don't think they'd approve of me going on a date with someone else—even Jude Braddock, whom they liked when we were kids—before my divorce is final. So I don't intend to tell them, and I also don't intend to let this fall out of the flirty friend zone.

It's not going to be easy if Jude keeps his game at flirt level ten. But I'm not about to ask him to tone it down.

8

JUDE

I'm actually nervous as I drive to pick her up. Clammy palms, accelerated heartbeat, dry mouth. I used to get like this around her when I was a kid too. In fact, this hasn't happened around a woman since, so this whole sensation is surreal. It kind of feels like déjà vu, and the last thing I want is to relive my brief, awkward history with Zoey.

It started out perfectly, once I finally grew the balls to make a move. I was walking her home after she babysat my sisters. We were on the beach and having our first real conversation in the two years we'd known each other. She told me she admired how passionate I was about hockey, I told her she was as beautiful as a sunset, and then…it started to rain. I pulled her under a lifeguard stand and kissed her like my life was ending…or beginning. It was goddamn poetic. But our date started with some family drama—hers—and ended with vomit. But now I'm going to get a do-over—one that involves nudity and orgasms. Lots of fucking orgasms.

That's my main goal here, to get her naked and worship her the way I wanted to when I was seventeen. In a way, that fateful night going horribly awry was probably a good thing. I might have disappointed her back then since I was a virgin. Despite discovering the ability to woo women around the age of fourteen, I didn't lose my virginity until I was eighteen. I'd perfected everything there was to perfect besides sex, but I had been waiting for someone special for the actual deed. Yeah, I fully know how hysterical that is coming from me now. But back then I'd wanted a connection—true, strong and real—for my first time.

My dad had given me the sex talk at fourteen. He said, "I'm a realist, son, and I know you're not going to wait until marriage. That's just not how the world works now. But you should know that it's a special, sacred thing, and you should share something more than hormones with whomever you're intimate with. Love would be what I'd hope for, but respect and friendship are the bare minimum. And remember, your first time only happens once, and having all three of those things is the only way it'll be memorable for you and the girl. Trust me. Also, when you do finally settle down, whether it's at twenty or fifty, don't do it unless you feel all three of those things down to your core, Jude."

Then he went on to threaten to murder me if I didn't use condoms every single time. I smile now at the memory. I didn't take all of his advice, at least not as life went on, but in the beginning, as a teenager, I took it to heart. I tried to follow it fully and completely, and so even though I'd come close a bunch of times, I held on to my virginity. Because I felt all those things—love, respect and friendship—for that wild, redheaded pastor's daughter, but the one thing I didn't feel around her was courage, and when I took my shot, it blew up.

The tap on the glass of my passenger window startles me back into the present. She's standing there, smiling, and I realize the doors are locked. I hit the button, and she climbs into my passenger seat. She looks more refined than the Zoey I was just remembering. Her hair has been straightened, the natural waves gone. She's pulled it back into a low ponytail. She's not as dressed up as she was when I dropped off the phone at her work, but she's in a loose, flowered tank top and a pair of linen shorts. The Zoey from under the life-guard stand would be in something tighter and shorter, but she's still fucking delicious. I've only seen her three times since we've re-connected, but each time it's the same feeling as it was when I was a kid. Seeing her makes me feel like I just discovered Dixie left me a Nutella cheesecake in my fridge the first day of the off-season. Lucky, elated and intent on devouring it...or in this case, *her*.

"What are you thinking?" she asks, her eyes searching my face.

I smirk. "I'm thinking what it felt like the first time I finally got my lips on yours."

There's a sharp intake of breath beside me, and it makes my smirk deepen. I glance over, and her porcelain skin has a pink glow to it as she smooths her hair, flustered. When she regains her composure, she says, "Best kiss of my life."

"That's because we haven't had our second one," I reply. "Yet."

She lets out a breathy laugh. "Technically, I think we did at Scooter's place. Just neither of us remembers it."

I grimace at the memory. "I can't say the words 'Boone's Farm apple wine' without wanting to gag."

"I still can't smell anything cinnamon flavored without think-ing of the Fireball we barfed everywhere. Repeatedly." She laughs again, and inwardly I want to die, but I laugh too. "So where are we going?"

"My friend Duncan and his girlfriend, Carla, are throwing a barbeque. Nothing big or crazy, just a few people."

"Is Duncan a teammate?"

"Yeah." I glance over at her. "You don't follow the Thunder at all, do you?"

She shakes her head. "Morgan's husband, Ned, watches hockey sometimes. I'm surprised your name didn't come up."

"Morgan? Your brother? He has a husband?" I glance over and she nods, her hazel eyes catching mine, looking for some kind of judgment or disgust like she did when we were kids and she first told me Morgan was gay, but she still finds neither because I've always believed love is love. Instead I give her a gleeful smile. "Please say you haven't told the sorority this yet. I love being the one to dash their dreams. They were all in love with Morgan."

"You're a jerk, you know that, right?" She smiles at me, and damn, if it doesn't hold the power of the sun.

I shrug, because I can't claim innocence, but in my defense my sisters give better than they get. Always. "So you never knew where I played? That I was right here next to you the last three years?"

"I thought you were in Milwaukee," she explains as I weave the car through the narrow streets in Duncan's new Nob Hill neighborhood. "In my defense, I didn't want to stalk a guy who blew me off."

"I swear on my career I didn't blow you off," I explain. "I stupidly left the paper you wrote your email address on in Maine. As soon as we went back for Memorial Day weekend, I emailed you. But you never responded."

"I ditched the Hotmail account for a school one," she explains.

"After the NHL draft, I didn't go back to Maine that summer because things got crazy fast with training, moving and finding an agent and everything," I tell her. "Not that it would have mattered, because your dad had already taken a job somewhere else."

"Sacramento," she elaborates, playing with the end of her ponytail for a second. "I did try to find you on Facebook. More than once. Couldn't find you or your sisters."

I nod. "Yeah, Facebook is a bitch for professional athletes and their families. So is Instagram and all social media, really."

"All athletes? Or just ridiculously good-looking, incredibly talented, single ones?"

"I'm sorry, did you say something after you called me ridiculously good-looking?" I ask with feigned innocence. "Because you didn't have to."

"Jude, you are way more cocky than I remember," she announces as I pull to a stop about half a block from Duncan's new address. I turn off the car, and we look at each other.

I lean on the console between us, my face close enough that I can smell the hints of jasmine in her perfume. "I'm a big boy now."

"You were a big boy before," she returns with a grin. "At least I think it felt that way, if I recall."

She opens the door and slips out before I can reach across and grab her, which is exactly what I was intending to do. Grab her, pull her into my lap and get that second kiss under our belt, and then let her get under my belt and see what she missed out on that first time.

But I have no choice but to get out of the car and join her on the sidewalk. I instinctively reach for her hand. And when our fingers lace together, it feels like the most natural thing in the world. We walk up the hilly street to the address Duncan texted me. I squeeze her hand a little as I confess, "I emailed you at your old Hotmail account a couple years ago on the off chance you still checked it."

"A couple years ago?" she repeats, her voice filled with disbelief.

"Yeah, you were on my mind." I look up at the address on the house we're passing and then back at her. God, I love her eyes. I've never seen another pair quite that color. They're mostly a dark amber but rimmed in a stormy gray with flecks of blue and green in them. "I never forgot about you."

She smiles at me. I use our joined hands to tug her a little closer as I turn and climb the steps to Darby's new house. "I wish I could remember the password to that account. I would love to know what you said."

I ring Darby's bell and stare down at her. "I'm kind of glad you don't. I was drunk when I wrote it. I think I asked if you were still prettier than a sunset and if I could have a do-over. I *might* have gone so far as to say it would be the best sex of your life."

She lets out a big, beautiful laugh, and I can't help but laugh with her. The front door swings open, and Duncan is standing there in a pair of shorts and a well-worn Captain America T-shirt. He gives me his usual gregarious grin, and then his eyes land on Zoey. "A fellow ginger!"

He grabs Zoey and pulls her over the threshold and into a hug. She lets him, probably because he did it so quickly she didn't have a chance to dodge him. I step into the house and untangle her from my goofball teammate. "Back off of her, you orange yeti."

He laughs and takes a step back, extending his hand like a normal human being. "Hi. I'm Duncan. It's my party. Well, mine and my girlfriend, Carla's. She's out back working the grill. She makes bitchin' barbeque chicken with this secret marinade."

"Hi. Zoey." I watch her shake his giant freckled hand, and I put an arm around her shoulders to keep him from spontaneously molesting her again.

"Welcome to my new *maison*," he says with a bad French accent and a grand sweeping gesture with his hand.

"It's lovely," Zoey tells him, and she's right. It is. Duncan's last place, a loft condo, was spectacular too, but his furniture and decorating choices left a lot to be desired, at least to anyone over the age of twenty-one. His living room featured a bunch of beanbag chairs and pillows on the floor. The dining room held a Ping-Pong table instead of a dining table. One wall was nothing but a series of old-school arcade games.

This place has none of that. There is a real sectional couch in the living room and throw pillows on the couch, not the floor. I spot a table, an actual table, not a Ping-Pong table, through the archway into the dining room.

"Did you hire a designer or something?"

"Carla," he says proudly. "It's all grown-up and shit, huh?"

I laugh. "Yeah. Impressive."

"Come on." Duncan motions us with his hand as he starts down the hall and through the massive marble-tiled kitchen. "Party's back here."

I take Zoey's hand again and follow him. His backyard is impressive for San Fran, where that kind of thing is a hard-to-find luxury. It's grassy, with a nice-looking oak tree in the corner for shade and a redbrick patio with a grill Carla is currently overseeing. There's also a hot tub at the other end.

"Hey!" Noah, another teammate of mine, calls out, lifting his beer toward us as we step onto the redbrick pavers. "I didn't know you were coming, Braddock."

I give him a wave and let my eyes scan the rest of the group. My teammate Brian is sitting on a lawn chair under the tree. A foot away Noah is shirtless, sprawled out on another lawn chair trying to catch the last few rays of afternoon sun. His girlfriend, Stella, and Brian's wife, Abby, are in the hot tub laughing about something and sipping margaritas. Sitting at the picnic table in the middle of the yard is Levi. Tessa is in his lap, her arm wrapped lazily around his neck.

Right. I actually forgot they were going to be here. That brings a smile to my lips. I haven't forgotten about them in a long time. It feels good.

They look up and see me, and Tessa lifts up and shifts so she's sitting on the bench beside her boyfriend instead of on him. That's for me. She's never forgotten my request to avoid PDA in front of me.

God, it feels like it was a million years ago, but it's only been ten weeks. I give them both a quick smile and look down at Zoey. "Hey, everyone, this is Zoey."

She gets a "hey" from Noah. A wave from the girls in the hot tub, who don't even bother to look over. Brian nods in her direction. Carla mutters a "welcome" from the grill but doesn't turn around. I've gotten more heartfelt greetings from mortal enemies on the ice. It's annoying, to say the least.

Levi stands up. "Hey, Zoey, have a seat." He motions to an empty lawn chair near him and Tessa. "I'm Levi, and this is my girlfriend, Tessa."

Tessa looks over. Zoey drops my hand. Tessa stands up. "Holy crap! Zoey?"

"Tessa! Wow! Hey! This is a week of crazy reunions for me, I guess." Zoey laughs and leaves my side to envelop Tessa in a hug.

She knows my ex? Fuck. My. Life.

The embrace ends, and Tessa yells, "Carla! Look!"

Carla finally turns away from the grill. Her eyes land on Zoey, and she lets out a small, startled squeal before shoving the spatula in her hand at Duncan and running across the lawn. "Oh my God! Zoey! What are you doing here? It's so good to see you!"

"Jude invited me." Zoey laughs and looks confused that she's repeating this. Clearly Carla wasn't paying any attention at all. Makes sense; she tends to ignore my existence. "I helped Tessa and Carla find the space for their salon."

"Of course you did," I say with an acerbic tone but a bright smile. "Awesome."

Duncan laughs. Out loud. The dick. "Zoey, what are you drinking?"

"Oh, umm, a beer would be good," she says, and Levi nods.

"I'll go with," I mutter and squeeze her shoulder before following Levi across the lawn and into the house.

He gives me a sympathetic smile as he opens the fridge. "I didn't see that coming."

"I didn't either," I admit. "Now Carla and Tess are going to badmouth me to her. Fantastic."

Levi hands me two Coronas. "Tessa won't. Carla might, but I don't think it'll matter."

I raise an eyebrow as I twist the cap off the beer, and he hands me a lime wedge from a Tupperware container in the fridge. "Why do you say that?"

"I don't know. I just have a feeling," Levi says in his typical confident tone. He could sell a steak to a vegan with that voice of his. It's one of the reasons why he's a great leader in the locker room.

He heads back outside, but I pause for a second and watch the scene through the kitchen window. Carla has abandoned the grill and is sitting at the picnic table with Tessa and Zoey, the three of them all smiling and yakking away. Ugh. This better not blow my chances of getting in her pants—again. Well, actually *finally* is more like it.

9

ZOEY

When I look at my watch, I'm surprised it's already ten thirty. The night flew by. Jude's friends are nice, and seeing Tessa and Carla again was fantastic. I still remember how full of hope and excitement they were when they walked into Penner Realty almost two years ago now. Adam was off having lunch with his dad and brother, thankfully, or he probably would have turned them around and ushered them back out the door. They were, as he would say, "small potatoes." We tended to take on large firms or franchises. But I loved their vibe, and I took them on myself instead of giving them to a newer, younger agent. The commission was so small it made Adam roll his eyes when it came in, but I was thrilled to help them. And I'm even more happy to know that the place worked out perfectly, and their business is thriving.

When I'm not catching up with Tessa and Carla, I'm watching Jude. I can't help it. I just can't believe I'm here with him. He jokes with his buddies and helps Duncan at the grill, but the whole time, he's staring at me as much as I'm staring at him. His eyes slide all over my body—I can feel them—as I talk with the girls or walk to the kitchen to help Carla and Tessa get the salads out of the fridge. During dinner he sits next to me, and he rests his hand on my knee when he's done with his food, his thumb making small circles on the outside of my thigh. It's barely a touch, his thumb is just grazing me, but it feels incredible.

"I can't believe you got rid of the Ping-Pong table," Brian moans to Duncan as he scrapes the last of the strawberry shortcake dessert off his plastic plate. "I used to love kicking your ass on that thing."

"Oh, it's still here, baby," Duncan replies proudly. "I got me a game room here."

Carla rolls her eyes, but she's smiling. "We had to get a three-bedroom just so we could have a dedicated man cave because I wouldn't let the entire place look like an arcade."

Jude's hand stills on my leg. "You guys bought this place together?"

Carla nods. "Yeah. Why do you think it has real furniture?"

Jude doesn't answer. All of a sudden his hand feels heavy and life-less on my leg. I watch Duncan's eyes slip over to Levi and then to Tessa before he stands up and announces, "Come on, boys, I'll show you my man cave. And, Brian, I'll kick your ass at Ping-Pong since you want it so badly."

Levi and Brian stand; Jude doesn't. Instead he turns to me, a look I can't decipher on his handsome face. "Go," I assure him, assuming he's worried about leaving me. "I'm fine."

He hesitates and then leans closer, so his lips are so close to my ear, they brush it as he whispers, "I'll be back soon. Miss me."

He stands and wanders into the house behind his friends. Tessa begins to collect the disposable plates. Carla grabs a fork and scoops up a chunk of what's left of the decadent dessert. "Oh, sure, you want to clean up here, but when I lived with you, I couldn't get you to put a coffee mug in the sink."

Tessa rolls her eyes. "I cleaned, you liar. You're going to miss an errant coffee mug when you now have to pick up dirty jockstraps."

Carla shivers dramatically, her nose scrunched up and her lips pursed, and Abby and I laugh. Then Carla smacks the back of her fork against Tessa's hand. "Stop. You're a guest now. Relax and let me clean up after you without complaining."

Tessa smiles. "I'm going to miss you, you psycho."

"We see each other every day at work," Carla reminds her. "Besides, you're going to have a new roommate who will come with benefits I didn't come with. Naked benefits!"

Tessa laughs again and smiles brightly. It's not hard to deduce she's going to move in with Levi. Abby finishes her margarita, and Carla moves to pour her another one from the pitcher on the table. "No. No. I'm going to have to deal with two toddlers in a couple hours. Can't be a hung-over mommy."

Carla turns to me and lifts the pitcher. "Any kids?"

I shake my head. "No. But I've got to work early, so I'm cutting myself off."

"Damn. I was hoping to liquor you up to get you to talk," Carla tells me with a grin. "I'm dying to know how you met Jude."

"I knew him as a kid," I explain, and before I can elaborate I'm greeted by three sets of falling jaws. "What?"

"I just...I didn't expect that," Carla stutters.

"I figured you met him at a bar or strip club or some team event or something," Abby adds. Clearly the alcohol has loosened her lips. "That's usually where he finds his women."

"Abby!" Tessa scolds and gives me a sympathetic smile.

Abby looks instantly embarrassed. "Sorry. But in my defense, who would have thought a woman could know him that long and still be talking to him?" she blurts out, and then covers her mouth. "I'm sorry."

Wow. She doesn't like Jude very much at all.

"So you're from Toronto?" Tessa asks me quietly.

"No. I met him in Maine. I used to live there when I was a teenager, and his family has a summer house there," I explain. "My parents moved to Sacramento when I started college, and we lost touch, but I ran into one of his sisters a few days ago, and well, then I ran into Jude. He invited me along tonight so we could catch up."

It seemed easiest to keep it vague like that. I remember Dixie saying she didn't want people to know she was related to him, and I'm not sure if any of them are in on the secret. Why are all three of them staring at me like I'm some kind of extraterrestrial?

"So, like, did you date him?"

Tessa smacks Carla's arm as soon as the question leaves her mouth. I laugh at them. "No. Not exactly. But I had a huge crush," I admit.

"I can see that," Abby replies, tucking her dirty-blond hair, ends still damp from the hot tub, behind her ear. "I mean, he's hot as hell to look at, and I imagine as an eighteen-year-old he was way less of a jerk."

"Abby!"

"What?" she asks Tessa innocently. "That was a compliment. Sort of."

"Come on, Tess, not all of us are as forgiving as you," Carla tells Tessa with a pointed stare. Tessa looks instantly uncomfortable and glares at Carla for a second before turning to me, her face morphing into a smile.

"Small world, huh?" she says. "That you know him and we know you. It's a happy coincidence!"

I nod, but I can tell there's something else, something more than even the disdain I'm seeing, behind this conversation.

"Hey, Sunset, I think it's time to get you home." Jude's voice fills the evening air, and I turn to find him standing in the doorway, one arm up on the frame, which pulls his white shirt up to reveal a sliver of tanned skin and the tip of an unbelievably cut external oblique muscle that until this moment I'd only ever seen on TV and movie actors.

"Sunset?" Tessa repeats.

"Childhood nickname. He compared me to a sunset," I tell them, memories of that crazy night filling my head. "He said I was fiery and glowing and breathtaking."

By the time I finish the explanation, I'm blushing a little. Not because the story is embarrassing—I still think it's one of the sweetest compliments I've ever gotten—but because they've got that "we've just seen an alien" look on their faces again. I stand and lean over and give each of them, even Abby, a quick hug good-bye and thank Carla profusely for hosting. Jude reaches for my hand again as I climb the stairs, and he leads me through the house. I can hear the boys yelling at each other upstairs in what I'm assuming is the man cave.

"I should say good-bye to Duncan and thank him."

"I did it for both of us, it's fine," Jude says. His tone is flat and a little clipped, and I wonder if he's in a bad mood suddenly, and if he is, why? As we walk down the steps to the sidewalk he slows his pace a little bit, and his grip on my hand gets looser. His thumb starts do-ing that circle thing again but this time on the heel of my hand. "So how was your time with the girls?"

"Good. I mean, how crazy is it that I know Tessa and Carla?" I re-ply as we make our way down the hill to his car. He just smiles. "But I will say, it was a bit of a grilling session after you left. And not the kind that requires a barbeque."

He steps in front of me and turns to face me, stopping us both even though we're nowhere near the car. His blue eyes are dark, murky, and his expression is defiant. "They're not my biggest fans."

"I was starting to catch that, but why?"

His eyes shift past me, over my head, probably looking out at the water visible at the bottom of the street. He takes a deep breath and exhales quickly and with force, and then he looks down at me. "I don't bring girls like you around to things like this."

"Girls like me?"

"Girls who..." He's searching for a word and finally says, "Girls who know me."

"So you bring strangers to friends' parties?" I ask, trying to give the moment some levity because it feels oddly dark. "Like homeless people off the street?"

He smirks that bad-boy smirk. "I don't usually bring anyone to parties, but I sometimes leave with someone if it's a big event and there's a girl there that isn't taken or I haven't already fucked."

Fucked. The word startles me. Adam would never use such a visceral word. But damn if it doesn't send a little shiver of desire skittering down my spine.

Jude looks at the horizon again and then back at me. "I play a game for a living, and I'm incredible at it. That means I not only love competition, I excel at it. I like the hunt-and-chase part of relation-ships. I'm great at it, but not everybody appreciates the dedication I bring to that aspect of relationships."

"You've had a few one-night stands." I shrug, and his blue eyes land on mine. I laugh. "Okay, so you've had a lot. Do you remember who you're talking to, Jude? Hooking up was my only extracurricu-lar activity in high school. I'm not going to judge you for that, even if they do. You didn't judge me."

He reaches up and wraps a hand around the base of my neck. It's gentle but primal at the same time, and for a quick, fevered second I wish he'd kiss me. But instead he says, "I loved that you were experi-enced, because I didn't know what the fuck I was doing."

I laugh and blush. He leans forward and presses his lips to my forehead in a small kiss and then, lips still brushing my skin, he says, "I wanted you to teach me everything you knew. Take me and my virginity and make me a man. I wanted it from the second I laid eyes on you."

"You laid eyes on me at barely fifteen."

"Yeah. So? I know what I want as soon as I see it. I always have." Jude dips his head so we're eye to eye and grins devilishly. "And you, Zoey Quinlin, are something I want."

He's using present tense, not past. That shiver, like a quake of electricity, runs down my spine again. And then he says something that sends reality, like a bucket of ice water, crashing down over my heated skin. "Let's get you home."

Home. I can't bring him there. Ugh. "Just drop me back off at the office. I'll find my way from there."

"Is your car there?"

"Yeah. And I don't want to leave it overnight."

He nods, and I'm relieved that he's okay with that answer. Until we're a block from my office and he starts to drive more slowly and says, "Where is your parking lot? Is it behind the building?"

"Umm…yeah, but I didn't park there."

"Oh. Okay, so where'd you park?"

Shoot. He's going to be all gallant and take me to my actual car. I underestimated his chivalry. I point to the front of my office. "I actually have to run inside and grab some paperwork and stuff. So just drop me here."

He pulls to the curb in front of my office, but as I reach to undo my seat belt and escape, he turns the car off. I blink. "What are you doing?"

"It's late, Zoey. I'm going to wait for you and make sure you get to your car okay," he offers and, damn, this would be so attractive if I weren't lying my ass off.

I lean back in the seat, my head hitting the white leather headrest, and close my eyes. "I didn't drive today."

He looks completely baffled, and I don't blame him. "Zoey, you need to talk to me."

"My current living situation is unconventional, and it's really best if you don't drop me off at home." I sigh. God, I hate this. The night was going so well and feeling almost magical. I was relaxed and content for the first time in a long time, and now this.

He unbuckles his seat belt too now and leans right across the console, reaching out and cupping the side of my face and turning me so we're eye to eye. "I'm only going to ask this once, and you need to be honest," he starts and waits for me to respond, so I nod. "Is it safe for you to live there with him?"

"Yes. I promise."

He says nothing at first, and those crystal-blue eyes search my face for any sign I might not be telling him the truth. When he's satisfied with what he sees, he exhales. "Okay. Because if he hurts you, emotionally or physically, then you have to tell me. Or someone."

"It's nothing like that, I swear. He just isn't signing the divorce papers." I pull away from his hand and rest my head against the seat again, pressing the heels of my hands into my eyes, suddenly weary. "He was supposed to get the business, and I was supposed to get the house. It was in the pre-nup, which he drew up, but now he's going to contest it."

I go on to tell him everything about how I was living in the hotel but the credit card was canceled and I maxed my only personal card to pay for it, so I moved back into the house and am hoping it pushes him into signing the damn paperwork. "And then this morning I got up and my car was gone."

"Gone?"

"It was a lease. A birthday present from him last year, and it was technically in his name." I huff out a frustrated breath. "So he returned it, but the joke's on him because I'm not a snob like him, and I'll ride a streetcar or jump in a cab. I even downloaded the Uber app, so he can suck it."

Jude listens without interrupting until I finally stop talking. Then he starts the car. "Buckle up and give me your address. I'm your Uber tonight."

I hesitate, but I know there's no talking him out of it, so I give him the address and reach for my seat belt. He doesn't say a word the whole drive, but the silence isn't uncomfortable. I can see him rolling this new information around in his head, trying to make sense of it. If he can, I hope he enlightens me, because I'd really like to know how to make my world right again.

"Which one?" he asks, slowing as we approach the iconic row of houses across from Alamo Square Park.

"Second from the end. The blue one that matches your eyes."

He smiles at that, but it's soft and without its characteristic hubris. He pulls to the curb a house away from mine, and I'm happy he's not right out front in case Adam is home and happens to look out the window. I don't want to give him any reason to start asking questions. I mean, not that I've done anything wrong. I haven't.

I unbuckle my seat belt and glance over at Jude, who is still wrestling with his thoughts.

"So the jack-off is making this impossible for you. Slowly pulling all your options, like your credit cards and your car, because he's trying to beat you down so you just walk away, forget the pre-nup and give him everything." He's not asking a question, he's stating the facts and he knows it. For the first time ever, I watch Jude's face cloud over with anger. I have never seen him look anything other than flirty, mischievous or gregarious. The darkness doesn't make him any less attractive. In fact, the tiny flip in my stomach means it makes him more appealing. Oh Mylanta.

"I'm not going to do that. I'm not going to back off or give up," I promise him, my voice soft but firm. "I'm not greedy, but I'm not walking away with nothing. I helped pay that mortgage, and I busted my ass to grow his business too, so I deserve my fair share of what we've built."

I can literally see the anger lift from his features, and that perfect mouth with the perfectly symmetrical lips pulls into a suggestive, roguish smirk. "Don't bust that ass. It would be a crime against humanity if it was busted."

"You definitely grew out of your shy side," I reply.

"I was never shy, I was inexperienced," he corrects and reaches over to push back my hair and then lets his fingertips trail over my cheekbone and down to my jaw.

"And now you're experienced."

"I can prove it." He leans closer and his tongue slowly slides out and wets his bottom lip; watching it is like watching a match scrape across a striker. Only the flames it creates burn inside of me.

I can feel his breath dance warmly across my skin, and his lips brush mine. And I know that this kiss is going to be incredible. The kind that wraps itself around your soul and bleeds its way inside, branding you with its heat and intensity for the rest of your life. When you're old, on your deathbed, it's remembering kisses like this that gives you comfort. That gives you proof that you lived, and lived well. Just like our first kiss did.

But I can't let it happen. Not now. Not like this. I pull away, reaching for the car door and swinging it open. He looks disappointed but not surprised. Still, I give him an explanation. "I'm still married. It's honestly just on paper but…I need to respect that."

"I understand," he replies. "And now I hate him even more."

I smile. "Good night, Jude."

"See you soon, Zoey."

"I hope so."

10

ZOEY

I'm eighteen again. We're alone in our mutual friend Scooter's one-room apartment just like last time. Only this time Jude's not drunk and neither am I, at least not on booze. I feel light-headed and deliciously warm, but it's not from all the Fireball and Boone's Farm apple wine we consumed in real life. Here, in this unreal moment, the warmth is from the feel of his bare skin, all of it from calf to collarbone, pressed against mine. The light-headedness is from the brush of his lips on my lips, the way his tongue sweeps my mouth and the soft scrape of his fingers as they make their way into the only piece of clothing I'm wearing—my underwear. And then he's touching my clit, and I'm moaning into that perfect mouth of his, and he's whispering back, "I want to make you see stars, Zoey. I want to touch you and lick you and push inside you, filling you up until you see nothing but stars."

"Jude…"

It's my orgasm that rips me from the dream and back into the cold light of day. I swim through the euphoria back to reality. I'm alone, in the guest bedroom in my house, with an ex-husband down the hall and nothing but my own hand pretending it's Jude. It's both the best and worst way I could have started today.

Orgasms are good even if they're not from someone else. And, damn, it's been a long time since I've relaxed enough to have one. But now it's going to make it that much harder to forget him and get on with my life. Because that's really what I have to do until this whole divorce gets sorted and Adam moves out. And then I should probably throw all my time and energy into my career, since it's so new. If I think about what my life needs, rationally, logically, like Spock or a robot or something, it needs a lot of things, but rekindling a spark with an old flame isn't on the list. But, damn, I want that most of all.

I sigh as I sit up and run my hands through my hair before opening my bedroom door and walking to the bathroom. Adam is coming up the stairs in running clothes, a sheen on his skin. He stops at the sight of me and stares. The look on his face is unpleasant at best.

"Good morning," I say casually, because I'm not going to let him suck away my post-orgasmic Zen.

"You sleep in that now?"

I look down at my white tank top and men's boxer briefs. This used to be my M.O. before I met Adam. In fact, I not only slept in men's boxer briefs and generic white tanks, I put them on as soon as I got home. And my hair used to spend more time in a messy top-knot than out of it. I didn't even own a straightening iron until after I met Adam and wanted to look more grown-up because he was so much older than me.

"Yep," I respond simply and yawn—loudly—without covering my mouth.

He's absolutely horrified, and I stifle a smile. "What happened to all the silk pajama sets I bought you?"

"Goodwill," I reply, stepping into the bathroom and closing the door. I lean against the closed door and lift my hands to my mouth to smother a giggle as I hear him swear and stomp loudly to his bedroom.

Okay, maybe that was uncalled for and kind of juvenile, but, damn, it was fun.

Twenty minutes later I'm dressed for work in a charcoal pencil skirt with a cream-colored sleeveless top and a pair of killer Louboutin heels. I decided to leave my hair wavy today, but it's pulled back in a low, messy chignon. I feel like a million bucks as I lean against the marble countertop and sip my English Breakfast tea.

Oh, how I've missed my teapot collection, I think as I glance at the row of stunning ceramic and porcelain beauties in various shapes and colors that line the long shelf above the eat-in nook. I glance down at the Wedgwood one—my favorite—that holds the rest of the tea I'm currently drinking. It feels good to be here again, despite Adam. I put a lot of love and care into this place. We hired a lot of professionals to help, but I still insisted on doing some of the work myself, like scraping the wallpaper off and replastering holes in the walls and painting the crown molding. I told Adam it was because I was a perfectionist and needed to do it myself, but the fact was it gave me an excuse to be alone, away from him. Because he never lifted a finger on this whole place. I once asked him to change a few casings for the light switches, and he paid the contractor to do it.

Adam walks in, dressed for work in a perfectly pressed summer suit. He runs a hand through his hair and makes a sour face at the sight of me. "I hear your lawyer finally contacted my lawyer."

"That's good."

"Unfortunately, no, it's not good," Adam says and stomps over to his precious thousand-dollar espresso machine. I hate that thing. It's like some kind of alien ship landed on the counter. "She's not being reasonable."

"She's supposed to ask for nothing more than the pre-nup outlined," I reply firmly.

"Yes, and that's unreasonable, Zoey." He sighs loudly, like I'm a disobedient, dim child. "The pre-nup states that it would be yours in the event of children. You didn't and can't give me children."

"That's not true. The pre-nup says the house is mine and the children's, not just *if* we have children," I reply sharply and place my teacup down on the saucer beside me with a shaky hand. "And I can have kids. The doctor only said it would probably take longer than normal."

"We tried for a year, Zoey, and you couldn't get pregnant. If you don't want to face reality, it's not my problem anymore." He rolls his eyes and hits a button so the ugly espresso machine rumbles and spits aggressively. "And as for the house, you didn't even come up with the down payment for this place. It came out of my trust fund."

"I worked for your company without my own paycheck for two years. And you wrote the pre-nup. I didn't ask for the house. You gave it to me."

"I gave it to our unborn children that will never exist," he snaps. "Because you're barren."

I stare at him. Did he really just go there? The doorbell rings, but we both ignore it. I'm rooted to the wood floor, anger making me rigid. "I loved you. I gave myself and everything I had to this marriage. I joined not only my assets with you but my life."

My voice is shaking and he looks annoyed by that, which makes me even angrier and more on the verge of tears than I was seconds ago. Still, I right myself, leveling my shoulders and holding his gaze as the doorbell rings again. "I am not going to be punished for something that is out of my control. And in the end, Adam, I'm happy we found out I might have difficulty conceiving, because it showed me what a mistake you were, how unworthy you were of me in the first place."

I storm past him and into the front hall to answer the door, because the bell is being rung *again*. I swing open the door and find Morgan standing there. My brother looks like he just stepped off a billboard, as per usual. He pulls off his aviators and smiles, but it fades almost immediately. "What's wrong?"

"Nothing. What do you want?"

"I thought I'd drive you to work since that asshole stole your car."

"Oh. Thanks." I take a deep breath. "Let me grab my—"

There's a loud crash in the kitchen. Something shatters. I turn and race back in there, Morgan right on my heels. I skitter to a stop in the doorway directly in front of a large chunk of my favorite teapot. The floor is damp with tea, and chunks of the expensive china pot are all over the floor.

My eyes land on Adam, and he shrugs. "I brushed against it while getting my travel mug."

"You did that on purpose."

"Hardly. I guess you left it too close to the edge of the counter, Zoey. You should be more careful." He takes a few steps, intent on brushing by me and leaving me with the mess, and I let him, because if he doesn't leave, I might stab him with one of the broken china pieces.

But Morgan has other ideas. He uses his six-foot frame to block the doorway. Adam sighs dramatically. "I don't have time for your protective-brother act, Morgan. I have a meeting."

"You're an asshole, you know that, Adam," Morgan says, refusing to move an inch. "I've always thought it, but now I can say it."

"Your opinion of me matters to no one, Morgan, because you matter to no one," he replies, his tone like ice. "Now move or I will call the police."

He doesn't move. Instead Morgan just smiles with the warmth of a wolf. "Go ahead. Call them and tell them you have an unwanted man in your house. I'll go upstairs and wait for them naked in your bed while I anonymously tip off the society page. I know they don't blink at divorce, but I doubt your Waspy rich family would like a homosexual scandal."

"I doubt your husband or the parents of the kids you teach would like that."

Morgan laughs. "It's a charter school. Very progressive. And Ned would know it's a lie and he'd go along with it. He hates you as much as…well, just about everyone else on the planet."

"What the fuck do you want from me, Morgan? It's just a fucking teapot."

"And it's just a fucking house, so stop being a petty bitch and give it to her."

I sigh. "Morgan, let him go. It's not worth it. *He's* not worth it."

"He should clean up his mess," Morgan argues, but I just shake my head.

"I'll do it. I just want him gone."

Adam smiles like that's some kind of victory to him. "See, Zoey? Now you're being agreeable."

I ignore the biggest mistake of my life and glare at Morgan. He relents and shifts so Adam can get by. A second later the front door slams as I grab a paper towel and start collecting the broken pieces of china. Morgan disappears. I hear his feet on the stairs but don't bother to ask him where he's going.

With the remnants of the teapot cradled in the paper towel in my hands, I step on the lever and open the trash can beside the fridge. Morgan reappears with one of Adam's expensive dress shirts in his hands. Before I can ask what he's doing, he drops it into the biggest puddle of tea on the floor and uses his foot to push it around, mopping up all the liquid.

"Great. That's just going to make things worse," I remark and cross my arms.

Morgan levels his dark blue eyes at me. "Is that even possible at this point?"

He's right. It's probably not. But just in case, I walk over to the shelf holding the remaining pots and carefully start to take them down and carry them, one by one, up to my room. I place them gently under my bed. As I return from hiding the last one, my phone beeps on the counter beside my empty teacup.

I walk over and grab it and open a text from Jude. I'm smiling at just the sight of his name, but when I open the message it's a picture of him—a selfie—and now I'm downright grinning.

"Who is doing that to your face?" Morgan asks with awe. "Christ. You look blissful."

"Language," I warn as I stare at the photo of Jude in bed, one arm tucked under his head, tattooed bicep flexed, eyes sleepy and seductive, soft, panty-wetting smile dancing on his lips, accompanied by the words Do I look tired? Barely slept. Couldn't stop thinking of u.

"I'm not the one who doesn't swear," Morgan retorts, reaching for my phone. "I have broken way too many commandments to worry about taking his name in vain."

He plucks my phone from my hand before I can stop him, and his eyes nearly bulge out of his head. "Holy sweet mother of Satan. He is still one hot little fuck stick, isn't he?"

"Morgan, seriously. Your mouth is a porta-potty." I grab the phone back and quickly save the picture to my gallery. "And yes. He is."

I grab my bag and make my way to the front hall. Morgan follows behind. "I Googled him right after you mentioned running into him, and I knew he grew up well, but those ad campaigns and hockey shots are nothing compared to bedhead nakedness."

I smile and turn to lock the door as Morgan steps out onto the front stoop. "Why is he texting you half-naked photos? Is he still crushing? Clearly he's still crushing. Are you going to hook up with him? You need to hook up with him."

I laugh and start down the stairs, scanning the street for Morgan's Mini Cooper. "I can't hook up with anyone until I make this divorce final."

"Show your lawyer that selfie so she knows what's at stake," Morgan advises. "No warm-blooded human would want you not to be able to fuck that."

"Oh Mylanta! Just stop."

"Seriously, Zoey, promise me you'll at least consider a rebound romp with him when you're free and ready," Morgan requests earnestly, which is kind of hysterical and weird at the same time. I don't know why we have this kind of relationship as siblings, but our sex lives have never been a taboo conversation. I know when he lost his virginity and who it was to—both times, male and female—and all the oddball details of his sex life before Ned. Luckily, he keeps his husband's bedroom moves a secret. I don't need to know that. "That boy looks like he's built for meaningless sex, and the internet confirms it."

"What do you mean, the internet confirms it?" I ask as he unlocks the Mini and we both slip inside.

He starts the engine and reaches for his seat belt as he elaborates. "He's slept around. A lot. And he never disappoints, apparently."

"Yeah, but for every woman who has actually slept with an athlete or celebrity, there are probably two more that claim to and haven't. It's the way society is," I say, not that I care, because Jude's past is his past.

"Okay, by that logic, if I disregard two out of three women who have said they've slept with him on the internet, then he's probably just approaching triple digits and not in them," Morgan replies and grins, but I know he's not even kidding. It doesn't matter. Jude's told me he sleeps around. I did too once, so who cares? I glance out the window.

"There's a dick pic."

My head spins around so fast, I'm surprised I don't have whiplash. Morgan laughs. "A dick pic? Like a picture of his dick? Jude's dick? On the internet?"

"Yes. Well, I mean, his face isn't in it, and apparently he denied it, but there's the corner of a tattoo in it. The edge of a fancy letter. Maybe an R or a Y. The pic is taken from a weird angle. He's lying on his side and it's shot over his hip and so it's a profile dick pic."

I laugh because this is ridiculous and also makes me light-headed, and that reminds me of my dream this morning, which, if I'd managed to sleep a little longer, would have involved the dick we're talking about and, sweet buttered biscuits, I am losing my mind. Morgan must have glanced over at my high-pitched laugh and seen my red cheeks and flustered expression. "Have you seen it?"

"The picture on the internet?"

"No. His dick," Morgan replies. "If you have, then you can tell me if the picture is real."

"No, I haven't. We both were too drunk to get that far, and then there was barfing and that was it, remember?" I reply quickly. "And even if I do one day, I am not telling you about it."

"And crying. There was crying," Morgan adds oh-so-helpfully.

"Right. And that was your fault," I remind him with a sideways glare. "You had to come out to Mom and Dad the same night I was supposed to get busy with Jude. You're the reason I haven't seen his wiener yet!"

Morgan's laugh fills the car, and I find myself smiling despite the shitty start Adam tried to give my morning by murdering my teapot.

Morgan pulls to a stop in front of my building in a loading zone and turns on his four-way flashers. "Let me run in and get a shit ton of your business cards so I can give them out to parents at my school."

"Really? That would be great, Morgy! Thank you." We get out of the car and make our way into the office. Anastasia greets me with a smile and gives Morgan a long, appreciative stare. "Morning, Anastasia. This is my brother, Morgan."

He waves at her and gives her a big, overly friendly smile. He might not be straight, but he loves attention from either sex. Anastasia grows an inch taller in her seat and pushes her Ds in his general direction. "Nice to meet you, Morgan."

I'm halfway out of reception, about to round the corner into the open main room where my desk is located, when Anastasia calls out after me. "You have a client waiting."

My heels squeak on the polished floor as I stop abruptly and look back at her. "I do?"

She nods. "Mr. Braddock from the other day. He's back."

The slowest, deepest, most obnoxious smile spreads across Morgan's face. "Oh, this is going to be good."

He passes me, and I turn and speed up my walk to catch up to him. I'm half a step behind him as he gets to my desk. Jude isn't there. He's a few feet away sitting in the chair across from Marti. Marti is smiling at him full of dreamy awe, like he invented the vibrator or something. Jude's blanketing the chair with his frame, legs spread, shoulders back, takeout coffee cups in each hand balanced lazily on each thigh. He's all confident, relaxed sex appeal.

He looks up as we both stop at my desk, and his eyes cloud over before he registers who Morgan is, but it hits him before I have to explain, which is good because I'm too busy absorbing that fleeting moment of darkness that overtook him. It was intense and possessive; it was effing hot.

"Morgan?" Jude stands up and strides over to join us by my desk.

"Jude Braddock, long time no see," Morgan exclaims, and they do one of those bro-hug things made slightly awkward by the coffee cups in Jude's hands.

"It's been a long time, man. You look good. How've you been?"

"You grew up nice," Morgan announces, and I cover my face with my hands.

Jude laughs easily, unbothered by my brother's overzealous compliment or the way he's clearly gawking, his blue eyes rolling slowly from Jude's shoes to his head, blatantly pausing on the front of his pants. "You turned out okay too, Morgan."

Marti is watching the whole scene with wide, curious eyes, and I'm watching in horror. I reach out and put my hand on Morgan's arm and squeeze, hoping he'll get that it's a signal to shut up. I look at Jude, who is looking at me with his trademark contradictory lively smile and penetrating eyes. Being his sole focus makes me tingle, as usual. I'm beginning to get addicted to that feeling.

"I brought you a coffee," he says and hands me one of the cups in his hands.

"Oh. Thanks." I take it with an apologetic smile. "I don't usually drink coffee. Only tea and chai lattes."

Morgan takes it out of my hand and raises it to Jude. "Thanks."

Jude smiles at him, but his eyes stay on me. I want to look away, but I can't. It's like he's got his own gravitational pull that controls the muscles in my eyes. Not that I'm complaining. I just hope our little audience doesn't notice how obsessed I am.

"Morgan, the business cards are on my desk," I say, still staring at Jude. "And if you don't go soon, you'll get towed. You're in a loading zone, remember?"

"Yeah, well, it's time for a new car anyway," Morgan quips, and Jude grins at that, finally pulling his eyes off me to glance at my brother.

No longer having eyeball sex with Jude, unfortunately, I manage to turn and grab the cards off my desk and hand them to Morgan. He takes them, sips the coffee he stole from me and holds up the cards. "Going to hand these out for her. She needs the business."

Wow. That makes me sound pathetic.

"Actually, that's why I'm here," Jude says, and those gorgeous baby blues slide back to me. "I want to sell my place and get a new one. And I want you to do it for me."

"You do?" Is he doing this on purpose? Because he knows I need the business? Or because it's an excuse for us to spend time together? Do I care either way? No. I honestly can't say that I do. All I know is that I do need the business, and I do want to hang out with him, so this is pretty much the best thing that could happen, regardless of his motivation.

"Yeah. I'm kind of sick of my condominium, and my sisters visit all the time, so I want something with more space." He shrugs and tilts his head a little. "A master that's away from everything so I don't hear them when they're up late giggling over wine or up early yammering over coffee."

"Zoey would be more than happy to help you out," Morgan volunteers for me, and I nod.

"I'll help out too. I probably have a lot of listings you'd be interested in," Marti pipes up and almost startles me. I forgot she was even in the room. "I know all the neighborhoods in the city like the back of my hand too."

"I'm sure Zoey can handle Jude all on her own," Morgan interjects and wiggles his bleepin' eyebrows. I am going to murder him.

Instead of bludgeoning him with the stapler on my desk, I put my hands on his back and push him toward the front door. "Thanks for the lift! Have a great day! Bye, Morgy!"

Morgan starts to wander in the general direction of the door, but he's still eyeing Jude as he does it. "Nice seeing you again. We should get together for drinks and catch up."

"That'd be great. Zoey mentioned you're married now. We could make it a double date," Jude suggests and drops an arm over my shoulder.

"Yeah, I guess that works," Morgan says, and I laugh.

"He's straight, jackass," I remind him in a loud whisper.

He feigns shock at my swear word, and Jude laughs, arm still draped over my shoulder like a warm, comforting blanket. "I am. But if that changes, you'll be my first call."

"Ha!" I squeak and cover my mouth, because that came out way too loud.

Morgan laughs too. "Day made!"

He waves at me and gives me the thumbs-up before finally leaving the building. Finally!

Jude looks at his watch. "Shit. I have to go. Training with the guys. Walk me out?"

"Yeah. Sure."

We're both silent as we make our way through the open area, weaving between desks to the front door. Anastasia gives Jude her best alluring smile as he passes, but he doesn't seem to notice. As soon as we're outside, he points down the street. "I'm parked over there."

And then he takes my hand as we start down the sidewalk. I let him but, honestly, it's confusing. Because every time he does it, it feels intimate, like we're more than just old friends reconnecting. But we aren't and we can't be right now. Still, I don't pull my hand away, because I like it, whether I'm supposed to or not.

"Are you serious about moving?"

"Yeah."

"And about me being your Realtor?"

"Of course."

I can't believe it. "Well, then there's stuff we have to do."

We reach his Tesla, and he stops and turns to me on the sidewalk. "Will this stuff mean we have to spend time together?" I nod, and he says, "Good. Then I'm in. Just tell me when and where."

"You'll need to sign a contract with me, and I'll need to see the place," I explain. "See if there's anything that needs changing or sprucing up before we take pictures and show it. And we'll need to set a price. If you tell me your address, I'll pull comparable listings."

He gives me his address on Broadway in Pacific Heights, and I grit my teeth so my jaw doesn't hit the floor. I know the building. It's only five years old, state-of-the-art, and every apartment in there is over a million bucks. This commission is going to be insane.

"Why don't you come by tonight around eight and see it for yourself?"

"Yeah. I can do that." I nod.

He steps closer, dips his head and kisses my cheek. I close my eyes and savor the feeling. But it's gone all too soon, replaced with nothing but a warm breeze as he steps back and walks around the car. Smiling, I watch him drive away. Jude's been back in my life for less than a week, and everything is turning around. He's my good luck charm.

11

JUDE

I give Duncan a little kick with the toe of my shoe as he lies panting like a dog on the grass. I squat and grip the huge four-hundred-pound tire and flip it one more time. Yeah, I'm showing off. Our trainer, Matt, chides, "Easy, Braddock. It's not a competition."

"Darby should thank the gods for that. He'd lose every time," I boast and then plant my ass on the tire I just flipped and try like hell not to pant as loudly as Duncan.

"This isn't part of my usual off-season training," Duncan complains, wiping the sweat from his face with the back of his freckled arm. "When I train back home in Minnesota, it's just kettlebells and wind sprints and easy stuff."

"It's not my fault you're here," I remind him. "Blame Carla."

"Yeah, I know." Duncan struggles to sit up. "But it's worth it to be with my girl all summer, right, Levi?"

Levi looks up from where he's resting next to the tire he flipped and chugs from his water bottle. He doesn't answer. Because he's living with Tessa and he doesn't want to say it in front of me. I figured it out the night of the barbeque. Tessa and Carla had been roommates, so if Carla is now living with Duncan, Tess has most likely moved in with Levi. The fact that he is squirming right now confirms it. He doesn't look me in the eye as he changes the subject. "I'm glad we've amped up our training. We've got to be better than we've ever been if we're going to have another record-breaking season."

I'm beginning to hate the way he and Tessa dance around their relationship in front of me. Like full-blown seething anger kind of hate it. It doesn't help me forget the betrayal, like I thought it would. It just seems to make it more obvious. So I grab my water bottle and squirt myself in the face, trying to cool down, and then I say, "You didn't answer the question. Is it worth it? Skipping a full two months at home with your brother and your friends to hang out with Tessa?"

He looks ridiculously uncomfortable—*physically* uncomfortable—like someone put itching powder in his jock kind of uncomfortable. He actually starts to squirm. "Can we finish this session so I can go home?"

Matt steps forward, ready to give us our next drill, but I raise my hand. "It's the off-season. You're not my captain right now, so I can say stop being a bitch and answer the question."

That makes his expression grow dark. Good. He stands up, water bottle clenched in his fist. "What the fuck do you want me to say?"

"The truth. Talk about your fucking life, and stop making everything more awkward by dancing around shit in front of me."

"You asked us to—"

"I asked you to maybe just chill out in front of me, but that was months ago."

"So you're over it?"

Both Duncan and Levi are staring at me with intensely curious eyes. I sigh and lift the hem of my shirt to wipe the water off my face. "I'm more annoyed now by the fact that you're trying to hide that you're together, even though I know you are, than the fact that you're actually together."

"Well, that's progress," Duncan says acerbically. I flip him my middle finger.

"It's worth it. I don't miss Laguna hardly at all," Levi confesses in his typical calm, honest tone.

Okay, yeah, that stings a little. But it's not because I miss Tessa or want her back, it's because I still am choked by the realization that I'll likely never have that kind of relationship with anyone. Because I'm just not wired that way, as much as I wish I were.

"Cool." I give him a nod. "I'm happy to hear you say that."

Somewhere in my heart I know that I am, even though on the surface it's just smoldering jealousy. Levi, being Levi, doesn't mention the fact that the scowl on my face doesn't match the sentiment behind my words. And Duncan, being Duncan, changes the subject.

"So that Zoey girl is a sweetheart," Duncan says as Matt motions for us to walk over to the agility ladders he's set up.

I smile and reach down a hand to help pull his lazy, out-of-shape ass up. "Yeah. She's perfect."

Levi's normally impassive face lights up like a Christmas tree. "So things are working out?"

"They will, I'm hoping," I say and stand at the end of the middle ladder while Levi and Duncan flank me on both sides. "She's definitely just as interested as I am, but she's got some personal stuff to deal with before we can…explore that interest."

Matt reaches for the whistle around his neck. "Crossovers. Five sets."

He blows the whistle and we get to it. I've been working out consistently almost all summer long. After the dick pic incident in Toronto, I came back here and had a lot of alone time, so I worked out during the day and spent most nights hanging out with Dixie. But I had still slept around a little bit, which is why another unsolicited hookup showed up at my place last night and woke me—and my neighbors—wanting sex. I turned her down and sent her home, but it made me realize Zoey can't get my place listed fast enough.

I need to move. I probably would have waited a little longer, and maybe even taken some of my unwanted visitors up on their un-requested booty calls, but now there is Zoey. I need a break from my usual habits, and Zoey is the perfect place to focus my energy—sexual and otherwise. She needs someone, and I am enjoying being that someone, even if it is only sadly platonic right now. I realize I'd rather have platonic with Zoey than anything else with anyone else right now.

By the time we finish this drill, Duncan honestly looks like he might die. Levi isn't too far behind, but he's better at faking it. My leg muscles are on fire, and it feels like there's not enough air in the world to fill my lungs. Matt seems to know our limits, even though it's only our fourth session with him. "Okay, kids. We're done for today. After you go for a slow mile-long jog for warm down."

Duncan swears. Levi groans and I grunt, but Levi sets the tracker app on his watch and we all start down the running path behind the gym. The pace is slow and easy. I could go faster, but there's no way Duncan can, so I don't try.

"Keep my mind off the fact that I'm killing myself here, and tell me more about the Zoey situation," Duncan begs through his huffing and puffing.

"She's a Realtor. She's going to sell my condo and find me a new place."

"You're selling your place?" Levi is shocked.

"You're selling your home to get into a girl's pants?" Duncan questions.

"No. It just worked out that I can sell my house and get in a girl's pants," I correct him. He tries to laugh, but it just makes him pant harder.

"So is the catch that you can't get together with her while you're working with her?" Levi wants to know as his app beeps and we turn around. "It would break a Realtor oath or something?"

"No. And even if that were true, I'd break the fucking oath and she would too," I say, and I'm confident it's a fact. I can feel our chemistry, like it's an entity unto itself. It's a living, breathing thing dancing between us when we're together. It's the same chemistry I felt when we were kids, but hadn't felt again until now. And it came back stronger than ever.

"Then what?" Levi wants to know.

"She's got to file her divorce papers," I admit.

"Holy shit, she's getting divorced for you?"

"Duncan, does Carla know how mentally deficient you are?" I ask and roll my eyes. "No. She was already separated for a while. The ex is just giving her a hard time on the settlement part."

"That sucks," Levi murmurs.

"It does, but she's tough. She'll get him to sign. And this idiot's loss is my gain. Zoey and I can finally pick up where we left off,"

I explain and grin. "I never thought that would happen, but it's happening."

"Is she going to be ready to jump into a serious relationship so quickly?" Duncan asks.

I laugh. "Relax, Cupid, I'm not asking her to marry me or anything."

"You're not?"

My feet slow even more at Levi's confused tone. I glance over, and he looks as baffled as he sounds. "Of course I'm not."

"Well, then…what are you doing?" he wants to know.

We're about twenty feet from where Matt is picking up the ladders we used, so I slow to a walk. Duncan happily joins, but Levi, never one to set a bad example, turns and jogs backward, a little slower than before, so he can stare at me befuddled while he waits for my response.

"I'm waiting until she's legally free to have sex with another man," I explain and lift my arms above my head to work out a stitch in my side. "Because I want that man to finally be me."

Duncan pulls his shirt over his head and uses it to mop the sweat from his red face. When he's done, he asks, "So this is just about sex again?"

"Have you met me? What else would it be about?" I smirk.

"You haven't always just been about sex," Duncan replies without thinking. When his brain finally catches up with his stupid mouth, he stops walking altogether. "I just meant that you aren't against serious relationships."

"I'm not against them. I just can't do them," I reply curtly as we get to the grass in front of Matt, and Duncan collapses. He's looking up at me like I'm a lost puppy or something. I don't like it, so I turn to look at Levi instead. His expression is stunned and confused.

"Warm down stretches," Matt barks.

"Jude, you were devastated when you found out that Zoey's parents had moved away," Levi informs me, like I don't know. "You were waiting to have sex with her."

"Jude? Braddock? He was saving himself?" Duncan sounds completely dumbfounded. Emphasis on the *dumb*.

"Yeah, and the second that goal became unattainable I fucked the hell out of Erin Moorehouse." I remind him of what I know he remembers, because I kicked him out of our room that night. "And then less than twenty-four hours later I did the same thing with her sister, Emily."

"You were eighteen."

"Yep. And ask your girlfriend how much I've changed."

Okay, that was out of line. Even I know that.

"Jude," Duncan says with caution as he starts to get back up on his feet. I'm sure he thinks he's going to have to get in between Levi and me to stop a fight. It wouldn't be the first time.

But even though Levi looks pissed, he refuses to act on his feelings. Exhibit A as to why he's a better player, friend, boyfriend and general human being than I am. "So Zoey is just another conquest?"

"Right now she's not even that," I reply and start toward the entrance to the gym.

"Warm down!" Matt bellows.

"I'll do it at home," I bark back and keep walking.

I know I seem angry, and I am. Levi doesn't get to make excuses for my behavior with women. He's not my best friend anymore, and even if he were, I wouldn't want him to do it. I know exactly who I was—who I am—and I don't need him to sugarcoat it.

I really didn't think twice about being with another girl when I was dating Tessa. In my head, they didn't mean what Tessa meant, so why did it matter? But it did matter, and it cost me Tessa. I just don't know how to be any other way.

I'm not bitter. Just realistic. Tessa once told me that maybe what was right for me was a partner who would look the other way. That comment was like a gnat burrowing into my soul and chewing away. Those words kept me up for more nights than I can count. What killed me was that deep down, I thought she might be right.

Zoey is lucky Tessa happened. And the fact is, she's been through too much with this asshole ex of hers to go through any more bad shit because of me. I just want to show her a good time. Remind her how sexy, beautiful, and unbelievably desirable she is, and then I want us to have that night we lost to booze and drama. Because I'm definitely going to be able to show her the best damn sexual experience of her life. But that's it. Sex. A much anticipated do-over, nothing more.

I'm not capable of more, and I don't want to hurt her.

12

ZOEY

Today turned out to be a really good day, and I didn't even have to chant a mantra once. When I got back from activating the cell phone Jude gave me, I had a commission check waiting for me from a small condo I sold last month. It isn't huge, but it's enough to pay my credit card off and make me more comfortable until the divorce is settled. But as the day progressed, my happiness started to mix with some nerves about going to Jude's condo. It didn't help that he had sent me a few innuendo-filled text messages and another selfie of him napping, the blankets pushed so damn low down his waist that I blushed.

Now I shift nervously from one foot to the other as I wait for the elevator to take me up to the fifth floor, where Jude's apartment is located. *All business,* I tell myself. *Keep it business. This is a huge listing for you. Take it seriously. Don't eye-fuck the client and let him make your panties wet.*

The elevator doors slide open, and I step out into the sleek, modern hall. I can't believe that he lives here. It's gorgeous. Not at all my taste, but definitely amazing. His unit is at the end of the hall. I knock on the door and feel oddly out of place. It takes him so long to answer the door that I worry he forgot—or changed his mind—or I dreamed this amazing opportunity. But then the glossy white door swings open, and Jude is standing there in nothing but a suggestive smirk and a towel. There are droplets of water on his shoulders and dripping from his wet hair. He clearly just got out of the shower.

A drop starts to slide from his collarbone, over his pec and down his torso. My eyes follow its path over every ripple of muscle in his stomach and down to the dark golden hair just below his belly button. He's decorated that perfect skin with tattoos. My eyes trace them. There's a red maple leaf on his right shoulder with a black silhouette of a hockey player in the center of it. On the inside of his left bicep there's a Stanley Cup with two dates written underneath—the dates he won it, I guess. And as he reaches up and runs a hand through his hair, trying to shake off excess water, I can see his surname, in big, beautiful, insanely detailed Old English–style lettering down the side of his torso, running from right under his armpit down to his hip. Braddock. I stare at the strong curve of the end of the K in Braddock.

There's the corner of a tattoo in it. The edge of a fancy letter. Maybe an R or a Y.

It's neither. It's a K.

"Eyes up, Sunset." He winks and reaches out and wraps an arm around my waist, pulling me forward for a hug.

Professional! My brain barks like a drill sergeant.

I place a hand on his damp bare chest to stop the hug and then swiftly step out of his grasp. "I can't hug you. You don't have a shirt on."

He looks amused. "Okay, come in and take a look around while I put on a shirt."

I scoot by him, careful not to touch any of his perfectly sculpted nakedness. I pull a pad and paper out of my purse and force myself to concentrate on the apartment. The first thing I notice, after he walks by and I give his towel-covered ass a good long look, is the flooring. It's wall-to-wall bamboo in a fabulous extra-wide plank. I walk down the long, wide hallway, glancing in the closet, guest room, powder room and small laundry room as I go. Everything is in great shape and decorated in classy neutrals except the guest room, which is a bold teal with a near-black trim.

"This building is hot," I say as I enter the main living space and see the door to the master bedroom, where he must have gone to change. "Units rarely become available, and when they do, they sell quickly and above asking."

"Good," he calls back, and I wander through the stunning kitchen that looks like it's never been cooked in. There's a huge island, and I trail my fingers across the stunning quartz countertop as I pass by on my way to the balcony. "How many square feet is this place?"

I pull open the sliding glass door to the decent-size balcony. I'm mesmerized by the phenomenal views of Sutro Tower, so I don't realize he's right behind me until he speaks. "It's just under fifteen hundred feet."

I jump a little, and his hands land on my hips, as if to steady me. I turn. We're less than a foot apart. "Can I get that hello hug now?"

His wet hair is curling a little bit at the ends. The white V-neck T-shirt he put on is clinging to his skin. He's still damp, and he's making me damp. I glance down. He's not wearing pants. He's only wearing underwear. Jet-black boxer briefs that cling to the curve of his ass and the wide muscles in his thighs and the very round package…

Be professional!

I take a step back onto the balcony and hold my notebook and pen up in front of me like a shield. "I can't hug you, you don't have pants on."

"So many rules, Zoey. When did you become a rules girl?" He grins.

I try to ignore it and ask, "And you're the only owner?"

"Yep," he says, leaning on the doorframe, with no intention of putting on pants, I guess. "I picked it for the view and the eco-friendly elements. Solar panels on the roof, and eco-friendly floor-ing, countertops and lighting."

"Yeah, it's still one of the top eco-friendly complexes in the city." I tell him what I found as I Googled his building. Okay, and maybe I also Googled him so I could see that dick pic Morgan mentioned. I couldn't find it, though. "It seems great all round. So why are you selling?"

"I want more space. And different space. I'm outgrowing this place, I guess." He shrugs.

I don't feel like he's telling me the whole story, but I stop myself from questioning him more. The fact is, I'm just his Realtor, and I don't get to delve into his personal life. But I want to delve into his underwear, which is worse than just probing him on his inner thoughts.

"It's hot out here. Let's go inside," I say and fight the urge to fan myself like a southern belle. "You can go put on pants."

He chuckles. "But you just said it's hot."

"Jude, who greets their Realtor in their underwear?" I blurt out and march through the kitchen to the large, open living room.

"Someone who has almost gotten naked with their Realtor," he replies and walks around the island, leaning his firm ass against it and crossing his arms. "And someone who wants to take the 'almost' out of that statement."

Grown-up Jude Braddock is bold, and I have to admit it turns me on. But that doesn't change the fact that this isn't a possibility right now. "Can we go over the listing please? Figure out price? Sign contracts?"

He nods, but there's a flicker of disappointment across his face. For the next twenty minutes we stand at the island, me on one side and him on the other, because I don't trust myself to stand right beside him, and we set a list price, and he signs the contracts to officially make him my client. He pauses before signing the last paper and lifts his eyes to mine. "You know this isn't going to stop me from hitting on you relentlessly, right?"

I bite back a smile. "We should keep it professional, Jude."

"There's nothing unprofessional about the way I seduce a woman, Zoey," he explains. "It's actually a fucking art form."

It's funny how I try to keep swear words out of my vocabulary, but when Jude uses them, it makes me want to crawl across the island and put my tongue in his mouth. That's the long-lost Zoey Quinlin coming back to life again. It feels good. Actually, it feels fantastic. He's watching me watch him, and that tantalizing smile reappears.

"Why are you smiling?"

"Because you are," he tells me, and I lift a hand to my face. Crap. He's right. I am. My revelation makes the smile on my face grow.

I bite the inside of my cheek to try to stop my wayward mouth, and I point to the paper his pen is hovering above. He laughs as he signs and slides the pile of papers at me.

"Thank you."

"Anything for you."

I shake my head at his tenacity. *Focus, Zoey*. "Okay, now we need to make a to-do list."

"To-do list?" he repeats. His hair has started to dry, and he's got a piece hanging down close to his eye as he leans on his elbows on the island. I want to reach out and brush it away, but I know if I do I'll end up running my hand through his hair and gripping the back of his neck and… "Zoey?"

I clear my throat and glance up at his air conditioning duct. Is that on? Why is it so hot in here? "A list of things you should change before the first open house."

A slow smile spreads across his perfect mouth. My temperature rises with every millimeter the corners of his mouth rise. I slip out of my suit jacket and walk over to his kitchen table and lay it over the back of the chair. I turn back around and catch him staring at my ass. Why does that make me want to smile? I am so bad at this professional thing.

"Eyes up, Braddock," I throw his line from earlier back at him. "First thing on the list: Put away personal items. Your hockey stuff. You don't want people to know who owns this place. Also, you should probably paint the guest bedroom. It's a little too unique compared to the rest of the house."

"I can start a to-do list," he says and reaches across the island to take my notebook and pen. I watch him flip to a blank page and start to write. "There. Done."

I'm drawn to that smile of his like a moth to a flame, and I find myself walking around the island to see what he wrote. I know with every ounce of my soul that he didn't write a single thing I said on that list, so I'm dying to know what he did write. I try to lean over and glance at the paper, but he pushes it farther away from me, so I end up right next to him, our hips touching. Jude wrote "Jude's To-Do List" and directly under it he wrote "Zoey Quinlin."

I burst out laughing, but he doesn't join me. Instead he uses the moment to move his strong arms, planting them on the island on either side of me. When our eyes meet, the laughter catches in my throat and fades almost instantly. He's smiling, but it's gone from mischievous to molten. "It's funny to you? That I want to finish what we started?"

"No," I manage to whisper. "It's insane."

He tilts his head, confused. "So you don't feel it?"

"Feel what?" Oh sweet snickerdoodle, he's so close. All I can smell is the clean, warm scent of his soap, and it's making me feel light-headed and irrational.

"The connection we still have," he explains, the warmth from his skin and the heat from his smile making me feverish. "The way I can feel you under my skin the minute our eyes connect. The way I feel you *here*." He moves one hand off the counter and down between us, cupping himself with his palm. "Every time we're in the same room."

I'm not pinned between him and the counter anymore. Moving his hand created an opening and I could slip aside, away from him, but the only things that move are my eyes. They drop down to watch him hold himself and give himself a slow, purposeful rub.

"I feel it," I confess in a whisper. The corner of the K in his Braddock tattoo licks at his hip bone and that rumored photo dances through my brain. I reach out and hold his side, covering the letter with my palm. His skin is warm and smooth and hard.

He moves his hand from the front of his underwear, and I stare at the long, thick line pressing against the fabric until he places his thumb gently under my chin and forces my eyes up. He's got a satisfied smile dancing on his gorgeous face. He's glad I'm staring at his hard-on.

"So why is it insanity to want to act on that kind of attraction?" he questions me. I have absolutely no response. "It's been a decade, an entire decade, Zoey, and yet you're still like a bomb that detonates inside me every time our eyes connect."

I swallow, even though my mouth is dry. "I'm married."

He sighs, and his eyes leave my face and follow his hand as it moves from my chin down my neck, his fingers tracing a line that sets goose bumps off like falling dominos in their wake. His hand glides along my collarbone, around to the back of my neck and up into my hair.

"I know. And somehow in the last decade you turned into a good girl." He almost sounds disappointed. "It's okay. I've waited eleven years. I can wait a little bit longer."

"For what? What are you waiting to do?" I'm needy. I know exactly what for, but I want him to say it. I want to hear the words come out of his sexy mouth, and I want them to be dirty. "Say it. Please."

His fingers twist and move in my chignon, and then suddenly my hair is free and tumbling over my shoulders, and his fingers move deeper into it and then curl. My hair is gently twisted in his curled hand and he tugs softly, tilting my head gently and leaning closer so his lips are near my ear. "I'm waiting to do all the things I dreamed of doing to you at seventeen. Spreading your legs with my hands and then spreading your pussy with my tongue. I'd never done that to a girl when I was seventeen, but I wanted to do it to you. I fantasized about feeling that part of you on my tongue, of tasting you, of watching from between your legs as you came."

"Holy fuck."

He grins at that. I can't see it, but I can feel his mouth pull open against my ear. He must remember my aversion to cussing and that I only do it when I can't control myself. He leans in so that his whole body, and I mean his *whole* body, is pressed against mine. The hard edge of the island's countertop must be digging into my lower back but I don't feel it. All I can feel is the weight and heat of his skin touching mine and the undeniable press of his erection against my hip. He is rock hard and it makes my stomach flutter wildly.

"And after I check eating you out off my to-do list I'm going to peel you out of your proper little suit and finally push my throbbing dick into your wet little pussy and fuck you long, hard and slow until we both explode."

I moan. It's only slightly louder and trembling as much as a hummingbird's wing, but it's a shameless moan just the same. He's moved his face from my ear and now we're nose-to-nose, and that tongue he's promised to fuck me with is sliding over his bottom lip, and if he tries to kiss me like he did last night I will not stop him. He can do anything to me right now and I would welcome it.

There's a noise. The scrape of metal. A click.

"Jude! So Match.com was invented by sadomasochists. I'm one hundred percent certain and would swear to it under oath." Dixie's voice echoes down the hall, and it's like a fire alarm screaming, sending us into panic mode.

Jude jumps back, and I rush to the other end of the kitchen, toward the table, stumbling over my own feet because apparently I can't walk in heels anymore—or, you know, at all.

"I mean, every guy it matches me up with is a complete mouth-breathing, crotch-scratching, parents'-basement-dwelling, unemployed, unmotivated, slack-ass hipster douchebag!" She wanders into the kitchen staring at her phone. "I'm deleting my account at this very—"

She looks up and freezes—mouth hanging open, hand in midair. I smile and wave. "Hey!" I reach for my jacket. "It's good to see you again. I was actually on my way home."

Dixie's eyes move to Jude, who, thankfully, is on the other side of the island, so she doesn't know he's only wearing underwear, and then she shifts her stare back to me. "Don't leave on my account. I'm just here to grab a dress Winnie forgot. She wants me to mail it back to her so she can wear it in Maine."

"So Mom took my advice and they're going to Maine?" Jude looks ecstatic.

Dixie nods, but she's still got a startled, slightly skeptical look on her pretty features. "Yeah. Early next month. I assumed she told you. She said she was going to call you."

"She might have. My phone is in my jeans."

Dixie's eyebrows lift. "And where are your jeans?" She starts to crane her neck to see over the island, and when she can't, she starts to move closer to him.

Jude, as bold and shameless as ever, steps around the island. Luckily, his hard-on is no longer visible or else I swear I would have thrown myself off his balcony. Dixie frowns and turns to me. I start to babble. "He's listing his place, and I'm his agent. We were going over paperwork."

"Yes, well, that makes sense. You can't enter into a legal contract in the state of California with your pants on." Dixie rolls her eyes.

"Nothing happened," I feel the need to tell her.

She smiles at me, and it's this odd mix of sympathy and amusement. "I'm sure it wasn't from lack of trying."

"I'm going to grab my jeans and then drive you home," Jude tells me and pads across the living room to his bedroom. "Dixie, feel free to get the dress, and then try not to let the door hit you on the way out."

I watch them go and sigh as I try to smooth my hair, which must be crazy. I walk over and retrieve my hair clip, which fell to the floor after he pulled it out. Thank God for Dixie because I was about to let Jude do anything and everything he wanted to me. I was powerless, and I was enjoying it.

13

JUDE

As we drive through the city to her place, Zoey stares out the window, and I mentally list all the ways I am going to murder my little sister for having the worst timing in the history of the world. If Dixie hadn't interrupted, I think I would have finally been able to get this gorgeous woman naked and underneath me. Actually, I probably would have gone for naked and on the counter, but whatever. Same difference. But Dixie had to barge into my place the way she always does—unannounced and like she owns it.

Zoey looked relieved when Dixie walked in, but I know it's not because she wanted to stop me. It's because she couldn't stop herself. She wanted to fuck me as much as I wanted to fuck her.

I turn onto her street and slow down, looking for a spot, because I intend to walk her to the door. There are a man and a woman on the sidewalk next to a car right in front of her place. Zoey leans forward when she sees them. I pull to a stop just a little behind them, hoping they'll hop in the car and leave so I can snag their spot.

"What are you doing?" Zoey exclaims, clearly panicked. "That's Adam! Don't stop! Keep driving!"

"Your ex?" I ask, shocked. I stare at him again. Huh. Not much if you ask me. "Why is he with some woman this late at night? And why can't I stop?"

"That's just his assistant, Minerva. She must have been dropping off files or something. She does that," Zoey mutters and leans closer. "She's gained weight."

My eyes finally move to the woman. She's shorter than Zoey, with long, sleek jet-black hair. It's dark out and she's wearing a navy trench coat, but it's not tied and the wind keeps blowing it back to reveal a pretty loose-fitting calf-length navy-and-white dress that does seem to be a little snug in her midsection. I turn off the car and hit the four-way flashers. Zoey stares at me, her hazel eyes about to pop out of her pretty head. "What the hell are you doing?"

I smile at the swear word. I love making her crazy enough to drop a cuss bomb. I open my door. "I'm walking you to your door."

"Jude! Don't!"

I ignore her, closing my door and walking around the car to open hers, since she clearly won't do it herself. Adam is looking up now—right at me. The woman is still talking to him, like I'm not even there.

"You need to let go of the house if it means getting her out of your life so you can concentrate on what matters!" the woman is saying. "This matters now. Not her. Not the damn house. Get a new house. You have the money!"

I want to turn around and find out what the "this" is that she thinks matters so much, but I don't want to make it obvious I'm eavesdropping. I can't help but think that this isn't a typical boss–assistant conversation. In fact, by the tone and the anger, these two have seen each other naked. I would bet money on it. I don't know if Zoey knows that, and I certainly don't want to be the one to tell her.

"Minnie, that's not the point!" Adam barks back, frustrated.

I pull open Zoey's door, and she glares at me, her face a frantic dance of anger and panic. I reach out. "Come on."

She ignores my hand and gets out of the car. I can't help but glance over my shoulder to catch Adam's expression. He was checking out the car at first, his eyes sweeping over it from the hood to the trunk. Makes sense. Not a lot of Tesla Model X's driving around. But then I see his eyes find Zoey, and I smile because he looks like he thinks he's having some kind of bad acid trip. No, you're not hallucinating, little buddy, it's happening. Your ex is trading up.

"Zoey?" he says, and I laugh at the pure disbelief in his voice.

"Adam," she snaps back at him as confirmation, but says nothing else. She walks past me and starts toward her front stairs. I shut her door and follow her. Out of the corner of my eye I watch the assistant pull her dark coat around herself, but she's not cold. It's a self-conscious move. She's uncomfortable.

Zoey must catch the move too, because her step falters, and she looks over at the woman. "Hello, Minerva. You making another one of your famous late-night contract runs?"

"She is. You know how she always goes above and beyond." Adam's tone is hasty. I don't know this tool, but even I can tell he's covering something.

"She's the superhero of the administrative assistant world," Zoey says and smiles genuinely at Minerva.

Oh man, Zoey, how are you so naïve? Weirdly, I don't think less of her for it, though. I just want to wreck this guy for taking advantage of her. He's probably been banging this secretary the whole time he was married. Zoey might not love him now, but she did at one point, and he probably violated that. She's a pastor's daughter: marriage isn't a joke to her.

"Who is your friend?" Adam says, and our eyes meet. I give him the biggest, most insincere smile I've ever given anyone and step forward, hand extended.

"I'm Jude Braddock. I'm a client of Zoey's."

He hesitantly stretches his hand out to meet mine. We're both trying to prove something with our strangle grips. "You look familiar."

"I play hockey for the Thunder."

That acid-trip look is back. "You're buying a house from her?"

"Buying one and selling one," I correct him and turn to Minerva. I give her a warm smile. "Nice to meet you. Minnie, was it?"

"Minerva," she corrects.

"Oh, sorry. I heard him call you Minnie. I guess nicknames are reserved for those who know you the most intimately."

Zoey is watching the whole exchange. When the wind blows and Minerva's coat catches in it, she yanks at it to pull it closed again, but it's too late. Even in the weak glow of the streetlights, I can totally see the baby bump. I glance over at Zoey. She saw it too.

"You're pregnant?!" Zoey exclaims, smiling.

"She's only three months along," Adam blurts out defensively.

Holy shit. It's his kid.

Zoey doesn't have the same revelation. She brushes by Adam and me to hug Minerva. "Congrats!"

"I'm actually four months along," Minerva explains; her voice is soft and filled with hurt because baby daddy just screwed up the date. She pulls back sharply and pulls at the trench coat again.

"Well, have a safe drive home, Minerva. Thanks for dropping off the files," Adam says briskly.

I glance from his hands to Minerva's and look up. "What files?"

I may not be willing to blatantly tell Zoey what's happening here, but I sure as hell am going to drop as many clues as I can. She deserves to know. My eyes lock with Adam's, and he knows I know. He bristles and punches his shoulders back, getting even more defensive. "They're inside my house. Why are you here?"

"Just dropping off my Realtor since you seem to have misplaced her car," I say and give him a smile so cold it would make lying naked on an iceberg feel warmer.

"I'm not here for contracts." Minerva's wobbly voice cuts through our aggressive banter. "I'm sorry, Zoey. I swear I didn't plan it, and it started after you two split up. If it makes you feel any better, I'm beginning to regret it."

Minerva turns and rushes down the street to her car. Zoey is standing motionless, bound by truths that were just thrown at her. I turn to Adam. He's not going after Minerva, the mother of his child, and he's not rushing to ease the harsh reality that just crashed down on his ex-wife. He's just standing there looking annoyed, like the whole thing somehow happened *to* him, instead of because of him.

My fists twitch, they want to connect with his arrogant face so badly.

"You have something to say?"

"Not to some professional rink rat," he says condescendingly; then he turns to Zoey. "I did not cheat, but I'm wondering if you can say the same, Zoey."

She lets out a hard, sarcastic laugh. "Are you kidding me right now?"

"I know math has never been your strong suit, but we've been separated over five months, and she is only three months pregnant."

"Four," I correct.

He glares at me. I smile. Now it's his fists that are twitching. Good. Bring it on, little man. But, sadly, he doesn't. He turns back to his ex-wife, who is looking like she's finally connected all the dots. "You want this house for her."

"For the baby," he corrects abruptly. "You convinced me this was a good place to raise a family. I'm the one with a family, so just do the right thing and step away."

She doesn't respond. He shakes his head in frustration and storms up the stairs and into the house. I stare at her as she watches him go. The wind whipping around us and rustling through the trees is the only sound. I'm suddenly petrified, because I don't know what to do or what she's going to do. Is she going to cry? How do I stop it? Is she going to snap and light the house on fire with him in it? Should I stop her? More than anything I just don't want her to be hurt. I think something in me would break if he broke her.

I step closer to her and reach for her hand. "What can I do?"

She turns to me, and I don't think I've ever seen another human being look so tired. "I'm going to give him the house."

"What? Why?" I ask, incredulous. "He's impregnated another woman while still married to you. No judge is going to give him anything."

"But he's right." Her voice is weak and on the verge of breaking. My heart clenches. If her voice cracks I will crack. "He's got a kid coming. He wanted something I didn't give him, and he went and found it. I want to find what he couldn't give me too."

"What is that?"

She looks around the street as if searching for something. The answer, maybe. She doesn't find it, or she doesn't share, because she goes back to her original statement. "This house was supposed to be filled with love and happiness and kids. Not me just stumbling around by myself. I don't need it. I'm not even sure I want it anymore."

I want to remind her that's not the point. The point is, she deserves to walk away with something from this marriage. He doesn't deserve to take everything from her. I hate that I feel like he's taken too much already, and it has nothing to do with material things.

"What do you want?"

She takes a deep breath and seems to hold it. She tilts her head up to the dark sky. "I want to feel something good again."

The words are carried to me on the wind, and I hear the slightest, tiniest crack in her voice on the word "good," and something in me snaps. She needs someone, and I want to be that person. I have to be, for me as much as for her. I'm in front of her before she tips her head back from the sky, and then I'm against her—all of me pressing into her—as I grab her around the waist with one hand and cradle her head with the other. And then I kiss her.

It's everything our first kiss was—rough, hard, unexpected and wanton. Her lips are soft and warm, and her tongue is perfect against mine. I've kissed a thousand girls in my lifetime, but the only time I've felt this kind of passion is with Zoey. It roars up from inside me; the deep ache of desire I've had for her isn't quelled by the kiss, it's intensified. When we finally break apart we're both panting.

"Jude...I have to go."

"I know," I agree. But I grab her head with both my hands and give her one last fierce kiss. She holds on to my arms while I do it.

When she breaks away, she immediately turns and runs up the steps. She glances back once before disappearing into the house. I walk back to my car and get inside. I'm torn. I want to stay. Just sit out here and wait, in case she needs me. But I know she'll be able to handle herself with that idiot ex of hers. And if she does walk away from the house, that's fine. I'll pay for a new one for her myself if I have to and let her pay me back whenever she can. I'm there for a lot of people in life—my mom, my dad, my sisters, even Levi—and I do it gladly. But I've never been as overwhelmed with the need to be there for someone as I am for her. I have to make sure she's okay. I feel like her happiness is mine.

14

JUDE

The next morning I wake up with a raging hard-on and a craving for pancakes. The problem is I can do something about only one of those needs. When I got back from Zoey's last night, Dixie was still here marathoning *Stranger Things* on Netflix. The girl is addicted to television but doesn't own one. Trying to figure her out has always annoyed the fuck out of me, so I stopped a long time ago. We get along a lot better now that I don't question her insanity.

Anyway, because I'd bet my life savings she crashed in the guest room, my stomach is the only thing I can satisfy. I never jerk off with my sisters in the house. None of them have ever bothered knocking in their lives, and I refuse to get caught. It would scar me more than them.

I stretch and try to think of generic things like hockey plays and what's in my fridge, but it's not easy, because last night with Zoey is all I want to think about, and that's not going to get my dick to deflate. I thought the night had peaked with our little dirty word exchange in the kitchen, but then I finally got to kiss her again and damn if it wasn't fucking perfect. Better than the first. I can't wait to do it again. And more. So fucking much more.

"Get up, dirtball!" Dixie's voice bellows through my entire apartment. "I made blueberry flapjacks!"

Okay, sometimes she's not a fucking nightmare. I roll out of bed and wander to my closet to find clothes. When I make it into the kitchen, she's drinking coffee, ass on the counter next to the stove, and there's a big pile of blueberry pancakes in the middle of the island. I grab one of my kitchen stools and reach for the maple syrup. My parents make sure I'm stocked, bringing a few bottles of the pure Canadian maple syrup every time they visit.

Dixie watches me pour. "Work up an appetite last night?"

"It's pancakes. I could eat six after a five-course meal," I say through a mouthful.

Dixie smiles at that and takes another sip of coffee. I keep shoveling heaven into my mouth. "You're lucky you're a hockey player. With your pancake addiction you'd be nine hundred pounds if you didn't work out for a living."

"Don't care. I'd eat pancakes every day even if I was a bus driver like Dad."

"Yeah, but it'd be harder to indulge your other obsession," she says with a devious smirk. "Those hot little numbers at the bar don't want to go home with the nine-hundred-pound guy who smells like maple syrup."

"You underestimate my charm," I retort.

"Doubtful," Dixie replies, putting down her coffee mug. "If your charm is so undeniable, then how come you were the only one with your pants off last night?"

"And there it is! The reason you made me pancakes. You're trying to get me to talk." I laugh and pour more syrup on what's left of my stack. "Why would I tell you anything? You're just going to call the rest of the sorority and find a way to tease me about this until I'm fifty."

Dixie jumps off the counter. "I won't tell Sadie and Winnie."

"Yeah, right."

"Jude, I won't."

I look up at that because she called me Jude, not ass-face or dirt-ball. That means she's serious. Her expression confirms it. Maybe it's the maple syrup clogging my brain or maybe it's just leftover eupho-ria from last night, but I decide to tell her. Everything. From the failed hookup when we were young to the flirting now. Then I tell her about the scene with Zoey's ex and his assistant last night.

"He knocked up the secretary? Could he be more of a cliché?" Dixie pretends to gag. "Ugh. Zoey must have had temporary insan-ity when she agreed to marry that turd waffle."

I chuckle. Dixie comes up with the best insults ever. She's been like that since she was a kid. It's like an art form for her. She walks over and leans forward with her elbows on the other side of the island. "What happened next?"

I tell her about the kiss. I probably shouldn't, but it feels good to talk about it, like I'm reliving it. Almost too good, because I can feel my dick start to chub. Shit. Thank God my sweats are loose. When I'm done, Dixie is staring at me with narrowed eyes, a fur-rowed brow and her lips pressed tightly together in a hard, flat line. I have no idea what the fuck that expression means, but it doesn't feel warm and fuzzy.

"What?" I haul another load of pancakes up to my mouth.

"I just...I don't know. I've never seen you like this." Dixie tilts her head, her blond bob hanging like a curtain, skimming her shoulder. "You like her."

"Yeah, Einstein. I kiss girls I like."

"You kiss anything with a vagina," Dixie replies. "The kissing isn't why I realized you liked her."

"Whatever." I shrug and run a thumb over the syrup left on the now empty plate and pop it in my mouth. "I know she's going to work today, so I'm going to swing by her office. Want to come, or do you have work?"

"It's Saturday, Jude."

I glance at the calendar on the fridge as I bring my plate over to the sink. She's right. Oops. I have a hard time keeping track of the days of the week in the off-season. "So come with me. She'll love to see you again, and I know you want to see her."

"I do," Dixie admits. "And watching you act like this is oddly enthralling."

"Thanks. I think." I rinse my plate and then grab her coffee mug off the counter and put both in the dishwasher because I know she won't. "Anyway, I want to see how she's doing and invite her to the charity game."

"Really? Like as your date?"

I nod.

"But you always go solo and pick up some horny, slutty fan." I glare at her. She shrugs unapologetically. "What? It's like common Thunder PR knowledge. Like lore or something."

"Yeah, well, even lore can be rewritten," I tell her and head to my bedroom again. "I'm going to shower. If you're coming with me, can you please try to keep your catty quips to a minimum?"

"I can try!" she calls after me.

Forty minutes later we're at Golden Gate Realty. Only Zoey isn't. Anastasia, her co-worker I met the other day, greets us at reception. She explains that Saturdays most agents are showing properties, and Marti had two showings that overlapped so Zoey offered to run one. She seems way too remorseful that Zoey isn't in the office and keeps almost begging to help me with whatever I need.

"No, really, Anastasia, it's nothing you can help with, but thank you," I lie with a smile.

"I'm working on becoming an agent as well, so maybe I can sell you a house one day," Anastasia explains with a wide smile and a flutter of her eyelashes.

"Anything can happen." I grin.

She leans on the reception desk and lets her fingers dust over my knuckles.

"What's the address on the listing where Zoey is now?" Dixie interrupts, her voice all business.

Anastasia gives us the address. Dixie's out the door with a terse "thanks" a second later, but I stop to give Anastasia a hug, because she wants one, I can tell. Outside, Dixie is standing by the Peet's Coffee. "Come on. I need a latte to calm my stomach after witnessing that."

"Witnessing what?" I open the door to the coffee shop and Dixie walks in.

"Hello! You. Flirting with Zoey's co-worker." Dixie waves her hand, pink nails flying in front of my eyes.

"I wasn't flirting with Anastasia," I argue. "I was just being myself."

She gives me a hard, exasperated stare. "I thought you liked Zoey."

"I do like Zoey. I have always liked Zoey."

"No. I mean *like* Zoey." Dixie exaggerates the word "like" as we approach the counter. She orders an iced caramel latte with coconut milk and starts to reach into her purse, but I pay the guy before she can unzip her wallet. My sisters all make decent incomes, but I make an obscene one, so I don't mind paying for things. In fact, I'd rather. They all gave up a lot of weekends and time with their friends because Mom and Dad were shuttling us to my hockey tournaments. I like to give them stuff and help them out so it seems worth it to them.

I wave off the change the guy tries to hand me as Dixie thanks me and we move to the corner to wait for her drink. "You talk about Zoey like she's something special."

"She is," I reply easily and run a hand through my hair. "She's the one that got away. The original and the one and only. That's special."

Dixie is staring at me with that "I sucked on lemons" face she's so great at. "The one that got away from…?"

"My bed." I can't believe she's so dense she needs me to spell it out. "I never got the chance to sleep with her. It was a fucking tragedy then, and it's still a tragedy, because her stupid pending divorce is keeping it from happening now. Luckily, though, this time neither of us is going anywhere, so I can wait it out."

The guy behind the counter calls out her order, and she reaches up and grabs it. Turning with a huff, she marches out of the coffee place, and I follow behind. Why the hell is she tantrumming right now? What is her issue? When I ask her as we walk to my car, she doesn't respond, only rolls her eyes, so I decide to let it go. If I'm lucky enough, maybe she'll be too bitchy to talk the entire ride to the open house Zoey is working, and I'll actually get to listen to the radio.

It works. Whatever has her pissed off at me keeps her quiet the whole fourteen-minute trip, but, sadly, I don't enjoy the radio. I'm too busy trying to figure out what her problem is. When I park the car, it hits me. "I'm not going to use her, Dix."

Our eyes meet, and I can tell that's exactly why she's pissed. "So it's not just about getting in her pants?"

"Of course I want in her pants. The sex is going to be phenomenal."

She wrinkles her nose at that last statement.

I turn off the engine and continue to reassure her. "Ease up, Dix. I know she's not some puck bunny. Jesus, I meant it when I said I liked her. She's amazing. Getting in her pants won't be the end of it."

"So you want to date her? Like seriously?" Dixie questions. "Because if you do, you need to stop flirting with other women."

Oh God, she's a broken record. "I wasn't flirting with Anastasia. And I don't think Zoey and I will date."

She actually looks heartbroken. "Why not? You like her!"

"Yeah. That's exactly why," I bark back, really fucking fed up with this conversation. "If I want her to keep liking me back, dating isn't the best idea."

She stares at me, eyes hard, mouth in a flat line. Then she shakes her head slowly, like she's in disbelief. "You are in for a rude awakening, Jude Braddock."

"What?"

Dixie's face relaxes, and she smiles. "Forget it. Let's go see Zoey."

We both get out of the car, and I lock it as we head toward the sleek, modern Bernal Heights home with the "Open House" sign out front. I reach over and grab her drink, taking a sip. She instantly starts slapping at me, so I relent and give it back before I can down the whole thing and really annoy her.

As we climb the stairs to the front door, a couple emerges from the house. They're smiling and saying something about having their agent get in touch, and then I see Zoey standing just on the other side of the door. She's all business in a short-sleeved loose black dress and a pair of pumps. Her tan, toned calves are on display, and I can't help but think about how great they're going to look over my shoulders.

The couple moves by me and down the stairs, talking to each other in excited voices about the house. Zoey's hazel eyes flare when she sees me, and then a smile bursts onto her face, and I suddenly feel taller, smarter, happier and just generally like a superhero. I grin back at her and step into the house. Without even thinking about it, I reach for her and pull her into a hug. I have to work to keep it casual because my hand on her lower back wants desperately to slip to her ass and as my head slips over her shoulder my lips feel drawn to her cheek, but I refrain. It's definitely not the place. Unfortunately.

"Hey! What are you doing here?" Then she sees Dixie over my shoulder and pulls away to go hug her. "Dixie!"

"Good to see you again!"

When they break apart, Zoey looks at me inquisitively. "Are you house hunting without me? Getting a head start?"

"Nah. This place is nice." I glance around the modern, open-concept first floor with gleaming white walls and cabinets and dark oak accents and floors. "But I want to stay closer to downtown, and I need a quick commute to Mission."

"Okay," she says. "So to what do I owe the pleasure?"

Pleasure. Man, do I want to show her pleasure. "I wanted to see you and make sure you're doing fine."

I glance around the house, not sure if we're alone. Her pretty smile falters, and she glances over her shoulder. Clearly there are prospective buyers somewhere in the house. I take a step toward her. "How'd it go after I left? This morning?"

"He was locked in the master when I went back in the house, and then this morning he was gone when I woke up." She sighs and runs a hand through her hair, which she must have straightened, because those waves I love are nonexistent today. "It's better this way. I have no idea what to say to him anyway."

I hear footsteps, and then an older woman walks into the kitchen where we're standing. She praises Zoey on the house and insists she "has to have it" and her agent will be in touch. Then she walks over to the counter near the six-burner stove and sheepishly takes a donut before heading out the door. I eye the donuts. They're from a low-end chain, nothing fancy, which is out of place. I've been to high-end open houses that offer sushi or gourmet cookies or even crudité platters.

She laughs at my reaction. "I know. Not fancy at all, but every time I bring the dollar donuts, they're gone in a flash. Novelty, maybe, or guilty pleasure. Whatever the reason, I feel like it also makes the open house a little more memorable."

Dixie walks over and reaches for one covered in pink icing and rainbow sprinkles. Zoey laughs as my sister takes a giant bite. I turn back to her and gently take her hand. I can't help it. If I'm this close to her and I'm not touching her, my fingers start to tingle. She glances down at our hands and back at me, the sweetest hint of a smile on her lips. The lips that felt like heaven against mine. I can only imagine how incredible they'll feel around my dick.

"What are you thinking?" she asks suddenly in a breathless whisper. "I swear your eyes just darkened a shade right in front of me."

I let my tongue play against my bottom lip. Her eyes drop to it and she squeezes my hand. Dixie groans loudly. "Do they make condoms for eyeballs? Because you two need them."

The front door opens and a tall, lanky guy dressed in golf clothes comes sauntering in. Zoey drops my hand and grabs an info sheet off the counter. She walks over and immediately starts charming him with the details of the house. A minute later the guy is off to wander around, but not before he gives her a long, appreciative glance from pumps to head. Zoey has already turned away from him, so she doesn't see the leering glance, but I do, and it makes jealousy flame inside me.

Zoey takes in my appearance as she approaches, and I can tell she can see that my mood has shifted. "Is everything okay?"

"You do all of these alone?"

"Open houses? Mostly."

"Is that safe?" I can't help but question. "I mean, random strangers and you alone in an empty house. It worries me."

For some reason the heat of jealousy is instantly replaced with the burn of embarrassment. I'm acting like a possessive boyfriend, and I'm not. I don't even want to be. And if I was her boyfriend, the last thing I would be is possessive. I was the polar opposite of possessive in my last relationship. I can't handle the way Zoey is looking at me with that sweet little smile, like she's amused and somehow flattered by what feels like some kind of meltdown to me. So I look away, and the only other person to focus on is Dixie, who is silently devouring the rest of her donut, watching the scene with rapt attention the way she watches her Netflix shows on my eighty-inch television. Yeah, that's not helping.

I decide to change the subject. "So I was wondering if you wanted to come to a game."

"A hockey game?" Zoey questions. "The season started already?"

"It's preseason," I explain. "Not league sanctioned. A bunch of guys from the California professional teams get together and play a bunch of guys from the local college teams. It's to promote the growth of hockey in California. Each year one of us picks a charity to donate the proceeds to, and this year is my choice."

"What did you pick?"

"ALS." I keep talking before she can ask me why. "It's tomorrow night, and there's a carnival in the parking lot afterward."

"Yeah. I would love to go." She says it easily, not a hint of hesitation and a bright smile on those perfect lips that she happens to have painted a delectable pink that reminds me of the color they were after our rough little make-out session last night. I swear to God my dick just quivered.

"Great. Oh, and I wanted to ask you what color you want me to paint the guest bedroom?" I ask, scratching at the back of my neck. "I was going to do that tonight."

"You're painting our room?" Dixie finally stops watching us and decides to speak. "But we picked that color! We love the teal."

"It's pretty," Zoey admits and gives her a sympathetic smile. "But it doesn't flow with the rest of the space, and it's a specific taste. We need the whole place to look pleasantly neutral. A light gray with soft white trim would work."

"I always thought it was ugly," I pipe up, mostly just to annoy Dixie. Without even turning around, I can literally feel her trying to eviscerate me with her eyes. "And you should probably help me repaint it. Since you're the reason I have to."

"In your dreams, butthead" is Dixie's automatic response.

"I'll help," Zoey says and meets my eye.

"Okay." I wasn't actually going to paint it myself, I was going to hire someone. I was just trying to take the piss out of my sister. But now that it means alone time with Zoey, I'm heading directly to the paint store after this. "Come by about seven?"

She nods. "Can we make it seven thirty instead? I have some stuff to take care of at the office and then I'm meeting with my lawyer, and I'm not a hundred percent sure how long it'll take."

"That works. See you then." I lean in to hug her and turn my face into her ear. "And if you don't have any painting clothes that you can get dirty, you can just do it naked. I won't mind."

The sexiest little giggle bubbles up from her, and she pushes me away. "That's really kind of you not to mind."

I shrug nonchalantly. "I'll even join you if you're uncomfortable. I'm that nice a guy."

"Join her with what?" Dixie asks like the annoying little sister she is.

"See you tonight." I give Zoey a wink and start toward the door.

"What are you joining her for? What am I missing?" Dixie whines.

"Say good-bye, Dick," I tell her, using the childhood nickname she hates more than anything on earth. I used to call her that instead of Dix. I did it once in front of some guys in her grade school and it caught on, apparently.

"Jerk," she hisses but turns and hugs Zoey. "Bye. Feel free to dump a bucket of paint on him tonight. And I'll see you at the hockey game."

"See you then!"

We get outside and Dixie asks me again what she missed in there. "I offered to paint naked with her if she didn't have clothes she wanted to mess up."

"God, that's so sleazy. You really just care about getting in her pants."

"It's a priority, yes," I confirm. "And also not your business, Dick."

"Seriously, you better not call me Dick out in public, like at work or anything," she warns, her voice as serious as a heart attack.

"Don't worry, Dick," I say as I unlock the car doors, and we both get in.

"Stop!"

I laugh and turn and glance out the window, staring at the house we just left.

After a minute Dixie waves her hand in front of my face. "Hello! Let's go! Is your penis overriding your brain again and you forgot how to drive?"

"I just want to make sure that guy leaves," I mutter, and as soon as I say it a car parks in front of the house, and a young couple gets out. I hope they're going to go into the open house too so Zoey isn't alone in there with the creepy gawker.

Not only does the couple open the gate and start up the path to the front door, but Creepy McStalkerson comes out the front door at the very same time. I actually sigh in relief, then I start the car and glance over at Dixie to make sure she has her seat belt on. She's scowling at me, hard-core.

"What?" I ask as I put the car in gear and drive away.

"I'm not going with your dumb ass to the paint store. I have to get home."

"Busy Saturday night Googling spoilers for your Netflix shows and hunting down new cat memes?" I quip and laugh at my own joke because honestly, that was hysterical.

"You know you're being a total self-destructive idiot."

"Because I'm making fun of the fact that you clog my email with at least three cat memes a week?" I ask and guide the car up a steep hill toward her apartment. "It's either laugh or cry."

"She's an amazing girl," Dixie goes on, ignoring my hilarity. "And for some reason she is completely into you. I bet she'd even admit it if I ask her. But you are pretending you don't feel the same about her, and I don't get it."

"I'm not pretending anything. I told you, she's hot, and I totally want to pick up where we left off, which was moments before sex," I repeat myself. "And I told you, I don't want to blow her off afterward or anything. I want to stay friends. Good friends. Hell, she could even replace Levi. I like her that much."

"She has a vagina. She can never be Levi 2.0," Dixie remarks flatly and tips her head back against the seat, a frustrated groan escaping her throat. "Stop being a moron. Did you learn nothing from Tessa?"

"I learned I can't keep a good thing going." I hit a red light and turn to stare at her. She's not just being annoying and invasive, she's being dramatic. Annoying and invasive are kind of her thing, but dramatic normally isn't. "I think that makes me the opposite of an idiot to accept reality, Dick."

"Argh!"

I force myself not to smile at her anguish. The rest of the drive to her building is quiet. When I finally pull to the curb in front of her apartment, which is above a sushi place, I turn to her. "Have you eaten at that place? I think I might grab some. I'm starving."

She remains silent, still scowling as she undoes her seat belt. She reaches for the door, and I can't help but remark, "You invented resting bitch face, didn't you?"

"Well, you invented restless dick syndrome," she snaps back. "And it's going to ruin your life."

"That's not even…is that an actual thing?" I ask, suddenly worried that it might be. I mean, hell, there are so many of those medication commercials curing things I never knew existed; this could be one of them.

Dixie lets out an exasperated breath and gets out of the car, but then leans back in. "It might be an actual thing. I guess we'll find out."

"What the hell does that mean?"

She slams the car door, and I watch her stomp across the sidewalk and into her building. When did she turn into a dramatic diva? Jesus. I hope that's just a phase. My stomach growls, and I pull the car over at an empty meter. Time to grab some sustenance, because I'm hoping to burn a lot of calories tonight.

15

ZOEY

I brace myself as I walk into the conference room behind my lawyer. I spent the last half hour telling my lawyer everything—including what happened last night. She looks like she's heard and seen it all; when I told her about Minerva and her baby bump, she didn't even blink. In fact, she smiled. "Honey," she said, patting my hand where it rested on the edge of her desk, "I know that must hurt, but it's essentially a winning lottery ticket. Is there anything you didn't get in the pre-nup that you want to add? Because the ball is in your court."

I shook my head. "I'm not even sure I want the house anymore. I just want this to be over so I can move on."

"And I just want you to have something to show for the pain he's put you through," Cordelia told me with a sympathetic tone to her voice. "Ned is family, which makes your brother family, which makes you family. And my family isn't going to get screwed by some rich asshole who thinks his shit doesn't stink. You're getting that house. You can sell it if you want, but it's going to be yours."

I didn't want to argue with her. I was hoping no one else would want to either. So now here we are walking into the conference room of her law firm, where Adam and his lawyer are already waiting. Adam doesn't look up from the table as we enter, and he never makes eye contact with me through the entire meeting. I don't know if it's out of guilt or embarrassment or just because he's an asshole. Probably the latter. His lawyer is a bulldog and tries to argue that because Adam has a pregnant girlfriend he deserves the house. Cordelia laughs in his face—she actually does! She reminds him that by having sex while still married, Adam violates any terms of the pre-nup, and I can now request spousal support and half of everything.

It's almost an hour of back-and-forth, and we're no closer to signing. So finally I say, "I'll sell it to you."

"Excuse me?" his lawyer says, and he looks absolutely horrified that I spoke at all. I guess it's not my place, but I don't care anymore.

I have so much to look forward to in my life—a new career, rekindled friendships with the Braddock girls and a rekindled...something with Jude. I just want to be done with this. It feels like a wound that keeps reopening every time I think about it or have to deal with it.

"I will sell you the house," I repeat. "Let's face it, no matter how you rationalize it, Adam, you fucked someone else while we were technically married."

"And you're coming home late at night with a professional hockey player who's had his stick in half of San Francisco," Adam counters. His tone, dripping with condescension, is like putting gasoline on the sparks of frustration that are already inside me.

"Slut-shaming? This is your thing now?" I laugh with no trace of gaiety. "He's a childhood friend and a client. I'm helping him find a place."

"Why, so he can bed the other half of San Francisco?" Both he and his lawyer snicker at that one.

"No, so he can fuck me," I blurt out, and my lawyer drops her pen with a startled clatter on the polished wood table. Adam's haughty smirk evaporates, and his jackass lawyer stops laughing. "But here's the thing, Adam. He hasn't had me yet. And he won't until the paperwork is signed, because I'm a much better person than you. You can hold out as long as you want. I can wait. But a judge is going to be far less charitable than I am. And Minerva only has five more months left. So actually, I changed my mind."

I pause and take a deep breath and then level him with a cold, hard stare. "I'm not offering you a chance to buy the house. I'm keeping it, and now you're going to pay me the value of the car you stole from me. And all the credit card debt I racked up when you made me live in a hotel is yours to pay and yours alone. Got it? Because if you disagree, we're going to court, and I will ask for alimony and half of that precious business you own on top of this."

Adam is turning the most awesome shade of red. I don't even try to stop the smile that starts to spread across my face. His lawyer starts threatening to keep this tied up for years, but Adam interrupts him, turning to me. "Zoey, please. Show me a little kindness. I know that's who you are deep down inside…"

He gives me a pleading look. It resembles the one he gave me when he begged me to start trying for a family. He's eight years older than me, and he felt like it was time. Men his age should have families. We were the only ones in our affluent social circle—which was really his circle—who didn't have kids. He thinks that look will work now? It only worked the first time because I thought I loved him. I thought having a baby might fill the holes in our marriage. I wanted to make it work. I want nothing more than for it to end now. "I'm being kind to the only person that matters now. Me."

His softened expression hardens up instantly. He would wrap his hands around my neck right now if he could. He turns to my lawyer. "Amend the paperwork, so I can sign it and be done with her."

Cordelia stands and quickly leaves. I sit back down and wait. The room is definitely a toxic environment now and it's a long twenty minutes until Cordelia is back with the updated documents. Adam angrily grabs the papers from her and signs them in an aggressive scrawl.

"Adam—" his lawyer starts.

"You were the biggest mistake of my life," he seethes, and the words don't even sting. Not even a little bit. I share the sentiment. I realized that when I didn't even care that he had gotten Minerva pregnant. What hurt that night, seeing her and finding out it was his baby, was the fact that Adam might be right. I may never have a baby of my own. As happy as I am that I never had his children, I do want children one day. With someone else. And the fact is it might not happen.

When he finishes signing, he shoves the papers back toward my lawyer and starts out of the conference room. "I'll be out of the house in an hour and have movers come to get my larger stuff by tomorrow." He pauses and looks at me with hard, cold eyes. "Have fun with your little rink rat."

"Congrats on knocking up your secretary!" I call as I start to sign the paperwork myself.

He storms out, his lawyer traipsing after him. I look at Cordelia. "You could have gotten even more," she reminds me.

"He can't give me what I want," I tell her and exhale a low, steady breath. "Now what?"

"I'll file this Monday. It can take up to six months to get it processed, but you can consider yourself a single woman as of today, Ms. Penner. Congratulations."

"It's Ms. Quinlin again," I promise, more to myself than her. We shake hands, and I leave her office feeling lighter and more hopeful than I have in longer than I can remember. And the only thing I want to do is see Jude.

I start to walk to the coffee shop at the end of the street to waste time so when I go back to the house Adam is gone. I don't need another verbal smackdown with him today, or ever again. Across the street from the Starbucks is a burger joint. It's got a few tables outside, and the patrons are enjoying what look like incredible burgers and big, thick milk shakes. My stomach roars, and I walk right over and plop myself down at a table. I order a burger with bacon and two kinds of cheese and a drunken orange creamsicle milk shake made with amaretto. Because fuck it, this is a celebration.

As I devour my meal I get a text from Jude.

Hope the meeting with your lawyer is going well. I can't wait to see you tonight.

I smile and wipe burger juice from my fingers so I can text him back.

He signed.

I take a long, decadent sip of the boozy milk shake. It's like heaven in a glass. I'm pretty sure I'll end up a little tipsy from it, and I'm looking forward to it. Telling Jude my divorce papers are signed is the equivalent of stripping naked and lying down in front of him. It means we're going to have sex. I'm glad. I'm looking forward to it, but I haven't had sex with someone new in more than four years. Hell, because our marriage was crumbling, I haven't had sex at all in over six months. And the last time Jude and I attempted it, it was a disaster, so the loose, warm, uninhibited feeling the amaretto will leave me with can only make this easier.

My phone rings about two seconds after I hit send on the text. Jude's naked selfie flashes across my screen, because I set it as his contact picture, and I quickly swallow down a chunk of burger as I put it to my ear. "Hi."

"Hi yourself," he counters in a deep, flirty tone. "You're divorced?"

"You bet your sweet ass," I say with a giggle. Yeah, this milk shake is already working its magic.

"Then why the fuck aren't you at my house yet?"

"We said seven thirty," I remind him, smiling like a cracked-out cheerleader just from hearing his playful voice.

"That's when you were just coming over to paint," he replies, and then his voice drops an octave. "Now you're coming over for more than painting."

Whoosh. Just like that, it's official—we're going to have sex.

"I need to go home and change," I explain. "I'm still in my dress from the open house."

"Just come over. Now," he demands, and the need in his voice shoots through me, landing between my legs. "I promise you won't need to worry about what you're wearing."

I take a long sip of the milk shake, finishing what's left, and then shove the last few bites of my burger across the table and lift my hand to catch the waiter's attention. "Be there in twenty."

I pay my bill and order an Uber. As my driver slogs his way through weekend traffic toward Jude's place, I think about how this feels right now. The ink on my divorce papers is barely dry, and I'm driving across town to have sex with someone. And I have zero hesitation about it. I mourned my marriage already. I spent the first two months devastated and broken. I couldn't eat, or sleep, or hold a normal conversation. I just wanted to be alone, and I had given up on anything ever resembling happiness entering my life again.

Then after a while I had no choice but to pick myself up. And then, as the pain subsided and the frustration started because he wouldn't sign the papers and he wouldn't leave the house, I was able to see the fatal flaws in my relationship with Adam—the warning signs I missed—and I had come to terms with the failure and the loss and just wanted to move on, even though I didn't know to what.

Now I know what I'm moving on to—a better life, one that I get to build all over again. One that may include Jude. Jude has always looked at me like he sees something I don't. Something special and valuable, and it mesmerized me as a kid. I was drawn to that feeling he gave me. My rebellion and liberal sexual tendencies may have made me seem confident and bold, but I was as insecure as the next eighteen-year-old girl. It was an act, a way to defy my parents and guarantee attention from boys. But Jude looked at me like I was everything I hoped to fool people into thinking I was—beautiful, smart, desirable and lovable. And he had popped back up in my life at a time when I thought I was faking it again, only to look at me like I was everything I pretended to be. And if he saw me that way—beautiful, bright, confident, desirable and lovable—then maybe I actually was.

The Uber stops in front of Jude's building, and I thank the driver, get out and make my way inside. Nervousness is starting to seep past the calming warmth the milk shake caused. It's like getting back on a bicycle. I'll remember how to do this. And the chemistry between Jude and me is stronger than ever. People with that kind of connection—that crackle of heat between them every time they look at each other—don't have bad sex. It's not possible. Right?

I need this to be the right decision. Because it feels right. Everything about being near Jude, including that searing kiss last night, felt right. And I need that instinct to be true. I can't handle being so wrong about something again. I honestly can't. I ring his bell, and he opens the door a second later. He's got pants on this time, and a shirt, and it's mildly disappointing.

"Sunset," he growls, and as it rumbles up through him, it rumbles down through me. I step into the apartment, and he lets the door close behind me, and then he grabs me. His arm loops around my waist, and he yanks me into him. Before I can adjust my balance, he drops his mouth over mine.

It's savage and primal and so damn perfect. I'm breathless, and when he pushes his tongue into my mouth, his whole body presses forward, making my back arch and further tilting my precarious balance. I'm dangling, helpless in his arms, and I want to do nothing about it. I just want to submit, so I do, opening my mouth and giving him all the access he craves. When the kiss breaks, he pulls me upright, and I grab his broad shoulders for that balance I can't seem to find. My heels are firmly on the ground now, but my legs feel shaky and weak, like I've never stood on pumps before, and my knees are slightly bent and turned in, and I'm pretty sure I look like Bambi.

"You okay?"

"I'm better than okay when you kiss me."

It's a silly confession, but he seems to like it, because he grins and his lips graze my jaw as he whispers in my ear. "Imagine how good you're going to feel when I make you come."

Oh. God.

He steps back, letting go of my waist, but I manage not to tip over. He takes my hand in his and leads me past the guest room, which is set up for painting with all the furniture moved to the center of the room with plastic tarps covering it. There are two cans of paint and some trays and rollers in the far corner by the closet. I feel a flicker of disappointment that we might actually paint tonight. But he leads me past that room, down the hall and into the master bedroom.

The sun is setting through the oversize window, throwing streaks of gold and pink across the walls. The only light on is a weird rock-like thing on the corner of his night table. It's glowing a yellow-orange, adding to the ethereal feeling in the room. His bed is made. It's huge. A California king platform bed wrapped in distressed leather. The comforter is simple white, but there's a dark gray cable-knit throw across it that matches the pillowcases, except they're silky, probably like the sheets. This is a bed meant for one thing: fucking. It's a crazy thought, but it's accurate.

His hands are on my hips, and he gently pushes me into the room. "You smell so great. Different, but good."

"Different?"

"When we were eighteen, you smelled like coconut and vanilla," he whispers against my neck. "Like suntan lotion and ice cream."

I smile. "Coconut body butter and vanilla shampoo. I was addicted to both."

"Now you smell like flowers and citrus," Jude says, his breath tickling the side of my neck. "Still good, just different."

"Good?" I repeat the word as he moves from behind me to beside me. I turn my head to look at him. His eyes are clear and the most incredible, opulent blue, almost ombre in the way they get lighter toward the edges.

He leans in, lips pulling apart slowly, tongue gliding over his bottom lip for a second. "The scent still makes my mouth water and my dick hard, so maybe 'great' would be a better word."

Some might consider Jude's words crass or foul-mouthed, and maybe they are, but they make me wet. His one hand leaves my waist and the other slips lightly over my ass, and then it's gone too. He walks over to a leather chair in the corner of the room. There's a small pile of clothing there. It's the only thing out of place in the whole room, and I wonder if Jude's a neat freak.

"I figured you could change into this, so you don't get paint on your dress." He holds up the T-shirt. It's got the San Francisco Thunder logo on the front, and when he turns it around, it's his name and number on the back.

"Are we really going to paint?"

"Would you rather do something else?" I nod. His smile grows again. "Tell me what."

"You're the bold one, not me," I reply as a hot tingle creeps up my cheeks.

"That's not true." He laughs lightly and walks closer. God, I hope he touches me again. "You were the boldest, most sexually aware human being I had ever known."

"Some things change," I say, because I know that's how it seemed to a seventeen-year-old virgin, but now...I feel shy and unsure, and all I can think about is how much I crave the feel of his lips on mine again.

He reaches up and brushes my hair, skimming his fingers through it. "So change back."

"It's not easy." My voice doesn't sound like my voice. It's softer and yet rougher at the same time.

He stops skimming my hair with the back of his hand and wraps his hand gently but possessively around the back of my neck. "Yeah, but it's worth it. Tell me what you want."

"I want to fuck you."

He smiles for a fleeting moment before his mouth crashes down on mine.

16

JUDE

Everything falls away. Time, space, my thoughts, the world. It all dissolves with the first velvety touch of her lips. This is finally going to happen. She's finally going to be mine. I immediately reach around her back and start to lower the zipper on her dress. She's gripping my shoulders, and then her hands move down, over my chest and across my stomach, until her fingers find the hem of my shirt and slip under.

She lets out the tiniest, sweetest little moan when she makes contact with my bare skin, and it makes the base of my hard cock tingle. Jesus, this girl is still perfection. Her hands move up, exploring and taking my shirt with her. I've got her zipper down to her lower back, and then I too find bare skin. Her back is smooth and warm, and I trace the line of her spine upward as my lips move from her mouth to her neck, and she tips her head back to give me access.

My tongue skims a path down the elegant curve of her neck, and my hands push her dress off her shoulders. It drops all the way down, past the curve of her hips to the ground. She's in a black silk bra and a white lace thong. Her skin is tanned, her stomach is taut and her breasts are full, and I want to put my lips on every part of her—sucking and tasting and marking her.

She's got my shirt up to my chest, her fingers still exploring my skin, her thumb skimming my nipple. I reach up and grab the back of my shirt and pull it over my head and off. As the shirt hits the floor, though, so does my stomach. The uncomfortable feeling is instantly followed by a wave of nausea so strong I have to step back. Her head snaps forward, her face a mask of confusion, but when her eyes land on me she starts to look concerned. "Jude. You're a weird color. Are you okay?"

I want to answer her, but I am scared to open my mouth right now, because another wave of nausea is cresting inside me. What the fuck is happening? She says my name again, but I barely hear it as I blow by her and straight into my bathroom. Swinging the door closed behind me, I pray it stays shut, but I don't have time to check. I only have time to drop to my knees and lift the seat before I literally lose my lunch.

Ten minutes later I finally think the mass exodus has stopped. There's a tentative knock on the door. "Jude?"

"I want to die."

"Yeah, it sounded pretty bad."

"No. It's not just that I feel like dying, I want to die," I mutter and slide away from the toilet bowl to lean against the cool tile wall next to the shower. My stomach rolls at the motion and I groan. Why is this happening to me on the night I'm about to get what I've always wanted?

"What's wrong? Why are you sick? Can I come in?"

"I think it might be food poisoning," I say as I start to get the chills. Dear God, why? Why now? "I ate sushi from some place I'd never been to before."

"How much?"

"A lot." My stomach rolls again, but something twitches lower. Oh God, I want to die. "You can't come in. I don't want you to see this. Maybe you should go."

I wait for a response, but I don't get one for a long time, and it kind of makes me panic, but then I have to throw up again so I concentrate on that. When I'm done—for now—I softly call out her name as I drop back onto the cool floor tile. She doesn't answer. Maybe she left? I mean, it's not like she's getting any action tonight. And she may be so grossed out she'll never want action from me. Ugh.

The thought makes the painful cramping move from my stomach to my chest. I don't want this to end—it hasn't even begun again. This feels deeper than just my dick talking too, which must be because I'm dying—I'm weak. I close my eyes and will this to go away. A few minutes later there's a soft rapping on the bathroom door.

"Jude?" She's still here. "I ran to the corner store and got you some stuff like Gatorade and Pedialyte. It's great for keeping you hydrated when you have a stomach bug. And I'm going to leave a blanket here too, in case you get the chills."

"Thanks!" I manage weakly. God, I want to ask her to come in here and let me lie in her lap, but I don't want her to see this.

"I'm not leaving, either. I'll just be in the other room, so yell if you need anything."

"You don't have to stay..." Oh God, why does talking make me want to barf again?

"I want to. I want to make sure you're okay," she says quietly. "Just yell if you need anything."

I hear her feet pad across the wood floor and the soft click of the bedroom door. I slowly get to my feet, trying not to agitate what's left of the vile food inside me. I will never eat sushi again. I make it to the door and pull it open. There are three Gatorades and a couple Pedialytes and the cashmere cable-knit throw from my bed on the floor in front of the door. I contemplate moving to the bed and lying down, but I have a horrible suspicion I still need to be as close to the toilet as possible. I snatch the blanket and an orange Gatorade and drag them back into the bathroom.

I must have fallen asleep at some point after a few more barfing episodes. It feels like I just blinked, but the bathroom is really dark, and there's nothing but night sky visible outside the bedroom windows.

I place my hands gently on my stomach. My whole body feels like I've gone a few rounds in an MMA cage match, but when I start to sit up there's no tsunami of nausea, so that's a positive sign. I think the room smells horrible. Or maybe that's just me. I get to my feet and reach for my toothbrush off the counter. It feels like it takes me ten minutes to go through the simple task of putting toothpaste on the toothbrush, and then I start moving slowly, like I'm walking in water, into my bedroom as I brush. My Himalayan salt lamp is still glowing, the only light in the room now besides the glow of the alarm clock, which says it's a little before one in the morning.

Zoey showed up at my house a little before seven. She must be gone now. I mean, why would she still be here when I basically almost upchucked on her. Oh my God, I'm a complete moron. Who eats sushi from some place under his sister's shitty apartment in a questionable area of town the night they're going to hang out with their lifelong crush? Me. I'm that idiot. Ugh.

I sniff. Yeah, it isn't the bathroom that stinks, it's definitely me. I want to go out there and see if she's still here, but not smelling like this. I make my way back into the bathroom, gently bending and scooping up the Pedialyte as I pass it. I spit and rinse off my toothbrush, putting it back in the holder before I open the shower door. I turn on all three showerheads, the two on opposite walls and the rain head. Holy shit, I have to play hockey tomorrow. Sure, it's just a charity game, but still. Right now I don't even know how I'm going to make it through this shower without a nap. Jesus.

I drop the only things I'm wearing—my jeans and underwear—to the ground and slowly step inside. The water is deliciously warm and beats the remaining chill from my bones. I lean forward, placing my hands on the wall, and let my head hang. Please may this be over. May I be on the road to recovery. I've only had food poisoning one other time, and it came on as fast and vicious as this but left within hours. I'm hoping this bout has a similar pattern.

My eyes open, and I notice a shadow outside the steamy glass door. Holy shit, is it Zoey? I say her name, and the shadow moves toward the door. "Sorry. I heard water and wanted to make sure you were okay."

Something surges through me, and for the first time in hours it's not bad fish. I push myself off the wall and reach for the shower door, swinging it open. It shouldn't be a great effort, but it leaves me exhausted and my muscles achy. Zoey's standing there in the T-shirt I had left out for her. I honestly never intended for her to wear it, but she looks sexy as fuck in it and nothing else. Well, maybe underwear, but the hem falls too low for me to be certain. She's pulled her hair up in a messy knot, and the tendrils that have escaped have rebelled against the straightening iron she used and have started to curl. Paint splatters—the muted gray I bought for the guest room—are all over her arms like freckles. There's even a smudge of it on her cheek.

"You actually painted the guest room?"

She nods and gives me a mouthwatering self-conscious smile. "I needed something to do while I waited to make sure you didn't die."

I smile. "Thanks."

"Jude..." Her eyes keep sliding down, and her face starts to glow pink, and then she bites her bottom lip. "You're naked."

I glance down. Right. I forgot. And not only am I naked, I am half hard. Oh, well. I look back up. She's got her eyes firmly glued to my cock, and it makes it start to grow even more. And that makes me light-headed, because I seriously don't have the physical capability for this right now. I hate the universe for that. I take a deep breath and reach out my hand. "You look like you need a shower too. Get that paint off you."

She finally looks up at my face. Her head starts to bob in a nod of agreement.

"Get in here."

She doesn't answer with words. Instead, she reaches for the hem of my shirt and in one fluid motion lifts it up and off her body. I was right; she's not wearing anything else under that except the pretty white lace panties I saw earlier. My eyes drift over pale, perfect skin and the swell of her breasts, and my eyes trace the outlines of her perfect pink nipples. My tongue travels along my bottom lip, and then she's moving; without taking off the underwear, she's stepping into the shower next to me. Before she can slip by, I wrap my arms around her and pull her to me.

Every part of her cool, dry skin presses against mine, and I press my lips to the skin just under the ear where her jaw meets her neck. I pull the tender flesh into my mouth. I feel her knees tremble. "Oh God, Jude..."

I hold her to me with one arm around her waist, but I'm so destroyed by this fucking sickness that it's making my bicep ache. Fucking hell. Once again I wish I were dead. It'd be easier to be dead than to have to deny myself her yet another time. My lips ghost hers. "I want you so bad right now...but..."

Her body tenses against mine. "Are you going to be sick again?"

"No. I'm just wrecked, though," I confess.

She slips out of my grip, mostly because I have the grasp of a toddler right now. Ugh. I can do nothing but watch as she steps deeper into the shower and the spray coats her, droplets wetting her hair and then descending down her body. My eyes slide over all that pale, supple skin to the white lace thong, which is soaked. I lean against the far wall of the shower, across from the showerhead she's using, and watch her move. She's beyond beautiful and sexy in a way I never knew was possible. The base of my cock tingles, and I can't help but wrap a hand around it.

She grabs my shampoo and squirts some into her hand. Her eyes watch my hand as I give my dick a slow, firm tug. I see stars, and not in a good way. Well, not totally the good way. I know if I do this—anything sexual—I'll pass out. She steps in front of me, pressing her hips against me, and reaches up and runs her shampoo-covered hands through my hair.

My eyes roll back in my head, following the ripple of pleasure that starts at the base of my skull and rolls down my spine. Oh God, this is amazing. The wet lace from her thong rubs against my thigh. I gently reach out and hook my hands into the sides and begin to push them down her legs. If she notices, she doesn't care. It's probably a bad idea. All it will do is further taunt me, when I know I can't do anything, but, damn, I just want to see her. After all these years and all this time I just want to admire the beauty of her naked body. I push her underwear halfway down her thighs, and then gravity does the rest of the work on the wet fabric. It drops to the gray-and-white mosaic tile floor below.

Her fingers are magic running through my hair, massaging my scalp. It feels amazing, but what feels better is the way my dick keeps rubbing against her stomach. She's naked, right in front of me, and I am too ill to do a damn thing about it. Depeche Mode was right: God really does have a sick sense of humor.

I manage to reach up and softly push her wet hair back from her cheek. She holds the back of my neck and gently pulls me forward, off the wall I'm leaning on, so that I'm under the water. I tip my head back so the shampoo runs back and not in my eyes. The motion pushes my cock harder into her belly, and the water allows it to slip and glide across her skin in a way that makes me shudder with gratification. I reach down and hold her hips so she can't move away and break the contact.

"Jude…"

"Just let me touch you," I breathe raggedly against her neck. "I've waited so damn long to touch you."

The fingers of my left hand trace their way along her hip bone and down, slipping easily in the shampoo lather that must have dropped onto her. She's looking right at me, her eyes delving deep into mine, and I can't look away; even if I wanted to I couldn't. But it's better this way, watching her reaction as my fingers slip between her legs and find their way through a new wetness that isn't caused by the shampoo or the shower. It's caused by the way she feels about me.

I know I shouldn't start something I'm physically unable to finish, but I can't help myself. I let my fingers part her slick folds and I push up into her. She trembles, it ripples through her from her toes all the way up to her face, and it's punctuated with a sound that's some kind of heated mix of a gasp and a pant. Her eyelids flutter, and my mouth parts, and the sound happens again as I move in and out of her and make certain my thumb rubs rhythmically against her clit.

Her fingers grip my shoulders with bruising force, and she moves her hips forward, causing that hard-on of mine to slide against her again in the most incredible way. And then I get light-headed. In that bad way. Fuck. In one slow, steady move I pull back, pressing my back into the wall and groaning as every part of us loses contact.

"It's okay, there'll be another time," she promises in a near-pant as she struggles to regain control. She steps out of the shower, and I reach behind myself and start turning the dials so the water stops. I turn my head so my cheek is against the tile and watch as she grabs a towel and wraps it around her body, tucking it into itself between her boobs like women always do. Then she reaches for another one, unfolds it and hands it to me as I take a wobbly step onto the bath mat.

"Why do we keep barfing the second we decide to have sex?" I ask her. I'm kidding, mostly. I mean, I know why it's happening—the first time it was because she drank too much and this time it's because of my questionable raw fish choices. But why do we keep doing this to ourselves when we could be doing each other instead?

She leads me out to the bedroom, tugging me along by the hand because I'm too frail right now to walk at a normal pace. I grab the Pedialyte off the counter where I left it, and when we get to the bedroom I lower myself gently onto the bed and twist it open. I take a small sip. It has a pretty distinct taste, so I can't pretend it's just water, but luckily the flavor doesn't send my stomach rolling again. I take another sip and lean back against the headboard. One of my legs is still on the floor, the other on the bed, and my fading erection is still big enough to tent the front of my towel.

She walks back into the bathroom and retrieves the shirt she left on the floor and her drenched undies. I watch her, riveted. I've seen a lot of naked women—in a variety of shapes and sizes—and they're all sexy. But something about Zoey presses buttons I didn't even know I had. Just watching her long, bare legs move and the fluffy gray towel rub against her supple thighs makes me feral. Every part of my body twitches and burns with the desire to touch her. Except my stomach. That just aches. Fuck.

"Guess I'm going home commando." She laughs and the sound makes me warm.

"They'll be dry by tomorrow," I reply and motion for her to come to the bed.

She hesitates. "I should probably get going now. I mean…you need rest, and if I'm here I don't see that happening."

"What do you see happening?" I find myself saying. I didn't think this out. The words just came out of my mouth. My eyes slide up her legs and over that damn fluffy towel that blocks far too much and keep moving higher until they lock with hers. "Show me."

"Show you?" she repeats, her tone soft and dripping in awe.

I shift, lean forward and take the hem of the towel between two fingers and give it a little tug. It doesn't fall off, unfortunately, but it inches down over the swell of her breast just a little bit. "Take off this towel, crawl up on this bed, and show me what you want me to do to you."

She's silent, and I can see the idea rolling about in her head like a bowling ball, crashing into her fear, modesty and insecurity and hopefully knocking them down like pins. She takes a tentative step closer to the bed. "Jude."

Just my name. Just a ghost of a sound. Oh God, how I want to make her moan that word. I shift again, and this time I don't take the towel in my fingers, I take it in my fist and pull—hard. It falls from her body, and she doesn't try to stop it. I smile. "Show me where you want me to touch you."

She's got her hands by her sides and she moves them, just the slightest bit, toward her hips. Fingers spread. "You want me to touch your hip."

She nods. Her hand keeps moving, to the center of her abdomen, just under her belly button and above the promised land. It's a battle to keep my eyes up, focused on her fingers. Thankfully, they move downward. I am glued to the gentle way they glide, feather light against her skin. Her index finger slips between her legs and my mouth waters. I don't even realize I'm leaning forward until my stomach starts to ache again.

"You want me to touch your pussy?" I rasp, glancing up. Her eyes are shut, head tilted back just a little. I glance back down; she moves her legs a fraction of an inch farther apart, giving herself better access. I absorb the pace of her hand, the movement of her fingers, learning what she likes so I can replicate it later.

"I want that," she admits in a throaty whisper, and her hand pulls away slowly, her finger comes out slick, and my cock jerks like it's being electrocuted under the towel. I swear it's trying to pull me toward her pussy. She moves another finger down to join the first.

My text alert cuts through the silent apartment.

"Are you fucking kidding me right now?" I roar the words, and it makes her jump, and then she laughs and kind of covers herself with her hands, and I laugh. I should ignore the damn phone, but I always worry a late-night call could be about my dad. Or one of the sorority needs me for something, like bail money. "I have to check that."

She nods, and so I reach for my phone, which I had plugged into a charger earlier in the night before the food poisoning debacle. I swipe open the message.

Hey sexy. I'm thinking we need another round. Can I come over?

It's a number I don't recognize and didn't program into my phone, so there's no name. I don't even want to try to wrack my brain to figure it out, and I certainly can't be bothered to respond. I drop the phone back on the night table but it's too late; she's already pulled my T-shirt over her head. The moment is gone.

"You look hot in my shirt," I tell her with a smile. "But not as hot as you looked out of it."

She opens her mouth to speak, but my phone rings. My phone

fucking rings. I glance at the number on the screen. It's the same one that texted me. Internally I string together every curse word I've ever known. "Take it off again."

Her eyes are on the phone as it rings on my night table. "You should answer that."

"Nah. I'm busy." She finally looks over at me, and I grin. "Trying to get you to take advantage of me." The phone keeps ringing. I contemplate picking up my Himalayan salt lamp and dropping it on the phone. Repeatedly. The only reason I don't is the same reason I don't turn it off, either—my dad. I haven't turned off my phone, or even the ringer, since he was diagnosed.

"Are you feeling better?"

"I was feeling pretty good when I was watching you play with yourself." That was blunt. She flushes, and it's so fucking beautiful.

"Should you get that?"

I don't know if it's the stress of the unknown stalker calling me or just my usual bad luck, but my stomach lurches again. I fight hard to ignore it. "It's a wrong number."

The phone finally stops ringing, but Zoey doesn't stop looking at it, her brow furrowed. "How do you know it's a wrong number? Is it the same person who texted you?"

I nod and repeat, "Wrong number."

My stomach churns, and I start to feel hot. Zoey's brow furrows deeper, and she steps closer, leaning forward to put a hand on my forehead. "You look flushed."

I reach up and grasp her hand by the wrist and move it away from my head. "You're the one making me hot."

She gives me a tight little smile which is followed by a roll of her eyes. "Jude."

I don't know if she was going to add anything after my name, because my stomach twists painfully again, and I realize this food poisoning is far from over. I run into the bathroom and slam the door.

It's only ten barftastic minutes later when I reemerge from the bathroom, after brushing my teeth again and rinsing with mouthwash. My stomach muscles ache, which is quite the achievement for the bad sushi, considering I do a hundred sit-ups daily without breaking a sweat, let alone causing an ache. I walk over to my dresser and pull out a pair of track pants, since I left the towel that was around my waist on the bathroom floor.

Zoey has left the bedroom, probably so she didn't have to hear me puke. I wander out into the apartment and keep wandering till I find her. She's in the guest bedroom, standing in the center admiring the new paint, and she's put her dress back on, damn it. She's facing the wall with the window across from the door, but she hears me come in and glances over her shoulder. "I think it's going to need another coat. You might be able to get away with just touching it up by the window, though."

"Yeah. Whatever." I honestly don't give a shit about the paint. "Why are you dressed?"

"Because it seemed more appropriate," she replies, turning around to face me. "It's late, and you're still very sick, and the last thing you need—"

"Do not say the last thing I need is you naked, because you're the only thing I need and the only thing that kept me from dunking my head in that toilet bowl and ending this misery."

She smiles at that, and it's fucking spectacular. She's so damn breathtaking.

"Are you feeling better?"

"For now. I'm hoping it lasts this time."

There's a knock on my front door. It makes my heart stutter, and then it fills me with dread. I start to say a silent prayer she didn't hear it, but I can tell by the look on her face she did.

"Is someone at the door?"

"No," I lie. There's another, louder, undeniable knock. She lifts an auburn eyebrow and crosses her arms over her chest. "It's probably a Jehovah's Witness or a door-to-door salesman or something."

She laughs at the ridiculousness of my excuse. I'm sure whoever is behind the front door a few feet outside the guest bedroom can probably hear her, she laughs so loud. That means they won't stop knocking and go away.

"A door-to-door salesman?" Zoey repeats and laughs again. "Is that a real problem in this building? Should I put it in the sales listing? Building lives in some kind of sixties vortex so expect encyclopedia and vacuum salesmen?"

I want to kiss the sarcastic look right off her face but there's another fucking knock, and she starts to move—past me and toward the front door. I grab her around the waist, halting her forward movement and pulling her into my torso. I kiss the curve of her neck and whisper urgently, "I don't want you to answer it."

"What if it's Dixie or a teammate in trouble or something?"

"It's no one I know. I swear," I promise her because it's true. Even if it's someone I've seen naked, which it probably is, it's not someone I know.

She hesitates, but when they knock again, she leaves my grip, unlocks and opens the front door. Standing before Zoey is a tall, sultry brunette I recognize from a couple weeks ago. She was the last hookup I had before running into Zoey again. Her name is…

"Who are you?"

"I'm Zoey. And you are?"

"Zoey, this is Kassie." I step past Zoey and into the hall, putting a hand on Kassie's shoulder. "Can you give us a minute?"

"It's Kasey," she snaps and gives me a look of pure, drunken venom. "And don't bother. I'm leaving. At least now I know why you weren't answering your phone."

She storms back toward the elevators. Well, it's actually more like a stomping stumble. I sigh, scrub my face with my hand and wait until Kassie…I mean Kasey is safely inside the elevator heading down to the lobby before I turn to face Zoey. Only when I close the front door and turn around, she's not behind me. I make my way through the apartment and find her in the kitchen grabbing her purse off the kitchen island.

"Please don't go."

She lifts her head, auburn hair tumbling in untamed waves, still damp from the shower, around her shoulders, and it reminds me of how she used to look coming out of the ocean in Maine. I suddenly long for those times when I was younger and innocent and hadn't made a million bad decisions that keep biting me in the ass.

"If you think you need me to stay because you're too sick, I'll stay. On the couch out here." She points to the living room. "But that's the only reason I would consider staying."

"Zoey." I sigh and feel my shoulders sag. "I'm sorry. I wish you hadn't been here for that."

She looks suddenly nervous. Maybe "nervous" isn't the right word. Worried? Whatever the emotion, it's painting her pretty features, causing her to avoid eye contact and tug her bottom lip in between her teeth. It gives her an air of vulnerability, and it kind of destroys me for some reason.

"That happens a lot?"

I could lie to her. I've lied so much to so many women, especially ones I'm trying to get naked, it's my natural instinct. And those lies start to fill my head: *"She's one of Dixie's friends." "She's just a confused fan with a crush." "I think she was looking for my buddy Eddie. He borrowed my guest room last week and brought her over after a night out."*

One of those stories would fly, convincingly, from my lips if this were any other woman besides Zoey. Although they're on the tip of my tongue as I look at her, uttering them feels impossible. So even though it brings a hot wave with it—of humiliation, not illness—I go with the truth. "Yeah. It happens a lot. It's gotten completely out of control since I got back from Toronto this summer, and it's one of the main reasons I need to move."

Silence. Nothing but silence. And then a soft "oh."

"I'm not proud of it, obviously," I blurt out as I fight the heat rising in me. Suddenly all my one-night stands seem pathetic.

"If I wasn't…" She pauses midsentence and bites her lip again. Oh, how I want to do it for her. "It's not my business, but if I wasn't here, would you have let her in?"

"No." The answer flies out of my mouth, and it probably sounds like a lie, like I'm saying what she obviously wants to hear, but it's actually the truth. I lean forward, my forearms flat on the island that's between us, my hands palms down on the cool surface, fingers outstretched like I'm reaching for her, because I kind of am. "I would have answered the text and told her I wasn't interested, and that would have avoided the phone call and the visit."

"Because you're sick."

"No." I shake my head firmly. "Because I don't want her again. I haven't wanted anyone but you since the minute I saw you again."

The words settle between us, shocking both of us if I'm honest. I've made that proclamation before, to one other woman, and when I did it, I thought I meant it, kind of. But this feels different. It sounds different. My tone isn't dripping in false confidence because I'm covering hesitation. And the declaration doesn't feel like a sacrifice in even the slightest way. It's just the simple truth. Holy shit.

She blankets my hand with her own, curling her fingers under my palms and squeezing gently. "Do you need me to stay?"

I shake my head. "No. It's okay. I'm not going to be able to stop harassing you to take your clothes off, but I'm also not going to be able to do anything about it if you do. So it's probably better for both of us if you head home."

Zoey laughs gently and lifts her hand, pulling her cell out of her bag. "I'll call an Uber."

I follow her toward the front of the apartment, grabbing her around the waist and kissing her gently on her cheek before moving to that delectable part where her jaw meets her neck and kissing her more firmly there, reaching up and biting her earlobe softly before pulling back. I'd love to pin her to the back of the door and sear a kiss onto those plump lips, claiming her mouth with my tongue, but that will lead to something I can't finish.

She leaves, but not before caressing my cheek and laying a gentle kiss on my lips that makes me regret agreeing to let her go home. I would love for her to just lie with me and keep those gentle touches coming, because it feels like she's healing me when she does it. I'm that much of a pussy after some bad sushi. Wow.

I grab the last Pedialyte off the kitchen island and head straight for bed. I swallow it down in big gulps, place the empty container on my night table and turn off the salt lamp. But I can't fall asleep just yet. After fifteen minutes I reach for my phone and text her.

Need to know you're home safe.

After a minute she texts back.

Home safe.

Now I can sleep.

17

ZOEY

"This is amazing!" I whisper, and I know I'm grinning like a loon. "He is amazing."

"Yeah. He's all right," Dixie says in a completely unimpressed tone.

I turn to look at her, but it's almost painful to pull my eyes from the ice. Watching Jude skate down there is mesmerizing. Dixie's dressed in a pair of high-waisted black dress pants and a white silk blouse. She's a vision of business casual, but it's kind of completely out of place in the arena, surrounded by boisterous fans wearing hockey jerseys, most with mustard stains from their hot dogs or wet spots from spilled beer. She shrugs her tiny shoulders at me. "I've watched him my whole life. It's gotten boring."

I shake my head and let my eyes find him on the ice again. His friend Duncan has the puck, and he's skating up the ice toward the other team's net. He passes it to Jude, and two guys from the college team skate straight at him. He does this ridiculously cool thing where he looks like he's going to skate to the right but then at the last second he spins to the left, pushing the puck through one of the college guys' open legs, and then skates around him to pick up the puck again. The two college team guys are left in the dust, well, if there were dust on the ice. Then Jude passes to number nineteen, who takes a shot and scores.

"Did you see that? It was insane!" I squeal at Dixie, who still looks unimpressed, as I jump to my feet with the rest of the sold-out crowd and clap wildly. I even let out a "woo-hoo" for good measure.

Dixie laughs. "Holy crap, you're hysterical." She leans in and whispers, "Do you want me to get you his autograph? I have connections."

"Ha-ha," I reply wryly but with a sheepish grin on my face.

Everyone settles back down, and I take my seat again next to Dixie, who never bothered to stand up and only gave her brother and his teammates a half-assed slow clap after that play. She yawns—freaking yawns—and then asks, "So have you found him a new place yet?"

"I have some places to take him to tomorrow afternoon," I tell her. "I was going to take him to three, but I've cut one off the list. It doesn't have a doorman."

Her eyes, which are the exact same cornflower blue as her brother's, fill with intrigue. "Did he ask for a doorman?"

I shake my head and then tuck an errant strand of hair behind my ear. "No, but he definitely needs one." I don't want to tell her why after last night I think he needs a doorman, so I change the subject. "Jude said the party afterward was totally casual. A carnival-type event."

"It is, but I'm technically here as Thunder PR, so this is dressed down for me," Dixie explains and then stands up. "I should go check on the setup in the parking lot, actually. You're okay here? You remember the instructions to get to the friends and family room afterward?"

I nod, and my fingers automatically go to the laminated pass on the Thunder lanyard around my neck. Carla leans forward from her seat behind me. "Don't worry. Tess and I will make sure she doesn't get lost."

"Perfect. See you all later."

"Later, Ms. Wynn," I say and wink.

She laughs and shakes her head as she walks away. Tessa leans forward now too and puts a hand on my shoulder. "You've really never been to a hockey game before?"

My eyes keep following Jude around the ice. "A couple high school ones, but nothing like this. They're all so skilled. Even the college team."

"So you've never seen Jude play before?"

I shake my head. "No, but I hope he invites me again. I love watching him."

"I hope he invites you too," Carla replies. "But if he doesn't, we can score you some extra tickets. If you're still into the sport after things with him end."

The arena seems to get chillier. I hear Tessa spit out Carla's name in an angry whisper. Carla's face is a mask of embarrassment and remorse as I turn to look at them. "I didn't mean…I just meant that if things don't work out. Not that they definitely won't. I mean, Jude could…and you could want to be together for a while. It's not impossible or anything. I was just saying we'd love to still hang out with you, no matter what."

Tessa hisses her best friend's name again and then covers her face with her hands in exasperation. It's sweet Tessa is concerned for me, but Carla's words don't throw me. Jude's been honest about how active his sex life was, and he made it clear last night that I'm his only focus now. "It's okay. I know you're not trying to be mean."

Carla looks instantly grateful. "I'm not. I swear. I just…I'm an idiot."

The final horn, or buzzer or whatever they call it, rings through the building. I turn back to the ice and my eyes instantly find the number eighty-eight as he circles by the bench and then leads his players in a line to shake hands with their opponents, whom they beat 7–5. Tessa and Carla stand and Tessa motions for me to join them. "Let's get downstairs. There's no press scrum or anything, so the boys will be out quickly."

I follow them down the concrete steps and past a security guard into a tunnel on the same level as the ice. This whole thing is so foreign to me, and I feel as out of my comfort zone as Dorothy in Oz. And I'm just about bursting with excitement to see Jude. The tunnel opens up into a wide concrete hallway with doors lining one side. The other women pause and turn to me. Carla smiles brightly, trying to make up for her blunder earlier, I'm sure. "Do you want to come to the locker room with me? We can't normally be in there, but because it's a charity game, this time it's fine. And it's fun to see Duncan all sweaty and panting when I didn't cause it."

Tessa and I both laugh. "Sure. Sounds like fun," I say.

"I'll meet you guys in the lounge," Tessa says and turns to walk the other way down the hall.

"Wait! Aren't you going to come see Levi all sweaty and panty and stuff?" I ask.

Tessa shifts back and forth on her cute little ankle booties, and her fingers twist together anxiously. "No, I shouldn't, but enjoy watching Carla climb all over Duncan."

She smiles, but it seems tight, and then she walks away. I follow Carla and try to mind my own business but I can't. "Is she fighting with Levi or something?"

"No," Carla says but doesn't elaborate.

"I hope not, because I remember she was just getting over some asshole who cheated on her when you guys were starting the shop," I muse as we follow the curve of the hall, and I start to hear boisterous voices. "She seems really happy with Levi."

Carla presses her lips together like she's trying not to say something and then runs a hand through her hair, feathering her bright blue streaks. "Levi and Tessa need to keep their relationship on the down-low right now. Not everyone on the team is in love with their love. It's a long story and not mine to tell, especially when I have a case of foot-in-mouth today."

She gives me another embarrassed smile, and I give her a sympathetic one back. "Please stop worrying about what you said earlier. I know Jude has had a colorful romantic history, to say the least."

Carla opens her mouth like she wants to say something more, but Jude's voice bounces toward us off the cinder block walls, and I lose the ability to do anything other than find him. He's standing about ten feet away in hockey pants and nothing else. His dirty-blond hair looks darker because it's damp with sweat and curling slightly on his forehead. His skin has a glorious sheen to it, and even though I know it's sweat, I have the irrational urge to lick it. Lick him. Oh man, I've got it *bad*.

He's talking to a woman with a handheld recording device pointed at him, and he's gesturing with his hands, one of which is holding a water bottle with the Thunder logo on it. He doesn't look like he spent most of last night with his head in a toilet, which is good. He glances over her shoulder and his eyes land on mine, and a slow, smoldering smile starts to bloom on his already handsome face.

The reporter notices and turns around. Carla takes my hand and pulls me closer, which is when I realize I'd stopped walking and was just standing there gawking. Jude says, "Thanks, Maria, for coming down to cover this. I'm sure I'll see you again when the season starts up."

"But you haven't told me why you picked ALS," Maria tells him.

"It's a debilitating disease that doesn't get nearly the attention it deserves," he replies. It sounds like a canned response, and it doesn't help that he isn't even looking at her; his eyes are still glued to me.

I notice Dixie behind him for the first time, and she's frowning, but she wipes it off her face quickly as Jude moves past Maria toward me. I hear Dixie say, "Come on, Maria, I'll get you some time with Levi Casco now."

"Hey, Sunset." He winks at me. Carla keeps walking toward the dressing room. "I want to hug you, but I've been sweating my ass off."

"I don't mind."

I step close, and he wraps his arms around my waist. His skin is hot and slick, and I'm sure he's making my shirt damp, but I love the way it feels to be in his arms more than I care about my shirt. I feel calm yet electrified at the same time, and most of all I feel safe. Protected not just from bad things that could happen but bad feelings like the ones that have plagued me since my marriage fell apart—you are not worthy, you are broken, you are unlovable.

He pulls away, but not before pressing his lips to my cheek and whispering, "You look amazing."

I pull back and glance down at my jeans, simple white T-shirt and cargo jacket. "The only way I could be more dressed down is if I was in pajamas. I didn't even straighten my hair."

"Yeah, and I love it." He takes my hand in his and gives it a squeeze.

"Is Dixie mad at you?" I can't help but ask.

"Probably. I mean, isn't she always?" he quips and tugs on my hand. "Come meet the guys. The ones who weren't at Darby's barbeque."

As we walk down the hall, I say, "She frowned when you ended your interview with that reporter. I hope it's not because I showed up. I didn't mean to interrupt."

Jude's face grows uncharacteristically serious and he slows. "It's not you. It's me. I didn't tell Maria, the reporter, why I picked ALS as my charity, and it annoys Dixie."

"Oh," I say and stop walking, because he's stopped now too.

He presses his lips together, as if trying not to speak, and then he sighs. "My dad was diagnosed with ALS a couple years ago."

The news consumes me like a dark cloud. "Oh my God, Jude. I am so sorry."

His eyes move down, staring at the concrete between us, and he drops my hand. "I know. Everyone's sorry, which is why I don't talk about it. I don't like people to feel sorry for me."

"Jude, people who care about you will always share your pain and wish you weren't experiencing it," I explain and reach for his hand again. "Your dad is an amazing guy, and so are you, and I wish you both didn't have to experience this."

"Thanks." He pulls me close again. "It sucks."

"Dixie probably wants you to talk about it with the reporter so that others going through it know they're not alone," I explain to him. "And because you have a lot of fans who would give to the charity because they want to do something for you."

"Maybe." He pulls back and gives me a small, sad smile, but then he takes a deep breath and changes the subject. "Let's go meet the guys."

He leads me down the hall and into an open door. The locker room is filled with people, most of them half-naked, sweaty, incredibly built men. I spot Carla right away as she stands in front of a shirtless Duncan. There are a few other women in the room too, standing near guys I assume they're dating or married to. Levi is by himself sitting on a bench shirtless with a bag of ice taped to his shoulder.

"Hey! Listen up!" Jude calls out, and the entire room instantly quiets and turns to him. I feel suddenly and overwhelmingly shy because all of them are staring at me, not him. "This is Zoey. Zoey, this is the Thunder. Most of them are great; just stay away from Eddie."

He points to a tall, dark-haired guy with angular features and a pervy-looking mustache that's perched above a pervier-looking smile. Everyone laughs, even Eddie, who doesn't seem the least bit offended by Jude's statement. In fact, he steps forward, in nothing but his underwear, which are ridiculous black boxers with drawings of cat heads and magnets all over them, and extends his hand. "Eddie Rollins. I hear redheads are real firecrackers."

"Umm…it's auburn," I mutter.

Jude chuckles beside me and leans in, whispering against my ear. "I told you."

"Hey, Zoey." Levi smiles and waves from his position on the bench.

"Are you okay?" I wonder if I missed him getting hit or something on the ice because I couldn't pull my eyes from Jude. "Should I get Tessa?"

He shakes his head, his eyes darting to Jude, and then they come back to me and he smiles again. "Nah. It's an old injury, just not one hundred percent better."

"It's a rough sport. We get banged up a lot," Jude explains and squeezes my hand again. "But after last night, I know you're good at nursing me back to health."

He leans down and kisses me lightly on my temple, and my temperature rises. The entire room is still staring at us, only now most of them look completely bewildered. I feel like an explanation needs to be given, so I blurt out, "He had food poisoning, so I painted his guest room."

Duncan laughs. It's a loud, booming sound that fills the room and, thankfully, draws all the baffled eyeballs to him. He looks down at Carla. "If I eat something rotten, will you finish painting our master bath?"

"Not a chance, buddy," she replies swiftly and gives him a little shove. She turns to the door and motions for me to join her. "Let's go meet up with Tessa before Rollins takes off his pussy-magnet undies."

Jude waves at me as I go. Pussy magnet. I cover my face with my hand and groan. "Oh God."

18

JUDE

The mini carnival wasn't actually that mini. The college we played was supplying a bouncy castle, a kissing booth and a few carnie games like a hoops game and a balloon dart game. Dixie was in charge of the Thunder's contribution. I knew it would be bigger than the college's, but she really went all out. There were bumper cars, a swing ride, a carousel and a spinning ride I would rather die than go on after sushigate. Speaking of food, she'd also arranged for several different food trucks, so people had a choice of everything from corn dogs to cotton candy to lobster rolls to tacos. She even hired professional clowns, who are walking around doing magic tricks and making balloon animals for the kids. I personally find it creepy, but the kids don't.

"This is insane," Zoey says for about the tenth time since I met her in the lounge and brought her out here. All the people who bought tickets to the game were given passes to the carnival in the parking lot.

"I'll be honest with you, I think this is the best one of these we've ever done," I tell her as we weave our way through the crowd and I smile and nod at people as we pass. That is part of the reason people buy tickets to this event, because the players wander around the carnival afterward, and they get to hang out with us. I feel better about this event than I did earlier tonight. Telling Zoey about my dad made me feel happier, which is weird. I hadn't told anyone else except Levi. I also found the reporter after I showered, on my way to the friends and family lounge to pick up Zoey, and told her exactly why I picked ALS for my charity. That had made me feel lighter too.

"I told the reporter about my dad," I say now.

She looks up at me with a reassuring smile and squeezes my hand in hers. "Do you feel good about it?"

"I do. Thanks for giving me a different perspective," I tell her and lean down and kiss the top of her head. I wish I could give her a real kiss, the kind too NC-17 for public. We've been wandering around the carnival for more than an hour. There's still about an hour to go before the event finishes, but all I want to do, all I can think about, is being alone with Zoey.

A couple, both wearing my jersey, with their son, who is also wearing my jersey, stop in front of us, and the dad asks if I'd pose for a picture with the kid. Zoey offers to take it so they can all be in it with me. She's been doing that all night too, not at all uncomfortable or annoyed with the interruptions to our "date." At least I hope she considers it a date, because I do.

After saying good-bye to the family, we make our way down the food truck aisle.

"Are you hungry?" I ask, but she shakes her head.

"You?"

"No. I did manage to eat before the game, and I think I'm over the food poisoning," I explain as we pass the lobster roll truck. "But I'm not going to risk anything and ruin another night with you."

"There's going to be a night with me?"

She is staring up at me, a purely fake look of innocence on her beautiful face. I grin. "I need to finish what you started in my bedroom last night."

She smiles at that. It's warm and inviting and so sexy it makes all the blood in my body move south. Before I can throw her over my shoulder and drag her out of here like the caveman she's somehow awakened in me, Carla and Tessa are standing in front of us. "They're doing an adult jump in the bouncy castle!" Tessa exclaims gleefully and grabs Zoey's hand. "Come with!"

Zoey looks up at me. "Bouncy castle with me?"

"After sushigate? No. Besides, I'm saving my energy for later," I explain, and Carla rolls her eyes.

"Okay. More bounce room for us!" Tessa exclaims, and she starts pulling Zoey away, with Carla in tow.

I look around and find Levi and Duncan taking pictures with two fans by the dart game. I make my way over there as the fans walk away. Duncan grins at me. "Great carnival. Best one we've done so far. I bet you're raising a shit ton of cash for ALS."

"Yeah, Dixie went above and beyond." I nod and I feel a swell of pride. As a sister she can be as annoying as being locked in a dark closet with a mosquito, but Dixie is incredible at her job, and an incredible daughter. I know she went out of her way on this, not only to impress Thunder management but because it's about our dad.

"Let's head over to the beer tent," Duncan suggests, so we start walking toward the tent at the end of the parking lot. "We can grab a cold one and then walk over and watch the girls in that inflatable boob bouncer."

"It's a kids' toy, Darby," Levi reminds him.

"Yeah, but when my girlfriend's in it, it's a boob bouncer," Duncan replies. "Her tits look great when they bounce too. Trust me."

"Oh, I will, because I'm not about to look and find out for myself."

"You can look; just don't touch," Duncan replies as we reach the counter for the beer tent. "What're you boys having? It's on me."

Levi orders a Molson but I shake my head. "Not drinking tonight. Don't want anything to interfere with my plans later."

Both Levi and Duncan look stunned by that statement, and I can't say I blame them. I've never turned down a free beer in my life. And one is not going to affect me, but I have never wanted to be stone-cold sober more in my life. If I'm finally going to be with Zoey I want to be in control of every minute of it so I can sear it into my memory forever. It's going to be great sex. It's going to be sweaty and sexy and dirty, and the only thing I want clouding my brain is an orgasm. Since I seem to have stunned them both into silence, something I should get a medal for, I keep speaking. "And about later tonight, I don't want it to be too much later, so I'm probably going to sneak out of here once Zoey is done bouncing."

They grab their beers as Duncan pays the guy behind the counter.

"So you can get to a little private bounce session?" Duncan asks and starts thrusting his pelvis like some horny middle schooler.

Levi slaps one of his notorious captain's scowls on his face. "There are fans and kids around, you moron."

Duncan immediately stops thrusting his hips but starts wiggling his bushy red eyebrows. I look past Duncan and his spastic eyebrows and over at Levi. "Can you cover for me? If anyone asks why I left, say it's the lingering food poisoning I had last night."

"You really did have food poisoning?" Duncan asks, incredulous.

"Yeah. Spent half the night on my bathroom floor."

He shakes his head and lets it hang in defeat. "You play better than me even when you're poisoned. The universe is cruel."

"I'm better than you. Deal with it." I pat his shoulder condescendingly but with a joking grin. "If I wasn't sick, I would have been able to finally get Zoey naked, and then tonight I wouldn't feel like I'm on the verge of a life-threatening case of blue balls."

Levi smiles at me. It's an honest, real smile, so it looks foreign. He hasn't given me one of those in forever. "Go. I'll cover. There's only about an hour left anyway."

"Thanks," I say, and the smile I give him in return feels way more comfortable than the ones I've been giving him lately.

We're in front of the bouncy castle now, and through the clear plastic wall I see Zoey bouncing away and squealing with laughter with Carla, Tessa and a couple other wives and girlfriends. Her hazel eyes are bright, her normally pale skin pink from exertion and her lips pulled wide in a blissful smile. She sees me and somehow that smile grows, and all of a sudden it's hard to take a deep breath. Shit.

She makes her way to the edge of the bouncy castle, and I walk over to meet her. She drops onto her perky little ass and half slips, half jumps out of the castle, giggling the entire time. I reach up and grab her waist as she does it to make sure she doesn't fall down. Her shirt lifts when she slips off the castle so my hands touch the taut, warm, smooth skin of her waist. Her slender fingers grip my biceps as she lands on her feet smiling, laughing, euphoric. It's as if her mood is contagious. I feel this tidal wave of happiness because of this giggling, breathless, beautiful woman, so without thinking, I press her into the side of the castle and kiss her. Hard. Long. Deep.

My fingers press into the spaces between her delicate ribs as her fingers grip tighter to my arms and the inflatable castle behind her gives just the right amount against her back, allowing me to press my body into hers without crushing her.

"Jude." Levi's quiet but stern tone brings me back to reality.

I break the kiss and the contact, except for our hands, which I link together. She sighs and murmurs, "Oh Mylanta."

It causes a burst of laughter to rumble up from my chest. "You still say that?"

She nods sheepishly, and a wave of nostalgia hits me. It fills me with warmth and makes me feel lighter. The last time I heard her say that, my dad was healthy, and I was young and knew nothing but wanted to learn everything. When my best friend hadn't stabbed me in the back and I wasn't so fucking jaded. "Let's get out of here, so I can do that again with less of an audience and less clothes in the way."

I lead us, with my head down, on a steady march to the part of the parking lot that's still being used for cars. We pass one of the clowns, and he waves a pink balloon dog in our general direction and smiles, and it's creepy as fuck and makes me shudder. Zoey notices and looks at me, her eyebrows pulled together pensively. "Are you scared of clowns?"

"Fuck, yes," I say firmly, and that makes her laugh. God, if I could bottle that sound, I'd make millions selling it as a cure for depression. "One night when I was about ten at the cottage I couldn't sleep. You could see the TV from the top of the stairs if you lay flat on the landing. I used to sneakily watch TV from there every now and then, and this one night my parents were watching *It*. I didn't even mean to watch the whole thing, but I was literally too terrified to move once I saw Pennywise."

"But you're an adult now."

"Have you ever seen a clown that didn't look like a psychopath? Seriously?"

She laughs again and does this crazy cute thing where she kind of hugs my arm, her head tipping to rest on my shoulder briefly, and I have this insane desire to kiss the top of her head, but I fight it because it seems silly.

"That guy is probably a simple suburban dad of two or something," she counters rationally.

"Yeah, dad of two who spends his spare time burying bodies under his kids' swing set in the backyard," I add.

"I guess I should rethink my clown costume for Halloween."

"Yeah, you should. Clowns are deal breakers."

"I wouldn't want to break any deal I might have going with you," she retorts, and her smile has slipped from cheery into flirty.

As soon as we get to my car, I glance back quickly to make sure the clown didn't follow us, and then I pull on her arm, swing her around and reenact the bouncy castle kiss, this time pressing her into the much less forgiving side of my Tesla. She doesn't seem to mind the hardness of the car or of the kiss, which is much more aggressive than the previous one. I am so fucking turned on by her I can barely control myself. I want to strip her bare right here. I've waited over a decade to have her, and now that it's imminent, it feels like it's been two decades.

"You better get your perky ass in my car so I can get us home, or else we're going to be charged with indecent exposure," I warn her. Thankfully, she knows from the growl in my voice that I'm not kidding around, and she quickly slips into the passenger seat as soon as I open the door.

I know we have to go to her place, because I am not risking some unsolicited booty call screwing this up again. I take her hand when we're in the car and keep it laced with mine, resting on the console between us. About five minutes from her place, she realizes where we're going.

"My place?"

I nod. "Is that okay?"

"Yeah, I just wasn't expecting it," she replies and looks suddenly worried. "Adam was supposed to have movers come get his stuff today, but I'm sure they're gone by now."

The slight scowl on her face doesn't fade, and I hate that. Still, I'm not risking uninvited guests at my place, and as soon as I get out of this car I'm putting my phone on silent. Nothing—ab-so-fucking-lutely nothing is going to ruin this for me.

I pull to the curb in front of her place because even the parking gods are helping me get laid tonight. Thanks, universe, if I could high-five you, I would. We both get out, and I reach around and put a hand on her hip as I follow her up the stairs. I'm sure the house is impressive. It's a San Francisco landmark, and between her ex's money and Zoey's good taste, it's probably decorated perfectly, but my goal is to not see a fucking lick of it. All I want to see is Zoey's perfect naked body spread out on a flat surface, and the only view I want to see is the one from between her legs as she comes on my tongue.

She twists the key in the lock, and the door swings open. It's dark, not a light on anywhere, but that doesn't bother me either. I use my grip on her waist to turn her around and even without light to guide me, my lips find hers perfectly. She melts against me and her mouth opens, allowing me to gain access. Her mouth is warm, welcoming and sweet, because she still tastes like the cotton candy I bought her earlier tonight.

I kick the door closed with the heel of my shoe and then turn her around so she's up against it. What is it about her that I have to dry-hump her every chance I get? I can't control myself because I've never felt a rush like the one I get when I'm pushing against her. I can't even begin to imagine how good it's going to be with no clothes. Jesus, it might kill me. I'm willing to take that risk.

She wraps one arm around my neck but reaches out with the other, groping against the wall for the light switch. I grab that searching hand by the wrist and gently but firmly lift it up and pin it between the top of the door she's pressed against and my palm. Then I reach up, take her other arm by the wrist and do the same.

When I drag my lips from her mouth to her neck she whimpers, and I swear it goes straight to my cock, which starts to throb it's so damn hard. "I am going to make it impossible for you to do anything but make that sound."

"Right here?" she whispers back, arching her neck like a good girl so I can have all the access I want. "Against the door?"

"Do you care?" I breathe against her ear before pulling the lobe between my teeth and biting down, hard but quick, and then sucking on it. She shivers that good shiver that has nothing to do with the temperature. "Do you want me so much you'd let me fuck you against the door? On the hall floor? On the stairs?"

"I would've let you fuck me against the bouncy castle if you wanted. In front of everyone. I don't care," she replies, and her wrists wiggle under my hands, trying to break free. I let go, but only because I want to have my own hands free to take off her clothes, not because I don't want her pinned to the door.

I push her jacket off her shoulders, and she steps out of her flats, reaches for the hem of my shirt and yanks it over my head in one quick motion. I toe out of my shoes, kicking them to the side next to where my T-shirt landed. Her lips are latched onto my neck, and her fingertips are grazing their way down my torso to my pants. She starts undoing the button and fly on my jeans, and I slip my hands under her shirt, but I can barely see the beautiful skin I'm revealing, which sucks, so I reach for that light switch and flip it on.

The hallway floods with soft yellow light, and I look up to see an antique light fixture with an old-fashioned Edison bulb. I'll have to admire that later, when my cock isn't throbbing in my pants at a life-long fantasy about to be fulfilled. I focus back on her perfect face, expecting to see lust in her eyes and the pink flush of passion on her high cheekbones, but instead she looks shocked. And not a good kind of shocked, but a devastated kind of shocked. "What's wrong?" I ask and slowly turn around because her eyes are focused over my bare shoulder.

The hall is empty. Not a table, not a picture, nothing. My eyes move to the opening into the living room and there doesn't seem to be anything in that room either. She starts to walk toward the archway into the living room, and I follow behind her. "You said he was going to move out his stuff, right?"

She nods, but it's in slow motion. "We had an itemized list. In the pre-nup. Not everything, but most stuff."

Her short sentences and the confused tone in her voice make me realize that shithead didn't stick to the list of what was his and what was hers. "He took it all."

She nods slowly. I reach for her shoulder, to squeeze it and pull her to me, but she starts walking, moving into the dining room. There's a painting on the wall and nothing else. It's of snow-capped mountains. "That was a birthday gift I bought him. He was supposed to actually take that."

She doesn't sound upset or even angry; she sounds indifferent. Unaffected. But her body language is telling me this whole thing has affected her—greatly. I follow her as she walks into the kitchen. All the cabinet doors and drawers are open, and most are empty, although there are a few random things, like a potato peeler and a cheese grater, which I would love to use on this asshole's balls if I were her. Then I notice the large, round oak table in the nook area and the high-back chairs around it. "He left the table."

"Because I hate that thing," she explains, and there's a hard, pained smile on her face. "Adam picked it out and brought it home and insisted we put it in here, even though it's too big and looks like it belongs in Dracula's castle."

There's a piece of paper in the middle of the table. If that fucker left a nasty note rubbing this in her face, I'll shove it down his throat. She walks over, picks it up, and sighs. "A check for the car he took. So at least there's that."

But then her whole body tenses suddenly, almost violently, and she bolts. Out of the kitchen and running down the hall. She takes the stairs two at a time and I can barely keep up, which says something. By the time I reach the upstairs landing she's already run into a room at the back of the house, flipped on the light and stopped dead just inside the doorway.

I walk up behind her.

"Of course. Of course. Of course," she whispers the words over and over, and when I reach out and touch her shoulder it's nothing but tightly wound, hard and shaking muscle. She's so tense I feel like she'll shatter. And then…she does.

She crumples to the wooden floor of the nearly empty room. There's nothing in here but two nightstands and some bedding on the floor. I walk around her and drop down to my knees in front of her. I try to pull her to my chest in a hug, but she pushes me away. She leans back against the wall next to the door, knees bent and palms pressed into her eyes. "He thought it was a stupid hobby. He made fun of me for it. At first jokingly and then bitingly, but of course he took every single last one of them."

"What?"

"I collect teapots," she explains and sniffs as tears well in her eyes. "He broke one a couple days ago, so I took them all down from the shelf in the kitchen and put them under my bed. He took them."

He's a petty piece of trash. If there was ever any doubt before, it's gone now. "You'll get them back. You'll get everything back. He screwed with a legally binding document."

A tear spills down her cheek. I follow its path, rage swelling inside me with every millimeter it slips. She wipes it away roughly and lets out a heavy, ragged breath. "No. I won't. I can't. I just can't anymore. He can have it all. Fuck him. I'm going to sell this place."

"But you love this place, don't you?"

She sighs. "I really did, but he's ruined it. Every room in this place feels like it's been tarnished now. He won. He ruined it."

She moves to stand, but I stop her when she gets to her knees, pulling myself to my knees in front of her and cupping her face with both my hands. We're kneeling in the corner of the room, face-to-face, and I slowly, purposefully cover her mouth with mine. The kiss is slow, sensual and deliberate. It's also a promise. A promise to take away her pain, to tear down the painful memories and replace them with good ones. I want to do that for her. I *need* to do that for me. She holds on to both my forearms, her fingers wrapped tightly, and pulls her lips from mine just enough to speak. "What are you doing?"

"Taking away the power you're giving him," I tell her, kissing her slowly again before adding, "You're going to make new memories in every single room of this house. With me. Starting tonight."

She hesitates for just a second, pulling back a fraction of an inch when I try to kiss her again. But then she blinks, her grip on my arms gets tighter and she kisses me.

19

ZOEY

Nothing makes sense anymore. I don't know how I got here—twenty-nine years old, divorced, with a shaky new career, in a pillaged house with my teenage crush convincing me to screw the bad memories out of my life. All I know is that as crazy, messed up and completely insane as my life has become, his offer is the only thing that feels right. So I kiss him.

I need something—anything—to feel like a victory. To bring me joy, peace, release, something positive. I need to feel something positive. So I kiss him, and I let him pull me to my feet and walk me over to the pile of bedding Adam left, probably only because he couldn't find enough room in his moving truck to take it, and I let him lay me back on it.

He lies on top of me, and the weight of his muscular body pressing into me sparks an explosion of incredible sensations—warmth on my cheeks and a tingle across my skin and dampness between my legs. He's right, I need to create good memories here, and he can do that. More important, he makes me feel good—and not just physically.

I run my hands into his hair and down his back, but then he pulls back, moving onto his knees between my legs. Then, as he puts his hands under the hem of my shirt and pushes it up, he moves his lips over the newly exposed skin, kissing his way up my torso. I lift a little so he can get my shirt up and over my head, and before I can drop back onto the pile of bedding, he cradles the back of my head in his hand, covers my mouth with his again, and lowers me gently. I feel cared for—worshipped—and then he cups my breasts through my black silk bra and I feel pleasure. Dear God, when was the last time that happened?

I arch my back, pushing myself into his hand. "You like my hands on you?"

"Yes." I sit up and reach out and press both palms to the ripples of muscle creasing his abdomen. "And I want my hands on you too."

He bends down so our lips meet again and reaches behind me to unclasp my bra. As the straps slip down my arms, I finish what I tried to start downstairs and undo his pants. I pull away from his kiss, lean forward and kiss his stomach, just above his belly button, as I push his pants off his hips. He's wearing tight black boxer briefs that feel soft and luxurious under my fingers, but I want them gone too. Before I can push them down, though, Jude is pushing me onto my back again. He makes quick work of my button and fly and then curls his fingers into the waistband of my pants. "Lift those beautiful hips, baby."

I do what he asks, and he tugs my pants off. My underwear goes with them. I don't know if he's noticed, though, because he's busy kissing his way over my lower abdomen, and then he's biting my hip bone, and then…yeah. He notices. His nose tickles the crease of my thigh as his hand moves under my knee to push my leg to the side, putting me on display for him. His lips kiss the soft skin on my inner thigh. My whole body is taut with anticipation. I feel like I'm actually made of glass because I know when he touches me there, when his mouth makes contact with the hot, pulsing spot between my legs, I will shatter.

"I'm scared to taste you because I know I'm never going to want to stop," he tells me, and then a grin flashes over his face. "But then again, I'm all about conquering fears."

His mouth is hot and soft as it covers my pussy, and his tongue lands directly on my clit and I shatter. All my thoughts, my worries, my pain over everything that's happened shatter. I pull air into my lungs and let it out in a soft, wanton moan. This is everything. His mouth between my legs, his tongue sliding over my slit and circling my clit—forget oxygen, food and water—this is all I need to live. I can no longer feel the sheets lumped up under my lower back. All I can feel is his tongue, because the only part of my body that isn't filled with a euphoric numbness is my clit. Every nerve ending in my entire body has migrated to that tiny little space, and it's the most glorious feeling I've ever known.

And then I feel his hand move from where it's holding my thigh open, and he pushes two fingers into me and gives me a firm pump, and I open my eyes. I'm compelled to look at him—to watch what he's doing to me. I've never had that desire before, but I've also never been this undone, and the fact that it's Jude—the perfect boy I never thought I'd see again—using his perfect mouth to make me come feels too unreal, so I need to watch.

His eyes are barely open, hooded with desire and focused downward as he pulls back the slightest bit to watch his fingers move in and out of me. And then our eyes meet, and he presses his mouth to me again and moves his tongue in a slow, flat lick over my clit, and I'm gone. My whole body is being devoured by heat, and everything goes black as my eyes roll back and my back bends and my thighs snap shut like a bear trap, pinning his head as I twist and pant. The orgasm is like nothing I've ever experienced before. It destroys me.

His tongue and fingers keep moving until my legs finally fall away. He thinks it's because I'm done climaxing, but I'm not. The crashing waves of euphoria are still going, I just can't seem to use the muscles in my legs anymore. He pulls back and smiles at me, but I can barely see it because my eyes are fluttering open and closed. He stands up, pulls a condom out of his wallet, then drops his wallet and his pants and underwear. He kicks the discarded garments out of the way and kneels between my legs again as he tears the condom wrapper open and slides it over his long, straight, thick dick.

We're going to do this. Finally.

20

JUDE

I drop forward, my whole body about to pancake hers, but I catch myself with my hands on either side of her head and stop in kind of a push-up position just inches over her beautiful, naked, clearly spent body. That's too bad, because I'm not done with her. Not by a long shot. As much as I enjoyed eating her out—and I honest to God loved it—it isn't my endgame. The moment I longed for at seventeen is right here, mine for the taking with no drunken mishaps or rancid food to stop me from taking it—her—this time.

I lower myself a little closer so my lips can make contact with her cheek. "We're not done making memories, Sunset. Get up."

"I don't think I can," she responds in a weak whisper.

"Wrap your arms and legs around me."

She wraps her arms around my neck and hooks her ankles behind my back. I start to sit up, moving to cradle the back of her head as I do it. When I'm standing, I move to the wall and press her back against it. Her warm naked body is pressed up against every inch of my torso and my shielded dick is twitching against her, begging for more contact and friction, glorious friction. She won't get rug burn this way and besides, I love fucking standing up. It gives me all the control, and I need that right now, because if I let her ride me, I would come in a heartbeat.

I move my hands to her sides, just above her perky ass, cupping a cheek in each hand, and I lift her just a bit, just enough, and she puts her hands on my shoulders to hold herself up as I reach down with one hand to position myself. I swear to God my hand is shaking. And then I feel her heat against my tip.

I push up and use my hand on her ass to lower her at the same time. She's slick and hot and I swear she's still having an orgasm. Her pussy seems to pull me in. She lets out a little gasping mew when my entire length is inside her, and I let out a breath I think I've been holding for a decade. I had plans to take this slow, but my mind and my body aren't on the same page. My mind wants to savor the slow burn, but my body needs to fuck—hard. And I can control my mind but not my body, not tonight.

I pull out and push into her—hard. I do it again, faster. And again harder, but there's something unfulfilling. That loss of contact, even though it's fleeting, as I pull out of her is disappointing. She must feel it too, because her legs tighten around my waist. Her hands bury themselves in my hair. She's trying to get closer, get me closer. I shift, pushing my hips into her, and start to grind. It's better and I grunt out the word "perfect" as I roll and push into her, my rhythm still fast, my motion still hard. She's still pulsing against my cock, and it's crazy good. Better than I imagined, better than I've ever had, and the realization makes me move harder and faster.

The look on her face is better than any look I've ever seen too. I've seen a lot of sex faces. I'm a fucking expert in them. The porn star ones with the big O mouth, the sexy kitten ones with the fluttering lashes and the gasping breaths, but Zoey's expression is better than all of those. Her eyes are glassy and wide, there's a smear of pink brushed across her porcelain skin and her bottom lip is caught under her top teeth. If you looked up bliss in a picture dictionary, you would see Zoey Quinlin.

I squeeze her ass cheeks in my hands, my fingers digging into the supple skin. I'll probably leave marks, and I like that idea. I move a foot back and bend my knees deeper and then grind against her again, twisting my hips a little on the way up. It changes the angle: I'm deeper, and it's somehow tighter. Pleasure sparks in my balls and ribbons of heat roll up my cock. I grit my teeth. I feel the tremor run through her, starting with a quake of her thighs and a tremble in her spine. Her teeth fall away from that lip they were grasping.

Her fingers twist in my hair, and she tugs, bending my neck back, so her lips can find mine, but I can't kiss her, I can't do anything but pant and make some sound I've never heard before, like a growl. She bites my bottom lip instead of kissing me as she moves to my neck, kissing and biting; I grind low and hard with that same twist at the end and another tremor grips her, but this time it reaches her pussy. She's coming again. She moans my name, her mouth against the vein in my neck I know is pulsing with the strain of trying to bite back the explosion building in me. The vibration of the moan against my neck and the rolling pull around my cock make it clear I'm fighting a losing battle, but I manage to grit my teeth and keep going until her tremor turns to a flutter. Then my vision blurs and I turn my head into her neck, let out a roaring groan and crush her into the wall as my flat hand slams the wall above her head and my body quakes with release.

It almost feels like I pass out for a second, like a long blink of a second, but I don't know. I guess I don't, because I'm still standing. Well, standing might be an exaggeration. I'm on my feet but I'm leaning on her body, and the wall, and I know full well if I weren't, I would probably have fallen down.

"Babe?" Her voice is soft and raspy. I wonder if it's a standard post-orgasm thing. I'm going to have to find out by giving her another one or two sometime soon. When I can feel my limbs again. "You're heavy, and I can't take a deep breath."

Oops. "Sorry."

My hands move slowly to her waist, and I bend and pull out just as her legs land on the ground. She wobbles a little and laughs self-consciously, which makes me, without thinking about it, smile and cup the side of her face tenderly. "Those legs of yours are giving me the ultimate compliment."

She laughs again and kind of covers her face with one hand and shoos me with the other. "Bathroom is down that hall on the right if you need to take care of things."

I look down. Right. I head to the bathroom and dispose of the condom, which takes less than a minute, but when I get back to the room she's not there. One of the sheets from the pile on the floor is gone too.

"Zoey?" I call. She doesn't answer, and I feel something tight and cold twist my stomach. Not at all the feeling I want after the best orgasm of my life. "Zoey!" I say it louder this time.

"In here!"

I let out a breath I didn't know I was holding and run a hand through my hair. Where the hell did I think she was going to go? This is her house. It's not like she's going to bolt. I walk down the hall. Her voice came from the other end, the front of the house. I walk into what must be the master. It's the whole front of the house, with a big bay window overlooking the park. It's empty except for a white wrought-iron king-size bed frame. It's intricate and delicate, with rounded edges and the metal curling and swirling in a looping design. It's completely feminine, which I'm guessing means she picked it out, so I'm kind of surprised he left it. After all, he seems to only want to take what she loves.

She's standing in front of the curtainless window wrapped in a sheet with wild red sex hair, which is so damn hot my dick tingles again. I try to ignore it, because I can't see her face, and she might be distraught again. I slowly walk over and kiss one of her exposed shoulders. She keeps her face forward, eyes surveying the empty, dark park below. "He wasn't kidding when he said he loathed my choice of bed frames. But I see he loved the expensive memory foam mattress. Dick."

She's not upset. She doesn't even sound angry. Her tone is resolute. Her mood seems calm and accepting. She finally looks over at me, and I can tell she's tired, even before she stifles a yawn. I wrap an arm around her. I'm honestly almost ready for round two, but she looks exhausted emotionally and physically, so I'll have to wait. She curls into my chest, resting her head near my collarbone. "You think he left a sleeping surface anywhere?"

"No. Dick." She yawns again.

He did leave the long, fairly thick seat cushion on the window seat and the oversize throw pillows. There's another window like this downstairs, and he probably left those cushions too. I lay the big cushion out on the floor just next to the bed frame and then grab the other pillows and lay them out too. "I'll be right back."

"Where are you going buck naked?"

I smile. "Don't worry, I'm not leaving the house."

I go downstairs. I was right: the prick did leave those cushions too. I carry them back upstairs. When I walk back into the room, I find her fast asleep on the long cushion, a throw pillow under her head. The sheet that had been wrapped around her is now spread out on top of her. I watch her for a minute, her breathing deep and even, her eyelashes fluttering just a little bit. I could go. Normally I would. I mean, I got what I came for; why the hell should I sleep on the floor?

I carefully place the long cushion I'm carrying down beside her. I take a deep breath, stretch and bend down to grab a throw pillow, then as softly as possible I lower myself onto the cushion beside her. I carefully lift the sheet over me, tuck my arm under the pillow, and curl up facing her. After a minute I reach out and push a piece of her hair off her cheek. She shifts, moving closer, her head curled toward her chest. I lean over and give her that kiss on the top of her head I've been craving.

21

ZOEY

I point to the herringbone marble tile backsplash. "See the detail? It's modern with a classic twist. Very high-end."

He lifts my hair off my neck.

"The appliances are all Viking. Best of the best."

His lips are on my neck just above my first vertebra.

I take a big step forward, hoping to break the contact before it breaks my willpower.

"Let's take a look at the first bedroom. All three have attached baths."

I manage to make it into the guest bedroom before he can touch me again. But now he's got a hand around my waist as he steps into the room and stands beside me. Thank God this is Marti's listing and she's letting me show it on my own. Jude is the polar opposite of professional right now, and there's no way Marti wouldn't notice if she were here. And she wouldn't miss the delighted look I'm having trouble keeping off my face either.

I point to the barn door on a track that separates the bath from the bedroom. "See, another classic nod, but if you step into the bathroom, you'll see the modern…"

His hand slips to my ass and stays there. Right next to the area that's bruising a little from the way he gripped it last night. Luckily, before I succumb to the flush that wants to explode like fireworks all over my face, his hand moves lower and I think he's going to drop it away from me completely, but then his fingers find the hem of my skirt.

I step away, moving into the bathroom. I reach up and move my hair over my shoulder, because I'm suddenly, but not shockingly, hot. "Here they used the same black and white…marble…as the kitchen…"

He's right behind me, his fingers ghosting up my sides. It's a dual attack because his mouth is ghosting my exposed neck. Before I can stop myself my head tilts, giving him better access, and my eyes close. "Is the shower in the master big enough to fuck in?"

"What?"

"I like to fuck in the shower. And the tub. And…"

His hands have moved up the front of my shirtdress, and he's now fully cupping my breasts. My nipples hardening also act as my wake-up call. Once again I move away from him. "All the showers are very big. See?" I point to the oversize glassed-in one in the corner and move closer to the window. "Jude, this is work. I'm working. For you. I should be professional."

"Yes, you should," he agrees, which I find odd, but then he grins that big, infectious, boyishly charming grin of his. "But you're working for me, like you said, and I don't want you professional. I want you naked and coming on my cock."

"Jude!" I flush. I swear even my toes are pink. I have to grab the counter beside me for support because a full-body flush apparently takes a lot out of a girl.

"Come on. Test the water pressure with me," he asks, stepping into my personal space again. I need to find the strength to stop him. If only I knew where the hell I put it…it's around here some-where…His hand goes under my chin and lifts it. Our lips touch, and I'm the one who pushes up into him, opening my mouth and granting him access.

I know it's inappropriate, but it's so damn good. He's great at kissing. I knew that when I was eighteen. He was rough then, but in a fumbling way, not a domineering one. And everything was so urgent then, which I assumed came from his inexperience and his rush to be experienced. Still, it was a turn-on. Someone so enthusiastic and into it. Kissing didn't feel like a forced march with seventeen-year-old Jude the way it did with other boys that age who saw it as their one clear path to some-thing more. Kissing twenty-eight-year-old Jude feels the same way; only now it will most certainly lead to more, and we both know it—and want it. But it can't happen here in this house with my hand on a counter next to a stranger's toothbrush.

"Jude. God, as much as I would love to get into another shower with you, it can't be this one," I explain as I gulp down air after that breathtaking kiss. "I could get fired."

"Even if I buy it?" Jude questions. "Like a you broke it, you buy it policy. You fuck in it, you buy it?"

I laugh, and his trademark grin grows. "Do you even like the place? You haven't even seen the other bedroom or the master."

"I don't like it. I know that already," he replies calmly, and I'm a little taken aback. "It's stunning. It's the right neighborhood, and it's got great views."

"And enough space. Three bedrooms."

He nods. "Yeah, but it's a condo."

"With a doorman."

"I was hoping for a house. A row house or a townhouse or something."

"They don't have doormen."

"I don't care about the doorman. It isn't on my must-have list."

"If you had a doorman now, you probably wouldn't have to be moving," I explain. "You just put them on a list and a doorman doesn't let them in."

"Who on a list? The sorority?"

I laugh and run a hand over the marble countertop. I can't believe he doesn't want this place. "Not your sisters. The clingers."

He looks like he's been slapped, he's that startled. The boyish smirk drops like a lead balloon. I know he's stunned, but I can't tell if he's angry or otherwise upset by me bringing up the fact that he has girls come back for seconds, like he's an all-you-can-eat buffet.

"Are you only showing me listings with doormen today?"

I nod.

"So that my...what did you call them? Clingers? Won't show up unannounced?" I still can't read his face, which is really stressing me out, because Jude is usually an open book.

"Yes." Like I usually do when I feel like somehow I stuck my foot in my mouth, I start to explain even more. So I can add an ankle in with the foot. Why not? "I realize that if you move, you're not going to give those previous girls a forwarding address, so you're safe there. But I mean future women you take home could do the same thing, and then you're moving again. And I know you can afford it, but we both know it's still a huge hassle."

"Future women?" He looks like he's been slapped again, and I want to think it's a good thing. Because I want him to be horrified by the thought of any other women besides me. I really, really want that, because I still have endorphins pumping through my system from the best orgasm of my existence. But I'm still looking for a doorman building because some deeply rooted insecure and broken part of me believes I was just another number to Jude, who clearly got so good at giving orgasms by handing them out to thousands like samples at Costco.

He crosses his arms over his very wide chest and the shoulders of his short-sleeved button-down stretch at the seams. Mylanta, if he busts out of that shirt, my restraint is going to rip like that fabric. "So you think I'm going to bring random women home to my new place for sex. Because you think I'm going to continue to have one-night stands?"

"I'm not…saying I…know…you're going to…do that," I sputter, the words coming out with oddly spaced gaps of silence in between them, like English is suddenly not my first language. "A great Realtor picks up on needs a client doesn't even see themselves and satisfies them."

I just quoted a seminar from a Realtor conference in San Diego I attended three months ago. Seriously? But at least it came out of my mouth in one fluid sentence, so I decide to go with it. "Like you need a central vacuum system. Because you're a neat freak. Probably the neatest bachelor I've ever seen, and your current place doesn't have that, so I'm also looking for a unit that has that."

I point to the vacuum outlet on the wall by the edge of the vanity.

"I have a Roomba that runs by itself every day at three and a maid service that comes two days a week," he explains, arms still crossed and no sign of that grin of his anywhere on his kissable mouth. "Now let's get back to the one-night stand thing."

"Do we have to?" I mutter.

"I'm just trying to figure out if you're doing this because it doesn't matter to you if I keep having one-night stands or if you just assume it matters to me that I keep having one-night stands," he says, and he lets one arm fall to his side while he reaches up and rubs the back of his neck with the other.

"What do you think?"

"I think I haven't thought about it," he replies, dropping both hands to his sides now and looking at me longingly. "Because all I've been able to think about is how good it felt to finally have you and how much I think I need to have you again."

"Sweet snickerdoodle," I whisper.

"Zoey? Jude?" Marti calls out, and I actually jump. "Are you still here?"

"Oh crap," I say, panicked like she's about to catch us doing something we shouldn't be doing. Jude finally flashes that smile of his, and reaches out and grabs my hand.

"Relax. We're clothed." He pauses, then calls out, "In here!"

I hear clicking—heels on the hardwood—and then Marti pops into view. She's in what she calls her lucky red wrap dress because she always sells a house when she wears it. She smiles brightly, but after a second on me, her eyes go straight to Jude. "Hey! Checking out one of the guest suites, huh? Isn't it huge? And the other guest suite is the same size with a matching bathroom, which you probably already know. Are you in love? You must be in love."

"What?" He spits the word out like he choked on it, and he looks like he was slapped again.

"In love with the condo?" she repeats. "Are you going to make an offer? No pressure, but I am bringing another client through in about twenty minutes. That's why I'm here. Of course I would love to sell it to you. Make your friend Zoey her first big commission."

Jude gives her his grin, and I can see her basking in the full charming, sexy glow of it, and I don't like it. I'm jealous now. Great. Because that's an incredibly attractive quality.

"It's an amazing place," Jude tells her. "Incredible. But I definitely want to see a few more places, since this is only our first tour of the day. If I lose out, then it wasn't meant to be."

"That's understandable." Marti nods; the smile stays firmly on her face. She really wants to help me sell him one of her places, though. She sends me three of her listings a day trying to get me to show them to him.

"I'm taking him to a new-build townhouse now," I say, even though I'm going to have to dig the info up in my email because I'd actually knocked it off this list because it didn't have a doorman. Jude smiles. "It's in Pacific Heights."

"No doorman?"

"No doorman." I can't help but smile.

Marti's eyes zip back and forth between the two of us. Jude leans in and gives Marti a hug, which she revels in, but I feel that green-eyed monster start to grow inside me again. What the hell? I used to watch Adam hug women all the time and never thought twice about it. Of course now he's impregnated his assistant…but still. Jude wouldn't do that. He just has to move to avoid women hunting him down for his magical orgasm powers. Ugh.

Jude starts to the door. I hug Marti too. She gives me a perplexed smile and whispers, "What's the thing about a doorman, is it good or bad?"

"I don't know yet," I reply honestly, which of course leaves her looking even more baffled.

I find the listing in my email and give him the address. Jude punches it into his navigation while I quickly call the agent and ask if we can squeeze in a tour. He says it's not a problem and urges us to tour all four available units. There's a passcode lock on each door and he texts me the passes. Jude doesn't talk much on the way there, and he certainly doesn't bring up the doorman conversation, which wasn't about doormen at all. But he does keep his hand on my knee when it's not needed for driving, so I have no complaints right now.

There's a war being waged between my heart and my head, between what I should feel and what I do feel. My brain says I'm freshly divorced with a barren house that I can barely afford to keep or refurnish, a potentially barren uterus and a career that needs to be kick-started. My heart keeps reliving memories of last night, and it feels his hand on my knee and my gently bruised butt and the sensations fill my stomach with butterflies and they're carrying hope on their wings. Light, effervescent hope that this—me and Jude—is something big and beautiful and right.

I need to know exactly why he doesn't want the doorman. Is it because he doesn't want to bring randoms home anymore, because he intends on only bruising my ass and only giving me top-tier orgasms? Or is it because he's smartened up and will be having his one-night stands somewhere other than his house? I need to know to crush the butterflies and the hope they're carrying, which is exactly why I don't bring it up again right now. Because I'm scared to know the answer.

22

JUDE

"This place is more my style," I tell her as we climb the staircase with the reclaimed oak stairs and the vintage banister to the second floor.

"Then I'm glad I changed my mind and showed it to you," Zoey replies. I'm walking up the stairs behind her, which was a planned move. I wanted to admire her ass. She turns to smile at me and catches me, but she doesn't call me out.

"The views are incredible too," I say, and she laughs.

The second floor has two bedrooms with a Jack and Jill bathroom and a den. She motions for me to go ahead of her. "Go on and check them out."

I walk by her, letting my fingers graze her waist as I pass, and as I turn into the first bedroom, she adds, "You're right, it's a great view."

I grin. I love when she's sassy. The bedrooms are fine, but I know having my sisters share a bathroom when they visit is a problem now. I was hoping for three full baths so they will stay out of mine. Zoey's phone starts to ring, and I watch her dig it out of her purse. "It's a work call. Sorry. Go up to the third floor. The whole thing is a master suite, and the views are incredible. The real views."

She smiles and says her name into the phone. I walk to the end of the hall and up the staircase there. She's right, the master suite is amazing. I walk into the master bath. It's unreal. The shower is huge but has a floor-to-ceiling window in it, which is weird to me. It showers the bathroom in light, but everyone on the street below can watch you shower. I step into the stall.

"Yes!" I hear her cheer loudly.

"What?" I call back.

"This couple I was wooing into hiring me that I thought was going with someone else changed their mind," she explains, her voice getting closer with every word. She appears in the bathroom doorway; her eyes sweep the room until she finds me through the glass of the shower. "They're going to sign with me!"

"That's awesome!" I feel a huge wave of genuine joy. I feel her happiness like it's my own.

She seems to finally absorb the fact that I'm standing in the shower. "What are you doing in there?"

"Trying to figure out why they'd put a window in it."

"It's one-way glass. So you can see out but no one can see in," she explains, and glances down at her phone. She's doing something, maybe emailing her new client. "The theme of this development is bringing the outdoors in. That's why there's so many windows and skylights."

I find something really kinky about the idea of being stark naked and watching people on the street below walk by. I put my hand on the front of my pants. "So it's brand-new, right? No one has lived here? All the furniture and stuff is because it's staged?"

I have this totally amazing idea blooming in my brain. Actually, it didn't start in my brain. She nods without looking up from her phone screen and starts to walk into the bedroom. "Yeah. A few people have moved into the complex, but a lot of the units are still empty, like this one, so if you want it, we could have some negotiating power. They want to fill them up sooner rather than later."

"This shower and the master are huge selling points," I call out as I undo my pants and reach up to pull my shirt over my head. "But overall, I don't think this is the place."

"Really? Because it's in a great area, with almost double your current space and no door—" She stops midsentence, and I'm assuming it's because she's staring at my bare ass. I'm facing the window, watching a girl jog by below and a couple stroll the other direction holding lattes.

"Jude!"

"I just want to test it out. I've never people-watched while I shower." I grin at her over my shoulder while I palm my erection. "The architect has one hell of a fetish, I'm thinking."

"Mother of all things holy, put your clothes back on!"

"Why?" I ask casually and turn to face her, hand still on my growing dick. "It's not like my dick is on display for anyone who walks by. Although it's too bad this isn't regular glass. My dick is worth being put on display."

Her eyes drop. I curl my fingers and give myself a slow tug. "Jude Braddock, you are crazy."

"What? You don't think it's a good-looking dick?" I ask and throw in a mock tone of indignation for effect. "I've seen some dick in my time, thanks to locker rooms, and let me tell you, this one is downright pretty. Long; thick; perfect head."

Her eyebrows raise, but her eyes don't, and I can feel her stare like a warm caress across my shaft. I am so going to fuck her in here. She really doesn't have a choice. She opens the glass door and doesn't tell me to get out, which is a good sign she's not going to need much more convincing.

"It's a very nice dick," she agrees softly. Her eyes rise to mine. "It does very good things."

She reaches toward it, and I move my hand away. She replaces it with her own. Her fingers are soft and warm, and her grip is firm. A ripple of pleasure rolls up from my balls and through my shaft. I make a noise in the back of my throat. Jesus, her hand feels almost as amazing as her pussy. I grab the back of her head and pull her lips to mine. As my tongue claims her mouth, my hand makes its way under the hem of her dress to claim something else. I brush the silk fabric of her underwear between her legs and it's damp.

"Let me fuck you here," I beg against her mouth. "Against the window."

"It's unprofessional," she murmurs, but she's letting me tug her underwear off. They fall to the floor. I wrap an arm around her tiny waist to guide her and start walking, moving us both toward the window.

She manages to step out of her underwear without tripping. "A good Realtor picks up on a client's needs and satisfies them." I throw her words from earlier back at her because I'm fucking brilliant when I'm horny. Once her back is up against the window, I go back to the hem of her dress and start lifting it up. It's one of those loose-fitting deals, so luckily there are no zippers or buttons to slow me down, and I can just lift it up and off her body. Only she's blocking me with her arms when I get the dress up to her chest. Our eyes meet. "Isn't it professional to satisfy my needs?"

Her response is to bite her bottom lip and lift her arms. The dress is on the tile floor next to my clothes in seconds. I spin her so she's facing the window. It's quick, and my fingers slide into her pussy before she catches her balance. Her palms land with a smack on the glass and she whimpers. "If I buy this place, I am going to fuck you here every single night, while you watch unsuspecting strangers walk by."

She turns her head and drops her cheek to the glass and lets out a pant as my thumb finds her clit and my fingers move quicker and harder. She tilts her hips and starts grinding herself against my hand. I push her hair over her shoulder and kiss the back of her neck, starting at the hairline and moving all the way down to her shoulder, where I give her a gentle bite, which causes another whimper. I keep kissing, dropping lower and lower, kissing her back, her side, the curve of her waist, one hand still playing with her and the other reaching for the condom in the back pocket of my jeans. I find the condom just as my lips reach her ass, and I bite down, much harder than I did on her shoulder, and my fingers curl inside her, and she arches her back and moans. Her pussy quivers right along with her knees, and I know she's about to come. I still my hand, and she makes a disgruntled sound. I smile as I tear the corner of the condom package open with my teeth.

Rolling it on with one hand while I raise myself to standing again, I move my hand from her center to her hip and pull her pelvis back so she's bending a little more at the waist. I bend my knees a little and rub my tip across her opening. "I want my dick to do those very nice things you mentioned earlier."

She reaches back for my hip, trying to push me into her, so I give her what she wants and in one strong, fluid thrust, I bury myself inside her.

"Holyfuckinghell."

I'd smile at the fact that I just made her swear, but I'm too busy trying to keep my eyes from rolling back in my head. She feels just as unbelievable as she did the first time. In fact at this angle, from behind, she feels even more fucking magical than the first time.

My pace is punishing—fast and hard—but she is doing the opposite of complaining, arching her back and pushing her ass into every thrust. I thought I would get a rush out of watching the people walk by while I fucked her, but I can't seem to take my eyes off her in nothing but heels and a bra bent over in front of me long enough to look out the damn window. Although I do like the way the sun is shining in on us, making her hair glow like fire and her skin gleam like porcelain, except where my fingers from last night have left light bluish streaks on her. Fuck, I hope that doesn't hurt too much.

I let go of her hip with my left hand and snake it lower. As soon as I find her clit she moans again. Honest to God, that sound moves my orgasm into the launch position. I grit my teeth. She moves a hand off the window and palms her own breast through her bra. I start moving in her harder but with shorter thrusts, flicking my hips at the end of each one.

She mews like a cat in heat, and my orgasm prepares for launch. Fuck. I pant with the effort it takes to hold off. It's my favorite part of sex, the last moments where my mind fights off the pleasure my body is compelled to release. The tingle at the base of my cock, the warmth that claws through my veins, the pulse in my balls stronger than my heartbeat. Those feelings usually only begin a good ten minutes into sex. With Zoey, they start the minute my cock touches her pussy, so the fight is long and glorious.

She shoves her bra down a bit and she's got her hand on her exposed breast, her fingers playing with her nipple. My hand on her hip gets jealous and slides up her body. I shove her hand away and take the breast for myself.

"Pinch my nipple," she begs breathlessly.

I honor her request, and at the same time I thrust into her, and my other hand pinches her clit.

She lets out a high-pitched moan, and her back arches before her whole body quakes. The feeling of her breaking apart around me is all it takes to light my own fuse, and I explode, letting out my own strangled moan. Just like last time, there's a moment where my vision blurs and my joints turn to Jell-O, and I barely manage to stay upright.

I pull out of her, even though I want to stay longer, and reach out for her arm, guiding us both over to sit on the bench at the end of the shower stall. She is about to sit beside me, but I tug her down onto my thighs. I wrap my arms around her, and she dips her head, and we kiss a shaky, slow kiss. "I think we need to do this in a bed next time as a safety precaution, because one of these days I'm going to pass out."

"Me too," she admits and laughs breathlessly.

She drops her head onto my shoulder. "We need to get dressed before another agent brings someone in."

She turns and kisses me again, then climbs off me and retrieves her dress and underwear. I pull off the condom and look around. I can't very well dump it in the trash here, and there's no Kleenex or toilet paper. I guess that wasn't part of the staging. Damn.

She's got her dress on again and is shimmying back into her undies when she looks over at me and seems to understand my predicament. She steps out of the shower and walks over to the counter where she put her purse earlier. She digs around and hands me a Kleenex. I wrap the tied condom in it and she takes it from me and puts it in her bag. "A good Realtor hides the evidence too."

"Is that so?" I laugh as I grab my pants and pull them on.

"It's in the training manual," she kids.

I pull my shirt on and step out of the shower. "I'm beginning to realize my last Realtor was terrible."

As we start to make our way out of the house, I take her hand in mine. "So are you thinking of making an offer?"

"It's definitely on the maybe list," I reply. "But I'd love to see something with three baths."

"I can line up some more places in a couple of days," she responds. "Although I don't think there's another listing with that kind of shower."

"That's okay. We're moving to beds for safety reasons anyway, remember?" I wink at her. "But no doormen."

The serene, happy look on her face falters a little. She lets go of my hand and opens the front door, stepping out onto the stoop. I follow her and wait as she closes it and makes sure it's locked. As we walk back to the car at the end of the block, I try to take her hand again, but she pulls away. Sighing loudly, she turns and looks up at me. "So why no doorman?"

I don't know why my heart jumps like it just got a shot of adrenaline. I knew when I brought it up again it would bring us back to this awkward conversation. Still, I'm suddenly filled with nervous butterflies. "Because you think I need one to keep uninvited hookups away."

"Don't you think you're going to need the help?"

I grab her around the waist and pull her to me in the middle of the sidewalk. I wonder if she can feel the way my heart seems to be running around my chest like a scared dog. "All I think, all I can think about, is how fucking much I love being with you and only you. I don't see that stopping anytime soon."

"So no doorman required."

"Definitely not."

Her eyes drop to my chest, but she's smiling. I do that stupid thing where I kiss the top of her head again. I told myself I wasn't even going to try to make a commitment again, and I'm not trying. It just happened with no effort at all. But it still terrifies me, because I don't know if I'll be able to keep from breaking her heart.

23

ZOEY

"That's the last of it, unfortunately," Morgan tells me as he and his husband, Ned, drop the couch in the middle of the living room with a thud. He stands and wipes at his brow dramatically before turning and tipping backward onto it.

"I wish we had more stuff to give you," Ned says with a sympathetic smile. "And that the stuff we had wasn't so dated."

The couch my overdramatic brother is stretched out on is an overstuffed clunky thing in a navy-blue and forest-green plaid fabric. Definitely not my style, but it's clean and free. It was my brother's in his bachelor apartment and it somehow migrated to Ned's parents' basement when the guys moved in together a few years ago. "Are you sure your dad doesn't need it?"

Ned shakes his head. "You're probably saving my parents' marriage. He would go down to the basement to work on projects in his workshop and take three-hour naps on this thing instead. My mom has been waiting months for him to fix the loose shelf on her spice rack."

I smile. "Okay, well, thanks for letting me have it. And the little bistro set for my kitchen."

"I'm parched!" Morgan announces.

"I've got lemonade or beer in the fridge; come and pick your poison," I say and wave him toward the kitchen as I start to walk. Ned reaches down and pulls Morgan off the couch, giving him a quick kiss as he gets to his feet.

In the kitchen I open the fridge. "So what'll it be?"

"Beer for me," Ned responds, and I reach for a Coors Light.

"Me too, but I'm actually more thirsty for information," Morgan says. I toss him a can of beer, and he catches and opens it. "What is going on with our hockey bad boy?"

I laugh. "He's ours, is he?"

"I crushed on him too, don't forget."

"Who are we talking about?" Ned asks.

"His name is Jude Braddock. He plays for the Thunder," I explain.

Ned turns to my brother and raises his eyebrow. "You have a crush on a hockey player?"

Morgan shrugs. "I did when we were kids. But don't worry. He's straight and totally into Zoey."

I take a sip of my beer, trying to use the can to cover my smug smile, but they both catch it. Morgan grins and Ned laughs. "That face says something has progressed since we last talked about him. Something good."

"We've…we're involved," I say, trying to sound casual, but I am not at all casual. Since the inappropriate and unprofessional but totally worth it sex in the newly constructed townhouse, we've seen each other every day. I've been sleeping at his house almost every night, and the one night I stayed here, on the air mattress I bought, he stayed with me. The booty call texts from other women only happened once so far. Well, once since the initial sushi poisoning night. Last night at a little after midnight. He scooped the phone off the night table and ran into the bathroom to answer it. I heard him whispering a firm but polite turn-down, and then he crawled back into bed and spooned me.

"Is the sex good? Oh my God, I bet the sex is mind-blowing." Morgan sighs and Ned rolls his eyes. He knows he's married to a pervy Nosy Nelly, and I think it amuses him more than anything.

"It's incredible," I admit.

"Yes!" Morgan shouts and pounds a fist into the air. Mylanta, he's a dork. "Is he wild? I bet he's wild and kinky. Give me a detail. Nothing that reveals anything about your girl parts but something about his boy parts."

"No!"

"She's no fun," Morgan tells Ned. "I thought it was Adam making her that way, but clearly she's lost her edge forever. I bet it's all boring and vanilla because of her. Poor Jude is probably wasting his talents."

"You're a dick," I tell him, not really offended by his insults. Well, not totally. But enough that it makes me want to prove him wrong, which I realize is what he's going for. "We had sex in front of a window in an empty house I was showing him."

Morgan fist-pumps again, and Ned's jaw hits the floor. "You did that?!" Ned looks stunned.

I cover my face with a hand. "I know. It's completely insane and wrong, but it's not my fault. He has a way of sucking the sanity right out of me."

"Like a vampire," Morgan adds helpfully. "He's a sexual vampire!"

"There are gay ones too. I dated one. His name was Enrique," Ned explains, and Morgan gives him a look, but Ned winks at him and turns back to me. "So are you two officially dating or just sucking the sanity out of each other? Not judging, just asking."

"I feel like it's too soon to say we're boyfriend and girlfriend," I tell him as I lean back against the counter. "I mean, I've been divorced about sixty seconds and Jude's been back in my life about five minutes. It's crazy to think this is serious already."

Morgan looks up at Ned with a "bullshit" look, and Ned looks up and gives the same look to me. "Are you telling us that or convincing yourself?"

I shrug and take another sip of beer.

Morgan puts his beer down on the table he just brought over and stands up and walks over to me. He grabs both my shoulders and gives me a little shake until I take my eyes off my can of beer and look at him. "Fuck timing. It really isn't everything."

"Morgan has a point, Zoey," Ned chimes in. "I mean, you did the sane thing already with Adam. You dated for a reasonable amount of time, you were engaged at an appropriate age, you got married after an acceptable period of time. And no matter how right the timing was on that, the relationship itself wasn't."

"True." I smile. "I'm not seeing anyone else and don't intend to, so I guess he's my boyfriend."

"Well, you should make that clear to him," Ned advises. "Because boys like him have girls throwing their bits at them everyplace they go. He sounds like he really likes you, but if he doesn't know the rules, he might not follow them."

I feel a little flutter of anxiety at that comment. Ned isn't wrong. I haven't dated in a long time, but when I did, I was a total guy about it. I could have sex and not at all believe it automatically meant some kind of commitment. And Jude's late-night drop-ins, phone calls and texts prove he definitely has girl bits being hurled his way.

"I'll have the talk with him when I see him again." I groan. "Ugh, it feels so high school but I will."

"So when will you be having sex with him again?" Morgan asks and clears his throat. "I mean see him again?"

"Tomorrow afternoon I'm taking him to see some more houses, and then he has a preseason game I'm going to," I explain. "Tonight I'm actually having a girls' night with Dixie."

"Has she asked about me?" Morgan wants to know and turns to Ned. "She had such a crush on me."

"Yes. Should I break the news to her?"

"Wait until she's had a little wine to soften the blow."

The doorbell rings. We all stare at each other, startled. I'm not expecting anyone, so I'm perplexed. I put my beer down and start out of the kitchen. Morgan follows, muttering, "If it's Adam the ass nugget coming to steal what little he left behind, I'm going to dick punch him."

"I'm sure it's not Adam." *Please may it not be Adam.*

I get to the front door and swing it open. There's a guy in a crisp blue shirt with a company name stitched on the pocket holding a clipboard. I look past him and see another guy opening the back of a big truck. "Ms. Quinlin?"

I nod.

He turns the clipboard toward me. "We're here with your new mattress set."

"I didn't order a new mattress set." I turn to my brother and Ned, but they look as confused as I am. I haven't told my parents about the furniture Adam took because it would upset them more than this whole ordeal already has, and even if I did, they don't have the money to buy me a new one. Especially not from this high-end store.

He points with the tip of the pen to a name under billing information. "Mr. Braddock purchased the set. This is the address he gave for delivery."

"Sweet snickerdoodle!" I gasp in disbelief and actually take the clipboard out of his hand and reread the name about twenty times.

"This boy deserves more than snickerdoodles, Zoey-Poey," Morgan tells me sternly over my shoulder. "He's a goddamn dream."

"Easy, honey," Ned tells him.

The delivery guy hands me the pen. I stare at it. Morgan nudges me. "Sign."

"But—"

"No buts. Sign."

I sign the delivery order, and the guy asks me where I want it. Ned leads him up to the master bedroom because I'm flustered. All I want to do is find my phone and call Jude. I walk into the kitchen, grab my phone off the counter and dial his number.

"Hey, baby, are you calling to ask me to break in the bed with you?"

I smile instantly. "Jude, you shouldn't have. I can take care of myself. I need to."

"I know you can, I promise," he replies. "You can consider it taking care of me. I had to have the trainer massage my back for half an hour after sleeping on that wonk-ass inflatable mattress you went out and bought."

"We could just stay at your place, then."

"I'm not done making good memories for you in that house," he says matter-of-factly with a teasing lilt in his voice. "We still have to make some in the shower—your shower—and the kitchen and the third floor. I need the bed to rest comfortably between rounds."

I don't say anything. I'm too busy enjoying the warm feeling that is swelling up inside me. "Well, when you put it that way…"

"So you'll keep it?"

"Yes, for your health."

"Thank you," he replies.

"Oh, and your place is officially listed. You can check it out on MLS," I add.

"Great," he says, and I can hear voices in the background. "Practice is about to start. I should go. I'll call you later."

"Okay."

"Don't break in that bed without me," he warns cheekily before he hangs up.

I put the phone down and walk back to the hall, where Ned and Morgan are seeing the deliverymen out. Morgan turns to me. "Seriously. This is exactly what you've needed for years."

"A new mattress?" I know exactly what he means, but I'm being sassy.

He gives me an overdramatic stare. "A gorgeous guy who cares enough to want you to sleep comfortably…"

That's true, but it surprises me that he's not making some kind of pervy remark. His blue eyes are sincere. He reaches out and hugs me. "Okay. Simmer down, brother."

"We've got to go," Ned says, grabbing Morgan by the shoulders and gently pulling him off me. "If I don't get him out of here, he's going to leave me for your boyfriend."

"Thanks again for the furniture."

They walk out the front door and down a couple steps, then Morgan turns back around. "You want to thank me? Send me a picture of his dick." Ned and I both give him horrified stares. "So I can see if it's the same one from the internet photo!"

Oh, right. I forgot about that. Jude's penis is on the internet. I don't respond; I just wave good-bye and close the door. Then I take the stairs two at a time and run into my bedroom and launch myself onto the new mattress. It's like landing on a cloud. Which, I smile as I think to myself, is an appropriate metaphor for how my life feels right now too. My life was in free fall and Jude is my soft landing.

24

JUDE

"Let's go!" Coach calls as he passes the locker room, the rest of the coaching staff following along behind him. Everyone is in their new Thunder training sweats that carry the Stanley Cup logo with the dates under it. Back-to-back is not something the team owner wants to forget or wants us to forget. Not that we could.

"That Zoey?" Duncan asks, pointing to my phone as I hurriedly tuck it back in my pants hanging on the hook in my locker. I nod, and he smiles at me. "Welcome to the club, buddy."

"Whatever." I blow him off, but I'm smiling as we walk down the hall.

Eddie overhears as he comes up behind us. "You get in that hot redhead's pants?"

I nod. "She's got a name. It's Zoey."

"Right, Zoey." Eddie grins. With the mustache he insists on sporting, he looks like a guy who would try to sell candy to kids out of the back of a windowless van. "So does her carpet match her drapes?"

For the first time ever I feel an animosity toward Eddie for one of his off-color comments, which I usually find amusing. But I also know I'll sound like a giant hypocrite if I tell him to shut the fuck up, so I swallow down my anger and try to play it off casually. "You'll never know."

"I can try and find out if you're done."

My feet have just hit the ice, and even though I'm furious I decide to skate away, fast. I want to punch him with my glove on and knock him out until the season is over, but I need to let it go because that dick pic already has me on the management's shit list. I don't want to start any team drama so I skate. Hard.

Ten minutes later the coaches have us doing passing drills, and Eddie is off with Noah at the other end of the ice doing goalie crap, so I have time to calm down. It's crazy that I'm this pissed off. He used to make lewd comments about Tessa a lot when I was dating her, and I never got irked. I knew Tessa wanted nothing to do with him, and I'd bet a year's salary Zoey wouldn't touch him either, yet...now I'm contemplating physical violence.

After twenty minutes of drills, Coach calls a break and we skate to the bench for Gatorade. Duncan smiles at me while Levi is crouched down beside him messing with his skate laces. Like Eddie, I haven't seen Duncan much since we started because he's defense and was doing drills with the defense coach at the other end. Now we'll probably scrimmage, followed by a shootout game. I'm looking forward to a few hard slap shots at Rollins.

"So you and Zoey wanna go to the movies with Carla and me tonight?" he asks.

I laugh. "What is this, 1952? Do you want to go to the sock hop together too?"

"It's just fun to hang out with other couples," Duncan replies, and he sounds offended. I instantly regret being hard on him, because he's honestly a great guy. "Or are you guys still in that honeymoon phase where all you want to do is be alone naked?"

"That phase should never end, Darby," I reply and squirt some green Gatorade into my mouth. "When it ends so should the fling."

"I'm not talking fling. I'm talking relationship," Duncan clarifies, and then his bushy red eyebrows pinch together, and he frowns.

"What are you doing tonight? Going to the movie with Carla and Duncan too?" I ask Levi. "Or are you and Tess having a quiet night at the malt shop? One milk shake, two straws?"

"You're in a mood," he says in a low, calm voice.

He's right. I am. "Sorry. I'm just kidding around. So you going out with Tessa tonight or do you wanna hang out?"

"Tess is in Seattle for work," Levi explains. "I was going to marathon something on Netflix and order something greasy for the last time until May."

"Wow. You're a wild child, Levi. Tessa should worry about leaving you alone." I'm just a bucket of sunshine today.

"You're dating, right?" Duncan asks out of nowhere. "It's not just fucking, right?"

I sigh. "I feel like you should be writing this on a note and passing it to me in history class."

I just called him immature, which makes me an even bigger asshole, because I already regretted being an asshole in the first place. Levi frowns at me, in case I'm not catching that I'm an asshole, because he's great like that. But something about sharing me and Zoey with these guys is making me uncomfortable. Like I'm covered in honey and wearing a sweater made out of bees uncomfortable. I don't know why. I'm having the best couple of weeks I've ever had in my life. She's not just a childhood wet dream come to life, she's a friendship rekindled and an ally in my life, which is something that I feel like I've been missing since everything went to shit with Levi. She's letting me talk about my dad, and I'm helping her forget a shitty time in her life. Maybe that makes it feel scary. Or maybe it's the fact that I've never felt so close to someone before.

Either way, though, Darby doesn't deserve to be shit on. I give him a friendly shove and a smile. "She's got plans tonight. Girls' night."

"Oh. Okay." Duncan still seems a little miffed as he shrugs and skates away to talk to one of our equipment guys about his glove or something.

"I'm going out for a little fox and hound," Eddie tells me, skating up beside me in his heavy goalie gear, his mask perched on top of his head. "Fox and hound" is his way of saying picking up women. He thinks it makes him classier than just saying, "I'm going out to try to get laid." The jury's still out on that, though. "Me, the new kid Payne, and Noah."

"Where?"

"Abbey Tavern, probably. SFU is back in session." He grins. "Time for a new college experience."

He's in his midthirties, so I realize how absolutely gross that is, because even I have started to feel pervy around college girls, and I'm only twenty-eight. He doesn't, though. And neither do two out of five college girls he hits on, because I've yet to see him leave a college bar alone.

I have no place to be tonight, and unlike Levi I'm not whipped. I can go out and have a good time without Zoey. It's not even that type of relationship. She hasn't tried to have the talk yet. My rule has always been that if it's not defined, I'm not confined. I actually thought about putting it on a T-shirt once.

"I'm in," I tell Eddie as Coach announces it's scrimmage time.

I skate toward center ice, and Levi skates beside me. "Really?" Levi questions, and I turn and start skating backward so we can face each other.

"Is this the part where you tell me what to do with my love life?" It's a challenge, as in I fucking dare you to lecture me after you fucked my ex.

His lips press together as if he's got to do that to keep himself from talking. Typical Levi. He likes to scowl and brood rather than say anything that might make him appear like he has a heart. I thought Tessa was getting him over that annoying personality trait, but I guess not. Not with anyone other than her, anyway.

I turn and skate faster. The scrimmage is high-paced because everyone is excited to be together again. Instead of using my energy to try to hit Eddie with slap shots, I focus on showing up Levi, because my frustration has been redirected. I actually play better than him, but it's a hollow victory, because I know his shoulder is still kind of wrecked. We hit the weight room next and then some cardio before the day is over.

I take an extra-long, extra-hot shower, because my back is still a little achy from Zoey's damn air mattress. We must have put a hole in it, because by the time I woke up this morning my ass was pressed painfully into the floor and my legs and head were wrenched up in the air. I had to get her that mattress. Not just to save my own back, but because I like fucking her in a bed. I discovered that when she slept at my place earlier this week. That was our first mattress experience, and it deserves repeating. Plus, I hate the idea of her on that cold, leaky air mattress whether I'm there or not. I get that she can't afford a decent mattress right now while the money from the divorce is still in limbo and her career, although picking up, hasn't taken off, but that's not her fault and she shouldn't be punished for it. That's why that prick took all the furniture. To punish her. My dad always said living well is the best revenge, and if I can help her get revenge, I'm going to do it.

I get out of the shower. Eddie is videotaping himself in front of the mirrors waxing his mustache. He's obsessed with videoing things. I usually don't care, and have even been known to mug for his camera, but today I ignore it completely. "So tonight is going to be great! I feel like I haven't gone out with you in forever."

"Yeah, it's been a while. Summer's been busy and everything," I mutter and give him a quick friendly smile. I walk out into our dressing area and Levi is tying his shoes on the bench in front of his stall. Eddie follows me out, still videotaping, and I'm about to drop my towel so I scowl at him. "Stop filming shit, okay?"

"Yeah. Sorry." He puts his phone down. "I won't put that one on Instagram. Just the one of me grooming my mustache. Women love that shit."

I don't say anything as I continue changing.

"They also love a good dick pic. Honestly, every chick I meet asks me if that one of yours is real. I wish I'd had some chick post my peen," he jokes, and I give him a tight smile.

Levi gives him a glare. He hates that that happened to me, but he hasn't told me outright because of the rift between us.

I bet he feels he and Tessa are the reason I went on a bit of a sex bender and ended up with a girl who would put my dick on the internet. I sleep around a lot—I mean, I did—but I wasn't a total idiot about it. I never allowed cell phones to even enter the bedroom. In fact, I always made a conscious decision to make sure the phone stayed in her purse, and the purse was in a different room than the one we were fucking in. If it was road trip hotel sex, I always made sure she left it by the door with her shoes.

But the girl in Toronto, well, I wasn't thinking. It was a rough week. My dad took a fall and was in the hospital. My mom was a bit of a mess about it. I had spent three days after that comforting the sorority and my mom, and once we got Dad settled back home again, all the heavy talk about when to move him to a care facility started up again, and I was still pissed about Tessa and Levi. So I went out with Eddie, who also lives in Toronto in the off-season, to blow off steam. Her name was Jennifer, and Eddie said he knew her, and she was a regular puck bunny. She made the rounds and she knew the rules. I wanted a quick and easy lay. I got my dick on the internet instead.

"Eddie, can you give us a minute?" Levi says. Like a lot of things that come out of his mouth, I don't think he means it to sound as serious and foreboding as it does, but his voice is so deep and rough that he always kind of sounds like the world is ending.

Eddie looks at Levi and nods, then turns to me, his eyebrows raised behind his captain's back. "I'll meet ya in the parking lot."

I nod and reach for my jeans, pulling them on. And then I turn back to Levi. He's standing now with his hands shoved in the pockets of his own jeans. "So listen, I know you're still upset about everything that happened, and I'm not about to tell you that you should be over it because I don't have any right to do that."

Fuck, are we really going to do this? Now? Here? He's the one who wanted so desperately to keep it out of the locker room last year, and now he's bringing it in. And the thing is, I don't even think he gets what the real problem is. That's why I can't get over it. That's why the rift between us is getting bigger instead of smaller.

"You don't have any right," I agree, and grab my shirt and pull it over my head way more aggressively than is required. I run a hand through my damp hair and sigh. "So can we stop having these types of conversations where you tell me you know you should shut up and you don't fucking shut up?"

"Jude, all I want to say is that if you're not over Tess, that's fine. It really is, but then don't screw around with Zoey," he says, and my blood begins to boil. "Tessa told me about her rough divorce, and she seems like a really nice person who really does like you. I—"

"I'm over Tessa." I interrupt him with this news flash, my voice hard as stone and just as cold. "I was over her before you started sleeping with her. And we're talking Zoey here. You know how I felt about her in high school. You really think I'm going to treat her like a puck bunny?"

He looks genuinely perplexed, and if my blood was boiling before, that expression on his face turns it into an inferno in my veins. "You don't get it," I say, "and that's the part that fucking makes me hate you the most."

The word "hate" causes his eyes to widen and his jaw to drop just enough that his mouth opens. He's hurt, but I don't feel any guilt about that. "I'm still staying away from you, and I'm still resentful because you were a brother to me. And you decided to throw that all away."

"It was her or you."

"You made it her or me when you picked her over me," I argue and shove my feet into my shoes without bothering to do them up. "You decided you had to start a secret relationship with her because it was easier on you than trusting me with the truth. You didn't care enough about our friendship, all ten years of it, to be honest with me."

"You would have been furious," he argues back, and his shoulders are rigid and pulled up sharply. "You *were* furious."

"Fuck, yeah!" I bellow, and I know if any of the coaches or staff are walking around the halls they can hear me. I just don't give a fuck right now. "I still would have been furious. She was my fucking ex-girlfriend, Levi. You broke the code. But I also would have accepted it eventually. I just wouldn't be reminded every time I look at you that you lied to my face. That's the difference, asshole. That's what you're not getting."

I storm out of the locker room. He follows me. "Jude! Wait."

I turn, briefly scanning the long narrow hall and all the doors along it to make sure we're alone, and then I step closer so I can keep my voice low. "We're teammates. I'm cool with that. I like playing with you, but that's all we are now. So I don't care if you trust my intentions with Zoey. You don't get to comment on my love life unless my dick ends up on the internet again, in which case, pull your captainly duties and tell me I'm embarrassing the organization or whatever."

"Jude, come on…"

"Bye, Captain. See you tomorrow at the preseason game."

"Are you seriously still not over your bromance breakup with Casco?" Eddie asks, and I frown as I lift my eyes from the foam on my beer and glare at him.

Eddie shrugs. "Being out with some warm and willing college chicks should be enough to get your mind off him is all I'm saying."

My mind isn't actually on Levi. It's on the teapot I saw in the weird little shop a few blocks over next to the place we ate dinner at. I haven't been able to get it out of my head since I saw it. The girls Eddie's been chatting up come back to the table. They peed in pairs because that's what girls do at twenty-one. The brunette who has her boobs pushed up so high in her V-neck sweater that they're basically a shelf under her chin looks at me. "Your beer is almost finished. Let me buy you another."

"No, it's okay. I'll buy a round for everyone," I tell her and smile.

She smiles back. "If I have another, I'm definitely going to miss my eight o'clock class tomorrow."

"Oh, no," I say, and I hope it doesn't feel as sarcastic as it actually is. I guess it doesn't, because she's still smiling as she puts her hand on my knee under the table.

"Oh, well, fuck it. I'll miss one class. It's worth it to let loose and have some fun," she announces.

Her friend claps in favor of the terrible decision and yells, "Shots!"

Eddie looks so happy he might cry. I try to smile, but all I can think about is how her clammy hand is probably making my jeans wet. It's gross. Thankfully, shots isn't just a mating call, it means we're getting up and going to the bar, so she lifts her hand from my knee. I follow along behind my brunette as Eddie walks beside the girl with the darker brown hair, his hand on her lower back precariously close to her ass.

I spot our rookie Carter Payne and Noah playing pool over in the corner, and I wave and start to head that way. Perfect excuse to get out of this shot situation. But the girl grabs my hand as I try to break away. "Where you going, gorgeous? You can't expect me to do shots alone."

I don't bother to explain she's got her friend, Eddie and his mustache to get drunk with. I just let her guide me to the bar. Maybe a shot of tequila will get that teapot out of my head. It was really unique, though. A pretty jade-green color with roses swirled right into the porcelain. I wonder if Zoey has seen anything like it.

"What should we do?" the one Eddie is macking on asks excitedly.

The one next to me, who I realize still has a grip on my forearm, announces, "I'm a baby when it comes to shots. I need something sweet that goes down easy."

She's looking right at me with that comment, and it suddenly feels like it's some double entendre, and now my forearm feels itchy from her clammy hand. Why the fuck is tonight a disaster?

I step up to the bar, pushing between two seats because it makes her let go of my arm, and the seats barricade me from any more unwanted contact. That's what it is, I realize, unwanted. Jesus, I'm not me right now. And then, as Eddie starts explaining how much fun these are with two people, I know I have to get the fuck out of here. Right fucking now.

His girl listens intently as he explains how you lick the salt off someone's neck, do the shot, and then bite the lime wedge out of their mouth. Her friend nods in agreement. "I've done a ton of these before. They're super fun!"

The bartender's looking at me, annoyed. I think I missed it when he asked me what I wanted the first time. I order four shots and drop money on the bar top before he even goes to prepare them.

Then I look across the room and wave Carter Payne over. He looks confused, but I just keep motioning. No rookie in his right mind is going to keep playing pool when his alternate captain is calling for him. So Carter puts down the stick and starts to weave his way through the crowd.

The bartender puts the shots on the counter in front of me with four lime wedges, then turns to hunt down a salt shaker. Someone is breathing down my neck, so I turn around. It's Eddie. "You going to do your signature move again?"

He's talking about the way I habitually drop the lime from my mouth a second before the girl puts her lips on it so it ends in a kiss. I've done it probably a million times. It's a lame-ass, cheap move as old and original as polyester. I've always known that, but it's never bothered me. Until now. I shake my head, and he looks like he might faint. "Really? Are you retiring it?"

I pat his shoulder. "I'm passing the torch, buddy. It's all yours."

He looks like I just gave him a winning lottery ticket. I can't fully absorb how sad that is. I honestly don't want to. Carter lumbers up to the bar just as the bartender plops down a salt shaker next to the shot glasses and lime wedges. "Hey, ladies, this is Carter. He's a new teammate, and we always like to let them do the first shot. What do you say?"

I'm looking directly at the brunette, and she's looking back at me, her face a mix of confusion and disappointment. "What about you?"

"I don't drink tequila." Luckily, no one calls me on that bold-faced lie.

Carter looks confused, but she's cute, so he's smiling. She seems to agree with the cute assessment, because she nods and reaches for a shot glass. I watch them do the shot, but her eyes are on me while she licks Carter's neck, which makes me feel gross again. When Eddie goes to do his shot with the darker-haired girl, he's grinning wildly. As soon as he drops the lime, as gracefully as a wild boar doing yoga, I turn and head directly for the exit.

No one notices, or if they do no one stops me, and that's what counts. On the sidewalk I take a deep breath and start walking. I'm not even sure where I'm going. I just know I'm not staying here.

25

ZOEY

I pour the last of the Pinot Grigio she brought into her glass and put the bottle back down in the small wine bucket. Dixie points to it. "That is the coolest thing. I need to get one of those so I don't have to keep pausing my Netflix show and running to the fridge to refill."

I laugh. She talks about Netflix a lot. I love good TV too, but Dixie's life seems to be nothing but work and Netflix. No chill. She's a bright, beautiful young girl, so that kind of bums me out.

"Yeah, well, Adam left a lot of the appliances and all the wine-glasses and gadgets because he hates wine. He only drank scotch," I explain as I take a sip of wine.

"Ugh. Scotch. Men think it's so sexy and tough. You know what's sexy? A man who can drink a piña colada with extra maraschino cherries and not think it takes away from the size of his penis," Dixie proclaims as she reaches for one of the grapes on the cheese plate I made and pops it into her mouth.

I'm laughing at the smirk on her face, which is so much like her brother's, and the oddly specific reference. "Is there a specific piña colada–drinking male you think is particularly sexy?"

"What?" She flushes. "No. I'm just being vague, not specific."

I can tell by the flustered way she answers that she has someone very specific in mind. This night just got interesting. But before I can weasel more information out of her, she changes the subject.

"I liked running into you the other morning." She smiles.

"I'm sure it's not the first time you've found a girl doing the walk of shame out of your brother's apartment at seven in the morning," I note and let out a sheepish laugh. Dixie came by to see Jude on her way to work a couple of days ago just as I was leaving to run home and change for work.

"Yeah, but it's the first time I've been happy about it," Dixie replies and runs a hand through her bouncy blond hair. "And was it really shameful? I mean, to me it's only a walk of shame if it's a tawdry, meaningless hookup."

Her blue eyes are laser focused on my face waiting for my reaction. It's cute. "It's not meaningless, no. Not for me, and I don't think for him."

Dixie's face morphs into another bright smile, but after she takes a sip of wine her voice becomes cautious. "Jude isn't exactly great at relationships. I mean, he hasn't had a lot of them to learn from."

It seems like she's apologizing for him. "He's doing fine so far. I mean, if he considers this a relationship. We haven't really defined anything."

I blink, stunned by the sudden change in her expression. She looks kind of horrified. "You guys should have the talk. I know it's awkward and everything, but Jude is…Jude is a better person when he's given rules."

"What does that mean?"

"It's just like I said: he's only ever had one serious relationship, and he didn't treat it very seriously," Dixie says and pauses to take a sip…no, a gulp…of wine. "I love Jude. I give him all the crap I can, but he's honestly the best brother and son that ever existed. I know he'll also be the best boyfriend, husband and father in the world one day too. He just might make a few mistakes on his way there."

"Whoa now." I laugh and take a big gulp of my own wine. "We don't need to talk marriage and babies here. We've been involved with each other for just a few weeks."

Dixie laughs sheepishly. "I know. Sorry! I'm getting ahead of myself. It's just we love you, and you and Jude would make such cute babies."

My smile twitches, but I manage not to let it fall. Dixie doesn't notice and keeps on talking. "He loves kids, by the way. He's so great with them when we visit the children's hospital with the team. I want him to have girls so we can teach them how to drive him crazy like we did."

The way she's talking is sweet, and she's so full of love and hope it's making my heart hurt. She wants to be an aunt one day. She wants her brother to be a father. I may not be able to provide that for them. That realization feels like a cold breeze invading the warm, dreamy cocoon I've been living in. *Relax, Zoey, you and Jude are nowhere near that.*

The doorbell rings. I'm not expecting anyone, but I'm happy for the interruption so we don't have to keep talking about this. Dixie instantly puts down her wineglass and climbs up on the back of the couch, craning her neck to see if she can see who is on the stoop from the bay window behind her. I laugh at her. "Are you still scared of serial killers and monsters?"

I'm kidding, but she gives me a pretty serious glance. "Yes. I am fairly certain you should always be scared of serial killers, like your whole life. And psychopaths. And clowns."

I burst out laughing at that and cover my mouth as I walk toward the front door. Whoever is behind it rings again. "What is it with your family and clowns?"

"Look through the little window at the top!" Dixie demands.

I do what she requests, and my heart starts doing gymnastics. "This is the hottest psychopath I've ever seen. I am totally letting him in."

I unlock the door and fling it open. Jude's perfect body fills the doorframe. He's in dark jeans and an untucked button-down shirt with a brown cardboard box tucked under his left arm. His mischievous grin has a darker element tonight, and the twinkle in his blue eyes seems to hold a serious glint. I almost have the urge to ask him if something is wrong, because that look, along with the fact that this is an unexpected appearance, makes me think something is. But I can't get a word out because his lips are suddenly glued to mine.

The kiss is a reflection of the way he looks—it's dark and moody and something Jude has never been before: needy. He grabs my waist with his free hand and pulls me to him roughly, but his lips brush mine softly. His tongue slides gently into my mouth, but his fingers curl tightly around my waist. It's one of those monumental big-screen kisses, and I don't want it to end. But Dixie lets out a sisterly groan, and he slowly, begrudgingly, breaks it.

"Oh God, gross," Dixie wails dramatically. "My eyes!"

"Sorry," Jude says in a decidedly un-Jude way, because normally he would shoot some kind of snarky comeback to Dixie. "I didn't mean to crash girls' night. I just wanted to see you."

Dixie and I exchange glances. Dixie's voice loses its sarcastic tone. "You okay, Jude?"

He nods and shrugs at the same time, which is the weirdest thing ever, and then holds up the box in his hand. "Yeah. I'm fine. I just want to give this to Zoey and thought I would swing by on my way home. I don't have to stay."

"Yes, you do," I blurt out, and his grin starts to lose that darkness. "I mean, you don't mind, do you, Dix?"

She shrugs. "No. I was going to head home after I finished my glass anyway." She looks at the glass in her hand, lifts it and tips it back, downing the rest of her Pinot. She reaches for her purse hanging on a hook on the hall stand and then hugs me. "Thanks, Zoey. We have to do this again when Winnie and Sadie are visiting."

"For sure."

She steps to the right, in front of Jude, and hugs him. "Are you sure you're okay?"

"Yes."

"Are you going to tell me what's in the box?"

"No."

She pulls out of the hug and gives him a motherly look. "Is it a sex toy?"

"Dixie!" I laugh and cover my face with my hands, because I'm not a hundred percent sure it's not a sex toy.

"Get out, loser," Jude barks at her, but it's jokingly. He walks over to the front door and opens it. "Are you parked nearby? Do you want me to walk you? Do you have that mace spray I gave you on your key chain?"

"Yes, no and yes," Dixie replies and pulls out her key chain to show him the little spray bottle, then she points at the mystery box. "That better not be a video camera. No sex tapes. Not that it matters for you with your dick already out there, but Zoey's dad is a pastor. Don't do that to him."

The minute the dick comment flies out of her mouth, Jude's head whips over to me. Our eyes meet and I know. It really is his dick on the internet. He looks away and turns back to his sister. "Thanks for that, Dixie. Have a *great* night!"

"Oh. Oh! Oops! Jude, I—"

He shuts the door on her and then leans against it and looks up at me. The darkness creeps back into his features. He runs a hand over his dirty-blond hair and then lets it hang—his head and his hand. I take a step closer. Just one. "I already knew about the cock shot."

"Oh. You Googled me?"

"Morgan did, and he told me about it."

He groans, and his hand moves back up to rub his forehead, but he's still staring at the floor under his feet. "Great. Your brother has seen my dick."

"If it makes you feel any better, he thought it was lovely." I know it's a dumb thing to say, which is why I say it. I want to lift the mood, his spirits and his head. It works, kind of. His head tips up, and his eyes rise a little. He looks at me from under his thick blond lashes.

He looks embarrassed, and it makes my heart ache. I take another step closer. "I don't care, Jude. It speaks more to the character of the person who did it without your permission than it does to you."

He stops breathing, for just a heartbeat, but he does it so quickly I can notice. "How did you know it was without my permission?"

"I just knew. I know that you wouldn't do that on purpose." I bite my bottom lip. Am I saying the wrong things? Should I just shut up? If I knew what was wrong, I could do a better job of fixing it.

A sad smile flashes across his face but then disappears. "You're the only one who assumed that. Everyone else assumed I knew it happened. I let it happen."

"I'm sorry." I take another step. He's still watching me with hooded eyes. My fingers are twisting together anxiously, so I pull them apart and point to the box. "That's for me?"

He looks at the box in his left hand like he forgot he was holding it. He finally pushes himself off the door, grows to his full height and hands me the box. It's heavy and nondescript with no label on it. I resist the urge to shake it and start to open the top. I pull back some white tissue paper and am greeted with gorgeous roses made out of rounded jade-green ceramic. I move to the stairs because that's the only place to sit in the hallway, drop my butt onto the third step, put the box on my lap and start to dig it out.

It's a teapot. I've never seen one quite so unique or beautiful, and I have seen a lot of teapots. I carefully run my fingers over the delicate roses in the ceramic and admire the way the jade color catches the light.

"I know it probably doesn't make up for losing your collection, but I thought you could start a new collection with this one." He's trying to sound casual, but it's strained. He's feeling vulnerable because he wants me to like it. And I really, honestly do. I like the teapot almost as much as the gesture, but neither compares to how much I like him. And that's really what is taking my breath away right now and making it hard to speak.

I gently put it down on the step beside me and stand up. I walk right over to him and grab his face in my hands and kiss him, long, slow and with every word I can't seem to find. The kiss just adds more intensity to the chemistry between us. He reaches around my neck with one hand, burying his fingers in my hair, and his other hand cups my ass, pushing me into him as he lifts his hips off the door to show me how much he wants me right now.

I want him too. I want to relieve the internal struggle or torture that he's trying so badly to hide from me. I want to soothe him and prove to him that no matter what is upsetting him, this—me, us—will always make it better. I let my hands move between us, finding his belt and then his button and zipper. Once I've got all of that undone, I move my lips to his neck and my hands push his jeans off his hips and I grab his ass in one hand. It's so unbelievably strong. Just solid muscle. I drop to my knees in front of him, fingers hooked into the waistband of his black boxer briefs. I place a soft kiss on the outline of his hard shaft through the thin, silky fabric. My eyes move up and find his clouded with lust as they stare back at me.

I lower the fabric, and his fingers slide through my hair again. I have honestly never wanted to blow a man like I do right now. I need to taste him, to feel him quiver against my tongue, to make him forget whatever it is that's got him so unnerved. I slide his underwear down and press my tongue to the base of his shaft, giving it a firm, flat lick. As soon as the tip of my tongue reaches the tip of his dick, I slide my way back down, this time opening my mouth and letting him slip right in.

This delicious sound rumbles out of him, deep, needy and

strained. His hands in my hair hold tighter as I slide up and down, swirling my tongue and sliding my free hand up to graze his balls with my fingertips. He's so hot and hard in my mouth, and I've never been more turned on by a blow job in my life.

"Baby, I'm close," he warns after a while and tries to still his hips. I feel the hesitation in his movement, but he can't stop completely, and I don't want him to. I suck hard, sliding my lips as far down his length as I can go without choking.

"Zzzzooooeeeeyyyy." I hear his head hit the door behind him, and with one hard thrust into my mouth he comes.

His legs actually give out and he slips out of my mouth as he slides to the ground. I swallow and smile at him. His eyes are glassy and barely seem to be able to focus and his breathing is labored, like he's run a marathon. I grin. That gets his glassy eyes to focus for a minute, and he reaches out and cups the side of my face. "Hey, now. Cocky smiles are my domain."

"Watching you come, knowing I can do this to you"—I wave a hand over his current state of general undoneness—"with just my mouth is the hottest thing ever."

I watch his own cocky grin start to take shape on his handsome face. He leans forward, his hand still cupping my face and his thumb lazily tracing my cheekbone. "Are you wet from blowing me?"

I nod. He starts to push himself off the back of the door. "I'm going to have to see for myself."

He puts his hands on the floor on either side of my hips, and as our lips connect he pushes me back onto the floor. He moves his mouth to my ear and balances on one arm as he slips the other down to shove the yoga pants I'm wearing to my knees; my thong goes with them. As soon as his fingers make contact with my pussy, my back arches and I sigh.

"I told you," I breathe. He's smiling against my neck, I can feel it.

"You know how amazing it is that *I* can do this to *you*?" Two of his fingers slide into me. "I've dreamed of the idea that you want me as much as I want you since we were kids."

I run my fingers languidly over the bulging bicep of the arm he's balancing on. His fingers feel so good I can barely keep my eyes open. But then suddenly they're gone, and before I can complain I feel the tip of his dick slip through my wetness as he guides it up and down my slit.

"Tell me you're on the pill. Please."

"I'm not," I admit and then softly add, "But I don't have STDs and my body hates babies."

He stills at that, his eyes finding mine with an inquisitive look. I bite my lip. I just ruined the moment. "I have some issues. I might never get pregnant."

"Is it impossible?" he asks in a gentle tone, but I'm sure he's lost his hard-on and is trying to figure out how to leave my house and never come back.

I start to move, trying to get out from under him and sit up, or at the very least get my pants up, but he won't let me. Instead he lowers himself so he's resting on top of me. His dick, thankfully, is still hard and pressing into my thigh, so at least I haven't totally turned him off. I can't look him in the eye, though—I'm too insecure—so I stare at the Stanley Cup tattoo on the inside of his left bicep. "Not impossible, but not easy."

He shifts, moving his dick higher; his tip nudges my slit again. Our eyes finally meet and he lifts a hand and pushes my hair back off my forehead. "If it was impossible, I would slide right into you right now, no condom, and let your pussy own me like your mouth did. But…"

He says he can't, but he pushes against me again, his tip slipping a little deeper, and I roll my hips a bit, causing it to slip even deeper. He groans and freezes. When he speaks, his voice is strained and airtight, like he's holding his breath. "We should still use a condom for now."

"Mmm…yeah," I reply, and I mean it, even though I shift my hips and take just a little more of him inside me. It feels so damn good.

"I don't want to stop…" He pushes just a little bit deeper. "But I want to be good…to you."

He pulls out completely and reaches for his jeans, where he pulls a condom out of his back pocket. "Put this on me."

I tear open the package, and he lifts himself, like he's doing a half push-up, so I can slip the condom over his rock-hard dick. As soon as it's on, I place him where he needs to be, and with one hard, long, magnificent push, he's completely inside of me. I hiss out an expletive, and he smiles as he presses his lips to mine. "Making you swear is almost as rewarding as making you come."

"You do both like a pro," I mumble back and rock my hips. I need him to get me there. I need to come now. This whole night has somehow turned into a bit of an emotional roller coaster and I need the release.

We go at it like wild animals on the floor of the front hallway. I'm pretty sure the wood floor is about to put splinters in my ass, but I don't care. I just care about him—the way he feels on top of me, inside me, the way he is sending sparks of pleasure shooting through my body, the way he's looking at me like I'm the reason he's alive. No man has ever looked at me like Jude does. "You're going to get on birth control," he pants into my ear as I teeter on the edge of what is about to be an earthquaking orgasm.

"O…" My mouth is trying to say "okay" but all I get out is the O, and then I fall into the heavenly abyss of orgasm.

I hate the pill. It's annoying and makes me moody, but I will do anything for this man. Because I love him. I bite my lip as my orgasm ebbs, because those three words want to explode from my mouth and I can't—not here on the floor while he chases his release. But soon. Soon I'll tell him, and I have a feeling he'll say it back.

26

JUDE

"I can't believe you bailed! What a bitch thing to do!"

If Eddie doesn't stop ragging on me about last night, I swear I'm going to "accidentally" skate into him tonight, even though he's my damn goalie. Ever since he walked into the locker room he's been harassing me about leaving him last night. I really don't want to hear it, for a multitude of reasons, one of which is that we've got our first official preseason game tonight, which should mean no pressure, because it's preseason, but Zoey is here so I need to impress.

I pull on my pads and look over at Eddie, annoyed. "Did you get laid?"

"Fuck, yeah."

"Then shut the fuck up," I retort and look over to Levi, who has just waltzed into the room, although clearly he's been at the arena for a while, because he's already wearing Under Armour and his shoulder pads. He was probably with the trainer getting his shoulder taped.

He must have caught what I just said and glances over at Eddie.

"What's wrong, Rollins? Braddock steal the woman you wanted? Again?"

Duncan chuckles from his locker, and Eddie flips him the bird while he answers his captain. "Nah, the bitch bailed and went home before one set of panties got dropped."

Levi's dark eyes fly so quickly to mine I feel like there should be the sound of tires screeching to accompany them. "You didn't stay out?"

I shrug and keep my eyes on my skates. "Called it an early night."

He drops down next to me and reaches for his own skates. "Could have swung by."

"I had other people to see," I say and finally look up. He's got a small but knowing grin on his face, and it radiates approval. He knows I went home to her, and he likes it.

"It's different." He says it low for only my ears, and it's a statement, not a question.

I hate feeing vulnerable and admitting my feelings for Zoey to anyone. It makes me feel like I've opened my own chest and am offering my heart up for people to fondle. He's the only one I ever let in, and that still feels like a mistake, so it's uncomfortable when I nod. "Yeah."

Everyone in the room starts to clap and cheer. Worst timing ever. My head snaps up, and I see Elijah Casco, Levi's little brother, walk into the room. His eyes are as big as saucers and he looks as skittish as a deer, but he's trying to hide it under a big smile. I turn to Levi. "He's playing?"

"He got called up from the AHL last night. He's going to back up Rollins tonight since Noah is out with a tight groin. See what he can do." Levi is beaming like a proud dad, which is great, because the Casco brothers don't have one of those.

I stand up and walk over and bear-hug Eli while the team all bellows different words of welcome. Elijah is only twenty-four. He was the hottest goalie at the college level. I thought he wanted to finish his degree, but at the beginning of his senior year he suffered a life-threatening injury during a game and dropped out of college shortly after, and the Thunder immediately signed him to their AHL team, the Storm. Goalies usually spend a couple years on the AHL team because there are only two spots on every team. But Eli is the best of the best, and if any goalie was going to jump the line it would be him. Especially with our backup being Rollins. Eddie is a good guy, but he was never a great goalie, and at almost thirty-five he's definitely reaching the end of his career. He knows it too.

"Good to see you in here," I tell him as we break apart.

"Good to be in here," he replies and grins. He's so much more laid-back and, well, fun than Levi.

"Good to see ya, buddy!" Eddie stands and greets what is sure to be his replacement one day—and sooner rather than later. "Sorry that I'm going to play so well you never leave the bench."

"Ha!" I bark out with a teasing grin. "Eli, you'll be in by the end of the first period."

"Nah, it's a mean-nothing game. Rollins might actually play well," Levi chirps, which is unheard of. He never joins in our childish taunts. Everyone roars at that except Eli, who is fiddling with the neck protector attached to his helmet, his face serious. I don't even think he heard us. My eyes slip to the still angry-looking scar across his neck.

Dixie breezes into the locker room, not a care in the world, even though a couple guys are still in nothing but their jocks. If she notices, she doesn't act like it. "Boys! Listen up!"

"Hey, Ms. Wynn," I call out because some part of me can't turn off the brother mode no matter how hard she wants me to. "Maybe knock before entering or something!"

She finally glances around the room and sees the various states of undress. Her eyes linger the longest on Elijah, who is actually fully clothed. "I'm not the Virgin Mary, Braddock," she tells me, her eyes taking an awful lot of time to move from Eli to me. "Nothing I haven't seen before."

I bite my tongue. She continues her announcement unfazed and clearly unaware that more than a few of my teammates are checking her out in her little black skirt and heels. "Not a lot of press here tonight because it's preseason, and the few that are here only want to talk to the Casco brothers, so everyone's free to go to the party afterward. No media scrum."

She turns on one of those heels and storms out of the room as quickly as she entered. "Jesus, that woman is all kinds of smokin' hot!" Eddie says after a long, low whistle. Every fiber of my being tenses. "I mean, she's like got a total stick up her ass, but she's so hot you want to take it out and replace it with—"

"Hey!" Levi snaps, his stern baritone stopping Eddie midsentence, thank God. I was about to lunge across the room and knock him out. "I know it's preseason, but let's focus, okay, Rollins?"

Levi's eyes move to me, and he nods a little. "Thanks," I whisper.

But of course Eddie, being Eddie, isn't done. "Come on, Casco, I know you're all married and everything, but the other single guys here know how hot she is. And she's just an intern, not an employee, so it's not like we can't, you know, try to see what's under that tight little skirt."

"They hired her full-time in June," Elijah corrects, which shocks me. I don't know how he knows that. Maybe he read a press release or something?

I tug on my skate lace so hard it snaps. I'm going to rip that pervy mustache off Eddie's face and feed it to him. Elijah stands up. "You know, Rollins, you should probably concentrate on the fact that I'm here to show you up and take your job, and not what's up the skirt of a girl way too smart to touch you with a ten-foot hockey stick."

We all look at Elijah and a couple of guys let out exaggerated "ohs!" His voice was light, teasing, but his face is tense, his jaw locked, his brows pulled together. I glance at his hands and they're fisted by his sides. I realize Levi must have told him Dixie was my sister, or he figured it out on his own. Maybe Dixie even told him herself, because I did see her talking to him a few times. Either way, it's the only reason I can think of that he'd be this pissed. Elijah is all about the inappropriate jokes and looking up any skirt he can, so it's got to be his loyalty to me making him stand up to Eddie.

"Easy, little Casco," Eddie replies, and he's pissed but trying to mask it. "Guess you have that uptight attitude in common with your big bro, huh? Come on, Jude, you know. You're single."

"I'm not."

It comes out of my mouth before I even think about it, and even though I hadn't planned on admitting that to anyone, not even really myself, it feels normal to have the words out there. Not just normal, but good. I toss the broken piece of skate lace in my hand in the garbage and stomp toward the door, teetering a little on my unlaced skate. "I'm dating Zoey, and even if I wasn't, trust me when I say I would never hit on Dixie or talk about her the way you are. And you should do what Eli said and shut the fuck up and concentrate on playing well so you don't make it too easy for him to take your spot on this team."

I storm out of the room in search of a trainer and new laces.

The game was crazy. We beat the San Diego Saints, barely, but we beat them, and it felt good to be out there competing again, even if it was only preseason. Levi was probably our best player, scoring two goals before he went to the medical room halfway through the second period because his shoulder started to act up. Eddie was definitely our worst, letting in three goals in that period, so they pulled him for the third and put in Eli. Levi didn't play the third, so the media didn't get their big Casco brothers moment, but it was probably for the best, since Eli looked shaky out there and let in an easy goal. Darby scored one, and I scored two back-to-back in the third, which took us to the win. I swear I played better knowing Zoey was in the stands watching.

After the game, Levi isn't in the locker room, so I do something I never do: I take it upon myself to give the post-game speech. Usually the coach does it if Levi isn't available. I even pushed Duncan into doing it once, since he is an alternate captain like me, but this time I don't shirk my responsibility. I'm feeling good about the way I played and, well, life in general, so I just do it.

"Nice work, boys!" I start, and they all look up. Duncan reaches over and lowers the music on the iPod he has hooked up to speakers. "We were rusty and a little shaky, but we pulled together and won. This was tough, and it was only preseason. After two Stanley Cup wins in a row, every team in the league wants to knock us down a peg. We need to use the animosity as fuel to make us do even better. Okay?"

There are a bunch of loud shouts of agreement. I see a few eyes dart past me, so I turn around, rubbing the sweat out of my eyes with my towel. Levi is standing in the doorway with a towel and a bag of ice taped to his shoulder. "Anything to add, Captain?" Duncan asks.

"What he said," Levi replies and gives me a nod of approval, and it makes my shoulders pull back in pride. No matter what our history off the ice, he's still the most pulled together, solid player and leader I know on the ice, so if he not only agrees with what I said but has nothing to add, it's a compliment.

Levi walks over to his brother, but Eli gets up and mutters something, then heads out of the room, still wearing half his equipment. Levi goes to his spot next to me and drops onto the bench. "He's still shaken up from the injury."

I look up and find his face worried. "That's normal, right?"

"I have no idea. He's the only goalie I know personally who has had an injury like that." Levi almost chokes on the words as he says them, and my heart clenches. Jesus, I remember when it happened and how I felt seeing it. I can't even imagine what it was like for Levi or for Elijah himself. "But you know this league, they need results every day, especially from rookies. He's going to be shipped to the minors and stay there a long time if he can't find his way around this."

"He will. I know he will," I say, trying to sound comforting because I honestly believe Eli is strong enough to get through any residual fear. The kid is as tough as he is crazy. Good goalies always are. I resort to what I'm best at to lighten the mood: teasing. "Speaking of Eli, did he grow over the summer? He's got to have a couple inches on you now."

"It's his hairstyle. It's like a foot off his head," Levi mutters.

"Sure it is." I smile. "Does he call you squirt yet?"

I'm a jackass for making fun of him, since Levi is three inches taller than me at six three, but it gets that morose look off his face, so who cares? Smiling, Levi rolls his eyes at my joke and changes the subject.

"So your girlfriend coming to the party tonight?" Levi asks. I nod and fight a smile at the word "girlfriend." I do not need to look like a lovesick puppy in the locker room. "Good. Tessa is dying to see her again."

"She's back from her work thing?"

"She's coming straight to the party from the airport," Levi explains.

"Cool. Zoey brought her work friend Marti, who I'm sure will love to meet Tessa and Carla and anyone she can sell a house to," I explain and pull off my shirt and start undoing my pads.

"I know it doesn't matter, but I'm happy for you, Jude," Levi says, and his serious tone, which most mistake for angry, is back.

I nod and drop my pads on the ground and look up. Eddie is watching Levi and me, his expression dark. I have no idea what his issue is, so I ignore him and turn back to Levi. "It matters. Thanks."

Levi looks shocked but doesn't say anything. He nods, and I get up and make my way to the showers, eager to get cleaned up so I can see Zoey.

27

ZOEY

Marti is twitching like a kid in a candy store as she looks around the massive, immaculate house. The party is the last one the Thunder will have with the Stanley Cup before the trophy heads back to Toronto and waits for the next team to claim it at the end of the season. That's why the management decided to throw a final get-together tonight for players and family at the owner's house. The owner is some incredibly successful tech businesswoman named Ryanne Bateman, which blew my mind. She is, according to Google, the only female owner of a pro hockey team, and also according to Google she is over forty, which is crazy, because she doesn't look a day older than me.

Marti is in awe of the house and this woman's wealth and power, and spent the first hour we were here whispering ideas on how to approach Ryanne and give her a business card, but all I could think about was Jude. He played amazingly tonight, and it was crazy, but it turned me on to see him dominate on the ice. And then he walked out of the locker room in that expensive blue three-piece suit with the crisp checkered shirt and the silver tie, and it was almost more eye porn than I could handle. I wanted to start unbuttoning his jacket and vest with my teeth right there in the friends and family lounge.

"We should get Jude to introduce us to her," Marti says as she sips her champagne beside me. "She probably buys real estate the way we buy underwear."

I smile, but my eyes are on Jude as he chats in the far corner of the living room with his sister. "I'll see if he can do it."

"I've already given out business cards to half the team," Marti says and nudges me so my eyes finally leave my boyfriend. "Zoey, you need to take advantage of some of these connections before I steal them all. You're the one who has to build a client base."

"I know. I will." I've already had a casual conversation with Abby, who just found out she and Brian are expecting their third baby and will be needing a bigger place before it's born. But I didn't want to treat my affiliation with Jude like a business arrangement, because it isn't. Of course I haven't told that to Marti, but she's beginning to figure it out.

"So I'll be honest with you," she says in a conspiratorial whisper while my eyes follow Jude's hand as it plays with the Windsor knot in his tie and then slides down the tie to where it's tucked into his vest. Why does his every move make my nerve endings dance? "I kind of want more than just commissions from some of these guys."

I nod, barely paying attention. "Go for it."

"Like you are?" That finally gets my attention, and I look up and find her eyes staring back at me with zero judgment. "Hey, honey, I am all for mixing work and play, as long as you both know what you're getting into."

"I've never been involved with a client before," I explain, despite the fact that she doesn't think less of me. "But Jude and I had a history we just couldn't forget."

"I figured there was more than just an old friendship, because from the second he walked into our office he looked at you like you were edible," Marti acknowledges with a smile. "Like I said, I see nothing wrong with a little good, clean fun. Who am I kidding? I actually like good, dirty fun better. And speaking of dirty, is that one single?"

I follow her index finger, which she lifts from the champagne flute she's holding and subtly points toward the buffet table. There, slobbering all over the roast beef slider tray, is Eddie Rollins.

"Eddie? Oh Mylanta!" I can't believe she's asking about him. "Yes, he's single. For a reason."

"Who is single for a reason?" Tessa asks as she suddenly appears beside me. She absently pushes her long, curled blond hair behind her shoulder as her blue eyes scan the room. "Have you seen Levi?"

"Tessa, this is my co-worker Marti. She came to the game with me tonight," I explain, and the two smile at each other and shake hands. "I leased Tessa and her partner the space for their business, and she just so happens to be dating Levi Casco."

Marti's brown eyes flare and she covers her mouth as she gasps. "Thor? You're dating Thor? Oh, girl, you are my idol. He's San Francisco's hottest bachelor."

Tessa laughs and blushes a little at Marti's use of Levi's "god of Thunder" nickname. "He is pretty hot, if I do say so myself. I haven't seen him in four days, so I'm in withdrawal."

"He's in the backyard drinking beer out of the Cup with Duncan and Carla, last I saw," I explain. "His shoulder had him sitting part of the game."

Tessa frowns in concern, but my eyes are attached to Jude again as he makes his way over. With every step closer, the tingle in my body gets stronger until I'm almost fidgeting. As soon as he's close enough, he circles my waist with his arm and kisses me softly. "Having fun, ladies?" he asks us all, and then turns and nuzzles my cheek with the tip of his nose. "Sorry, Dixie needed to talk to me about a charity thing I did."

"Look, there's Thor!" Marti announces and points. Levi is walking into the house from the open back doors. Well, it's not exactly doors. The whole back wall is glass panels that retract so it opens completely to the backyard.

I watch as Tessa and Levi's eyes connect, and both their faces start to glow at the sight of each other. Her smile is so big and beautiful it makes me smile. She starts to move toward him, and he excuses himself from a conversation with the elegant team owner and some guy in a suit and starts toward her. I'm expecting this sappy moment complete with a giant reunion kiss but...it doesn't happen. They hug, but it's so quick I almost miss it because I blinked. They bow their heads close and whisper something that's probably sweet—or better yet, sexy—but that too is brief. Marti notices the restrained quality of the whole thing too, and shoots me a sideways "what the fuck" type of glance. I just shrug and look to Jude for some kind of explanation. He's not paying attention; his eyes are on my shoulder where he's softly pushing back the one tendril of hair I have purposely let fall away from my sideswept low ponytail. "You look amazing tonight."

I look down at the cocktail dress I'm in. I went for something fun and flirty with a tight top but flared at the waist—and it has pockets, which automatically makes a dress a ten for me. "That's the first time you've given me a compliment when I'm dressed up."

"You always look good, but I like you best dressed down. Or not dressed at all," he whispers, and then his voice drops even lower and his lips graze my neck as he adds, "This little loose curl is going to be the death of me."

He sweeps a hand over that loose tendril again, his fingertips scraping my neck and making me wish I brought a backup pair of panties. "Speaking of backups…"

"We were speaking of backups?" Jude asks, and I realize he's got me so frazzled I'm not making sense.

I take a small step away from him and point to Eddie. "Is he single?"

"Of course. Why?"

"I think he's hot," Marti announces and puts her empty champagne glass down on a passing waiter's tray. "Does he need real estate?"

"He might need to sell his place here one day soon," Jude replies and shrugs. "He's single, but be warned, the only C word he's about is conquest, not commitment."

Marti doesn't seem the least bit concerned. "That's what they say about you too."

We both look at her. Jude's face is suddenly void of its usual amusement. His hand stills at my neck. Marti instantly realizes her mistake, and while her cheeks turn as red as her dress, she quickly adds, "And everyone was clearly wrong about that. Besides, the only C word I'm interested in ends in o-m-i-n-g, and if he can make me do that, the rest will sort itself out."

She marches away, toward Eddie. "Well, that was an overshare of epic proportions," I say, because it's silent now and feels awkward.

Jude laughs, and his hand tightens around my waist. "Hey, I admire a girl who goes after what she wants and doesn't expect more than she's going to get. That's why I had a crush on you way back when."

I smile. "And now?"

"Why do I have a crush on you now?" he asks, and I nod, pulling my bottom lip between my teeth out of nerves, even though it'll ruin my lipstick.

Before he can answer, a female voice, soft, smooth and dripping with confidence, interrupts. "Mr. Braddock. We haven't had a chance to chat yet tonight."

We both look up, almost startled, like we forgot we were in public. I kind of did for a minute there. "Ms. Bateman. Thanks for giving us one last big night with Lord Stanley," Jude says with his usual flirtatious smile, which shouldn't bug me because I know it's genetically impossible for him to smile any other way. But still, it kind of does when it's directed at such a stunning, put-together woman. "This is my girlfriend, Zoey Quinlin. Zoey, Ryanne Bateman, our team owner."

We shake hands. Her grip is firm, her hand is cool. I feel like my skin must feel clammy next to hers, and I should care but I don't, because he just called me his girlfriend. "Nice to meet you."

"You too." Ryanne smiles, and it's authentically warm. "You must be quite a woman to get our biggest social media problem to settle down."

"Ouch!" Jude laughs. "That was blunt."

"And accurate," I add, thinking back to the dick pic, and I'm grinning because…I'm his girlfriend. Ryanne laughs and reaches out and takes my empty champagne glass from my hand.

"That astute comment deserves another glass of champagne." At that announcement three waiters converge on us. I nod gratefully and take a flute. Jude does too.

"Well, do make sure you drink some of this from the Cup later," Ryanne tells me and grins. "It's a ridiculously unhygienic tradition, but I swear I bought the team just so I could do it. Jude, you and Levi better make sure I can do it again sometime soon."

"We'll do our best."

She floats—seriously, it looks like she's floating under her long, clingy aubergine dress—toward Elijah Casco, who's holding a tall fruity-looking drink, twisting the umbrella in it as he talks to Dixie in the corner of the dining room. "Holy moly, she's something else."

Jude nods. "She is unique. She says she got into hockey because her dad liked it, and she bought the team in his memory. I think she bought it because she likes fucking athletic younger men and because it makes her money."

My breath catches in my throat, and I nearly spit my mouthful of champagne back into my glass. "She fucks the team?"

Jude chuckles at my horrified whisper. "Not the whole team. It's not like sexual harassment or an initiation ritual or something. She doesn't even live in San Fran. She's based in New York, so she's hardly ever here, but when she is and she throws these little shindigs, she usually ends up with one of us."

The champagne turns to acid in my mouth, and I have trouble swallowing it down. He notices, and his hand presses softly into my lower back. "Not me. I haven't slept with her. She offered to blow me at last year's Stanley Cup party, but I politely refused."

"But she's gorgeous and clearly not looking for a commitment, which was totally your thing," I blurt out like a raving lunatic, because only a lunatic would say something like that to a guy they want a commitment from.

Jude slides his hand completely around my waist and pulls me against his side. "I'm glad you said 'was.'"

"I hope it's 'was' because I'm your girlfriend now," I whisper back, and my heart swells as the words leave my mouth.

He grins and kisses my cheek. "That's right. Now can we get home so I can get naked with my girlfriend?"

"I should make sure Marti is okay with me ditching her," I say and look around the room, but I can't find her, so I start to walk toward the backyard. Jude laces our fingers together and follows behind.

As we enter the backyard, we pass Abby and Brian, who smile at us, and then Carla, who is sitting on Duncan's lap on a lush lounger by the fire pit. As I scan the crowd for my co-worker, I spot Tessa and Levi in the corner. They're almost hidden against the high bushes that line the property, holding hands as Levi's hulking frame almost blankets her. His head is dipped down and they're talking, but if either moved a fraction of an inch they'd be kissing. Levi catches my eye and takes a definitive step away from his girlfriend. Their hands untangle and he gives me a small, quick wave.

"Levi really isn't into PDA, is he?"

"What?"

"They just always pull apart when they think someone is watching."

Jude leans down, nuzzling my neck again. "Can we just find Marti and get out of here so we can do things to each other with no one watching?"

"Fine." I laugh.

Marti, it turns out, is drinking champagne out of the Stanley Cup and having some kind of flirty, borderline dirty conversation with Eddie Rollins. She's fine with us cutting out early and Eddie assures me he'll "take care of her." Ugh. Well, I know Marti is a big girl and knows exactly what she's getting into.

The drive home is quick, and as soon as we get in the house, I'm all over Jude. I can't help myself. Everything about him tonight is a turn-on. From the way he played on the ice, to the way he looked in the three-piece suit, introducing me as his girlfriend, all of it. By the time I get him into my bedroom, his pants are at his ankles and his suit jacket and vest are somewhere on the stairs, as is my dress. He picks me up, which I don't expect, so I squeal, and he laughs as he drops me on the bed and climbs on top of me. His kiss is one of his demanding ones and it's amazing. Jude, I have decided after all these weeks, has three types of kisses. The demanding one, which is forceful and dominant, the kind I don't even bother to try to keep up with—I just let him claim my mouth. The gentle one, which is sweet and soft with this simmering passion that makes me melt. And the needy one, which I've only experienced that time he showed up unexpectedly with the teapot. That one is forceful, but not in a dominant way, in a searching way. He's searching for acceptance with his tongue, teeth and mouth, acceptance and love. I match that one with every graze of his lips and push of his tongue, because I need him as much as he needs me. God help me, because I only have broken pieces of a heart left, but when he kisses me like that, I want to give them all to him.

He grinds into me one more slow, seductive time before breaking the kiss and pulling away. His right knee drags up the inside of my thigh, followed by his left as he pulls himself up to sit on his heels between my legs.

His eyes are roaming my body as he tugs at the Windsor knot in his tie. "How are you so fucking beautiful?" he exclaims in an exhale.

I reach up to still his hand and grab that tie to pull him back down on top of me, but I'm too late. The tie slips out of its knot and off his neck when I pull on it. He grabs it from me and I flop back on the bed, my hair flying up around me before fanning out across the pillow. I lift my arms again to reach for him, and he grabs both my wrists and I feel the silky tie slide around them.

His body covers mine as he pushes my arms over my head. His lips find the spot where my jaw curves up to my ear. He bites down, and I shiver with pleasure and move to wrap my arms around his neck, only I can't. He's wrapped my wrists in the tie and tied them to the metal bed frame. He pulls back to look me in the eye and he smiles. "Can I?"

"Yeah," I say easily, which is weird because I've never wanted to be tied up before. Never even really entertained the thought, but with Jude, it turns me on, and I'm excited to see where this goes.

"Good, because I am going to take my time tonight," he says as his blue eyes roam again down my legs and back up, to my stomach and over my ribs, to my breasts. He's undoing his shirt slowly, button by button, and it's so damn sexy. "I want to taste you and tease you without your hands on me so I don't get distracted."

His eyes are sliding up my neck now, and when they land on my face our eyes lock. "I want you to fuck me."

"Holy shit," he almost gasps. "Don't say that."

"Why?"

"Because I'll fuck you."

I bite my lip to hold back my smile and then whisper, "Good. Fuck me, Jude. Please."

His mouth comes crashing down on mine. His hands tug at my underwear and easily shove them all the way down my legs. I break the kiss to move my lips to his neck, because I've learned it's a weakness for him.

"I want to feel your pussy quiver on my tongue," he growls against my shoulder.

"I want to feel your dick quiver inside me," I counter, and I spread my legs a little farther so his hips fall into the space I make.

"Zoey, when you talk dirty, it's the hottest thing in the damn universe," he confesses and grinds again, his hips pushing up, his cock rubbing against my inner thigh.

It's not enough. I don't know what the hell is happening, but I'm suddenly and completely overwhelmed with the urge to make him fuck me. Everything else he's promising, his tongue, his fingers, his mouth, are all amazing, but I can think of nothing but his dick inside me. I want it. I want it now. I want it so badly my skin is feverish, and I feel like I have to struggle for a breath.

"Please fuck me, Jude," I beg. I'm actually full-on, without a flicker of regret, begging him to fuck me. "Hard. Fast. Rough."

He kisses me hard again. Our tongues push against each other as his hips roll and mine twist, and I feel his tip bump my entrance. He feels it too, because he grunts a little and pulls his hips back, like a good boy. He may be coming to his senses, but I am losing mine. I yank against the restraints and swear again.

"Jude…" I tug again. The metal of the bed frame creaks. "Do it again."

"I want to…" His words are wrapped in groan.

"Do it. Touch me there with just your cock. Please." I twist and push my hips up as he swings low, and it happens, his dick so warm, so hard yet soft. It bumps and then he pushes. He pushes into me—ever so slightly—but his tip slides into me. And then it's gone.

"You want me?" How is that even a question? Why is he in such awe?

"God, yes. I've never wanted anyone the way I've always wanted you," I confess hoarsely, and I wrap my legs around his waist, hooking my ankles behind his lower back.

He grinds his hips, pushing his perfect cock into my perfect space—once again just the tip. He's breathing hard already; his face is twisted like he's struggling internally both physically and mentally. I bite my lip and sigh and turn and kiss his shoulder because it's the closest thing to my mouth, and then I nip the skin there. "Please."

"Zoey, God…" He kisses my neck and whispers against my ear as his hips push up. "Tell me to stop."

No. I can't. I won't. I'm suddenly the wild, restless and completely reckless teenager he always thought I was—the one I wanted to be. "Fuck me, Jude. Fuck me like I'm the only thing you want."

And he pushes—hard—sinking into me quickly and fully. My back bends and the air evaporates from my lungs. Something like a whimper twisted around a gasp makes its way from my open mouth. He's inside me, bare, and it's perfect. He moves, a little out and all the way back in, and makes his own new sound—a groan and a grunt and his voice is someone else's—darker, deeper, rougher, needier as he pants out his words. *Fuck. Zoey. Jesus, this. So good. You're perfect. I can't. Ah. Uh.*

Physically, emotionally, everything inside me is making love to him right now. My heart, my head, my body. I've never felt like this.

Never knew there was something this intense. Every nerve ending in my body pulses stronger and stronger until it's too much. The world goes dark and I fall apart—my mind and my body melting. I don't even realize I'm pulling at the tie around my wrists as I thrash until Jude reaches up and roughly smacks a hand over mine, pressing both my palms gently against the metal frame. My eyes crack open in time to see him come. His face is flushed, his expression wild, and a noise tears out of his throat, raw and heavy.

Oh my God, I love him.

He's got everything—all of me is his. I can't stop it. I can't get it back. It's too late. My heart and soul are his. In one clumsy motion his hand on the bed frame yanks at the tie as his body drops onto mine.

"You're free," he pants weakly into the pillow next to my left ear, where he's buried his face.

My hands are numb, but I move them up into his hair anyway. My eyes close and fight to quell the bliss and fear and confusion that are blowing through me like a tornado with the power to lift and tear apart everything. "I'm so not free."

He doesn't hear me. I didn't think he would. I'm not even sure the words actually formed. But the realization did.

28

JUDE

I'm terrified. The all-consuming rush of my orgasm immediately turned into an even vaster swell of panic. My pulse won't stop racing, my breath won't fill my lungs again, and I can't stop sweating, so I roll away from her onto the other side of the bed, and then I immediately sit up, so my back is to her. I need to calm down, and I won't do that if I look at her. I push my fingers into my hair, pressing the heels of my hands into my temples.

"We just did that." Her voice is low, soft and stunned. "Oh God, we did that."

"I've never lost control like that. Not with anyone," I admit, still struggling to catch my breath.

"You're freaking out. I'm so sorry. I shouldn't have…" I feel the bed move slightly. She must have sat up. I have to look at her. I need to calm down and look at her. "I'm sorry. I shouldn't have let it happen…"

That weak, wobbly admission is like a slap to my senses. I twist to face her. The room is mostly dark, but even in the shadows I can see her devastation. Her complexion is ashen, and her eyes are wide and watery. I cup the side of her face with one hand. "Come here."

She inches across the mattress. I move, meeting her in the middle, and then lie back down, pulling her with me. She snuggles close, her legs tangled with mine, her cheek against my bicep, but her body is stiff.

"You think I'm worried about the lack of protection?" I feel her nod against my arm. I look down at the top of her head. "I'm not."

Her head tilts up, and I see skepticism and confusion in her gaze. Makes perfect sense, because I don't get it either. I should be losing my ever-loving mind. I've never had sex without a condom. Not ever. I was a freaking zealot when it came to covering my junk. I never took chances, and I never made mistakes.

"But you're freaking out." My heartbeat starts to stumble like a drunk person as she reminds me. She presses the palm of her hand down firmly on my sternum. "Your heart is still pounding."

"Yeah. I've never lost control like that. I told you," I repeat and slowly force air into my lungs. I am going to fucking beat this feeling before it becomes a full-blown panic attack and I ruin everything. I'm not panicking over the condom—or lack thereof—I'm losing my mind over the realization that I am completely, madly, inconsolably in love with her.

Which means I suddenly feel like I have no control over anything, and she can completely wreck me. I didn't expect to end up here. I didn't think I could. I thought this was just going to be fun. A distraction, a blast from the past, a final shot at a long-lost conquest. But I didn't conquer anything. I surrendered. Without even knowing how to, I gave her my heart.

"You've never had unprotected sex?" Her voice is quiet, slow and calm, like she's trying not to startle me. She knows I'm still freaking out.

"Never."

"Not even with your girlfriend? She wasn't on the pill?"

My heart gallops even faster. "What girlfriend?"

"Dixie said you had one a while ago," she murmurs. "She wasn't on the pill?"

"She was. I just didn't," I murmur, and I feel her head move. She's looking up at me, I know it, but I don't open my eyes. "It just never happened."

"You've never had an accident?"

"Nope. I'd never risked anything with anyone." I wish we would stop talking. About this. About everything. I don't want to talk. I'm scared if we keep talking I'll tell her I love her, and that's not okay. Not right now. I can't expect her to deal with that knowledge when I can't even deal with it myself. Holy shit, I'm a train wreck. "Tired."

I say it softly, slowly, like I'm about to fall asleep, even though I couldn't sleep right now if I swallowed a bottle of Ambien. I tighten my grip on her, hugging her closer to my side, and she puts her head down on my bicep again.

Twenty minutes later she shifts, rolling onto her side, her back to me. She's been asleep for a while now. I wait, pressed into her back, for another forty minutes, the whole time watching her eyelashes flutter and running through a billion reasons in my head why this is okay. Zoey isn't going to hurt me. I won't hurt her. It's fine. This is good. We're good and we're going to continue being good. This is what I thought I wanted with Tessa—I have it. It's real this time. It's right.

Still, I can't fucking calm down. Adrenaline won't stop racing through my body. Two hours later, when I know sleep is not coming maybe ever again, I slip out of bed. I move through the house in the dark, gathering all my discarded clothing as I go. She's got a small chalkboard on the wall next to the fridge. I grab some chalk and, next to the grocery items she's jotted down, I scrawl a note. Then I head to the front door, twist the smaller lock on the back of the handle so it locks behind me, and close the door.

I just need time to think.

29

ZOEY

Waking up this morning to an empty bed instantly made my blood run cold. He freaked out last night. I get it. We did something stupid. I mean, I'm not on the pill. I also can't get pregnant without a shit ton of tries—more than six months of trying had resulted in nothing, so I know one time with Jude was likely to bring the same results. But he's never done this before. He freaked. Understandable, but he seemed to be calming down. He calmed me down enough that I fell asleep.

When I get downstairs, I see the note on the chalkboard.

Z, Couldn't sleep. Call me when you wake up. Yours, J. OX

Okay. That makes me feel a little better. I make my way back upstairs and dig my phone out of my purse. I have less than half the battery charge left, so I walk over to the nightstand to plug it in, and that's when I see Jude's phone on the floor. It's half under the bed, with one side touching the leg of the nightstand. It must have fallen from his pants pocket when we were pulling off each other's clothes.

And he was in such a rush to get the hell away from me, he left it behind.

I push the thought from my head. I have to give him the benefit of the doubt. It was late and dark and he just forgot it. Simple mistake, and not a sign of abandonment. I put his phone on the table next to mine and head into the bathroom to get ready for work. Twenty-five minutes later his phone is beside mine on the kitchen table as I steep my tea when it chimes and the screen lights up. I glance down and automatically read the text message filling the screen by accident or habit or whatever. I just do. And I instantly regret it.

The message says: Great seeing you last night. You are full of surprises! Can't wait to see you again.

The name on the message is Kina. I don't know a Kina. He does, obviously. And he saw her last night. After he left my bed? I shake my head. I don't know that. Maybe it's someone from the party. A fan or someone who works for the team or a teammate's wife or sister or something. It could be meaningless. It could be innocent. But it could also break my heart.

I can't sit here with my thoughts anymore so I get up, dump my tea in the sink and head to work. All I want to do is call him, but I can't because he doesn't have a home phone, only the cell phone currently in my purse with a message from Kina. Argh.

He'll figure it out. He'll come to my work for the phone or to my house for it tonight, and we'll talk it out, and everything will be fine. Because I need everything to be fine. I want it to be fine. I deserve fine.

Marti is already sitting at her desk when I walk in. Well, hunched over her desk is a better description. She's got both hands wrapped around a venti cup. She looks presentable to the common person, but I know her too well by now. Her hair is up in a topknot, and she's wearing the jeans and black silk shirt she keeps in the desk drawer in case of emergency.

"You haven't been home," I announce as I walk around my desk. "I'd ask where you were, but I think I know."

She looks up, and I expect a sheepish smile, but instead I get a tight one. I drop my bag on my chair. "Everything okay?"

She nods. "Yeah. The sex was satisfactory. Both times," Marti explains, and I try not to cringe. I just don't find anything about Eddie Rollins attractive, so I really hope she's not about to give me details. "But he is a chatty drunk. And he's not a good teammate."

I lift an eyebrow. Okay, this I kind of want to hear. "How so?"

"Well, he doesn't seem to like Jude much. I think they had a falling-out, because he was bitching like he was scorned or something," Marti mutters. "Man, you'd think Jude stood him up for prom."

"What did Jude actually do?" I can't help but ask as I sit my butt on the corner of my desk so I can face Marti. I probably shouldn't be asking. I mean, gossiping is a bullshit thing to do. But…he has me feeling all needy and insecure after disappearing.

Marti sighs and fidgets, playing with the edge of the plastic lid on her coffee cup. "He says Jude gave him shit about locker room talk. Chewed him out in front of the guys."

That's not bad. I mean, maybe to a dirtbag like Eddie, but to me it's a good thing. I shrug and feel my shoulders loosen, because I was tense and didn't realize it. "I have a feeling Eddie is probably pretty hard-core. I mean…not that he'll talk about you."

Marti laughs, unperturbed. "Oh hell yes, he will. But I don't care.

Maybe it will help the guys remember my name when they need to buy or sell a house."

"Marti!" I laugh, and she smiles, but it falls off her face pretty quickly. Too quickly. "What?"

She goes back to fiddling with her cup. "After round one, before round two, he took me on a walk down memory lane about how much fun Jude used to be…and how his adventures with women were legendary both in number and antics."

I nod. "Yeah. I know."

Marti glances around the office to make sure none of our co-workers are too close. "His hockey stick is on the internet," she whispers and points at her crotch just so I know "hockey stick" is a euphemism.

It makes me laugh. "I know that too. It's fine. Believe it or not, I was a very liberal wild child when I first met Jude. We're not judging each other on the past. Besides, he was single."

She looks even more uncomfortable. "Not always, according to Eddie."

"I know he had a girlfriend for a while."

"Did you know it was Tessa?"

Everything stops. My heart, the blood in my veins, my lungs, my brain. Marti clearly sees the incomprehension on my face, so she clarifies. "The girl dating Levi Casco. She was Jude's girlfriend."

What? Why? How? I don't…I can't understand. A flood of memories start making sense. The way all the hockey wives and girl-friends don't seem to like Jude. The way Levi and Tessa won't touch each other when Jude's in the room. I thought it was because they were anti-PDA but they're trying to be subtle for Jude. Carla once told me that some people on the team aren't okay with Tessa and Levi being together. She meant Jude. He's not okay. Why? Because he loves Tessa? No. Yes? I don't know, and it's making me feel even more humiliated. Why didn't he tell me?

Marti stands up, grabs her phone off her desk, takes my hand and leads me through the office to the tiny conference room. It's empty this early, so she pulls me inside and shuts the door behind us. She literally has to move me toward a chair and push on my shoulders to make me sit down. Internally I'm grappling with which emotion I should let overtake me.

Anger that he didn't tell me this right away. Paranoia about why he didn't tell me this at all. Sadness because he didn't want to tell me this. Humiliation because clearly everyone I've been around in the last few weeks—Tessa, Carla, Levi, Dixie, Jude, Eddie, the rest of the team and now Marti—knew and purposely left me in the dark. Like an idiot.

Marti swims into view, sitting down in front of me and blocking the wall I'm staring at. She puts her phone on the table between us. "Eddie was drunk and had major verbal diarrhea, so he was just blurting out everything. He said Jude and Tessa were dating and that Jude cheated on her, so she dumped him. Then I guess at some point she and Levi started dating, and Jude lost it when he found out. Eddie's big concern was it happened in playoffs and made Jude a pissy bitch that wasn't fun to party with."

"Tessa?" I repeat her name, and it feels painful suddenly. I remember when I met Carla and Tessa and took them to see potential business locations. Tessa was quiet and even seemed a little depressed. I remember Carla saying I shouldn't think Tessa's mood was due to her lack of interest in the places I was showing. It was because she was going through a breakup.

A breakup with Jude.

"I knew you didn't know, and I wouldn't think that was too big a deal normally," Marti tells me, her voice calm and almost reassuring. "I mean, I would normally believe that Jude thought it would be awkward to tell you, or he hadn't found the right moment…But then Eddie started the audiovisual part of his drunken homage to Thunder drama."

Her hand moves to her phone. "Eddie was trying to show me how much fun Jude used to be. He kept showing me pictures on his phone of them partying. Mostly from his summer in Toronto after they won the Cup. There were a couple videos too of them in a hot tub with a bunch of girls."

She's pulling something up on her phone, and something in me starts to squirm like an animal in a trap. "I don't want to see him with another girl, Marti."

"That's not what I need to show you," she assures me and pauses, her eyes filling with sympathy. "I emailed this video to myself after Eddie passed out. I don't even think he understood the significance of it when he showed it to me, but I do."

She hits play and turns her screen to face me. It's a video of Jude in just a pair of wet underwear, sitting on the edge of a hot tub. The background is dark night sky with some building lights twinkling like this hot tub is on a roof. I can hear girls chattering and splashing and Eddie's pervy laugh.

"Dude, look around you. There's plenty of pussy to drown your sorrows in," Eddie's voice says off camera.

Jude takes a sip from the beer bottle he's holding and runs a hand through the overgrown beard he's sporting. Water drips from it. This has got to be very soon after winning the Cup. That's a playoff beard.

"I'm not sad. I'm pissed. She had to pick my best friend? It would be like me fucking Carla. I might have fucked other people, but it wasn't anyone she knew."

That beer in his hand is definitely not his first because his words are sloppy. Someone off camera splashes him, and I see the water drops hit him, but he ignores it. Eddie speaks again. "So give her a taste of her own. Fuck Carla!"

"She's Darby's, you jackass," Jude barks. His eyes narrow angrily, and then he sips his beer again. "But that's a good idea. I should fuck one of her friends. I mean, Carla's not her only one. I could find another girl she knows and parade that in front of her face."

"Just make sure she's hot," Eddie advises and laughs.

Someone splashes Jude again, and he smiles this time as a voice whines, "Jude, come play with me."

He grins at Eddie, which is essentially grinning at the camera, and puts his beer down. "But first I'll try out your drowning in pussy idea…"

The camera follows him as he lowers himself into the hot tub, chest-to-chest with a topless blonde. I close my eyes. I think I'm going to be sick. I stand up. Marti does the same, and as I turn toward the door, she puts a hand on my arm. "I swear I didn't tell you this to be a bitch," Marti pleads sincerely. "I just know if it was me, and I really liked him, I would want to know. Before I liked him even more, you know?"

I nod. I'm not mad at her. I know she's not being vindictive. She's trying to be a friend. I want to reassure her, but I can't right now. I can't do anything but get out of here. I need to be alone. I open the conference room door. Marti must know I'm leaving because she says, "I'll have Anastasia send your calls to me, and if anything urgent comes up, I'll text you."

I nod again, but pause and manage to find a shred of my voice, but only a shred. "Can you email me that video?"

"Okay."

I turn and walk as fast as I can out of the office.

30

JUDE

I should be sleeping. I only have two hours before I have to be at the airport to meet the team for our trip to the White House to meet the president and be congratulated on our Stanley Cup win last season. I didn't sleep a second of last night, but it was worth it, because I managed to calm myself down and get my head on right again. I would have headed straight back to Zoey's house at five when I was finally ready to go home, but I had locked the door on my way out. And then I reached for my phone and realized I didn't have it, so I gave up and went to my place.

Which is why I'm getting ready to head to her office instead of grabbing some much-needed winks—because I need to make things right with her more than I need rest. I'm hoping she'll let me take her to lunch so I can talk to her away from her office and spend some quality time with her before I'm gone for three days. I grab my packed bag off the bed and carry it into the kitchen.

Dixie is sitting on my island, cross-legged with her shoes on, eating a bowl of cereal. My face automatically contorts in revulsion, and

I smack at her leg. "Get your shoes off my counter! Why are you so gross?"

"Why are you a hypocritical OCD clean freak?" she counters with a mouth full of Fruity Pebbles. "You can't stand a dirty house, but you'll stick your dick in anything."

Her crass insult makes me think of where my dick was last night. I feel hot, like I'm going to blush. I don't fucking do that, so it weirds me out. She must see that weirdness on my face, because her blue eyes flare. "What? Am I missing something? What did your dick do and with who?"

"Stop being a pig, and be a proper little sister for once, would you, please?" I shake my head in disgust, but she's not buying it. "For the record my dick is the cleanest thing on me. I get tested every three months and you know that."

"Yeah and you always bag it. I know. Dad bought us all condoms when we turned sixteen, but I'm betting the conversation you got was a lot less pro-abstinence than ours," she says, referring to the sex talk my parents gave my sisters.

I shrug. "And FYI, I'm dating Zoey now, so the dick jokes can stop, okay? I don't want you teasing me like that in front of her."

She puts the mostly empty cereal bowl down beside her hip and a little coconut milk slops out the side and lands on the counter. "You can date someone and stick your dick in someone else. It's kind of your thing."

I sigh. Loudly. "Why the fuck do you have to talk about my dick? Stop it. And for the record, this is different."

Dixie looks floored, but starts to nod slowly. "Yes, it is different. Why?"

"Excuse me?"

"Why is it different?" she repeats and tilts her head as she waits for a response.

I glance at the clock on the stove. "I have to go. I want to take her to lunch before we go to DC."

"I was going to ask for a lift to the airport," she replies.

"Too bad. I don't even know why the PR team is coming. They didn't last year," I mutter and pick up my bag again.

"We're doing our own retreat there, not going to the White House with you. We're just sharing the plane," Dixie explains. "And trust me, I'm as unhappy as you. I was going to go down to the cottage early and get it ready for Mom and Dad."

"Right. They're leaving tomorrow, right?"

She nods and jumps off the island as I turn to leave, blocking my path. "You didn't answer my question. Why are things with Zoey different?"

The words are right there on the tip of my tongue. *Because I love her. Because she's my soul mate. Because for the first time in my life all I want, all I can ever think of wanting is this one perfect person.* But I don't think it's right to tell Dixie any of this before I tell Zoey.

There's a knock at the door. "Expecting someone?"

She shakes her head, blond hair flying. I put down my bag and walk to the door, Dixie right on my heels. Before I can twist the lock there's another knock and Zoey's voice fills the air. "It's another booty call dropping by unexpectedly!"

I frown. That's not funny. Even Dixie's not laughing. I open the door, and as soon as my eyes sweep over her face, I reach for her. "What's wrong?"

She steps out of my grasp. Her skin is abnormally pale and she's clutching her cell phone in a shaking hand in front of her chest.

"You mean besides the fact that you left without a word in the middle of the night?"

Dixie makes some weird noise in her throat.

Zoey's voice sounds funny. Hard but weak. She sounded like that when I found her in the lobby of the hotel, and I hated it then, and I hate it now. I start to reach for her again, but she looks at my hand like she's trying to light it on fire, so I pull back and grip the doorframe. "I was just coming to talk to you about that. Come in."

She shakes her head. "Okay." She crosses her arms over her chest. "Talk."

"Something tells me I should be somewhere else." Dixie's voice fills the air, and then she's pushing me out of the doorway so she can leave. She stops in front of Zoey and touches her shoulder. "Call me. Whatever happens here, you're my friend. Call me."

She heads toward the elevator, but not before throwing one hell of an angry glare at me. I watch her push the elevator button and then pull my eyes back to Zoey. "Zoey, please come inside."

"I don't think I should," she replies and presses her lips together for a moment before adding, "Because I want to. I want to go in there and have you feed me whatever line you think of to make me believe you didn't run to another girl last night after having unprotected sex with me."

"Unprotected?!" Dixie repeats, clearly judging the fuck out of us. Fucking great.

I grab the doorframe again and lean my upper body into the hallway because I have a feeling if I actually step toward Zoey she'll leave. "Come inside."

She shakes her head, dark red waves tumbling everywhere. "I

don't want to believe your lies. I want to hear the truth. So just give it to me."

I hear the ping of the elevator arriving, but I know my sister is still standing in the hall and isn't going anywhere. "Zoey. Come inside. I swear I won't feed you lines. I just want some privacy."

"I didn't plan that last night. I don't know what I was thinking. I wasn't." Her hands unfold and drop to her sides, and she looks at her phone. "I just wanted you so badly and I…didn't think."

"I didn't think either. Until after, and then I thought too much." I reach for her. I can't help it. I have to touch her. I manage to grab the sleeve of her long silky shirt. She doesn't pull away, but she doesn't let me capture her hand either, so I just cling to the fabric. "Baby, I just got overwhelmed. Not by the sex but—"

"Who was your last girlfriend?" she interrupts, her eyes lifting from my hand clinging to her sleeve to meet mine.

"Why does that matter?" It's not an answer, but I don't care. It's irrelevant. "The past is the past, right? You said you don't care."

"Did you date Tessa?" The minute Zoey asks the question Dixie sucks in a breath so loud we both hear it. Oh my God, I hate her right now. Truly.

"Go. Home!" I bark, glaring at Dixie.

She nods and punches the elevator button again. It must still be there from when she ignored it the first time, because the doors open instantly, and she disappears inside. As they close, I turn my focus back to Zoey, who looks like she might cry. Fuck. She yanks her arm away from me and the fabric of her shirt slips from my fingers.

My blood is starting to boil. "Come inside."

I step toward her and manage to grab her wrist before she can step away. She lets me pull her into the entrance, but she takes a step back. I reach up with the other hand and push my fingers through her hair to cradle the back of her neck and turn her so her back is against the inside of the doorjamb and she can't back her way into the hall again. She's rock hard, every muscle, nerve and tendon taut. I press my forehead to hers. "I shouldn't have left last night. I'm so sorry. I wasn't freaking out about the sex."

She puts her hands flat on my chest. Well, one is flat on my chest, the other is still holding my cell phone so it's pressed against my chest. She closes her eyes and takes a shuddering breath.

"Did you date Tessa?"

"Yes." I tighten my fingers in her hair. I'm scared to let go. My eyes are pinched shut, and I'm scared to open them. I don't want to see her face. I'm scared of how she'll look at me.

She reaches up and wraps her hand around my wrist, pulling my hand from her neck. My eyes open as she uses her other hand, the one pressed to my chest with my cell phone, and pushes me back a few steps. Her eyes are swimming in unshed tears. "Take your cell."

"Zoey, please. Let's talk about this," I plead, reaching up to grab my phone before she lets it drop from her grip. "She's with Levi now."

"Yeah. And you hated that," she announces, her voice unsteady as she pulls her own phone out of her purse and starts to fiddle with it. I open my mouth to speak, but she suddenly turns her phone screen toward me, and a video starts to play.

I recognize myself instantly. I watch the whole drunken, gross spectacle, my heart beating slower and slower with every sickening frame. And then I hear myself slur angrily, *"I should fuck one of her friends. I mean, Carla's not her only one. I could find another girl she knows and parade that in front of her face."*

My eyes fly from the screen. There are tears sliding slowly down her anguished face. "I know what you're thinking, but you're wrong, Zoey. I swear."

"I'm thinking I love you," she confesses and shoves her phone in her bag with a shaking hand. "I love you, and that makes me feel like an idiot. Like I'm that crazy person repeating the same mistake, expecting different results."

"I'm not a mistake. We are not a mistake."

"Was I revenge? Was I a way to give Tessa a taste of her own medicine?" She doesn't give me time to respond. She just wipes at her tears and keeps on talking. "I'm someone she knows and a teenage fantasy. Two birds, one stone."

"You really think I'd do that?" I ask, my voice as broken as hers now.

"You're that guy in the video. You said it." She sniffs and steps backward, into the doorway.

"I'm not that guy anymore." I hate that I have to tell her this. That she doesn't see it.

"No, you're the guy who leaves in the middle of the night after sex to go meet up with Kina," she replies, and I freeze. Fuck. How the fuck does she know that?

My expression—the shock—must look like guilt to her, because her face falls even further, and fresh tears start to fall. "I'm such a fucking idiot."

As she storms to the elevators, something inside me snaps. Or breaks. Maybe it just dies. But I'm suddenly swimming—drowning—in a level of pain I've never felt before. And it's making me wild with rage. "You really fucking are," I snap and her eyes widen. "If you can't see how I feel about you, how I am around you, then you're a fucking idiot."

She's furiously punching the elevator button over and over, but she stops and turns to me. "I'm different? Me? The barely divorced, barren, teenage whore with little more than a house to her name?"

Holy shit. How can she talk about herself that way? "Stop."

The elevator doors open, and she steps inside. "You left me to spend the night with someone named Kina, so no. I don't feel very different at all."

And then she's gone.

"ZOEY!" I yell so loud my throat hurts, but she disappears into the elevator anyway. "FUCK!"

My neighbor's door flies open, and he stares at me, pure annoyance across his features. "Dude. What the fuck?"

"Fuck off," I snarl and head inside, slamming my door.

It's over. Everything is over.

31

JUDE

Levi is looking at me like I'm fucking insane. I don't care. I don't care about fucking anything anymore. I shove my clothes in the drawers in the dresser nearest my bed and ignore him completely. I know it's not going to last. Levi will make me talk to him. I wish the coach hadn't put us together on this trip, but it wasn't just about the White House, it was about team bonding, so they made us double up. And I know sticking me with Levi was purposeful. Coach knows something got rocky between us last season, and this is his attempt at fixing it. But Levi is the last person on the planet I want to spend the next seventy-two hours with.

There's a knock at the door as I slam shut a drawer with the last of my things. Levi's bed is closest to the door. He's been sitting on the edge of it watching me with dark, serious eyes. He leans over and twists the knob. Duncan walks in, smiling and adjusting the backward Thunder baseball cap he's wearing. "Anybody starving? Wanna grab a bite?"

"I could grab something," Levi says. "But something light. Coach has a team dinner planned, remember?"

Before Duncan can reach back and close the door behind him, Eddie appears, and I realize there is someone I want to be around even less than Levi. He's in shorts and a tank top with "Spread 'Em" written across the front, and he's holding his phone up. At first I think he's taking a picture.

"Don't," I growl. All three of them turn to look at me with surprise on their faces. "No fucking pictures."

Eddie, the piece of shit, laughs at me. "It's video. Snapchat. Like a million chicks follow my account."

I storm over to him and whack his hand. Hard. The phone goes flying across the room. Levi ducks as it sails over his head and hits the wall above his bed. Eddie swears at me. "Dude. What the fuck!"

Duncan runs a hand through his crazy red hair and sighs. "Shit, Jude."

Levi does that thing that he does where he somehow makes himself seem bigger than his six-foot-three frame and moves to stand between Eddie and me, his back to Eddie and his eyes leveled on me. "Darby, Rollins, go."

He's using that tone he has that no one would dare contradict. Duncan nods and gives me one last confused glance before turning to the door. Eddie grabs his phone off the floor, grumbling under his breath, and it's more annoying than nails on a chalkboard.

"And this is a video-free weekend. In fact, anytime I'm around, video is off limits."

Eddie scowls at me. "Jesus, it's not like I'm the one who put your dick on the web."

I take a step toward him, but Levi blocks my way. Duncan grabs Eddie by the shoulder. "Come on. Let's go. See you guys at dinner."

"Not if I see you first!" Eddie bitches at me.

Duncan shoves him out the door and closes it with a hard thud. Levi hasn't taken his eyes off me since I hit the phone. "I'm going to talk to management. We should ban all social media from these fucking things. And from game nights and practices and from the fucking locker room. We shouldn't even be allowed social media accounts. They're fucking garbage anyway."

"You want to tell me what this is really about?" he asks, calmly folding his arms over his chest.

"He only uses those accounts to get fucking laid," I reply.

"Yes, well, he needs all the help he can get," Levi replies with a poker face. "He doesn't have your happy, easygoing charm."

That's a dig at my current mood. Levi is making fucking jokes. My rage reaches lethal levels. "Must be nice to be able to joke about everything. Is that what happens when a girl loves you back? I wouldn't know, but good for you. Now if you don't mind, I'm going to take a fucking nap, so good-bye."

I turn and storm over to my bed. I sit on the edge and kick off my shoes before pulling my shirt over my head and throwing it on the ground. I drop back and cover my eyes with my right forearm. The room is silent. He's not saying anything, but he's not going anywhere either. That lasts a couple minutes; then I hear him move around the room, but I don't hear the door, so I know he didn't leave. A second later his voice fills the air.

"What happened with Zoey?"

"It's over," I tell him, but my voice is hoarse. "And don't ask me what I did, because I will fucking punch you in the face."

I hear him sigh. "I don't think you did anything, Jude. At least not on purpose."

Okay. I definitely wasn't expecting that. I move my arm and open my eyes, looking over to find him sitting on his bed with his back against the headboard. He's looking over at me, his face soft with concern, not the hard lines of judgment I would expect. Because it's how he usually looks at me when the topic is women. I'm so stunned I don't know what to do or say.

"So what happened?" he prompts.

"She found out about Tessa," I confess and sit up. "That we used to date."

Levi swallows and looks uncomfortable. "You didn't tell her about all that?"

I huff out a frustrated breath and run a hand through my hair. "No. I couldn't figure out how to say, 'Hey, I cheated on my last girl-friend, you know that nice girl you like so much, but it all ended up working out because she was in love with my best friend anyway.'"

I move off the bed and grab my shirt off the floor, and Levi swears under his breath. "Jesus, Jude, you have a way of twisting the fuck out of everything."

"Whatever. Honestly, I don't care about what happened with you two. I'm actually truly happy for you," I reply, pulling my shirt back on. "Yeah, the situation could have been better, but I now know what you always did. I never loved her."

"But you love Zoey," he finishes for me. I drop down onto the corner of the bed and nod. "I think she loves you too."

"She did. Or she thought she did, and it made her feel bad," I mutter, trying hard not to completely lose it. "I didn't tell her about Tessa, which maybe she could have forgiven, but I kind of freaked out last night after sex. And maybe she could have forgiven that too, but then she saw a video Rollins made in Toronto this summer, and she saw a message from Kina on my phone and…"

I pause because my voice seems to have disappeared. I swallow hard and heave a heavy sigh of regret. "Fuck, Levi, even I would run after that."

"Whoa, whoa. Slow down," Levi says and leans forward. "What video? And who is Kina? And why would you, of all people, freak out about sex?"

"I don't want to talk about it, okay?" I bark and stand up.

"No," he barks back. "If you're going to start raging on teammates, I have to know why. So I can fucking fix it."

"It's not your problem to fix. What are you going to do, date her too?"

I'm so full of pain that I can't help but inflict it on others. It oozes out of me like pus from a wound. God, I fucking hate myself. Levi's face freezes and then hardens. "For the rest of my fucking life I will regret how I handled things with you when it comes to Tess. I was a coward and an asshole and you didn't deserve it. You don't have to keep reminding me."

I turn away from the door and walk back over to my bed. God, what I would do to be anywhere else right now. Levi rubs the back of his neck, staring at the carpet between us. I know I have to stop punishing him. I know he's telling the truth. And I know that in the end, no matter what kind of fucked-up rocky road we took to get here, Tessa, Levi and I are all exactly where we should be.

"I'm sorry. That was shitty," I say quietly, and then I swallow down my belligerent pride and tell him what he needs to know. "Zoey and I didn't use a condom last night."

His head darts up. He's got the best poker face of any person I've ever met. Nothing shocks him, or at least he never shows it—until now. He looks downright flabbergasted. This would be hysterical if I weren't destroyed. "You? Unprotected? You own a crate of condoms."

"Yeah, but we got carried away." I sigh and lean forward with my elbows on my knees. "It's no big deal."

"It's one of the biggest deals, Jude," Levi remarks, eyes still wide.

I laugh. "I know. But it didn't feel like a big deal. It felt right."

His expression has changed from stunned to baffled. I really should be enjoying this. "She's on the pill, right?"

"Nope. And I knew that," I explain, and his eyes grow wide again. "Yeah, that's still not why I freaked out. I thought, what's the worst that happens? She gets pregnant? I can't see myself with anyone else ever again anyway, so…I can deal with that. That's honestly what ran through my head."

"That's…"

Now he's speechless. The guy who has an answer to everything. Seriously, I wish I could enjoy this. "Insane? Stupid? Ridiculous?"

"Unexpected," he replies.

I smile at that, but it makes my chest hurt. "I'm different with her. She makes everything different. I mean, she did."

He rubs his jaw, scratching at the stubble there, and sits back down on his bed. "So let me get this straight. You had sex with her and freaked out because you weren't freaked out, and left? And then she found out about Tessa and some video Rollins made? So all of that made her break up with you?"

I nod, closing my eyes and pushing my palms into my eyes. "The video was me being a drunken ass. I was talking about you and Tessa."

He doesn't respond right away. When he does his voice is cautious. He is sick of being hurt by me. "What did you say?"

I look at him, and I know he can see the regret all over my face. "Something about how I should date someone Tessa knows so she feels what it's like to have that shoved in her face."

Levi lets that roll around in his head, and within seconds he makes the connection Zoey obviously did. "Zoey and Tess knew each other. Shit. Zoey thinks you were just trying to hurt Tessa?"

I nod. "Between that and the running out after sex and the text from Kina on my phone, she's done."

"Who the hell is Kina?"

"She's that nurse from the children's hospital," I explain, and I fall back across the bed, staring up at the ceiling. "I couldn't sleep when I freaked out, so I went to an all-night diner and Kina swung by there for breakfast with some other nurses when her shift ended. She recognized me and said hi. I asked her about that kid we saw when we visited with the Cup. I wanted to know if he was doing better. Anyway, she said he was out of the woods and cleared to go home this weekend. I said I'd love to give him and his family some tickets to our home opener. She said she could arrange it, so I gave her my number. I had forgotten my phone at Zoey's, and I guess she texted and Zoey saw it on my screen."

I prop myself up on my elbows to gauge his reaction. He's just staring and blinking, trying to absorb the whole story. "You're not sure if I'm lying or not, are you?"

"I mean...no. I think you're telling the truth; it's just...you've told lies like that before when you're hiding shit from a girl," Levi confesses, and I can't even be upset with him. It's the truth.

"Yep." I try to fill my lungs with air but it hurts. "Zoey's just come out of a bad marriage. And her ex knocked up his secretary sixty seconds after their marriage ended, so she's rightfully jaded. And my reputation gives her no reason to believe me. I don't even blame her. This is me fucking up again."

"Man, Jude, I'm sorry," he whispers. "Maybe if you just give her a couple days…"

I shake my head and drop back flat onto the bed again, this time closing my eyes. "No. It's better this way. I'm too much of a fuckup. I've known she was too good for me since I met her. Guys like me don't keep girls like that. After all the shit I've done, I'm not going to get a happy ending, and I'd accepted that until she walked back into my life."

"So don't accept it now."

"Just let me catch a nap," I growl back, because I am so done talking about this and feeling this and I just want to be unconscious. "Please, Levi."

"Okay, but know this, Jude…you deserve her," he says quietly, and a second later I hear the door open and close. I sit up, yank my shirt off and drop my jeans and then throw back the covers. I crawl into bed and lie there and think of her. Nothing but her.

32

ZOEY

"Hello?"

"Stop."

I blink and pause the video on my computer. "Stop what?"

"Watching the video I sent you of the Thunder meeting the president," Morgan replies sternly.

I lean back in my chair and shift the phone to my other ear. "If you didn't want me to watch it, then why did you forward it to me?"

"Aha!" he blurts triumphantly. "You're watching it. You're obsessed with it. Because you're obsessed with him!"

"I'm not obsessed," I reply and sigh. "I loved him."

"You still do, so talk to him," Morgan replies. "Work this out."

"I don't even know if he wants to work it out," I mutter. "If I was just a way to get back at his ex."

My mind is still reeling with everything. The Jude I heard and saw on that Rollins video was nothing like the guy I've been spending almost every waking hour with for weeks. That Jude was mean, selfish and coldhearted. I never saw any of those traits in him. Was I oblivious, just lost in old feelings and the need for someone to care about me after my marriage blew up? Or was I blinded by lust? Was I just another one of the millions of girls fooled into thinking they were special to him?

"So he hasn't called or emailed or texted?"

"Nope." I take a deep breath. "And I have an open house this afternoon at his condo. I was going to get Marti to handle it, but she's got her own showing."

"Is he going to be there? You can talk to him then," Morgan suggests.

"No, they have three days off before the first game of the season, so he went to Maine," I explain. "His parents are there."

"I just want you to be happy, Zoey," he replies quietly. "You deserve it."

"Thanks, Morgy." I smile. "I have to go to Jude's now. Talk tonight?"

"Sure."

I hang up and busy myself with the pre-showing tasks. Printing info sheets, gathering my signs, driving to the store and buying helium balloons and donuts. I get to his place twenty minutes before the open house. Once I dump everything on his kitchen counter, I glance around. He left it pristine, but I know that's not uncommon for him. He's absurdly neat. It's cute. I inhale, trying to clear my thoughts, but this place smells like Jude. Crisp and yet earthy—like an ocean breeze wafting through a pine forest. My heart starts to ache so strongly I want to clutch my chest.

I whimper. I didn't even realize I did it until I hear the deep voice filled with concern. "Zoey, are you okay?"

I spin, a scream about to be unleashed from my lungs. But then I realize it's Levi. I gasp for air. "Crap! Levi, you scared the life out of me!"

"Sorry." He gives me a small smile. "The front door was open."

"Oh. Right. I was just setting up for the open house," I explain and glance at his hands. He's holding an envelope. My eyes rise to his. "Jude's not here. He went to Maine, I think."

"Yeah, I know." Levi nods. "He flew out from DC with Dixie."

He holds the plain white envelope out to me. "He asked me to bring you this."

I stare at it. Across the front is one word: *Sunset*.

"Thanks," I say, but my voice is barely above a whisper. My heart is suddenly galloping in my chest. I need to calm down. This could be something as simple as instructions about the open house, or something as horrible as him terminating my Realtor agreement. Or it could be him professing his undying love. That's why my heart won't stop racing, filling my entire being with hope.

"I heard you know about Tessa," Levi says, and he looks as awkward as he sounds as he rocks on his heels and shoves his hands into the pockets of his jacket. "That he and Tess used to date."

I nod. "I don't know details, and I don't want to, but—"

"Actually, I think it would probably help clear this up if you did know some details," Levi interrupts. "I think he probably gives them to you in that letter. But, from my perspective, I just want you to know that Jude is an amazing guy, and he had every right to be pissed about how things with Tessa and me developed. But it was his pride wounded, not his heart. He wasn't heartbroken over her. I swear that's the truth. But he *is* heartbroken now."

I just stare at him wordlessly, because I don't know what to say. I want to believe him so badly, though. He nods toward the letter. "Read it. And I hope Tessa and I see you at the home opener."

He turns and leaves. Before I can do anything more than stare at the envelope, there's a knock on the door. A couple walk in with big smiles. "Is it too early?"

"No. Please, come in."

I shove the envelope into my purse. An hour into the open house there's a break and I'm alone. So I reach for the envelope and carefully open it, my hands shaking. It's a simple, neat printed note on DC Four Seasons stationery.

Zoey,

I know that video looks bad and I know everything else does too. But I also know I love you. I love you in a way I've never ever loved anyone. I can't just let you go. Please don't let me go. Come to the place it all began and let me win you back.

Love you always, Jude

In the envelope, behind the letter, is a boarding pass for a flight from San Francisco to Portland, Maine. The flight leaves tonight at eleven. I dig my phone out of my purse and dial my brother's number with shaking hands.

"He sent me a ticket to meet him in Maine," I blurt out as soon as he answers.

"So what do you need me to do? Water your plants? Give you a lift to the airport?" Morgan replies swiftly.

I laugh. "Actually, I was calling to ask you if I should go, but I've got my answer."

"Are you going to listen to your much wiser older brother?"

I take a breath. "Yes."

33

JUDE

I'm rocking slowly back and forth in the rocking chair on the screened-in porch. It's chilly and the only body parts that are warm are my hands, because they're wrapped around a mug of steaming coffee. The sun is going to rise soon.

She hasn't texted. She hasn't called. Levi did, so I know she got the ticket and the note. But I have no idea if she's going to come. The realization that she might not creates a pain in my chest that's suffocating, and it's why I couldn't sleep. I hear a racket inside the cottage. My parents' bedroom is just inside the front door, to the right of the living room. I stop rocking and listen.

Their door creaks, and then I hear the sound that's become too familiar. The thump and shuffle of my dad and his walker. "I'm fine, Enid. Go back to sleep. I'll holler if I need help."

His voice is scratchy from sleep and hard from the fact that he hates the way everyone has to fuss over him now. I decide not to get up and go see him. It'll only annoy him more. So I start rocking again and sip my coffee. A minute later he's in the doorway. His walker makes a thump as it hits the old wood plank floor. I look up. "Morning, Dad. Want some coffee?"

I had planned ahead, knowing he'd probably be the first one up and he likes having his coffee on the deck; I'd brought out a full thermos and an extra cup. He smiles at me with the same big, mischievous grin I inherited. But I don't know if I'd still have it after a diagnosis like his. He really is my fucking hero.

"You're up early. If there wasn't hockey practice, I used to have to tip your bed to get you out of it before noon."

I chuckle. "You only tipped the bed once in my entire life."

"Yeah, but I'll never let you forget it." He chuckles too. I notice his words aren't slurring like they tend to first thing in the morning or late at night. I know it just means he's having a good day and nothing's actually changed, but it still makes me happy. I pour him a coffee as he clumsily makes his way into the rocking chair next to mine. I'd already blended it with organic butter, so it comes out frothy and hot, thanks to the thermos. I introduced him to what's called bulletproof coffee this past summer because it's supposed to be good for the brain.

He smiles and takes a sip. "Butter in coffee. Who knew?"

We sit in comfortable silence for a few moments, both of us rocking and drinking our java. I try not to think of the fact that I might not have many more mornings like this left with him. But then the only other thing my brain wants to focus on is Zoey, and that hurts too. Fuck…why does everything have to suck?

"The sun is starting to rise," he murmurs, bringing my focus to something that doesn't suck. "Sunrises are always so damn amazing down at the beach."

My dad used to wake up for sunrise every single day we spent down here. When I was a kid, I just didn't get it. I loved sleeping in, but I never got to do it much thanks to hockey practices. And at home my dad usually worked the early shift and had to be at work by six in the morning, so he never got to sleep in. That's why the fact that he still got up at the crack of dawn here on vacation always confused me.

I put my mug down on the ledge of the table between our rockers. "Wanna go see it on the beach?"

He smiles, but it's fleeting. "I can't manage it anymore, Jude."

I stand up. He's wearing a gray tracksuit. I'm in a pair of sweats too and a Thunder hoodie. I clap my hands. "We're going to the beach!"

"Jude." He shakes his head. "I'd love to, but I can't manage that boardwalk, and the sand is too uneven for my walker."

"I'll piggyback you up and down the boardwalk, and there are benches right there at the dunes. It'll be great. Come on!" I say and wait for him to consider it. He's a proud man. I know the idea of his son carrying him isn't a pleasant one, but who the fuck cares if he gets to see the damn sunrise the way he loves.

He puts his mug next to mine and then leans forward, hands on his walker in front of him. He looks up at me. "Can you grab my camera off the desk?"

I'm grinning as I nod and dart inside to grab it. Ten minutes later I'm panting like I've played every shift in an entire game. My arms and back are burning from the exertion, but my dad is sitting on the bench at the end of the boardwalk smiling and snapping pictures as the sun crests the ocean.

"This never gets old." He sighs and snaps another shot before resting the camera on his lap. He glances over at me. "So why were you up so early?"

"Lot on my mind." I shrug and watch the sky start to turn pink and purple.

"A lot of pretty redhead?" he inquires, and I turn to stare at him. "I might have heard Dixie telling Winnie things got botched up with the Quinlin girl."

Goddamn Dixie. "Yeah."

"A little?"

"Maybe a lot." I sigh and lean my elbows on my knees. I point. "You're missing it."

He looks out at the sunrise but moves his hand to my shoulder. "You're more important than some colors in the sky, Jude."

I smile. I can't lose him—not ever. But especially not if I don't have her. I feel a wave of sadness and fight the tears it wants to bring. I do not cry. Not ever and especially not in front of Dad. He's got enough shit to deal with. "I'm trying to fix it. And even if this first attempt fails I'll try again."

He nods and lifts his camera to grab a couple more shots. Then he puts it down and rests his hand on my shoulder. "I think it'll work out. I always liked that girl."

"Me too." I sigh and sit up and take his camera from him. It's digital but kind of old. I have to remember to get him a new one for his birthday next month. I turn it and aim it at us.

"What are you doing?" he wants to know as I lean into him.

"Selfie," I explain.

"Is that a Kardashian thing?" he asks, and I laugh. He laughs with me, even though I know it's a legitimate question. My dad doesn't know a thing about social media. Doesn't even have a Facebook account.

I snap a couple shots and turn the camera around to check them out on the screen. We're laughing in all of them, but my favorite is the one where he reached up and ruffled my hair. I have to make sure to download that one so I can print it and frame it.

When we get home, I help my dad up the three steps to the porch. Once he's on the porch, I go back down to get the walker. We'll have to put in a ramp next summer. We probably should have already. A car rumbles down the street toward me. We're on the last block before the beach so it's a dead end. Most of the cottages around us are closed already for the winter. And it's early, so who is…it's a taxicab.

It stops at the curb in front of our place, and she gets out, pulling a small carry-on bag with her. She looks tired and a little disheveled and like the most beautiful thing I've ever seen. She stops on the edge of the sidewalk as the cab pulls away.

"I didn't know if you would come," I say, my voice raw.

"Really?" She gives me a timid smile. "Because I did."

"Zoey Quinlin!" My dad's voice suddenly booms from the top of the stairs. "You're still a beauty!"

"Mr. Braddock!" She grins and waves. "You're still a handsome devil!"

"And still a charmer." He laughs, and his eyes find mine. "Jude, why don't you bring your girl and my walker up here. You can offer her some butter coffee and I'll go lie down. That beach adventure left me in need of a nap."

I motion for her to climb the stairs. I'm hoping the fact that she used the ticket also means that she's going to stay with us, because that's what I'd intended. Still, if she wants a hotel I'll book her one, because it doesn't matter. All that matters is that she's here. I can make this right.

I follow behind her up the stairs, carrying my dad's walker. He's already hugging Zoey by the time I get up there. I give the walker back to him and watch him carefully, without making it obvious I'm watching him, as he heads back into the living room and to his bedroom. After he closes the door, I turn to Zoey and extend my hand. She takes it without hesitation, and I'm about to lead her back onto the porch for some privacy when there's a stampede on the stairs.

Fucking great.

"Oh my God. Dixie wasn't lying!" Sadie bellows. "She's actually here!"

"Zoey!" Winnie hollers and runs right at us, wrapping Zoey in a hug. "I can't believe you came!"

"I told you he invited her," Dixie says, smiling as she jumps down the last step with a loud thud.

"Can you all shut up? Dad just went to lie down and it's barely nine in the morning," I chastise.

"I know, but when a sign of the apocalypse happens, you wake up pretty quick," Sadie explains and turns to Zoey. "A beautiful, smart girl we all adore giving my brother another shot is a total apocalyptic moment."

Zoey laughs, which is better than correcting Sadie. I really hope that means she's giving me another shot. Dixie grabs Zoey's bag from her and hands it to Winnie. "Come into the kitchen and sit. You must be hungry. Sadie can make her awesome cheesy bacon quiche."

"Sure!" Sadie replies happily, and they start to try to pull Zoey into the kitchen.

"I'm starving, but I think your brother and I need to talk," she explains, and her beautiful hazel eyes find mine.

"You can talk to him later," Winnie says. "I mean, you're staying with us, right?"

She glances at me again. "If that's all right."

"It's more than all right," I say.

"Good. I'll put your bag in my room, and Sadie can feed you, and Jude can beg you to take him back later. When you have a full stomach," Winnie announces and runs back upstairs with Zoey's bag.

Zoey looks at me over her shoulder as my sisters pull her off. "It's okay. We've got time."

She smiles and lets them drag her to the kitchen.

The sun is setting before I get a moment alone with her. After my sisters made her breakfast, my mom and dad got up, and they had to spend time with her. They wanted to know everything about the last eleven years of her life and her parents' lives and Morgan's life. And by then she was yawning every five seconds, and she was starting to get circles under her eyes, and I realized she might not have slept well on the overnight flight. So I urged her to take a nap.

It was one of the hardest things I've ever done—letting her go upstairs without me—but I knew she needed rest, and if I went up there, I would definitely not let her do that. I'd want to talk and then I'd want to have sex. And both of those aren't ideal with the sorority and my parents a floor below in a cottage with paper-thin walls.

I decide to go for a run on the beach while she naps to avoid thinking too much and to avoid being bothered by the sorority. I run seven miles. When I get back I'm drenched in sweat and my legs feel like Jell-O. I open the door to the porch and pull my shirt off and use it to wipe my face. I hear someone groan in disgust.

"Dear God, I see enough sweaty half-naked men at work. I don't need to see it here," Dixie says. I glance around to make sure my parents are nowhere to be found, and I flip her the bird. She just smiles. "Zoey is up."

"Yeah?" My heart rate isn't going to slow down anytime soon now.

"She just got out of the shower, so you should get in it so you don't stink while you grovel," she advises.

"Thanks. Which room is she in?"

Dixie lifts an eyebrow. "Winnie's, so don't get any ideas."

You have to go through Dixie's room to get to Winnie's. It's the worst possible room they could have given her, because it means I'll never be able to sneak in, but I'm guessing they know that, which is why Dixie is smiling at me deviously.

"I should have been an only child." I head to the bathroom and take a quick shower. I wrap a fresh towel around my waist and grab my dirty clothes before heading upstairs. I hit the landing at the same time Zoey walks out of Dixie's room. She's in a fresh pair of jeans and an off-the-shoulder sweater. Her hair is in a simple ponytail and she's barely wearing makeup. I take a step closer to her and reach out and graze her cheek with my fingertips. "You look beautiful."

She blushes and smiles. "I feel better now that I've slept a little."

"Good." I nod. "Do you want to get out of here? Just the two of us?"

She nods. This time she steps closer to me. "It's probably time we talked."

"Yeah," I agree and watch her as she moves a hand to my chest. She places it just under my left collarbone and then slowly lets it slide down my bare, wet skin. "I just gotta throw on some clothes."

She nods again but doesn't stop trailing her fingers down my body. She's at my stomach now and still moving south. I take another step. Her fingers reach my towel and curl around the terry cloth, fingertips pushing their way between my hip and the fabric. I reach up and slide my hand behind her neck. I start to pull her lips to mine.

"Oh, no! Not in this house!"

Sadie's voice is like a siren going off. We jump apart and I drop my dirty clothes in order to keep my towel from falling. Zoey turns fire engine red. I turn and glare at Sadie as she comes out of her room across the hall. She ignores me. "Come on, Zoey."

When I get downstairs Zoey is sitting with my entire family around the dining room table and my mom is setting up the Monopoly board. Mom looks up at me and smiles. "We've ordered pizza from Bill's and we've invited you two to play, but Zoey said you had other plans?"

I nod. "We're going to walk down to Old Orchard and grab some food."

"Okay then. Have fun!" my dad says way too casually, and then he follows it with a very uncasual wink.

The sorority stays quiet for once, and it makes me think maybe Sadie is onto something with that apocalypse thing. We make our way out of the house as the sun starts to set. The air is salty and chilly. I ask her if she needs a warmer jacket.

"I'm okay," she assures me and points up the street, away from the main road that'll take us into town. "Let's walk on the beach."

Suddenly, I'm seventeen again, walking her home from babysitting. It's a good feeling but also sad. If only I could go back and start over from there. Not lose touch with her, not let her go, not waste time. But she's here now—in my life and my heart—and I have to fight like hell to keep her here.

"Your dad sure isn't letting his illness get him down," Zoey says.

"He never lets it affect his personality. At least, not in front of us," I reply as we make our way up the boardwalk. "And he's having a good spell right now too, which helps."

"You're an amazing son, you know that?" she whispers. "I've always thought that since we were kids, but seeing you with him now solidifies it."

I feel my chest grow tight. "I try."

"You succeed," she replies firmly and smiles.

We make it to the sand and both toe off our shoes. As I walk beside her, our free hands not carrying our shoes keep brushing, so I finally take hers and lace our fingers. She doesn't pull away, so I gain the confidence I need to speak. "Kina is a nurse. She works at the children's hospital. We went there a few weeks ago with the Cup, and after I left your place the other night I went to an all-night diner and ran into her."

It's too dark to read her expression so I just keep talking. "She is helping me get home opener tickets to a kid I met there. That's it."

"Okay."

"You believe me?"

"Yes." It feels like she's forcing herself to say that, and I hate it. "Why didn't you tell me about Tessa?"

"Because I was embarrassed about it," I admit.

She kind of shrugs. "I'm sure it wasn't easy to have her be with Levi if you were in love with her."

She's watching the cool sand in front of us carefully. Too carefully. She's avoiding looking at me. A few feet away, between us and the ocean, is a lifeguard chair. Not the chair from the rainstorm when we were kids, but it looks exactly the same. I pull her over to it and turn her to face me, pushing her back gently up against one of the long legs of the chair. I hate admitting this to her. I hate how it makes me look and feel, but I want her to know.

Her hazel eyes find mine because I gently cup her chin and force her to look at me. "I didn't love Tess. That's why the way I acted makes me an asshole. I should have let her and Levi be together without creating a shit ton of drama for him and the team. That video Eddie took was me being a drunk asshole with wounded pride. That's it. I forgot I even said it, that's how little I meant it. And I didn't know you knew Tess, and when I found out I didn't even think about it. Not like that."

I kiss her because I want her to feel the truth in my words. It's slow and sweet, and when I pull back, I can't help but whisper, "You're the only person I've ever loved."

She pulls back, pressing the back of her head against the wood behind her. The wind is blowing lightly and some strands of hair escape her ponytail and dance around her face. I reach out and brush them back, my fingertips skimming her cheek. She drops her shoes and wraps both arms around my neck. "I love you too. And it scares me because I've been broken by someone I loved less than I love you. So if you hurt me...there won't even be pieces left."

I step into her, dropping my own shoes in the sand next to hers and wrapping my arms around her back. We cling to each other like this for a long time. I bury my face in her neck and kiss her there gently and then lift my lips to her ear. "I won't destroy you. Because it would destroy me too."

Finally our lips connect again, and the kiss is intense—tongues and lips and moans and whimpers—as the ocean waves crash around us. I'm not hungry anymore, at least not for food. All I crave is her, and I know it's a craving that will never be satisfied. But thankfully, it's not one I'm going to be denied, either.

34

ZOEY

Early the next morning he groans as I untangle our naked bodies and reach for my clothes on the floor. He stops me by reaching around my body and palming my breasts, pulling me backward as he rolls my nipples between his thumbs and fingers. I'm instantly ready again, which is insane because after the sex we had last night I should be done…and walking funny.

I land sort of across his chest, my head falling over his shoulder, which puts his lips in the perfect position to kiss my neck. I close my eyes and enjoy the sensation. "Baby, your dad is probably up already and the rest of your family will be soon."

"So we'll be quiet," he whispers, his hands slowly making their way down my naked stomach.

We never made it for food last night. We stayed under that life-guard chair for hours kissing and talking until the talking turned to moaning and the kissing turned to petting and then we wandered home. His family had all turned in for the night, thankfully, so no one noticed when he pulled me into his room. The sex was different—and not just because we had to be silent and keep it slow to avoid making the bed creak or the headboard hit the wall. Emotionally it was more than anything I'd ever felt, and the orgasm was so intense it blinded me.

His fingers slip between my legs, and I can tell from the way he bites down on my shoulder that he likes what he finds. "Mmm…" he whispers. "My breakfast is ready."

"Wha—"

I don't know how he does it, but suddenly I'm flat on my back on the mattress instead of splayed across his torso and he's hovering above me. The flurry of motion makes me squeak, so he covers my mouth with his hand. "Quiet, Sunset."

He nudges my legs apart with his knee and moves between them. His head is between them before I can comprehend what's happening and then, as his tongue slides over me, pressing harder at my clit, there's no way to comprehend anything except the divine pleasure he's creating. I close my eyes, arch my back and thread my fingers into his hair. The pleasure rolls through me stronger and stronger with each pass of his tongue. He's just plain masterful with his mouth, his tongue moving slowly and with purpose. He's enjoying this almost as much as I am.

I feel his fingers move from my thigh to join his mouth. But I don't feel them. I move my hips, as if searching for them. I can feel him smile against my pussy. "Tell me what you want."

Jude loves dirty talk. "I want you to fuck me with your fingers. Please."

Two fingers join the party. He goes straight for the big show and curls them as he presses into me. He hits that spot that turns everything upside down inside me. I bite my bottom lip and hold back as much of my groan as possible. But a tiny whimper escapes. And then he does it again, but this time he sucks on my clit at the same time, and a hot ripple of ecstasy rolls from my clit through my entire body. My legs try to snap shut, clamping down on his head, and my hands fly from his hair and land on the pillow beside me as I turn my head into it to muffle any sounds as my body shakes with release.

He pulls his fingers out and moves his mouth away much more quickly than I'd like. My pussy is still quivering, but he's got other plans. He's holding his cock in his left hand and stroking it, hard. His thumb moves over the top, sliding through the ample moisture there. He drops forward, catching himself with his right arm beside my shoulder. And then I feel the tip of his dick as he guides it up and down my pulsating slit.

We were careful last night, making sure he was wrapped up before he went inside me. We haven't talked about how stupid we were or how we can't be that stupid again, but we both know it's true. We're not new to each other, or even these feelings, because I think we both knew they were there when we were kids. But we are new to exploring them, and even though I think we can handle anything now, we shouldn't test that theory.

But his tip is so warm and hard, but in a soft way, and every time he guides it along my slit my still pulsing pussy wants to swallow it whole. My hips inch down, without my consent, which causes the whole tip to disappear on the next pass. Jude's eyes find mine. "You're still coming."

"Mmm...hmmm...yes," I pant and try to still my hips but I can't. He clearly can't control his either because halfway through another slow pass, he stops and pushes into me. It's slow and only halfway, but it makes my whole body catch fire, and I arch and moan, and he has to let go of the base of his dick and drop a palm over my mouth again. Right. His whole family is probably able to hear any noise we make.

His thick, sandy-colored eyelashes flutter. He grunts quietly and pulls out completely. In fact his whole body lifts and he's back to kneeling between my thighs. He points a finger at me. "You're going on the pill as soon as we get home," he whispers sternly.

"Yes, sir." I give him a wobbly mock salute. "Now will you find a condom and push that perfect cock all the way into me, please?"

He groans happily and palms his cock again as I shush him. He grabs a condom out of his bag on the floor at the end of his bed and wastes no time covering himself with it. I reach out for him, to pull him down on top of me, but instead he pulls me up. "Wanna ride me? Because if I'm in charge, I'm not going to be able to stop myself from plowing you into the headboard."

I smile and crawl up into his lap, wrap my arms around his neck and cover his mouth with mine, pushing my tongue inside to play with his. He starts to lie back, bringing me forward with him. His right hand is wrapped around my waist but his left has reached down to grip his cock again.

I drop my legs on either side of his hips as I feel his tip move across me again where I'm warm and wet and waiting. If he's giving me the control, I'm taking it—all of it. So I break the kiss and whisper, "Cowgirl."

Before he can respond, I've spun around so my back is to him and I'm replacing his hand with my own as I hold his dick and slide down onto it. His hands go straight to my hips and latch on as I start to move. I arch my back, tip my head back and close my eyes as I ride him, focusing on nothing but the way he fills me up and how, when I roll my hips just so, it sends sparks of pleasure through my body.

"You're so incredible," he murmurs in a quiet grunt. "How did I get so lucky?"

"I'm lucky," I whisper and roll my hips again. Oh God, I'm so close…

He's moving behind me, and I don't realize he's sitting up until his hands move from my hips, one reaching to cup my breast and the other reaching between my legs. "Look at me, baby."

I twist my head as much as I can, and his beautiful face swims into view. He squeezes a nipple and rubs my clit at the exact same time, and my orgasm hits me like a train. He kisses me to trap the moan that's about to fly from my mouth. When my orgasm slows, the kiss breaks and he falls back and starts thrusting under me, which is great because I'm spent. A few minutes later he grabs my ass in both hands and shudders under me as his own orgasm hits. I rock my hips with his erratic thrusts to help him ride it out.

When his hips stop moving, I shakily lift myself off of him. He grabs me and pulls me down beside him, kissing me hard on the lips. The sound of voices downstairs is our reality check. I put a hand on his bare chest and push myself up, glancing around for my clothes again. I grab my underwear and bra off the floor. He's watching me with a glassy look in his light blue eyes. There's his trademark smirk dancing on his lips. "I can't wait to do that again."

I laugh. "Well, you're going to have to, because right now I have to sneak out of here without your family finding out."

He frowns, but it's fake, as he gets off the bed and gets dressed. A couple minutes later I'm standing right behind him as he cracks the bedroom door and peeks out into the tiny hallway. He glances over his shoulder. "Okay. You head into your room. I'll head downstairs."

I nod, and we both tiptoe into the hallway. He gives me a chaste kiss just as Dixie walks out of her room, texting furiously on her phone. She doesn't even look up as she walks by. "Ew. Gross. I knew you two would ignore the rules and bang."

She keeps walking down the stairs without another word. I giggle and Jude rolls his eyes before kissing my cheek and following her downstairs.

When I come back down a couple minutes later, his whole family is around the dining room table having breakfast. They all call out greetings, and I know Dixie kept our secret, so I give her a grateful smile. She winks back. After breakfast we have quick showers, separately, unfortunately, and say good-bye to everyone.

He has a team dinner tonight, and he's asked me to go with him. It hurts my heart a little to see him say good-bye to his family, especially when he hugs his father. Later, as we wait to board our second flight, from Boston to San Francisco, my phone rings. I step away from Jude and answer it in my best business voice, since I don't recognize the number. It's another agent, and she has a full-price offer on Jude's condo. I tell her I will get back to her within twenty-four hours and hang up.

They've started boarding our flight, so Jude and I walk to the gate. "That was an offer on your place. Full list price, but they want to close in fourteen days."

"Shit. Well, that's great, but now we've got to get serious about finding me a new place," he says. "It'll be an extra hassle if I'm homeless during the season. I spend so much time in hotel rooms on the road it'll suck to do it here too."

We hand our tickets to the attendant at the gate, and after she scans them Jude takes my hand as we walk down the tunnel to the plane. "You can stay with me until you find a place," I offer.

He stops walking. "Really?"

I shrug and smile. "I have a feeling you'll be over a lot of nights anyway. I mean, I hope so."

"I was planning on it."

"So then, it's settled. You can crash with me if we don't find you a place in time."

He pulls me into a kiss. "Thank you."

My heart flutters. I'm sure he'll find a place before he has to move. San Francisco has a million options in his price range. But still, I kind of hope he doesn't. I really like the idea of having him in my place. He fits.

35

JUDE

When we land in San Francisco we part ways, which I hate. But she needs to run to the office and get the paperwork to close the deal on my condo and change clothes for tonight. I need to change too, and all my clothes are at my place. I hate being away from her, even for a couple of hours.

I walk into my condo and look around. I'm not going to miss it. It's a total fuck pad. I knew that when I bought it—that's *why* I bought it—and it was perfect. But I'm not that person anymore. I just want Zoey. I walk into my bedroom and start unpacking my bag from Maine. My phone rings, and it's the cottage number.

My dad's voice fills my ear after I say hello. "Just wanted to make sure you and Zoey got home okay."

"We did." I smile and drop down onto my bed. "Thanks for letting her stay with us."

"She's family," he says happily and adds, "Or at least I have a feeling she will be."

"She will be," I agree easily. "Eventually. If she'll keep me."

"I've only ever seen one other woman look at a man the way Zoey looked at you," my dad says quietly. "And it was your mom looking at me. Now, granted, I'm much more handsome and charming than you, but…"

I laugh and he joins me. When our laughter dies down, I tell him, "I love you, Dad, even if you're delusional."

"I love you too, Jude. And I'm glad I'm not the only one," he replies and then adds, "I'll talk to you later. Your sisters are taking your mom and me for a lobster dinner. They're even paying."

"Have fun, and don't eat them into bankruptcy, or else I'll have to support them." I laugh and say good-bye.

Almost two hours later I pick up Zoey. She looks amazing in a short green dress, and she's wearing her hair in a low sideswept ponytail. I can't wait to mess it up later. But right now we have things to do that require clothes, unfortunately. I reach across the middle console and take her hand in mine. She smiles. "Where's dinner?"

"At an Italian place near Washington Square, but I need to run an errand first, and I wanted you to come along," I explain and turn onto the freeway.

Fifteen minutes later when I pull into the parking lot of the children's hospital, she looks suddenly anxious. "Jude, you don't have to prove anything to me."

"I know," I return, and hop out of the car. I make it to her door before she can open it and help her out, keeping our hands joined as I walk into the hospital and up to the floor Kina said Christopher is on now that he's out of isolation.

We turn the corner off the elevator. Kina bounces up from her seat at the nurses' station as soon as she sees us, but her smile falters when her eyes land on Zoey. Still, she rushes around the desk. "I told his mom you were coming. She's expecting you. We both agree you are the sweetest guy ever for doing this."

"It's not a big deal," I reply and add, "Kina, this is my girlfriend, Zoey. Zoey, Kina."

"Nice to meet you." Zoey smiles at her.

Kina nods and turns back to me. "He's in room 442 until tomorrow, when he's discharged."

"Thanks." I pause and pull two envelopes out of my jacket pocket, handing one to her. "For your help."

She rips it open and then throws herself at me in a hug. I don't expect it, and I have to drop Zoey's hand to untangle myself. "Thank you! I've never been to a home opener. I'll get to see you raise the Stanley Cup banner. That's the coolest thing ever. Thank you!"

"Sure thing. Have fun," I reply casually and wrap an arm around Zoey's waist as I lead her down the hall toward Christopher's room.

When we're out of Kina's sight, Zoey whispers, "You don't have to keep your arm around me. She got the point."

I blink. "I actually didn't do it to prove anything. I just like touching you."

She smiles at that, and I lean over and kiss her cheek.

Christopher is ecstatic to see me and over the moon about the tickets and the VIP passes. His mother is almost in tears when she thanks me. I tell her how happy I am Christopher is recovering and that I can't wait to see them tomorrow night. As we walk back to the car, Zoey stops me in the middle of the parking lot and lays one hell of a kiss on me. It's amazing, but even more fulfilling is the look of happiness and pride on her face. I know I'm a good guy, and I never really cared what other people thought. But I care what she thinks.

She kisses me again once we're back in the car, and I warn her that if she doesn't stop we're skipping dinner and heading straight back to her place, so she pulls back. "I'm starving."

The restaurant for the team dinner is a small mom-and-pop place. The team has booked the whole place, so it's private. There are two long tables, and we sit at one with Levi and Tessa across from us and Carla and Duncan next to us. Eddie, thankfully, sits at the other table. The conversation is light and fun. No residual drama. The food is fantastic, and I think Zoey has a legitimately good time. I know I do.

Our coach gives a speech, followed by Mr. Carling, who's Dixie's boss and the head of team relations. Then they pass out our Stanley Cup rings. Out of the corner of my eye, I can't help but notice Eddie with his phone up. He's either filming video or taking pictures. Probably Snapchatting the hell out of it. Zoey leans closer, the tip of her nose nudging my cheek gently. "You're scowling."

"Sorry." I smile at her and wrap an arm around the back of her seat. "Rollins and his fucking social media crap again."

The coach calls my name, and I stand up and accept my ring. I sit back down and open the ring box. It's huge and full of diamonds. Zoey looks stunned. "Holy shit, that's worth more than my house. It's beautiful."

I smile and leave a lingering kiss on her cheek. "Not as beautiful as you."

When the night is over, I can't wait to get out of there. I can think of nothing but being alone with her. She excuses herself to use the restroom with Tessa and Carla, and I make my way to the front of the restaurant with the boys.

Levi smiles at me as I approach. "Things seem good."

"Things are great," I admit with a smile. "Oh, and I'm moving. Sold the condo."

Eddie overhears and drops his phone and turns to me. "Your place was epic. Why sell?"

"Because I've outgrown the place," I reply.

"Please. It's the perfect place to bring chicks," Eddie argues, and Levi shakes his head.

"I think he doesn't have a use for that anymore."

"Yeah, sorry I didn't tell you it was on the market," I quip. "I could have sold it to you for double since you love it so much."

Eddie groans dramatically. "First Darby gets whipped by Carla, then you move Tessa in, and now he's giving up a hookup palace. What's next? Someone pops out a kid?"

"Been there, done that, doing it again," Brian pipes up, Abby wrapped around his waist. "And I hope all you fuckers get that lucky."

We all laugh, except Eddie, who groans again. Tessa, Carla and Zoey rejoin the group. As we wait for the valet to bring the car I kiss her, long and hard on the mouth. She's flushed from the act and the public display. "What was that for?"

"Because I can," I whisper back. Beside me I see Eddie with his phone up again, filming himself and Brian. Our eyes meet, and he quickly drops his arm.

"I was Snapchatting me and Brian, not you or anything else," Eddie explains.

"It's fine. Snapchat me," I say, and when he doesn't move, I say it again. "Come on. Snapchat me."

Eddie looks skeptical, but he points the phone at me. I hold up my ring. "Stanley Cup champs, everybody." A few of the guys standing around hoot and holler. I still have one arm wrapped around Zoey. "Only thing prettier than this ring is my girlfriend."

And then I kiss her. Tessa and Carla clap. Duncan whistles. Eddie groans and stops the video. I pull away from her and level him with a serious stare. "Snap that or I'll bitch-slap you again."

I'm smiling, so he knows I'm kidding…mostly. He nods and hits a button on his screen. "There. You're officially off the market. Happy now?"

"Very," I reply.

"Me too," Zoey whispers against my ear. "Now get me home and I'll show you just how happy."

36

ZOEY

"Oh my God, that was amazing!" I can't help but gush as soon as the final buzzer sounds.

Carla smiles at me. "Duncan did great. He's going to get sex tonight. But only oral, because he didn't score, he only assisted."

Tessa laughs and turns to me. "They wager sex acts on every game. It's ridiculous."

"Yeah, Jude would be getting it whether he scored or not," I explain with a smile. "Mostly because I can't deny myself."

They both laugh. Tessa wraps an arm around my shoulders and gives me a squeeze as we step into the elevator that'll take us down to the family lounge level. "I'm really glad you and Jude worked everything out."

"Me too." I glance up at her and grin. "And I'm glad things didn't work out for you and Jude."

She bursts out in a shocked laugh. Carla does too and shakes her head. "You know I hated Jude when he was with Tess, and after, of course. But with you…he's different. And he's growing on me."

I smile. "Good. Because he's a really great guy."

The elevator opens and we step off into the hallway, flashing our passes at the guard before making our way into the friends and family lounge. Levi is the first to show up, his hair still damp and his hands still tightening his tie.

"How's the shoulder?" Tessa asks, worry on her face.

"Sore. But not worse." Levi sighs. "It's going to be a long season if this doesn't heal up."

He leans in and steals a kiss, then he turns to me. "Jude is going to be a little longer than normal. He's taking Christopher on a little tour. He said you could join him. He's in the training room, I think."

I smile. "Thanks. See you guys later."

I head out of the lounge and down the hall to the left. There's a state-of-the-art gym there and some medical rooms for doctors to treat injuries as well as a cardio room. As I round the curving concrete hallway, I see Christopher with his mom, but Jude isn't with them. The kid is beaming like a spotlight he's so happy, and his mom looks equally thrilled. She recognizes me and waves.

"Did you have a good time?" I ask, even though I know the answer.

"Oh my gosh, the best day of my life!" Christopher exclaims and then proceeds to tell me about every single moment. It's totally adorable, and my love for Jude grows with every excited word. He did this for this kid out of the goodness of his heart that I love so much. Christopher finishes his almost three-minute tale with a yawn.

His mom smiles. "He needs to rest. Please thank Jude again. He's still giving the tour to Christopher's nurse, but I needed to get this little guy home."

"I will. Have a great night." I watch them go and continue down the hall. I wonder if he's still in the training room or if he's back in the locker room. As I try to decide whether I should turn around and head back to the lounge, I hear a female voice. It's squealing. The sound is coming out of the open door just ahead of me on the left. It's the weight room.

I freeze. I don't know why, but I can't move. And then I hear a slightly whiny, very flirty "Come on, Jude." Now I'm really not able to move. It's like I'm made of stone.

The only thing that moves is my head as I turn toward the open door. I can see into the room, just a little bit, and I feel like I should look away, but I can't. I see a wall and the edge of some kind of weight machine. I can also see Jude's shoulder and part of his back. He's wearing the red Under Armour shirt he wears under his equipment. His hands are on his hips, and his posture seems tense.

"I didn't invite you tonight for this," Jude explains sternly. "I was just being polite because you helped me out with Christopher."

"Oh," the woman says, sounding startled. It's got to be Kina because Christopher's mom said Jude was still with her. But clearly she wants a tour of more than the arena. I watch as her hand lands on his shoulder. "Well, you have my number. In case anything changes."

He takes a step back, causing her hand to drop, and crosses his arms. "It won't change. Hope you had a good time at the game. I'll just get someone to escort you out."

He turns toward the door and sees me standing there. He looks shocked. I'm finally able to make my feet move, and I walk swiftly by the entrance to the door that leads to the parking lot. He darts into the hall, I think to stop me. "Zoey, wait! It's not what you think."

I smile at him. "Yeah, it is exactly what I think."

I turn to the security guard at the door. "I think Jude needs your help making sure his guest makes it back up to the concourse."

Jude realizes I was going to get the security guard and nods at him. "Yes. Please."

Kina steps out into the hall, looking a bit peeved. Oh, well. She ignores me completely and gives Jude her best flirty smile. "I meant what I said."

"So did I," he responds firmly.

The security guard steps in between Jude and Kina. "Right this way, ma'am."

"I'm not a ma'am!" Kina replies, horrified, but she follows him to the door that leads outside.

Jude walks over to me. "I just want you to know that—"

I grab his face in my hands and kiss him before he can finish the sentence. It's way too deep and passionate for a public kiss, but I don't care. He doesn't seem to mind at first either, as he wraps his arms around my waist and pulls me closer, his tongue moving over mine. But then he breaks the kiss first and glances nervously down the hallway, moving his hand to shift the growing hard-on I felt pressing against my stomach. "Jesus, Zoey, I have to get changed and shower in front of a bunch of guys now."

"Sorry," I reply with a smile that says "not sorry."

He grins back at me. "You're going to pay for that later."

"I hope so," I reply, and we walk down the hall back toward the dressing room and lounge. "I hope I pay for it for a long, long time."

"You will." He leans over and kisses me quickly. "I promise."

Epilogue

ZOEY

Seven Months Later

I smile and have to talk myself out of doing a victory fist pump because the doctor's waiting room is kind of packed. So instead I text Jude.

Sold another place! Boom!

His response is instantaneous, which means he's out of the team's practice.

Aren't you the sexy real estate rock star. Let's celebrate! I'll take you to lunch.

The Thunder have a week off before they start playoffs and he's kind of been using his free time to follow me around like a puppy. Not that I mind. I like spending time with him, which is why I haven't really been trying to find him a new place to buy. I know he doesn't really want one, and I don't want him out of my house. Living with him has been perfection.

I text back that I'm at the doctor's office. He wants the address and says he'll pick me up here, so I text it to him just as the nurse calls my name. I get up and follow her into the little room. This is a follow-up visit. I'm here to pick up birth control. I should have gotten on this months ago, but work got crazy busy and Jude was moving. I needed to help with that, and then he was on the road a lot, and I got the flu at one point, so it just never happened. We were fairly careful and using condoms…mostly, but we're both ready to not have to be careful.

Dr. Kane walks in and smiles at me. "Hi, Zoey. How are you feeling today?"

"Great." I smile. Dr. Kane has been my doctor since I moved to San Francisco. She's the one who broke the news about my angry uterus. "Just here to grab that prescription."

"For the birth control." She nods and sits down on the little stool, my file open in her hands, and wheels over so she's right in front of me. "As you know, since you admitted you'd been a little less than careful with your boyfriend and you've had some breast tenderness and irregular periods, I wanted to do some tests before I gave you the prescription."

"Irregular periods are nothing new," I remind her, because it's been that way my whole life. And, although I'm not going to admit it to her, I think the tenderness in my boobs is probably from so much sex with Jude. The sisters are never left out of the action…and there's a lot of action.

"Yes, well…do you still want children?" she asks quietly.

The question throws me off, but it shouldn't, because she knows I was trying with my ex-husband. "Yes. Jude would make a fantastic father, but we're not in any rush. And he knows I might not be able to."

"You're able to," she replies, and at first I think it's a pep talk. She tried really hard to make it clear when she first told me about my issues that it wasn't infertility. That I could still conceive normally, but it would probably just take longer than usual. But there's something in her eyes that makes my heart feel like it's been electrocuted. "Zoey, you're pregnant."

"I'm what?"

"You're pregnant," she repeats as clearly as the last time. "I'm not sure how far along, but if you hop up on the table we can do an ultrasound and figure this out."

I don't speak. I don't move. I don't even breathe until my lungs start to scream and then I gulp in a breath. Dr. Kane leans forward and takes my hand. "I know this is unexpected. I assume you and your new boyfriend aren't trying?"

"No." I can't get my heart to stop thumping or my eyes to stop watering. I'm scared but not upset. I mean...a baby? Jude's baby? "What about my angry uterus?"

She laughs because that's not a medical term, and I sound like a moron. "It was happy that day, I guess. Now if you're okay with it, why don't you hop up and we'll do the ultrasound."

I nod because I don't know what else to do, but my whole body is numb.

Twenty minutes later I am in the elevator heading down to the lobby. I would have been done ten minutes earlier, but I turned into a blubbering mess, and the doctor wanted to counsel me while I used up all her tissues. She actually asked me if I wanted to keep it. That's not the issue here, and I made that clear. It's too soon, it's crazy and it's in no way planned, but I want this baby. Jude's baby.

I think he'll want it too. But I'm still scared to tell him.

The elevator doors open, and I step into the lobby and he's all I see. He's sitting by the entrance, looking down at his phone. I didn't expect him to be here yet and definitely not out of his car. I can't tell him here in a public lobby of a medical building. I was hoping I'd at least get to do it in the privacy of his car. If I were a stronger woman, I would wait till we got home tonight, but...I am not that strong.

He glances up, sees me and gets to his feet. He's grinning his typical Jude grin, and I wonder suddenly if the baby will have his smile, and then I laugh. But I'm crying. He is a foot away and sees the clusterfuck of emotions on my face with the tears and the giggling and he immediately looks terrified. "Oh my God, what's wrong?"

He pulls me to the leather bench he was just sitting on and gently eases me down to sit on it. "Is it your parents? Is it Morgan? Did something happen?"

I shake my head. "The doctor told me..."

Every ounce of color drops from his face. His left hand is cupping the side of my face and I can feel the warmth drain from it. "Are you...sick?"

Oh God. I'm such an asshole. With what he's gone through with his dad, I shouldn't scare him. "No. I'm sorry, I didn't mean to...I just...we should have been more careful. I didn't think my uterus would like you."

He looks completely baffled. I pull the picture the doctor gave me out of my pocket, but before he even looks at it, his face goes white again. "Are you saying...Did I...Are you...?"

I hand him the image. He takes it with a shaking hand. I know he's not seeing anything but swirls and blobs. That's all I see when I look at it, but Dr. Kane swears one of those blobs is a baby. A healthy seven-, possibly eight-week-old baby. My voice is a squeak when it comes out. "Adam and I tried for a year and nothing, but somehow you and I take a few chances and…"

I drop my hand with the picture onto my lap, and he grabs my face in his hands, using his thumbs to brush the tears off my cheeks. "I love you."

I nod. "I love you too. I just…I just don't want you to feel trapped."

He hugs me fiercely, then pulls back and looks me in the eye. "Trapped? Are you kidding me? Baby or no baby, I don't want to go anywhere. You're stuck with me, Zoey. I'll be honest, I'm a little terrified, but I'm definitely more happy than scared. Shocked but happy."

I hug him again as a small wave of calm emerges in the sea of panic inside me. He pulls me to my feet and holds my face again. "This is unplanned and crazy, but it's us, Zoey. We'll be fine."

"You can still get your own place," I whisper. "I mean, you're welcome in my place if you want to stay, but you don't have to."

"In case you haven't noticed, I've been giving my Realtor a hard time about everything she shows me," he replies as we start toward the exit, his arm wrapped snugly around my shoulders. "I've never had any intention of getting my own place."

I smile, and happiness starts to overpower the fear and the panic. "I hoped that's what you were doing."

He pushes open the glass doors, and as we step onto the sidewalk we're face-to-face with Adam. Of course. Penner Realty is just around the corner. That's why I initially picked Dr. Kane—it was convenient. He looks up and sees us there. Jude grins at him. "Hey, Aaron."

I try not to smile, because I know he did that on purpose.

"Adam," Adam corrects and looks at me. "What are you doing here?"

"Seeing Dr. Kane. She's still my doctor."

Adam looks tired and stressed. I almost feel bad for him.

Jude obviously doesn't as he announces, "You might want to avoid this block because we'll be here a lot for baby checkups. It might get super awkward."

"Baby checkups?" Adam parrots.

"I'm pregnant." The words still feel so foreign.

"But that's impossible," Adam barks out.

"Guess it just took the right man." I hear the words leave my mouth but even I can't believe I uttered them.

Jude grins, kisses my cheek and winks at Adam before we march past my ex. When we get to his car he kisses me, long and slow. "I love you, Zoey. And I am the right man. And I'll spend the rest of my life making sure you and the baby always know it."

I hug him tightly. "I have no doubt."

Look for *Slammed*,
Dixie & Eli's story,
coming in
December 2017

ABOUT THE AUTHOR

Victoria Denault loves long walks on the beach, cinnamon dolce lattes and writing angst-filled romance. She lives in L.A. but grew up in Montreal, which is why she is fluent in English, French and hockey. You can visit her online at www.victoriadenault.com or facebook.com/authorvictoriadenault.